Thief in the Myst

By Ben Hale

To my family and friends,

who believed

And to my wife,

who is perfect

The Chronicles of Lumineia
By Ben Hale

—The Master Thief—

Jack of Thieves

Thief in the Myst

The God Thief

—The Second Draeken War—

Elseerian

The Gathering

Seven Days

The List Unseen

—The Warsworn—

The Flesh of War

The Age of War

The Heart of War

—The White Mage Saga—

Assassin's Blade (Short story prequel)

The Last Oracle

The Sword of Elseerian

Descent Unto Dark

Impact of the Fallen

The Forge of Light

Table of Contents

Map of Lumineia

Prologue: Margauth

A solitary figure stepped from the forest and ascended into the pass. The birdsong faded as he climbed, giving way to the mournful howl of the mountain wind. Black granite replaced bright trees and gurgling brooks, the stones roughly hewn and tossed into a semblance of a highway. Towering peaks blocked the fading light, casting the road into shadow. The wind gained a shrill tone as if to warn intruders, the chill piercing his skin.

Dressed in a cloak of black trimmed in green, the man kept his face cowled as he climbed into the mountains. His pace was unhurried as he picked his way past fallen boulders. An empty sheath lay on his back, the ancient material inscribed with runes and glyphs. Another scabbard hung from his belt and carried a thin sword.

The canyon curved and a decrepit citadel came into view. Built into a massive cleft between two mountains, Margauth had once been a mighty fortress. After the fall of the Verinai it had been abandoned until the Cult of Skorn had appropriated it for their use.

A great wall curved before the fortress, its battlements broken and layered in grime. The wooden gate had long since rotted away. Through the gap an uneven courtyard was visible, the surface strewn with ancient weapon stands and rusted blades.

A sheer cliff rose beyond the wall, its surface carved into the features of a giant beast. Jaws protruded from the rock, the fangs bared as if the very mountain yearned to roar. Light glimmered from the gaping mouth, and the rumble of drums echoed from within. The great windows above the mouth were shaped like eyes, the contours of the stone twisted in fury. The fortress gazed down upon the road as if daring the man to approach.

He paused to meet the citadel's gaze, and a faint smile tugged at his lips. Then his eyes dropped to the hovering sword that blocked the entrance. Anchored to a chain, the sword glowed with fire and swung about, searching for a target.

Rumored to be uncontrollable, the blade carried countless curses that had been added over the years. Unless a token of Skorn was shown to the blade it would not be pacified, and even a rock troll would be cut asunder. The cult claimed Skorn himself had forged the blade, unaware of the truth.

The blade leapt forward, straining against the chain. The man reached out to it and grasped the spine of the blade. It spun, attempting to break free and sever his arm. He held it in an iron grip and forced it aside, gliding forward to grasp the hilt with his free hand.

"Remember your Master."

The blade hesitated as if it understood his words, and relaxed in his grip. The man stepped to the chain and withdrew a small vial from a pouch at his side. Dribbling a few drops of acid onto the mithral binding, he watched as the liquid ate its way through the bond.

Free for the first time in eons, the sword shivered in ecstasy. The man reached to his back, sliding it into the empty sheath. It quivered in sublime relief and lay still. The man stepped away from the still sizzling chain and strode to the fortress.

Although the cult had thousands of followers, no guards were placed outside, their leaders assuming the blade was sufficient deterrent for intruders. The man strode through the cracked and weathered courtyard to the main door and reached for the handle. It creaked as it swung open, the hinges protesting the movement.

The great hall contained a scattering of light orbs. The green glow cast the space in a sinister light, making the shadows dance in disturbing patterns. Broken chandeliers hung from the ceiling, their metal brackets cankered with rust. Dust coated the walls and the floor, marred by

11

thousands of footprints. He made his way through the rotting furniture and cracked pillars to the stairs at the back.

Shouts and screams touched his ears, growing louder as he ascended. At the top he reached the doors facing the front of the fortress. Light glowed from the cracks in the paneled door, flickering and brightening before flashing green. The screams came to an abrupt end but the shouts increased, gaining a rhythm of intonation and reverence, unifying into an avowal of worship.

He grasped the handle and swung it open to reveal a large amphitheatre contained in the mouth of the fortress. Huge stone teeth formed the battlements at the rear, and a mirroring set of fangs protruded from the ceiling high above. The floor had been carved into benches that overlooked a wide platform.

At the center of the stage a pair of statues depicted two men locked in mortal battle. The statues resembled those placed in temples of the Church of Light, yet here Skorn stood above Ero rather than beneath, his sword raised for the killing blow. Ero's mythical staff lay broken on the ground, and the god was helpless to stop his impending death.

Men and women lined the space dressed in ceremonial cloaks of black and green. Most were homemade, their stitching haphazard and the cloth drawn from a cheaper cotton. The Cult of Skorn was condemned by the populace and governments alike, but since the cult's members were known only to each other, the governments of Lumineia could not punish them for their vile practices.

The man made his way between the ranks of fanatics, working his way toward the stage. Caught up in the chanting of the ceremony they paid him no mind. Then he spotted what they were worshiping.

A trio of figures stood on the platform over a sobbing fourth. On his knees, the man lifted his arm to the woman raising the sword above him. Bound in silver ropes, the captive trembled with fear. His features were hidden behind the mask of Ero, but his voice was audible from behind the mask.

"Please!" he cried. "I have a family—a farm! *Please, let me go home!*"

"A willing sacrifice!" the woman standing over him shouted, eliciting a rise in the chanting.

The man shook his head, emphatically denying her avowal but the mask on his face distorted his voice, making his words echo with the tinge of worship. Dressed in an ornate cloak of green, black, and gold, the high priestess held aloft the blade, its edge glowing red with heat. She cried out again, stoking the ire of the crowd. Then she looked down upon the broken man.

"What will you give to Skorn?"

The man struggled to flee but the silver ropes held him fast. The woman flicked the blade, her expression filled with glee as he recoiled in fear. Then the newcomer stepped onto the platform and strode toward the group. His appearance went unnoticed until one in the front row began to shout. The outburst spread like wildfire, causing the leaders to turn and face him. Then the man peeled back his cowl.

Although inured to violence, the cultists were still shocked by his appearance. Four ragged scars rent his flesh, tearing and pulling from temple to chin. The claws of the great cat had marked his flawless features, but his dark eyes glittered from between the scars.

"You *dare* to interrupt a sacrifice?" the leader demanded, recovering first.

"Carvia," the man addressed her, "your leadership here is no longer necessary."

Shock flitted across her features at the use of her real name, and then rage took its place. "I know not how you passed Skorn's blade, but your life ends here. Willing or no, you will be sacrificed to him." Her eyes flicked to the man at her side. "Bind him."

Her two companions leapt forward, but the man drew the previously bound blade and plunged it into the first. Releasing the handle, he willed it to withdraw and strike the second. Both bodies struck the stage and the sword glided above them, fire bursting up the blade.

The shouts reverberated into silence as Skorn's blade glided among them, free and leashed to the newcomer's will. He smiled and advanced upon Carvia. The sword spun around her, the tip gliding past her throat. She ignored it, her eyes fixed upon him.

"Who *are* you?"

"You have worshiped me for eons yet know not my face?" He laughed mockingly and gestured to the statues behind her.

Disbelief contorted her features but her eyes flicked to the statues. "You claim to be the god Skorn?"

He rotated to face the crowd. "I have slumbered for eons, but come to take my place at your head. Now I call upon you to recognize your master . . . and kneel."

Grappling with the suddenness of his claim, several cultists shifted their feet. One took a step forward and raised his hand to protest. Skorn's blade darted to him, plunging deep before retreating. The protest died on his lips and he slumped to the floor.

The man in the Ero mask struggled to his feet, and in the silence his relieved sobbing was clearly audible, even through the magic of the mask. He stumbled toward Skorn, raising his hands in relief. Skorn rotated to face him and smiled. The sacrifice recoiled from the expression, and then shrieked as the hovering blade plunged into his back. He slumped to the floor and the bloody blade withdrew before stalking the spectators once more.

One of the most fervent cultists dropped to his knees, crying out in worship. As if a dam had broken the others followed suit, and the thousands of fanatics dropped to their knees. Skorn basked in their chants before turning to Carvia.

"Your will or your life," Skorn said. "Either way, I will have my sacrifice."

Her gaze flicked to the dead, and then she too dropped to her knees. "Master," she whispered.

Skorn smiled and faced his cult. For now, they would be his army, the most loyal kind he could ever desire. He constantly found it amusing

14

that they viewed him as a god. He was Skorn, but even the cult that worshiped him had no idea of his true identity. Only the Eternals knew the truth, but he'd been careful to keep his presence secret.

After he'd escaped from Ero, the Thieves Guild had been the perfect place to hide—until Jack Myst had arrived. Skorn's smile turned into a scowl as he thought of him. Skorn yearned to kill him for what he'd done, but Jack was the only one capable of retrieving what he sought.

Skorn's gaze swept across the army of fanatics, a smile twisting his scarred features. His blade swung about, hovering over those with defiance in their features. At the sight of the sword they lowered their eyes and joined the building chant. Skorn allowed it to build to a fever pitch before silencing it. Then he spoke in the deathly quiet.

"Your sacrifice has been accepted," he said.

"Our will is Skorn's!" they cried, repeating the phrase with increasing fervor until the teeth of Margauth seemed to shake.

Skorn's dark eyes glittered. His return to power had begun.

Chapter 1: Rock Trolls

Jack Myst ascended to the cottage roof and wrapped himself in his cloak. The material of the shaden cloak bent the shadows, causing him to fade into the darkness. Then he settled in to wait. The roof belonged to one of the king's groundskeepers, so the building remained vacant at night. Guards would occasionally pass by and peer into the windows, but Jack had no fear of discovery, at least not from the men. The rock trolls were another matter entirely.

Theirs was a recent contract and one that heightened the castle's defenses a hundredfold. Only twenty rock trolls patrolled the castle and the grounds, yet they were more dangerous than thousands of the standard guard. In the month since Jack had been watching he'd never seen a troll out of place.

A female rock troll approached the cottage shortly before midnight, and Jack eased himself deeper into the shadow of the chimney. As she neared, Jack recognized her as High Captain Arana, the leader of the rock troll contingent in the city.

At nine feet tall and layered in muscle, she had skin as tough as boiled leather. Spiked tattoos covered her upper body, every inch marking a kill. The rock troll's Sundering displayed her history of battle—a visual challenge for every foe.

Jack controlled his breathing as she came to a halt in front of the cottage and slowly circled it, her eyes scanning every shadow large enough to obscure a squirrel. Her eyes slid across his form and then flicked to him. He resisted the urge to bolt but tensed his body, readying himself to flee. Then she moved on and he released a slow breath.

At least it wasn't Tryton.

When he'd first come to scout the castle, the rock troll king had just finished negotiating the contract. He'd almost caught Jack—twice. Jack had chosen to halt his stalking until Tryton had departed north. Then Jack had resumed his survey of the fortress.

Not prone to patience, he reminded himself of his purpose and continued to watch the guards. Like every night, he fell to pondering what he knew. It felt like a lifetime since he'd infiltrated the Thieves Guild and learned the true identity of the Guildmaster.

Skorn was an ancient, a member of a race presumed dead for eons. He'd sent Jack's mother to steal a map left by his people, but she had taken it and disappeared. Years later Skorn had found her. He'd sent thieves to bring her back but she'd refused, and been killed in the ensuing battle.

Jack would have died that night without the supreme sacrifice of his panther. In giving his life, Shadero had transferred much of his physical attributes to Jack. Jack's druid magic had been extinguished, but his body had been permanently enhanced as a result.

Jack had spent six years preparing himself to infiltrate the guild that had killed her. He'd hunted three men within their ranks, but his quest had not ended with their deaths. Shelt had died from his injuries years ago. Nemeth had been taken by the dark elves into the Deep. As the leader of those who'd killed his mother, Kuraltus had suffered as much as Jack had. Orn had taken his memories and forced him to be what he was not, a killer.

Do not be what I became.

He scowled, irritated that his mother's words continued to hold him to his oath. He'd sworn not to become a thief and so he'd left the guild. Then he'd found his mother's memory orb from which he'd learned the truth, that the man he'd defeated was an ancient. The information sent him on a trail of answers that eventually led to the castle at Terros.

You're still a thief, Jack, he imagined her saying.

I left the guild, didn't I?

Are you here to steal? she seemed to challenge.

Curiosity, he corrected.

She seemed to grunt in disapproval, but that only made him smile. He'd heard the distinct sound hundreds of times in his youth. Every time he would disobey, or think he'd tricked her, she would tighten her lips and make that sound.

—A motion drew his gaze and he shoved the memories aside. A pair of human guards had deviated from their assigned path and approached a troll to engage him in conversation. The door he guarded lay on the east side of the castle. Because of its distance from anything vital it had always been unguarded, until King Tryton had noticed the weakness and placed a rock troll at the portal.

The troll ignored the humans but they persisted, growing irritated with his silence. The troll had been trained from birth for the purpose of war, his discipline prevented him from losing focus. Still, he grew annoyed and lowered his gaze to order them back to their track.

Jack leapt from the cottage roof and bolted across the sloping grounds, counting the seconds. He needed five to make it past the rock troll's view—but the troll looked up in four. The troll barked an order for the soldiers and they recoiled. He sprinted around the turret and searched the shadows. His massive greatsword glittered in the moonlight as he spun about, searching for any hint of movement.

Fifty feet above the troll, Jack hung from his shadowhook, clinging to the side of the turret. The troll looked up and called out for the guards to bring torches, but before they returned Jack slipped onto the turret roof. His heart hammering in his chest, he counted the minutes until the troll muttered to himself and returned to his post.

The near catch brought a smile, and Jack resisted the urge to drop a pebble onto the rock troll's head. Instead he aimed his bracer toward another roof and activated his shadowhook again. An inky thread exploded from the bracer and streaked across the dim sky, fusing to the shadows on a neighboring roof. Activating one of the runes, Jack leapt off as the magic drew him in. He swung to the neighboring roof and then lowered himself to the wall below.

He reached the battlements and slipped through the shadows, gliding around the courtyard to a door that entered the castle proper. Below, a handful of soldiers fidgeted outside the stables, their helms catching the torchlight as they turned.

Jack reached the door into the keep but it swung open. On instinct he leapt above the door. His toes found purchase on the door's border and he held the wall with his shadowhook. Unfortunately, the two guards exited with a torch in hand.

". . . don't trust the trolls," one growled. "Just a few years ago they decimated an army we sent into the north."

"Aye," the second agreed. "Yet the king is even talking about augmenting their contract to lead the castle guard."

The guards came to a stop, and the light from their torch brightened the wall. Jack's shadowhook began to slip and there was nothing to hold. He caught a crack between two stones and held on.

"Blasted trolls . . ." a guard said, his voice trailing off as his eyes drifted up. His features widened with shock when he spotted Jack spread on the wall like a giant fly.

Jack grinned and dropped between them. He caught the torch handle and smashed the wood into the man's face. Then he spun to the second and struck him in the throat, preventing his shout of warning. Jack slid behind him and wrapped his hand across his mouth.

"If it helps," Jack whispered, "I don't like the troll's presence either."

The man struggled in his grip until Jack smashed his skull into the wall. He crumpled to the stone without a sound, but the dancing torchlight drew a shout from below.

"Oi!" a man called up. "What's the commotion about?"

Jack held the sputtering torch so his face remained in shadow and leaned over the battlements. "Willis stubbed his toe!"

The captain jabbed a hand toward him. "Get back to your route!"

"Yes, captain," he said.

He turned away and knelt to tie up the two guards. "You'd think your captain would know the names of his men," he murmured, "or at least which Willis is on watch tonight."

He felt a flash of gratitude for Tryton. Due to the troll's presence Jack had spent a week in the taverns of Terros, and overheard a Private Willis complain that there were several with his same name on the castle guard.

When the guards were bound Jack dragged them into a storage room and shut the door. Mentally he accelerated his timetable and slipped to the keep. He paused on the threshold and returned to the unconscious guards.

"Sorry, my friend," he said as he removed the man's uniform.

He took a moment to don the persona of a soldier, and adjusted the false jaw and hair that obscured his features. Then he strode inside. His effort was rewarded when he passed a guard ambling down the hall. The woman threw him a bored look which Jack returned.

"Blasted trolls," he said.

The woman grinned and repeated it before passing him by. Jack smirked in her wake before turning down another corridor. Twice more he passed guards on his way to the basement levels of the castle. Both failed to look beyond his uniform.

Sprawling and disorganized, the castle's very shape had created an unintended defense. He lost his way several times until he found the right stairs leading into the basement. Descending close to the great hall, he avoided the pair of rock trolls within and made his way to the King's Vault situated beneath it.

He'd expected a rock troll as a guard, and he was not disappointed. The hulking figure stood motionless outside a dwarven-made steel door.

20

Jack came to a halt around the corner and reached up to dim the light orb. If he was fortunate the rock troll would come to investigate, allowing him to slip by.

The rock troll merely glanced at the extinguished light, his eyes turning suspicious. Silently cursing their race, Jack used the dim light to point his gauntlet to the ceiling and ascend into the shadows. As in most of the castle, the ceilings in this chamber contained decorative bars that held short banners. Grasping one, Jack activated the enchantment on his second gauntlet, muffling all sounds in the immediate vicinity.

He used the banners to advance across the ceiling and carefully lowered himself behind the rock troll. Even with the muffling charm active, he touched the floor like it was about to explode and gingerly brought his weight onto the stones.

He was close enough to see the rise and fall of the rock troll's back as he breathed. A litany of white scars twisted the tattoos. It was the closest Jack had ever been to one of their kind, and he felt the urge to reach out and poke him in the back. To watch one be startled would be no end of amusing, but would probably cost him his head.

He eased himself to the door and slipped a lock pick into the keyhole, glancing over his shoulder every few seconds at the troll. Even though he had the muffling charm active, he controlled every motion. He was not prone to fear but a nine-foot rock troll with hundreds of kills to his credit stood behind him. Jack could hear the leather sliding against the troll's rough skin as he shifted, the sound just outside the range of his muffling charm.

After an interminable moment the lock gave, and he moved his picks to the second. His patience was rewarded when it too gave, allowing him to turn the handle and ease the door open. He slipped into the stygian darkness and then slid the door shut. Then he withdrew his lightstone from a pouch in his thief's webbing and activated it to its dimmest setting. The faint glow beamed across the room as he held it aloft, illuminating the strongroom.

At twenty paces across it was smaller than he'd expected, yet filled with a vast assortment of valuables. Coins, gems, and jewelry spilled from overflowing chests. Memory orbs overloaded shelves and were interspersed with enchanted weaponry. Old shields hung from the few bare walls, their surfaces covered in dust.

He advanced through the piles of wealth, resisting the temptation to dive into them. This time he had a different purpose, and after a few minutes of searching he found what he sought. Forgotten beneath a jeweled dagger sat a book the size of his palm. When he opened the cover, light blossomed from the paper. It solidified into a hovering page fashioned of glowing letters.

He reached up with his free hand and flicked the page to the side, examining the lettering. He grunted in irritation when he found the text of unfamiliar origin. The book was one of the few relics from the extinct ancient race that had inhabited Lumineia over forty thousand years ago. He shouldn't have been surprised at the language.

He closed the book and pocketed it before returning to the door. He paused when his eyes fell upon a massive sapphire. The jewel had been carved in the shape of a snarling cat. Black jet had been added to the face, giving the creature dark eyes. Unable to resist, he reached out to it.

His fingers probed the shelf beneath the cat and he sensed the tingling of power attached to the hind leg. He smiled and withdrew an anti-magic dagger to sever the trap. The tingling faded and he sheathed the blade. Then he picked up the cat.

A piercing shriek exploded through the room as a second trap triggered. The banshee curse crushed his muffling charm and rose into a furious wail. He cringed against the sound. In a single motion he drew his anti-magic dagger and plunged it into the pulsing rune underneath the cat's position, silencing the curse. As he sheathed the knife the door crashed open.

He spun to find the hulking troll framed in the doorway, an expression of fury twisting his features. The troll pointed his enormous sword at Jack.

"Submit or die, thief."

"I've never been good at either."

The troll shifted into a combat stance. "Then it appears I get to kill you."

"If you can," Jack said with a grin. Then he exploded into motion.

Chapter 2: Undaunted

Jack placed a foot on a lower shelf and leapt, twisting into a flip. The troll's sword flashed in his wake, crashing into the shelf and sending artifacts tumbling to the floor, setting off a chorus of banshee curses. Jack soared over the troll's shoulder and landed in the doorway. Curses exploded throughout the room as the wounded shelf collapsed, narrowly missing the troll as he leapt aside.

"You missed," Jack said.

The troll roared at him and surged toward the door, but Jack was already sprinting down the hallway. Even with Jack's enhanced speed, the troll gained ground, his giant legs pumping like a warhorse.

Jack raced around the first corner, running up the wall to prevent himself from crashing into it. Sprinting down the hall, he caught a decorative knight's armor to swing around a second corner. Six steps later he heard the crash of the armor and glanced back—and dived to the floor.

The troll had caught the knight's spear and yanked it free. Then he hurled it at Jack with lethal accuracy. Only Jack's reflexes saved his life, and the spear sailed over his shoulder, slicing a shallow line through his tunic.

"Do you always destroy what you guard?"

Jack's laughter caused the troll to growl and accelerate even faster. Jack swerved around another corner—and found a second troll. The newcomer was already racing toward him, his heaving footfalls causing the floor to shudder. Jack slowed, buying himself precious seconds to think. Then the trolls reached him and swung their blades in unison. The greatswords cleaved the air, one going for his neck, the other for his waist.

Jack rolled his body into a horizontal spin that carried him between the blades. The swords came so close he felt the cold from the metal as it streaked by his face. Then he was through the gap and landing on the opposite side. Slipping around the second troll he accelerated down the hall.

"Do you *train* to miss?"

The trolls bellowed their fury and surged into pursuit, but Jack had already turned another corner. He reached the stairs and took four at a time until a pair of guards appeared at the top. They shouted in alarm as Jack reached them. He leapt to the handrail and rebounded over their heads, landing in a sprint.

They gave chase but cried out in dismay when the two trolls plowed through them, knocking them to the floor. Jack glanced back in time to see one of the trolls veer off and disappear down a side corridor.

Jack turned a corner and slipped into an open door, closing it softly behind him. He turned to find himself in the kitchen with several cooks staring at him. A couple of dogs ran on a belt, turning a spit on which a turkey roasted. One cook stood with a ladle over the bird, a dark liquid dripping onto the sizzling meat.

Jack raised a finger to his lips to silence the cooks as the troll passed, but the troll slid to a stop and began to retreat. Realizing his hiding spot would not last, Jack turned and wove through the tables and cooks, making his way for the opposite door. To his dismay a female troll swung it open and stepped into the kitchen, straightening to her full stature. High Captain Arana drew her sword but stood her ground as Jack retreated to the center of the kitchens. Behind him the first door open and a troll ducked through the opening.

"How did you know I would come in here?" Jack asked Arana.

"I didn't," she replied, "I sent trolls to every exit."

The cooks shifted uneasily, with several scurrying out of the way. One woman squeaked in fear and fled amidst a cloud of flour. He grinned as she huddled with the others and then he gestured to Arana.

"I suppose you want me to surrender."

"The castle guard has been summoned. You can either remain until they arrive, or die on your feet."

"He made his choice," the troll growled from Jack's back.

Jack grinned at his tone and looked to find the one who'd caught him inside the strongroom. "Does the damage you do come from your wages?"

The troll sneered at him and took a step forward but Arana barked an order and he came to a halt. Then Jack heard the pounding of feet and rush of bodies. The sound continued to mount as soldiers converged on their location.

Jack shrugged and used the motion to distract from easing his hand crossbow into his grip. He thumbed the trigger to activate it and the bow sprang into place. Arana noticed the weapon and a small smile crossed her features.

"Do you mean to harm me with such a tiny weapon?"

"Of course not," Jack scoffed. "I mean to escape."

He raised the weapon and pointed it at the large light orb above his head. Pulling the trigger, he sent a piercing bolt into the glass. It exploded in a shower of sparks. Men and women screamed as the room plunged into darkness. Lit only by the cooking fires, the tables and kettles cast long shadows. Jack retreated into them.

"Hold your ground," Arana said. "Kill him if he attempts escape."

Jack's laughter seemed to come from everywhere. "I have my own door, troll."

A wall exploded, sending bits of stone and burning wood sizzling into the kitchens. Arana took two steps toward the opening before noticing the explosion had not broken through. She spun back to the door but Jack was already there.

"You have my gratitude, high captain."

She charged after him as he sprinted into the grand dining hall. A handful of soldiers were rushing toward him but he leapt for the long table. Fine china scattered at his passage, shattering on the floor.

"Kill him!"

"That's the King's own plate!"

"Stop him before he breaks the—"

Jack swerved to kick the glass goblet reserved for the king. Renowned as the king's cup, the goblet had been a family heirloom for centuries. Jack's boot hit the cup and it went soaring toward the hearth. The guards sucked in a collective breath as it shattered on the stones.

"We all know how ugly it was," Jack said from atop the table.

He pointed his shadowhook toward the ceiling and sent a thread of darkness streaking away. Blades and arrows descended upon his shadow but he glided out of reach. Alighting on the dark chandelier, he used it to leap to the next. Crossbow bolts streaked past him and clattered off the ceiling.

"Raise the light!" Arana bellowed.

Realizing she knew his shadowhook would not operate under illumination, Jack cast it at the wall and swung toward the archway that led to the great hall. A trio of soldiers stood in the opening and raised their arms as if to stop him. He crashed through them just as the light brightened in the dining hall. He tumbled across the soldiers, narrowly missing being impaled by a loose sword. Then he regained his footing and sprinted into the great hall.

Enormous dwarven-crafted pillars lined the space, aimed to point all eyes to the throne at the head of the chamber. The floor had been polished to a mirror shine, and reflected the darkened chandeliers hanging from massive beams. Enormous stained glass windows lined the upper walls, the patterns depicting great kings from past eras.

The current monarch had commissioned his own portrait to be placed above the main entrance to the hall. Larger than the others, the glass showed a striking man standing with his foot above a vanquished foe. The sun shone upon his face and his upraised sword. Recently completed, the glass had been conspicuously cleaned, making it brighter than the portraits of his predecessors.

Jack raced between the pillars and angled toward the main gates, but two trolls stood rooted in his path. He saw the glint in their black eyes and knew they would not be moved. A glance revealed soldiers pouring into the hall from all sides, closing the trap.

Still sprinting, Jack pointed his shadowhook toward the rafters above. The moment it attached he leapt to a pillar. Rebounding off its surface, he leapt to the one opposite, all the while shortening the length on the chord.

"There's nowhere to go, thief!" a voice roared, and he recognized it as the king's.

The guards fell silent but continued to stream into the hall and surround Jack's pillar. Jack alighted on a huge beam and looked down at the king's entrance. Still dressed in his bedclothes, the man appeared rotund and old, causing Jack to grin.

"My liege," he called, offering a mock bow. "Your window fails to capture your largess."

"I'll have your head on a pike!" the king roared, his face reddening with embarrassment.

Jack feigned a languid pose and ignored the threat. "But I suppose it couldn't be helped. Your belly alone requires its own window . . ."

Another intake of breath reverberated across the hall, and the king's face blackened with fury. His jaw worked but no words came out, and Jack wondered if the pulsing vein on his forehead would burst.

"But rest easy, my Lord," Jack called. "I'll make certain your craftsmen have another attempt at capturing your girth."

Laughing at the man's sputtering rage, Jack sent his shadowhook streaking into the rafters once more and then swung toward the window.

A stillness filled the hall, as if every soldier could not comprehend what Jack was about to do. The next instant his body crashed into the glass, shattering the image and sending colored shards cascading to the floor. Instinctively the men ducked but the trolls merely shielded their eyes, the glass bouncing off their bodies. As the sound of cracking glass faded one voice filled the hall.

"I WANT HIM DEAD!"

Soldiers rushed about, charging the main gates as the rock trolls sprinted outside. In seconds the hall had emptied and soldiers filled the grounds. Shouts and orders punctuated the night but Jack was not to be found.

As the minutes turned into hours it became clear the thief had escaped. The king stomped about roaring for his guards to search the city. With all their attention outside, no one noticed the figure slip back through the broken glass and descend to the floor.

As they searched the city and grounds Jack removed the false jaw and other items from his face and dropped them down a privy. Leaving the persona and the guard's clothes behind, Jack donned a servant's garb and entered the servants' quarters. Slipping into an empty bunk, he attached a false nose and then pulled a blanket over his shoulders. While the guards frantically searched for him he slept soundly with the other weary servants.

The next night the city guard found the shopkeeper he'd used to build his persona. Even as they arrested the perplexed man Jack ambled out of the castle. He trudged toward the exit as if he'd just completed a long day toiling on the castle floors. Troll and human guards paid him no mind, and several minutes later he was in the streets of Terros.

Jack passed irritable guards that had been out all night, and managed to keep the smile from his face. Once he was out of sight he removed the false nose and tossed it in the gutter. Then he withdrew the book he'd taken and examined the cover.

"Let's find someone that can read you, shall we?"

Chapter 3: Answers

Word spread quickly of the theft and the king's mood. The monarch's foul disposition contrasted sharply with the men in Jack's caravan headed north. He joined the group in a mercenary persona, and listened to the other guards share wild theories about the thief that had taken from the king's own castle. Few liked the king, and much laughter was had at the man's expense. Jack didn't hesitate to contribute his own thoughts, and smiled at the rumors they would start.

After a week's journey he slipped away and took the eastern road to the Library of Worchestan. He rode hard through a forest of elder and cedar trees. Two days later he crested a rise in the road and a village came into view.

Built around a pair of staggering towers, the settlement catered to the travelers who had journeyed a great distance in order to study at the library. Rumored to contain an archive that dated back to the Age of Oracles, the towers had been built by a fabled monarch known for his pursuit of knowledge. The man had commissioned the library to be constructed of the strongest materials and paid a handsome sum to a group of dwarven engineers to build it. To their credit, it had withstood wars and the elements for nearly twenty thousand years.

Each of the two towers loomed over the trees. They rose to hundreds of feet high, with each level housing books, memory orbs, and other records. Although the elves claimed to have the greatest collection of written history, their archives paled in comparison to the Library of Worchestan.

Jack entered the town and found a stables that would hold his steed. Then he advanced through the twilight to the southern tower. He found the door unlocked and strode past the drowsy guard.

A great spiral staircase wound its way up the core of the tower, leading to a labyrinth of alcoves, chambers, and study rooms. The rooms were filled to the brim with ancient tomes from bygone eras.

A handful of men and women toiled at ink stained desks, painstakingly copying from nearly illegible books. The scent of paper, leather, and dust filled the air, causing him to rub his nose in irritation. Then one of the men spotted him and approached.

"What do you seek, traveler?" he asked.

"I wish to learn of the ancients," Jack replied.

"Ah," he said, his eyes lighting with curiosity. "Such a topic is rarely requested. Is there something specific you wish to know . . .?"

The man waited expectantly but Jack merely smiled and waited in turn. When it became clear he had no intention of sharing any more, the man's expression tightened.

"You will need to speak with Attendant Loth," he said. "I will summon him."

His curt comment heralded his departure, and Jack turned his gaze on the library. Several minutes later the scribe returned with another man before departing without a word. Jack's eyes settled on Loth, unsurprised by his appearance.

The weathered old man resembled an aged apple. His smile creased the wrinkles, reshaping them until his features almost disappeared. His snowy hair reached past his shoulders and was tied at the back of his head, yet the strength to his gaze belied his age.

"You are not the first to seek the ancients," he said, and a shrewd smile appeared on his face. "But I suspect you may be one of the few to understand them."

"What makes you say that?"

31

"Those who come here always seek answers," he replied. "But I can always tell the ones that know a little truth . . . and want more."

Jack grinned and gestured to himself. "I'm Jack Myst."

"Loth," the man said, his grey eyes twinkling with amusement. "Come with me."

Turning about, he led Jack to the steps and worked his way down. After three levels Jack began to wonder how the old man managed to use them without his body giving out. As if reading his thoughts, the old man chuckled.

"We are not as frail as we look, traveler."

"That is well," Jack replied easily, "because you look like a stiff breeze might topple you to the ground."

Loth laughed and agreed. "Moisture destroys the archives, but the dryness destroys our flesh. You can see which we favor."

He chuckled to himself and continued to descend to the very bowels of the library. The steps grew dark and the air stale, indicating the level was rarely used. Loth pressed on to the base of the stairs. Then he stepped to a bracketed light orb and reached out to it. His touch caused it and several others to brighten, illuminating a circular room with eight corridors. Choosing one, he advanced away from the stairs.

Openings were placed on either side, and Jack saw more bookshelves and memory orbs placed on them, all covered in dust. Loth passed them by until he reached the final opening. Upon entering, he reached up and touched the light orb. It did not brighten immediately but slowly glowed to life as if reluctant to wake.

"Everything we have about the ancient race is stored in this room."

Jack looked among the shelves, but only four lonely books and a single memory orb sat in view.

"A wealth of knowledge," Jack said dryly.

Loth smiled, wrinkling his face once again. "Their civil war took place over forty thousand years ago. Precious little lasts that long."

"And yet I have encountered dozens of ancient artifacts in less than a year," Jack said.

Loth's eyebrows shot up. "It appears you have a tale to tell."

"Telling it would only put you in danger," Jack said.

"Then what do you wish of me?"

Jack gestured to the books. "Have you read them?"

Loth nodded, creasing his wrinkled jowls. "Most are a retelling of the Ballad of Ero and Skorn."

Jack grunted in irritation. His mother had made him memorize the lengthy ballad as a child, and aside from keeping him from a noose at the elven city of Azertorn, it had done little for him.

"Fairy tales will not help me," he said. "But a man that can read their language can."

Loth strode to one of the books and picked it up. Opening it, he thumbed through the pages until he found what he sought and then offered it to him. Jack examined the text and nodded when he recognized it.

"Can you read it?" Jack asked.

"Some," Loth admitted. "But it has not been spoken in eons, so the pronunciation is unknown."

"I don't need to hear it," Jack said, and withdrew the book he'd taken from the king's castle. "I just need to understand it."

Loth's eyes widened when he saw the book, and then turned shrewd. "The king would not give that up for any sum—unless it was taken without his knowledge."

"Perhaps it was."

Loth's eyes glowed with amusement. "If I should discover the thief, I will be certain to turn him in."

Jack grinned. "So you know of this book?"

33

"Many years ago the king summoned one of my colleagues to attempt to decipher it, but he would not let it be taken from his strongroom. We refused to bring our records south in order to translate it. The impasse means it has never been read."

Jack handed it to him and Loth reverently accepted it. A soft smile creased his wrinkled features and he slid his thumb across the binding. Then he began to speak, murmuring his thoughts aloud.

"The binding and cover have not been dimmed by age and are made of a peculiar material that endures better than anything we possess. Inscribed are the words, 'to mankind, may it bring you peace'."

He eased the cover open and, as before, light poured from within, flowing into a page above the book. Loth carefully placed the open tome on a pedestal situated near the front of the room and reached up to turn the ethereal page.

"What does it say?"

"Control your impatience," the old man chided. "It is difficult enough to read without you hovering over my shoulder."

With difficulty Jack held his irritation in check while the old man muttered to himself. Occasionally he shifted to the books and memory orb in the room in search of a particularly difficult translation. Every time Jack queried him Loth said the same thing.

"Patience, my son."

As the hours passed, Jack's stomach began to grumble, and he asked Loth where the kitchens were located. Deep in the thrall of his translation, the old man muttered incoherently and vaguely pointed upward. Blowing out his breath, Jack exited the room and went in search of food. An hour later he returned in a better disposition and took a seat on one of the benches in the archive hall. While he waited he examined the other ancient books and struggled to make out the tiny scrawl of long dead attendants.

The ancients had been small in number, some saying their entire race never surpassed a few hundred souls. Jack found several theories as to their origin, but the one he found most intriguing said they did not hail from Lumineia at all, but came from another realm. Perhaps they had only intended on staying for a short time, but a civil war had decimated their ranks.

The book finished by retelling the Ballad of Ero and Skorn. Most tellings of the ballad described Ero and Skorn as god and devil, both wrestling for dominion over Lumineia. With the power of his staff, Ero ultimately triumphed, casting Skorn into a pit of eternal torment.

In the version Jack had learned as a child there had been no mention of the ancients, but here the telling alluded to men and women that did not age, that had power beyond any of the races. It also contained additional verses that described Ero and Skorn. Both had spawned religions based on their faith, but little was said as to what caused the original rift.

Abruptly weary, Jack closed the book and rubbed his eyes. Then he rose and entered the room to find Loth still poring over the ancient book.

"What did you—."

"It's stunning," Loth said, turning excited eyes upon him. "It's a detailed account of the ballad, yet it's written in an entirely different form."

Jack folded his arms, his annoyance sparking. "I didn't go through all the trouble to borrow it just to read the ballad again."

"You don't understand," he said. "This is written like it's an *actual record* of the events, meaning the ballad we have is an interpretation of *this* book." His eyes glowed. "This is the original."

Jack was intrigued. "What does it say that the ballad doesn't?"

"As many historians have suspected, the god Ero and the devil Skorn battled for rule over Lumineia. The ancients were caught up in this conflict, ultimately perishing in the fight. What is clear from here is that Ero and Skorn didn't *rule* ancients, they *were* ancients, and . . ."

Loth continued to speak but Jack didn't hear his words. The truth that had hovered in front of him suddenly clicked into place. His mother had left an orb revealing the truth, that Orn was a living ancient. The man he'd battled for control of the Thieves Guild was not just any ancient. He was *the* ancient, the very devil that ballads told tales of, the name that inspired fear among every race in Lumineia.

"Skorn wasn't a god," Loth said, drawing his attention.

Jack's features tightened. "He was an ancient."

Chapter 4: The Ancient Keys

"I have to tell the others of this discovery," Loth said, and started for the hallway.

The man's words yanked Jack from his thoughts and he stepped in front of him. "That would be unwise."

"But a truth of this magnitude—"

"Will get you killed," Jack said with such force that Loth stopped and met his gaze.

"Truth cannot harm us."

"It can if Skorn has returned."

Loth snorted in disbelief. "You cannot mean that an ancient remains alive."

"Until recently he was the Guildmaster of the Thieves Guild. I did not know who he was but I thought I'd killed him. Now I wonder if I was successful."

Loth regarded him with a mixture of doubt and curiosity. "There are too many questions to ask, so I'll ask the one most obvious. If a former god now walks the earth, why did he need to take possession of the Thieves Guild?"

"Me," Jack said. "He wanted a thief capable of stealing an ancient map of Lumineia."

"Did you see the map?"

"I did," Jack said. "And then I destroyed it."

Loth's expression turned to ash and he passed a hand over his face. "Why would you destroy something of such value?"

"Because he wanted it," Jack replied. "And if he can, he would harm everyone and everything."

"And you care about the people?"

Jack laughed. "I care about stopping him."

"Why?"

"Because he doesn't think I can."

"Is that all it takes?"

"For me it is," Jack said, and reached for the book.

Loth stepped to it first. "Please," he said. "I implore you not to destroy it."

"If Skorn knows I have this book, he will kill anyone who has touched it."

"I swear I will put it where it cannot be found."

"You'd risk your life on that?"

"I gave my life for knowledge long ago," he said with sudden force. "I would do so again without hesitation."

Jack stared at his blazing eyes and then shrugged. "As you will. But speak of it to no one, or your life will not be the only one forfeit. He would burn this library to the ground to keep his secret."

Loth nodded and closed the book. Then he turned back to Jack with a strange expression. "You speak as if he has something to fear."

"He doesn't," Jack said, and then paused. "Or perhaps he does. One so zealous to protect their identity must do so for a reason. The question is, what haunts his dreams?"

"Or who," Loth mused. "If one ancient is alive, perhaps there is another."

"Like Ero?" He laughed, but Loth did not.

"Let us hope not," he said, his tone becoming grim. "For history has a way of twisting with time. He may have fought Skorn, but that does not mean he is our ally."

"If he lives," Jack countered. "No one has heard of an ancient for thousands of years. I doubt there are more hiding about."

"Perhaps," Loth said. "But you would do well to be cautious."

Jack turned away and strode for the stairs. "Caution has its place, my friend. Now I must go and ensure Skorn died."

"And if he didn't?"

Jack glanced over his shoulder. "Then I steal his life for good."

Loth shuddered, and then nodded. "Will you share what you learn with me?"

The earnestness in the plea caused Jack to sigh. "If I am traveling this way again, I will visit and share the tale."

"I'll have a mug of ale ready for you," Loth promised.

Jack grinned. "Farewell, old man, and do not forget my warning."

Loth tapped the book and then slid it into his white robes. "I have seen no such book, my Lord."

Jack laughed at the indignation in his voice and then departed. Exiting the way he had come in, he retrieved his horse and mounted. For the next several days he worked his way west until he reached Galignon, a small fishing village north of Terros. From there he took a boat south. Landing in the kingdom of Talinor, he disembarked and crossed the breadth of the kingdom to reach the great Evermist swamp, home of the Thieves Guild.

It was the first time he'd returned since defeating the Guildmaster, and the clinging mist elicited a smile. He'd spent several months in the guild before battling Skorn. At the time, Jack had thought he was simply a man named Orn, one who had gone to great lengths to hide his identity. It wasn't until after the battle that Jack had returned to his childhood home and found the memory orb left by his mother. There he'd learned the truth. Curiosity had driven him to find more, and that path had eventually taken him to the king's castle in Terros.

But had he killed Skorn?

The question had nagged him since he'd learned the Guildmaster was an ancient—even more now that he knew his true identity. The last he'd seen of Skorn, he'd been wounded and stumbling into the Evermist while two massive rayth cats stalked him. The cats would not have given up the pursuit, meaning Skorn would have had to kill or evade them, both of which were unlikely. Jack's thoughts turned to the ancient map Skorn had sent him to steal. One did not look for a map simply to possess it, so what location did he seek?

"I want what's rightfully mine," Skorn had said.

But what did Skorn want to find? Had he already gotten it? Was he even alive? Jack blew out his breath in disgust and quickened his pace. Two days after entering the Evermist he reached the Thieves Guild and paused on the edge of the lake.

The dark castle rose from an island in the still water, its walls covered in moss and vines. Mist clung to its walls and crept about its towers, obscuring much of the fortress. Once a mighty stronghold, the citadel had been forgotten by the other races and appropriated by the thieves.

The citadel exuded menace yet felt like home, the emotion contrasting with the surge of guilt. He'd entered the guild not to become thief but to find his mother's killers. She'd taught him the evil of being a thief, so he'd never expected to enjoy the occupation.

His earliest memories of his mother had included a strict adherence to a life of honor. At the age of eight he'd stolen a dwarven knife from a merchant cart. When his mother had found it she'd dragged him across mountain and plains before they found the merchant near Torridin. The taciturn dwarf had rapped his knuckles hard enough to make them bleed.

"It's just a knife," Jack said sullenly as he soaked his hands in an icy stream.

"A knife or a crumb of bread, it matters not." She took his hands and set to binding his wounds. "What you don't pay in coin you pay with honor."

"I don't even know what that means," he said.

She nudged his chin, forcing him to look at her. The sadness he saw there finally made him listen.

"All men are born with a measure of integrity," she murmured. "Some choices nourish it while others will waste it. A thief pays for each theft with a fragment of his soul until nothing remains, and their heart is as black as their desires. Will you be a man of honor? Or a thief?"

He thought of his father, who seemed to drink more with each passing year. "Does father have honor?"

"No," she said, her lips twitching with regret. "You must look to those who give when they have little, and only take when it will heal."

Jack still didn't grasp her meaning but he nodded anyway, and was rewarded with his mother's smile.

"I won't steal again," he said.

The memory faded and Jack stared at the Thieves Guild. Promising himself he was only here for answers, he managed to suppress the guilt. Then he reached behind a tree and caught the lever that raised the bridge. The submerged span rose above the surface of the water and Jack advanced across the bridge, avoiding the pair of alligators that had been caught on its surface.

He reached the door and caught the handle, but paused. What if Skorn had retaken the guild? What if Jack hadn't heard news because his friends had not been alive to send it? He quelled that thought and stepped inside. Then he made his way to the Guildmaster's office, the highest room in the fortress.

He passed Iron Hall, and a glance revealed a number of familiar thieves. He grinned at the surprise on their faces and his doubts faded away. Several fell into his wake, whispering to each other about his return.

"She will be pleased he has returned."

"But will he take her place?"

"Why would we want him to?"

Someone cuffed the speaker on the back of his head. "Do you not know who he is? That's Jack Myst, the liberator of thieves, the cheater of death."

Jack grinned but did not slow. A few minutes later he reached the doors leading to the Guildmaster's office. His smile widened as he thought of seeing Thera again, the barbarian turned thief. The thieves had called her Beauty, and with good reason.

Beauty's skill with body magic made her a formidable thief. Her desire to punish the Guildmaster for killing her sister had made her a formidable ally. When he'd left she'd been the obvious choice for the next Guildmaster. He swung the door open and stepped inside, coming to a halt.

Instead of Beauty it was Lorelia standing behind the desk. Tall and statuesque, she was the most beautiful elf he'd ever seen. Her golden hair flowed down her back like silk, and her bright blue eyes shined with excitement.

"Jack Myst," she drawled, a smile spreading on her features. "I thought you'd never come back." She glided forward and put her arms around him, drawing him close. She stopped short of kissing him, her expression teasing. "I missed you, Jack."

43

Lorelia had always been a vixen until the Guildmaster's memory magic had broken. Then he'd caught a glimpse of what she'd kept hidden. She'd been somber and timid, afraid even. Jack studied her but saw no hint of that identity. Then he recalled her final words to him when he'd left.

One who wears a mask recognizes another.

Jack feigned ignorance and slid his arms around her back. "Does this weary traveler get a kiss of welcome?"

She giggled and slipped away, returning to her desk. "What brings you back to the guild? I have a juicy assignment if you're inclined to rejoin our ranks."

"I have my own assignment," Jack said.

"Are you certain?" she said, her eyes twinkling. "It involves stealing a young bride before she's added to a harem."

"Tempting," he said, "but not this time. I came back to find Beauty."

Her grin turned into a very attractive pout. "You wound me, but I should not be surprised. You two were as thick as thieves before killing Orn." She grinned at her words.

"I actually thought she would be in that chair," he said, gesturing to the Guildmaster's darkwood desk.

"She is talented," Lorelia said, "but we both know she doesn't want to be a thief forever. Besides, she is still just a class three."

Jack peaked an eyebrow at that. To gain ranks within the guild one had to face the Machine, a multi-level wall built to kill climbers at every stage. Skorn and Kuraltus had been the only class four thieves among the guild, and none had ever survived to level five. The last Jack had heard, Lorelia had been a class three.

"When did you get your fourth rank?" he asked.

"Shortly after you left," she replied. "You left us in disarray, and someone had to pick up the pieces. Before it came to bloodshed I suggested we resolve it on the Machine, and I proved myself capable of taking what you cast aside." Abruptly she smiled, her anger sinking out of view. "But six months is a lifetime for us, so I'll happily welcome you back into the fold."

"And Beauty?"

Lorelia waved her hand. "She left the guild and hasn't returned."

Jack frowned at that. "Not even to visit? Where'd she go?"

"She returned to the barbarian mountains."

"She went home?" Jack asked in surprise.

"Yes," Lorelia said. "But why are you so concerned?"

"Because they will kill her," Jack replied, and turned toward the door.

Lorelia darted to him, reaching his side as he grasped the door. "Is this about Orn?"

He stopped and turned back. "Why would you ask that?"

"I think he survived."

His curiosity piqued, he folded his arms. "What do you know?"

"I know what he wants." She flashed a smug smile. "And why he still wants you."

Chapter 5: Skorn's Quest

Jack followed Lorelia through the fortress to the archives. Built into one of the turrets, the library stored the records of past assignments. Upon entering the Thieves Guild he'd used it to access the chamber and search for information regarding his mother. The library was also where he'd learned that Beauty harbored the same resentment toward the guild, and where she'd become his ally.

At a hundred feet tall the tower was hollow from foundation to peak. Books lined the walls of circular balconies, their titles illuminated by light orbs bracketed between the shelves. The scent of paper and dust wafted across the space, tinged with the smoke drifting from a fire in the hearth.

Lorelia strode past the fire and ascended to the third level. There she made her way to a strongdoor ensconced between two shelves. Producing a nine-pin key, she pushed it into the door and tapped her Guildmaster's signet ring above the lock. The echo of the tumblers mingled with the buzz of enchanted traps being deactivated. Then she swung it open and entered.

Jack followed her into the private study room. Large and open, the chamber contained a table and a few chairs, but the paintings on the walls had been removed. In their place sheets of parchment covered every inch and were interspersed with glowing yellow light orbs. Then Jack recognized one of the papers.

"You kept it all?" he asked, surprised and impressed.

It was everything from Skorn's office, all the papers and parchments that had blanketed his walls when he'd been Guildmaster. He'd kept intricate star charts, drawings, and maps that had gone unseen until Skorn's demise. Jack had thought they were the works of a madman. Now he knew they were the secrets of an ancient.

"He left behind a great deal," she said. "I cast a mirror charm to reflect everything onto the orbs, and then used the reflections to move it down here to study."

She reached towards the orbs and yellow tendrils of magic seeped from her fingers. Reaching out to the orbs she caressed them to life. As they brightened a series of images appeared about the room, detailing the scattered parchment and the star maps on the ceiling. Jack grinned when he realized the pieces of parchment had been placed in the same order they had been before.

"How thorough," he said.

She smiled at his praise. "It took a couple of months to sort it correctly, but it's exactly as he left it. Most of it is indecipherable, but a few things have become clear."

She stepped to two images prominent among the mess. One drawing depicted a red knife with barbs on both sides of the blade. The other resembled the first, but the barbs were larger and twisted in intricate patterns, while the metal itself was blue.

"At first I thought these were weapons," she said, "but I did some digging, and they're actually keys."

"Keys to what?"

"The Vault of the Eternals."

"The what?"

She laughed. "That was my response. Apparently the Eternals are a group of individuals that call themselves the guardians of Lumineia."

"How ostentatious of them."

"My sentiments exactly," she said wryly. "Nevertheless, it seems Orn wanted to access the vault, and it requires both keys to enter. I cannot say why. I believe the map from Azertorn showed the location of an entrance to the vault."

Jack moved to her side and examined the keys. "Where did these keys come from?"

"That's the interesting part," she said, her blue eyes brimming with curiosity. "Apparently these particular keys once belonged to Lord Draeken."

"Draeken was one of the Eternals?" Jack asked, surprised at the reference.

He'd learned some history from his mother and knew that Draeken had nearly destroyed Lumineia ten thousand years ago. But if just one Eternal could do such damage, who were the others? And what did Skorn want from them?

"From the little I can gather, Draeken was an Eternal until he was rejected from their group. Apparently he knew they would want the keys so he disguised them as daggers and had them hidden."

"Where?"

"One lies hidden among the Azure people, while the other was placed among the dark elves."

"You've learned a great deal in just six months."

She snorted in chagrin. "I admit, I became obsessed with solving the puzzles he left, but the answers were initially slow in coming. Fortunately, I had a breakthrough recently and was motivated to find the rest."

"So he wants these keys to access the vault," Jack mused. "But I doubt he'll do it alone. He's demonstrated a penchant for avoiding attention. I wager he'll send others to search for the keys—if he hasn't already"

"But who can he send?" she asked, sweeping a hand at the fortress. "The thieves no longer follow him."

48

Jack's brow furrowed in thought, and then a thought caused him to frown. "I can think of one group that would serve him, the Cult of Skorn."

She raised an eyebrow. "Why would they obey him?"

"Because he *is* Skorn."

She stared at him and then burst into a laugh. "You think our Guildmaster is a god turned devil—who now walks the surface of Lumineia as a thief?"

He folded his arms and glared at her until her amusement faded. "It's true," he said.

"You can't be serious," she said. "He's not a devil—"

"But he *is* an ancient," he said.

She started to laugh again but then understanding lit her eyes and her smile faded. "That would explain a great deal," she said slowly.

"We know the ancients were far more intelligent than we are," he said, "and that they killed each other off in the Dawn of Magic."

"That was forty thousand years ago," she pointed out. "And they obviously weren't immortal if they could be killed."

"True," he said. "But perhaps they had magics we don't understand."

She turned back to the wall of parchment and pondered that. Then she looked back at him. "If he really has taken over the Cult of Skorn, it means he has a veritable army at his command. I wager he has already sent parties to search for the keys."

A sly smile crossed Jack's face as he realized what she was suggesting. "You want to steal them first?"

"I thought you'd never ask."

He laughed at the anticipation in her tone. "What if he already has them?"

49

She jerked her head. "The cultists are anything but thieves. Even if they know exactly what to look for, they'd be hard pressed to find and steal them in so short a time—especially from the dark elves."

"So we go for the Azure key first," he said.

She gestured to the red knife. "They likely thought the same thing, but stealing from the azure is a brutal affair. The islanders are fractured into dozens of tribes, all with their own chief. They're not too fond of outsiders, either."

"Then we find the cultists," Jack said. "They're certainly there already, so we shadow their search and take the key before they do."

"A sound plan," she replied, "but one that would be unwise to carry out alone."

"I don't play well with others."

"So you've said," she said with a grunt of amusement. "But in this case we cannot afford to go it alone."

"What if Skorn left spies in the guild?" Jack asked.

She looked away, her features tightening. "It's possible. He was the Guildmaster for over two decades. Some may still be loyal to him."

"Skorn has a way with manipulation," Jack said. "Even those we think we can trust might betray us."

"Then who can we trust?"

"I trust Ursana and Gordon," he said. "They were instrumental in defeating Skorn, and I doubt their allegiances have changed."

She nodded in agreement. "I'd like to add Thalidon and his brother."

"Brother?"

"Roarthin," she said. "Turns out Skorn kept him locked in a secret cage for twenty years, and used him to force Thalidon to maintain the Machine and our tools."

Jack's eyebrows shot up. He'd known about Thalidon's brother, but the dwarven smith had made no mention of what Skorn had done to him. The manipulation would make both the dwarves hate Skorn.

"They stayed here?" Jack asked.

"They left shortly after you did," she said. "But I suspect they would return for this assignment. I can send Ursana and Gordon for them."

"What about Beauty?"

Her lips tightened. "What about her?"

"No one hates the man more than she," he said. "And her talent would be an enormous asset. I'll go after her while you gather the others."

"I'll come with you," she replied.

"I can find her on my own."

"Have you ever been to the barbarian mountains?"

"No."

"Then I'm coming with you."

Noticing the steel in her eyes, he resigned himself to her companionship. "As you order, *Guildmaster*."

She flashed a dazzling smile and slid close to him. "I look forward to our nights together."

He laughed and slipped out of reach. "I expect you to cook."

"Because I'm a woman?" she asked, indignant.

"Because you're an elf," he replied with a grin.

Her high laughter echoed off the walls of the chamber. "I'll cook if you share the tale of the castle at Terros."

He peaked an eyebrow. "Tracking my movements, are we?"

"Always, Jack," she said, and her smile reminded him of a rayth cat.

"Not much to tell," he said. "I slipped past the rock trolls and breached their strongroom."

"And what did you steal?" she asked as she extinguished the magic in the room.

Jack opened his mouth to answer but thought better of it. "Some secrets are meant to stay hidden."

"Did it help you learn of Skorn?"

"Actually, I learned that bit from my mother," Jack said, and used the half-truth to hide the truth. "She left a memory orb that detailed who he was."

"It's too bad you didn't find it earlier," she said. "That would have saved us a great deal of strife."

"Perhaps," he replied, and followed her from the room. "But he would still have been formidable."

She locked the door and turned to him. "Is there any chance he's dead?"

"We'll know when we reach the Azure Islands," he said. "If the cultists are there, we'll know he sent them."

Her expression turned serious. "What do we do when we retrieve the keys?"

"Destroy them," Jack said as if it were obvious. He smiled as he imagined Skorn's reaction to the keys' destruction.

"I'm confident Thalidon and Roarthin can handle that," she said. "I'll gather my things and appoint an interim Guildmaster. Meet me outside on the docks in an hour."

"Who will take over while you're gone?"

"Kuraltus," she said.

A surge of anger engulfed him, and then he reminded himself that the elf had been manipulated into killing his mother. Once the memory magic had been broken the elf had returned to his former self, and then left the guild.

"When did he return?" Jack asked.

"A few weeks ago," she said. "I don't think he had anywhere else to go."

"And you trust him?"

She strode toward the door. "He's changed, and he's more than capable. Besides, he helped me decipher Skorn's secrets."

"He served Skorn for a long time," Jack said with a frown. "Even if he now remembers who he is, it's possible he is still loyal to Skorn."

"Nonsense," she said with a dismissive wave. "But if you want to be sure, I'll summon him to my office. You can hide in my bedchamber and listen through the door." She smiled at the suggestion.

"As you order, Guildmaster," he said, "but I think I'll just wait right here."

Jack strode to the door but stopped on the threshold, turning back to the room. He had the unsettling thought that he was missing something. As the scanned the room he struggled to identify the nagging doubt but realized it was probably caution. Skorn had been plotting for thousands of years, and a single mistake would seal Jack's fate.

And cost him his life.

Chapter 6: A Dead Foe

They strode to the office and Lorelia sent a guard to summon Kuraltus. Jack drifted to the wall and leaned against it, curious and irritated at the same time. It looked like she wanted to talk but his gaze remained fixed on the door. Respecting his silence, she sat at her desk and set to work on a pile of parchment.

"He's different, Jack."

He didn't respond. The first time he'd seen Kuraltus he'd been killing Jack's mother. Years later he'd found him inside the Thieves Guild beating another elf for his failure. The cruelty on his face had been evident in the hardness to his gaze, the twist to his lips. Then Jack had learned the truth about Skorn, and his power to rob men of their memories, twist them into broken shadows of their former selves. Kuraltus had been a servant of Skorn for two decades, not because he wanted to, but because he'd fallen victim to Skorn's memory curse.

Jack had hated the elf until they'd languished in an elven prison together, and Jack learned how much Skorn had taken from Kuraltus. But the elf had still killed his mother, and Jack wasn't certain he could dismiss the hate he'd felt for so long. He slipped a hand to his back and felt the reassuring hilt of his dagger on his spine.

The Kuraltus that stepped into the room was vastly different from the one Jack had known. His clothes were tailored and neat, the coloring brighter than most thieves'. His eyes were bright, the smile on his face warm and friendly.

"Guildmaster," he said. "I understand you summoned me . . ."

His eyes found Jack and he came to a halt, his smile fading. "Jack," he said quietly. "It's been a while."

"Last time I saw you," Jack said, "we were escaping from Azertorn."

"The first time you saw me, I was killing your mother."

The blunt assertion caused Jack to scowl. "You said you weren't entirely in control of yourself."

Kuraltus sighed and looked away. "I was trained on Sri Rosen to be a soldier. Did you know that? When I returned I fought for my people with honor, and even reached the rank of lieutenant. I was stripped of my rank because I refused to follow an order to kill a human child. Instead I slew my corrupt captain." His eyes flicked to Jack.

"Orn removed the best of me like a vulture feeding on a carcass, the bones picked clean of anything worthwhile. For twenty years I lived thinking that was all I was, and obeyed him because I could not remember ever making a different choice."

"He manipulated many," Lorelia suddenly said, her voice turning bitter.

"You can only be manipulated if you allow it," Jack said.

"Say that again when he holds what you desire," Lorelia said. "You just need to look at Thalidon for an example."

"Orn steals what makes you whole," Kuraltus said. "I didn't know why I was killing, or why I did his bidding. My only thought was obedience."

"I refuse to believe in being forced to act," Jack said. "Our choices are our own."

Lorelia was on her feet. "Not when you care about someone, Jack. *You* may not care about anyone, but everyone else on this world has someone they love."

Stung, Jack turned on her. "I'm not as callous as you think."

"Does that mean you care about someone besides yourself?" Lorelia demanded.

"Skorn?" Kuraltus said, catching the name. "Don't you mean Orn?"

"One and the same," Jack said.

He shook her head in confusion. "Either way, he is dead, is he not?"

Jack turned away from her anger to meet his gaze. "Do we know for certain?"

"The other thieves tell the tale often," Kuraltus said. "He was wounded by your hand and stumbled into the Evermist with two rayth cats stalking him."

"We never found a body," Lorelia pointed out.

"The mist swallows much," Kuraltus said with a shrug. "How many could escape two rayths?"

"I did," Jack said. "Before I defeated him he dropped me in a pit with them."

Kuraltus raised an eyebrow. "You escaped *and* got them to serve you? I wager there is more to that tale."

Jack smirked but did not elaborate. "If I could escape, it's possible he did."

"Does it matter?" Kuraltus asked. "If he survived he cannot return here. All his tools of memory magic are destroyed."

Jack and Lorelia exchanged a look, and Jack shrugged. "You trust him, so tell him."

"Tell me what?" Kuraltus asked.

"It seems that my predecessor in this office was a member of the ancient race."

Kuraltus started to laugh until he noticed the irritation in Jack's face. "Orn? An ancient?" he jerked his head. "They died off eons ago."

"This one didn't," Jack said. "And his name is Skorn."

"You think he was named after a fallen god?" Kuraltus asked.

"He *is* the fallen god," Jack said.

Kuraltus laughed again. "How much ale have you drunk today? Ero and Skorn are just myths to frighten children."

"What if they weren't?" Lorelia challenged, coming around her desk to stand in front of him. "Myths are based in truth, after all."

"But gods walking among us?" Kuraltus asked, and snorted in disbelief. "I've seen that man bleed—and so have you."

Jack said, "We know the ancients existed because their relics and buildings are scattered throughout Lumineia."

"But—"

"And it stands to reason that Skorn and Ero were among them. We all know the ballad references the Dawn of Magic."

"Yes, but—"

"Skorn is an ancient," Jack said, annoyed at the elf's continued doubt. "And if he did survive, I intend to stop him."

Kuraltus shook his head but a glimmer of confusion had appeared in his eyes. Instead of disagreeing, he gestured to Jack.

"If what you say is true, his intentions are grander than our guild."

"Which is why we're going to stop him," Jack said with a grin.

Lorelia smiled. "And I'm going with him."

"What about the guild?" Kuraltus asked. "Our thieves are just beginning to trust and follow you."

"I want you to lead them in my absence."

His eyes widened. "You trust me that much?"

"You were a class four for a reason," she said. "And you weren't the only one affected by his memory magic. They trust you, as do I. Guard them while I'm gone."

"What about you?" Kuraltus asked, turning to Jack. "You would trust me as well?"

Jack stared at him but the hatred he'd felt for so long was absent. The elf before him was not the same one he'd hunted, and Jack could see no trace of the Kuraltus that had served Skorn with unwavering loyalty.

"I don't hate you anymore," he said. "Let's leave it at that."

"How can you forgive me after what I did to your mother?" Kuraltus asked.

Jack shrugged and stepped to the door. "I returned your memories."

"How does that make a difference?" Kuraltus asked, his expression more confused than before.

Jack's lips twitched into a smile. "Because the one that killed my mother was the evil Kuraltus. And I killed him."

The elf laughed. "As you say," he said. But his humor quickly faded at the realization of what Jack had said. He swallowed as tears came to his eyes. "So you forgive me?"

"No need," Jack said. "I killed the elf that killed my mother. *You* haven't done anything to me. I'd suggest you keep it that way."

"Nevertheless," Kuraltus said, "you have my gratitude."

Jack laughed and stepped into the hall. A moment later Lorelia joined him. When the door banged shut she caught his arm, forcing him to face her. Her eyes were bright with wonder.

"You surprise me, Jack."

"You make it sound like I did something grand."

She leaned up and kissed him on the cheek. "You did."

"I killed a foe," he said. "That's the furthest thing from grand."

Her features turned irritated. "Why do you insist on saying that? We both know the truth and—"

"Stop trying to twist my words," he said. "I meant what I said."

She blew out her breath. "You can be aggravating, you know that?"

"I know," he said, a smile playing on his features. "That's part of my charm."

"Blasted thief," she muttered. "You're going to make me regret going with you to find Beauty."

"I said you had to cook."

She sniffed. "I don't recall agreeing to that."

He frowned and turned back to face her. "You know what I said."

Her smile turned purely devilish. "See? I can be aggravating as well." She laughed at his consternation and strode away.

He caught up to her and descended at her side. "I'm glad you're coming," he admitted. "But this doesn't make me part of the guild."

She turned, forcing him to halt. "Did you enjoy working with Ursana and Gordon?"

He shrugged. "Of course, but I'm not a thief anymore."

"Then why steal from the high duke of Talinor?" She poked him in the chest.

"Now how did you know that was me?" he asked, a smile tugging at his lips.

He'd infiltrated the high duke's strongroom to find a record of ancient artifacts. The tome had dated back to the Age of Oracles, when the Verinai had collected such items. Listed among the items had been a book the king of Griffin held in his castle at Terros.

"Who else has the skill for it?" she asked shrewdly.

He laughed at her insinuation. "You really have been tracking my movements."

"I wasn't the only one," she said. "The guild views you as our liberator, and tales of your exploits invariably find their way to me. They respect you, Jack, and more than a few want to work with you."

"I liked working with Ursana and Gordon," he admitted, and then recalled what his mother had asked of him. *Do not be what I became.* He looked away and repeated, "But I'm not part of the guild."

"They weren't the only ones you worked with," she said.

He grinned at her anger. "Working with you is *always* a pleasure."

She grinned. "And the barbarian mountains are nice this time of year."

"Only if you like freezing to death."

"What if I do?" she said, and her smile turned mischievous.

He could not resist her excitement. "When do we depart?" he asked.

She gestured toward the steps. "You get the provisions. I'll gather my things and meet you at the dock."

"I look forward to our journey."

She laughed again and abruptly kissed him on the cheek. "It's good to have you back, Jack."

"I didn't say I was."

She laughed and slipped away without answering.

Chapter 7: Lorelia's Secret

He watched her depart with a grin on his face. He was loath to admit it, but the prospect of working with guild thieves again was appealing. Besides, going after Skorn alone would be unwise. Then he wondered what he'd just committed himself to. Lorelia was not the type to be dissuaded, and she always had her own agenda.

He strode to the kitchens and gathered a pack of supplies. He'd expected things to be different, but the cooks still required him to pay for the food. Exiting the hall, he dodged thieves wanting to talk to him and made his way to the dock at the eastern side of the fortress. Then Forlana stepped in front of him.

She grinned and folded her arms. "Jack," she drawled. "I hear you are using personas for your work. Your guise at the Terros castle was particularly effective."

He smirked and feigned ignorance. "Why does everyone assume that was me?"

"Am I wrong?"

"No."

She laughed and surprisingly stepped close to embrace him. He hugged her back and gestured to her. "I didn't forget everything you taught."

"I'm sure you tried," she said with a smile, and then turned away. "If you ever need help with a persona, you know where to find me."

"I'll do that," he said, and meant it.

He watched her go, thinking of the assignments they had completed together. For the moment Forlana was herself, right down to her characteristic bald head, but she could disguise herself so even her children wouldn't know her. On impulse he caught up to her.

"Did you know Morissa?"

Forlana peaked an eyebrow at that. "I haven't heard that name in twenty years. How do you know about her?"

He hesitated, and decided on a half-truth. "My mother knew her."

"Then she was fortunate," Forlana said. "Morissa was the best of us, and not just for her talent."

"What can you tell me about her?" Jack asked.

Forlana regarded him for several seconds and then shook her head. "More tales than you have time for. Come when you have time and we'll talk over a mug."

The glint in her eye made him wonder how much she suspected, so he offered a nonchalant shrug. "I'll see you then."

His desire to know more about his mother warred with his desire to keep his past private, but he strode past her before he could give anything else away. She didn't say a word and he didn't look back. When he stepped outside he found Lorelia already there.

"Took you long enough," she said.

"I like to be thorough," he replied, forcing a smile.

"I bet you do," she said.

He laughed and tossed her the second pack. "Let's go. It's a long way to the barbarian strongholds."

They boarded the small boat and Lorelia activated the enchantment that would take them east. As the boat glided across the murky water Jack turned his thoughts to their adversary. He settled into a seat across from Lorelia.

"How long did you search for Skorn's body?"

She swept her hand at the swamp. "A week. As Kuraltus said, the Evermist has a way of swallowing corpses." Then her eyebrows pulled together. "Do you really think he survived?"

"*I* could have escaped."

"Perhaps," Lorelia said, "but two rayth cats could kill a rock troll."

Jack thought of the rock trolls in Terros and shook his head. "I'm not certain about that."

She threw him a sly look. "Just how many were there at the Terros castle?"

He grinned and told the tale. For the rest of the day they laughed about past assignments, and Lorelia shared tales of the thieves under her command. Jack found himself wishing he'd been present, and wondered what would have happened if he had.

They stayed the night in a small cottage hidden in the swamp, and the next on the edge of the Evermist. During one of Jack's past assignments he'd alienated an entire Amazonian tribe, so they picked their way through the jungle with great care. After several days traveling through oppressive heat the ground curved upward, rising to the peaks in the distance.

The jungle gave way to a forest on the knees of towering peaks. The ground continued to rise until they were forced to pause and adapt to the higher altitude. The next night they broke through a line of mountains and reached a sprawling series of valleys. It was early fall but snow dusted the ground and dark clouds threatened more.

"The Bearkiller tribe should be on the northern steppes," Lorelia said, breathing hard.

Jack wrapped his cloak tighter about his shoulders and cursed the cold. He'd tried to shave his stubble but the stream's water nearly froze his hair to his flesh. From then on his slight beard gathered frost.

"The sooner we are out of these mountains, the better," he growled.

They advanced out of a pass and took a game trail north. After months in the lower altitudes his body refused to accept the cold. His shaden cloak had been enchanted with warmth in mind, but was no match for the blistering wind. After an hour they pulled their blankets from their packs. Wrapping those atop the cloaks, they pressed forward, working their way across the slope.

Although it was only mid afternoon it felt like twilight. Snow began to fall from black clouds. The wind caught the flurries and drove them sideways, churning the snow into a blizzard. Realizing the elements were not going to abate, Jack stopped and turned back to Lorelia.

"We need to find shelter!"

He was forced to shout over the howling wind. She nodded emphatically and they moved toward a stand of giant pine trees. Stepping beneath the branches of one, they huddled in the well created by the canopy and began snapping dry branches. Lorelia laid them into a small bed and then pointed a shivering hand outside.

"I'll get more wood! You start a fire!"

Jack's frozen fingers fumbled his attempt. Even with the enchanted sparklight the wind kept snatching the flame the moment it appeared. He repositioned his body to block the wind and then tried again. To his immense relief the fire glowed to life and licked into the smaller branches. Lorelia returned and began feeding larger branches, so Jack braced himself for the biting wind and ducked into the open.

The wind assaulted him like a dwarven warhammer, nearly knocking him sprawling. He gritted his teeth and pushed into the gale. Snow had already covered much of the ground but he managed to find an armful of dead wood. He returned to find a crackling fire blazing in the protection of the tree.

He set aside the firewood and moved toward the heat. He breathed a sigh of relief as it washed over him but couldn't stop shaking. Then he spotted Lorelia using both blankets to form a large bed between the fire and the trunk.

"Plan on sharing?"

She flashed a grin, her lips blue from the cold. "The fire will help but it isn't enough. We'll have to share the bed."

He smirked and pushed the pile of wood within reach, and then climbed beneath the blankets. Lorelia slid into place beside him and they removed their cloaks from inside. Then they huddled together, shivering as the storm wailed outside.

"Are you warm?" she asked.

"Getting there," he said with a tight laugh.

They took turns adding sticks to the fire but kept it small. Too large and it would light the tree on fire. Too small and the wind would extinguish it. After a while Lorelia fell asleep and Jack kept watch. Whether from the storm or nightfall, the region faded into darkness.

Beneath the tree snow still managed to fall upon them, gradually increasing the weight on his side. At first he thought it would make him colder, but it seemed to act like an extra blanket, and gradually warmth trickled through his limbs.

Lorelia's shivering began to fade, and after an hour she rolled over to face him. With their bodies pressed together he was close enough to see every fleck of blue in her flawless eyes. Her hair lay in disarray but that only served to enhance her beauty. She smiled at him as if aware of his scrutiny.

"Are you comfortable?"

"I can feel my toes again."

She chuckled and eased closer, tilting her head in invitation. He accepted, leaning in to kiss her soundly. Warmth flooded his frame and he pressed harder, drawing her to him. She responded in kind, her hands tightening on his back. Then he opened his eyes.

And her face flickered.

He instinctively withdrew and stared at her. She tried to kiss him again but he leaned back, studying her features intently. She smiled at him but he caught the tightness of her lips and knew it to be forced.

"What's wrong?" she asked.

He scanned her face, confused and uncertain at what he'd seen. Then his eyes flicked to hers and he noticed the trace of fear. Suddenly the truth clicked into place.

"How much is an illusion?" he asked.

She winced as if he'd struck her, and then her expression hardened. "You don't understand."

"You spoke of masks before," he said. "And you're certainly talented enough with light magic to maintain a guise charm."

"If I did have a mask, what makes you think I'd remove it for you?"

"Because I know the truth," he said. "And anyone wearing a mask wants someone to know who they really are."

For a while the sounds of the crackling fire and the shrieking wind engulfed them. Then her expression became pained and she swallowed. She slowly reached up and touched the amulet at her throat, sending a shimmer of light across her features. The enchantment seeped into her skin, revealing her true face. Jack stiffened in surprise, causing pain to lance across her features.

"Tell anyone and I'll kill you," she said, and rolled away.

Jack reached to her back but his fingers stopped short of touching her clenched shoulder. Then he slowly withdrew his hand, the image of her face still fresh on his mind.

Her face was narrow, as if two stones had pressed her skull. The skin on one cheek drooped, misshapen and lumpy since birth. Scars crisscrossed the other side of her face, marring the only part of her features that had been normal.

"I'm sorry," Jack said. "I was just surprised—"

"I'll take first watch."

"Wait—"

"Too late, Jack."

The fury in her voice drove him to sigh and lay down facing away from her. He wanted to console her but could not find the words, and eventually he fell asleep. Deep in the night a poke in the ribs woke him up. He rolled to face her but she refused to look at him. Resigned to feeding the fire, he grappled with her secret.

Warm and lost in thought he became drowsy, and the next thing he knew he was waking up in the morning. Filtering through the branches the sun shone on his face, indicating the storm had abated. He grunted at the lapse and reached for a log to place it on the fire. To his surprise another hand picked it up first.

Covered in a furred gauntlet, the scarred hand added the log to the fire and retreated. Jack followed it to the owner and found a man seated beside the flames, a massive maul resting on his knees.

Jack reached for his dagger but spotted a second barbarian leaning against the tree. A third shifted in his peripheral vision, and then another appeared. Jack rotated back to the first and the barbarian's features twisted with rage.

He nudged Lorelia awake. "We don't need to find the barbarians anymore."

She didn't look at him. "Why not?"

"Because they found us," he said.

Chapter 8: Brother

Huge and forbidding, the man was a veritable giant. His black hair hung free down his back but his beard had been braided like a dwarf's. Scars marred his face, cutting across his nose and angling down his cheek. Blue and red paint accentuated the scar in vibrant patterns.

The giant wore studded leather armor lined with fur, and a massive cloak made of bearskin. Encased with iron, the bear's skull formed the barbarian's helmet. As fearsome as it was, the armor did not compare to the weapon. Animal fangs and steel spikes protruded from the knobby maul, its sheer size enough to crush a foe's head like a ripe melon.

Jack yawned and sat up. "I'd ask you to make yourselves comfortable, but it's clear you already have."

The leader glared at him. "We don't care for spies in our lands."

He snorted. "Who would spy on this wasteland?"

Some of the barbarians hid smiles but the leader was not amused. "Take them," he said. "I'll decide their fate after the battle."

"Battle?" Lorelia asked.

His gaze flicked to her. "You chose to make your camp on a sacred battlefield between our clans. The bones of generations sleep beneath you."

"And you still haven't resolved the conflict?" Jack sniffed his disapproval.

The barbarian scowled and stood before pointing his maul north. "Let them witness the battle before we take their heads."

Jack opened his mouth to respond but a pair of large hands caught his arms and pulled him out from under the pine tree. He barely had time to don his cloak before he was shoved into the snow. He caught his balance and turned to snap at them—and then sucked in his breath.

Thousands of men and women surrounded the tree in disorderly ranks. Many sat on downed trees, sharpening axes and swords. Others were occupied with drinking from great barrels of mead, their songs echoing across the slope. Whetstones ground on steel as barbarians sharpened their blades, the distinct sound carried by the frigid wind. Despite the conflict of the previous night Lorelia shifted closer to him as they trudged through the snow.

"Any ideas?"

"Find out what happened to Beauty. And keep our heads."

"As detailed as ever," she said acidly.

"Have you ever considered that your persona is nicer than you are?"

She growled at him with such venom that one of the barbarians laughed approvingly. "She sounds like one of our kind," he said.

"I'm not," she snapped at him, but that only caused him to laugh again.

The barbarians brought them higher on the hillside until they reached a trio of youth crouched around a fire. Bearing a great double-bladed axe, the one in the center stood in greeting, his eyes lighting with curiosity.

His features were young and his beard short, yet he towered over the other two. In spite of his height his body lacked the characteristic girth of the other barbarians, suggesting he had not stopped growing. His black hair hung braided and tied, covering the wolfskin that adorned his back.

"Golic," the giant said, shoving Jack toward the group. "Make sure they watch the battle."

71

One of Golic's companions growled in dismay and he stabbed his broadsword toward Lorelia. "I will not forego a battle to do a woman's work."

The man stepped forward and struck him, sending him sprawling into the snow. "It wasn't a request, Ather. Don't let them escape." Then he turned his gaze on Jack and sneered. "The chief wants to kill them himself."

They turned and left. When they were gone Golic gestured to Jack and Lorelia. "Join us at the fire. I'm sure you're cold."

"Freezing," Jack said, and slipped into the seat vacated by Ather.

"You're a prisoner," Ather snarled. "Not a guest."

The youth reached out to strike him but Jack pulled a knife and touched the blade to the main's groin. Although Ather outweighed Jack by fifty pounds, his fist came to a halt.

"I'd prefer to be a guest," Jack said.

Ather's gaze would have charred a steak but he did not move, and the standoff lasted until Golic spoke.

"I'd take another seat," Golic said easily, a smile tugging at his features.

Ather snarled at him and retreated. "Watch them yourself, Golic. I'm joining the battle."

With that he snatched his sword from the ground and stomped away. In his absence Golic motioned Lorelia to the empty log across from him.

"You may be dead by nightfall," Golic said, "but you may as well enjoy the fire while you can."

"Do you always speak of death with such ease?"

"Death stalks us all," Golic said with a shrug. "Then we go to Ero or Skorn."

Jack and Lorelia shared an amused look at the mention of the devil. Then Jack gestured to Golic's other companion.

"And do you feel the same?"

The blond youth grinned and nodded, and Golic said, "He has been ordered to silence until his third kill."

Jack's gaze shifted back to Golic. "Do you treat all guests so well?" He held his wrists up like he expected to be bound, causing Golic to laugh.

"They didn't bind you because you are not a threat."

"Is that why they didn't take our weapons?" Lorelia asked.

Golic turned to her with amusement. "Our people do not consider you a danger."

The other barbarian nudged him and made several hand signals, and whatever he said made Golic's smile turn wry.

"He says our arrogance has been our downfall in the past."

"Arrogance always leads to destruction," Lorelia said, her eyes on Jack.

Jack ignored her. "Your chief said this was a sacred battleground."

Golic laughed with a trace of bitterness. "I could go into an exhaustive tale of how a rival clan wronged us, but I suspect it would be meaningless to you. In short we battle each year. The victor claims the region as their own, while the defeated must return to the higher mountains where food is scarce."

"Can you not share it?" Jack asked.

"Probably," Golic said, "but that would mean forgiveness, an act foreign to our people. Feuds are rife among the clans, and bloodshed is frequent."

"Can you forgive one who flees your lands?" Lorelia asked.

Golic's smile faded. "Is that your purpose here?"

73

"We seek for one named Thera," Jack said. "She was a daughter of your people until her sister fled and was killed. Then she went after the Thieves Guild."

Golic went rigid. "What do you know of Thera?"

"She journeyed here but never returned."

Golic lowered his voice. "If the chief knows that she lives, she will be hunted and killed."

Jack noticed the spark of worry in his eyes. "Why do you fear for her?"

"She is my sister," Golic said quietly.

Jack raised an eyebrow. "When is the last time you heard from her?"

"Three weeks ago," Golic said. "She sent me a message that she wanted to visit. She was supposed to arrive a week past but never came. Instead I received another message."

"What message?"

Golic fished a scrap of parchment from his pocket and handed it to Jack. "I admit I don't understand its import."

Jack unfolded the parchment and read the script. He'd expected it to be written in her handwriting and the ornate script confirmed it.

Orn survived. I spotted him in the southeast of Terros near Margauth. Golic, make sure he comes after me.

Thera.

Jack grunted in irritation and read it a second time. Noticing his reaction, Lorelia reached out and took the note. She cursed when she read it.

74

"You understand it?" Golic asked.

"It was intended for me," Jack replied.

Golic jerked his head. "I don't understand."

Jack crumpled the note and tossed it into the flames. "I've never been so disappointed to be right."

"Skorn's gone to Margauth, to the cult of Skorn," Lorelia said. "You were right."

"The cult of Skorn?" Golic asked, his tone darkening. "Why would Thera go there?"

Lorelia shook her head in confusion. "She pursues our former Guildmaster."

"We need to find her," Jack said, and rose to his feet.

"You think her in danger?" Golic asked, rising as well.

Jack barked a laugh. "When is she not?"

A distant horn blew. Long and haunting, it caused the barbarian camp to fall silent. Then an answering horn came from within the Bearkiller camp, bringing the horde rushing together to form ranks.

A man stepped from the southern tree line and plunged his sword into the snow. For an interminable moment the world seemed to hold its breath. Then barbarians exploded from the forest and roared. Bellowing at the men above them, they charged up the snowy slope.

"The Manhunter tribe has swelled in number," Golic said with a frown.

The Bearkillers released an answering roar and charged. Their great boots kicked snow into the air, sending small flurries billowing across the battlefield. Weapons were drawn and the glint of steel reflected in the sun.

Heedless of the snow the two armies came together in a crushing impact of blades and bodies. Steel rang against steel, plunging into flesh. The wounded cried out in rage and pain. Blood stained the snow, turning the white to scarlet.

"They kill without cause," Jack said in disgust.

"Perhaps," Golic said quietly. "But we know no other way."

"Knowledge must be taught," Jack said. "And it's time such senseless conflict came to an end."

"They will not listen," Golic said.

"Then they will die," Jack said bluntly. "And if you had half the intelligence of your sister you would know that."

Golic sighed and bowed his head. "Your words are harsh, thief, but they are not without truth."

For several minutes they watched the battle unfold. When Jack spotted Ather take an axe in his gut, he released an angry breath.

"I think it's time we take our leave."

Lorelia nodded in agreement. "Before the battle comes to a close and your chief decides he wants more blood."

Golic turned away from the battle and stared at them. "If you wish to flee we will not stop you." His silent companion nodded his head in assent.

Jack peaked an eyebrow at him. "How much will it cost you?"

"A good lashing," Golic said with a shrug, "but I consider it a price well paid for a friend of Thera's."

"How do we escape the valley?" Lorelia asked.

"There's only one way out," Golic said, "and therein lies your dilemma."

Jack folded his arms at the barbarian's tone. "So how do we get around the battle?"

76

"You can't," Golic said, and gestured toward the battlefield. "The only way out is through them."

Jack turned to the battle and a wild grin spread on his features. "Let's go steal ourselves an exit."

Chapter 9: Enraged

"You want to go *through* them?" Lorelia asked.

"Why not?" Jack asked, grinning at the prospect.

Lorelia shook her head. "I don't like our chances."

He gestured to the raging battlefield, which had already spilled to the cliffs on one side and into the forest on the south. The pass lay on the opposite side like a massive doorway in the mountains.

"They are more than distracted," Jack said, "so just stay on the move and we'll emerge on the opposite side."

"We will pretend to pursue you," Golic said.

"You don't need to pretend," Lorelia said. "You couldn't stop us if you tried."

Golic appeared doubtful but his silent companion bore a wide grin on his face. Jack ignored them and stepped down the slope. He checked his weapons and shouldered his pack. Then he strode toward the battle. Lorelia was quick to catch up to him.

"You think you can run into a raging battle and emerge unscathed?"

"Of course," he said.

"Your arrogance will get you killed, Jack."

"Do you see another way?" Jack asked.

She ground her teeth together but didn't argue. "What's the plan?"

"Stay on the move and don't engage."

"I'll do what I can with my magic," she said.

"Just don't fall behind," Jack replied.

They had drawn close to the battle and he had to raise his voice to be heard. His words drew the attention of several of those fighting. The Bearkillers wore mostly wolf and bear furs, while the Manhunter Clan used rabbit and mountain goat hides for their clothing.

The fighting barbarians from both clans glanced at Jack and Lorelia, but Jack continued his unhurried pace. When he reached thirty paces he began to accelerate through the snow. The barbarians saw them coming and reluctantly turned to face him.

Jack stepped on a rock and leapt over their heads. He came down at their backs and kicked a foot out from under a Manhunter. He went down, giving Lorelia the gap she needed to breach the outer line. When she landed at Jack's side they sprinted into the fray.

Jack darted behind a pair locked in mortal combat, and then ducked a stray swing from an axe. Spinning past them, he leapt a downed man and then dived to the ground. Sliding through the snow he passed through a trio of Bearkillers.

Lorelia used her magic to bend the light, obscuring her form and distracting those around her. One barbarian leapt toward her with upraised maul, but she sent a burst of light into his eyes, causing him to cry out and miss. Their passage did not go unnoticed, and barbarians from both sides began to shout.

"Skorn-blasted fool!"

"Someone kill the cowards!"

Jack stood up in indignation. "Cowards *flee* from battle, you Skorn-cursed whelp!"

The barbarian's face turned red and he charged after him. Jack darted to the side, leveling a punch into his gut that knocked the wind from his lungs. Even winded he managed to swing his broadsword in an arc that would cleave Jack in two.

In a flash of movement Jack ducked and spun. Then he rose and leaned back, kicking the barbarian in the stomach to send him sprawling. As the man landed with a grunt Lorelia sprinted by.

"You're not supposed to engage, remember?"

He turned and raced parallel to her. "They're more irritating than I anticipated."

A sword swung for his chest, but he launched himself into an effortless flip that carried him over the weapon. Landing in the snow, he carried his momentum into a roll that allowed him to evade two barbarians bashing each other with shields and hammers.

He came to his feet in a run and kept pace with Lorelia. "On your right," he called out.

She grinned and came to an abrupt halt. Unable to compensate, the barbarian that had lunged for her slipped in the snow and crashed to the earth. Lorelia taunted him as he slid by. Her grin caused him to roar in fury.

"Don't engage," Jack said with a laugh, and her smile widened.

Deep in the thrall of bloodlust several barbarians mistook him for a foe, and moved to intercept him. Jack flicked his hand and his crossbow dropped into his palm. Thumbing the activation trigger, he pointed the tiny weapon as the bow sprang into place.

He fired once, sending an explosive bolt into the snow at their feet. The detonation failed to pierce their armor but flipped them into the air. As stunned forms rained down on their companions Jack leapt the smoking crater. One of the barbarians stumbled after him but Jack stooped to pick up a shield. Spinning, he hurled it at the woman. The heavy metal struck her in the gut, knocking the wind from her lungs and dropping her into the snow.

They reached the heart of the conflict and Jack was forced to slow. Dodging blades and bodies, he wove his way through the raging battle.

He interrupted duels with abandon, laughing at the annoyance on the men's faces. Then he reached the Bearkiller chief.

Jack stepped on a dead body and leapt over the huge man. Locked in a duel with two Manhunters, the man looked up in astonishment as Jack sailed over him. Jack smirked and flicked his dagger out, pinging the barbarian's helmet.

"I think I'll keep my head."

He landed and darted away. Enraged, the barbarian chief smashed his maul into the two Manhunters and charged after Jack. The chief made no attempt to evade the fighting men and women, and smashed his maul into them as he crashed through the battle.

Empowered by body magic, his blows knocked huge men sprawling. Shields were shattered and weapons snapped in two. The Manhunters joined together, desperately trying to halt his charge but the chief would not be stopped. He exploded through their ranks and sprinted after Jack.

"I'll crush your bones to dust, you little runt!" he shouted.

Lorelia angled her path close to him. "Do you have to anger *everyone?*"

"Does everyone have to anger so easily?" Jack countered.

The Manhunter chief stepped in front of them and raised his sword, but his attention was not on them. Jack and Lorelia parted and flowed around him as the man braced for the impending impact.

"We battle once more for this sacred ground—"

His challenge ended in a grunt as the Bearkiller chief knocked him sprawling and pursued Jack with relentless focus. The chief bellowed his rage and several of the other Bearkillers joined him. Confused but obedient, the Bearkillers joined the procession until hundreds charged after their chief.

The shift in battle escalated, with the change in momentum spreading across the battlefield. Following their chief's example, the whole of the Bearkiller force began to turn toward the thieves.

81

Recognizing the thieves as the reason for the battle's interruption, the Manhunters roared and joined the pursuit.

"Congratulations," Lorelia said acidly. "You've managed to incur the wrath of *both* clans."

"They live in the north," Jack retorted. "You would think they'd have thicker skin."

The chaos was spreading ahead of them and barbarians from both sides lowered their blades and looked about in confusion. As more barbarians turned their focus upon them, Jack veered to an enormous Manhunter bearing a huge spiked axe.

"The Bearkillers say your mother is an ugly mutt."

The man's eyes nearly burst from his skull and he looked down at the trio of Bearkillers he'd been battling. His war-painted features contorted with abject fury. Even inured to battle the Bearkillers recognized their dire predicament and stumbled back.

"We don't speak about your mother!" one shouted.

"He isn't one of us!" another added, pointing his sword toward Jack's fleeing form.

"LIES!" the giant bellowed.

Still attempting to placate him, the Bearkillers retreated. He charged after them, swinging his sword with lethal abandon. The Manhunters not following Jack saw his charge and followed, howling in glee. Across from them the Bearkillers reacted in kind, surging forward to counterattack.

The forces pursuing Jack and Lorelia crashed into the battle and the scene dissolved into chaos. The Bearkiller chief struggled to advance but the knot of struggling bodies would not be moved. His bellowed orders were lost in the confusion. Moments later Jack and Lorelia burst from the battle and sprinted up the empty hillside. When they had put some distance between themselves and the battle they came to a halt to catch their breath.

Jack looked down at the chaotic scene with a wild grin. Instead of two armies battling for supremacy, the conflict had fractured into pockets of men and women striking at each other in confusion. The giant man Jack had insulted continued to rampage across the battlefield, while the two chiefs could not reach each other through the press of bodies. None seemed aware that they were not even on the correct battlefield anymore—the entire battle having drifted to the gulley at the side.

"That was harrowing," Lorelia said.

"Why?" Jack replied. "They didn't want to fight us."

"That changed when you taunted their chief."

"What did you expect me to do?" Jack asked. "Slip by without a word?"

"That's what any normal thief would do."

Jack sniffed and returned his gaze to the battlefield. "I told you. I'm not a thief."

"Then what are you, Jack?"

It irked him that he had no answer, so he didn't give one. "We survived, didn't we?"

"A few cuts," Lorelia said, "but nothing substantial. You?"

"I got snow in my boots."

A laugh burst from her lips. "We waded through ten thousand enraged barbarians and you are complaining about snow in your boots?"

"It's cold," Jack said. "And I've decided I hate the snow."

"How can you hate the snow?"

"How can you not?"

They turned away, but Jack caught sight of Golic on the opposite side of the battle. He'd descended into the fray and fought with a valor

83

that drew his people to him. In spite of his power he did not fight like the others and seemed to spare as many as he slew.

Jack smiled as he thought of Beauty. She too had disliked bloodshed, and even though she'd been trained for it, she forewent combat when she could. As Jack realized the similarities between the siblings he was forced to wonder about their parents. The little Jack knew of their father indicated no compassion had come from him, meaning that their kind hearts had likely come from their mother.

Jack's thoughts turned to his own mother, who had been a thief prior to his birth. Why had she kept her past as a thief hidden? Unbidden, Lorelia's question echoed in his mind.

Then what are you Jack?

As the sounds of the battle faded behind them he wondered why his mother hated being a thief. Was it because she was ashamed of what she'd done? Or ashamed of what Jack *would* become? He scowled as his gut tightened. He couldn't deny how much fun it was to be a thief, but what else was there?

Swear you won't be a thief, his mother's words echoed in his mind.

I already did, Jack thought, but his words were laced with regret.

Chapter 10: Beauty

They made their way south until they reached the western pass. Once they were through the mountains they slowed their pace. They kept a sharp eye on their back trail, but no barbarians appeared to be pursuing them. When they finally descended out of the high mountains Jack breathed a sigh of relief.

"I thought I'd never be warm again," Jack said.

"I wouldn't call this warm."

Jack grinned but couldn't argue. The wind carried a bite that heralded the coming winter. Even though snow had yet to fall in the valleys, the air was scented with it. Still, the difference from the high mountains was stark enough that Jack undid his cloak and brushed the lingering speckles of ice from its surface.

"What are we going to do about Skorn?" Lorelia asked.

He shrugged. "Find Beauty and get the keys before Skorn does."

"Do you *ever* make a real plan?"

He frowned at her acerbic tone. "Do you have a better one?"

"Actually I do," she said. "If our infamous Guildmaster really has joined the Cult of Skorn, he's got himself an army."

"So?"

"We could send another group of thieves to retrieve the second key," she said. "I am the new Guildmaster, after all."

"Have you forgotten how dangerous he is?" Jack asked. "Sending another group would just get them killed."

"Why?" she challenged. "You think you are the best of the guild?"

He sidestepped the loaded question. "Other thieves would not be prepared for what they would face."

"They can handle a few cultists."

"Have you forgotten who leads them?" Jack asked, irritated now. "He knows the guild's tactics. I'm not inclined to have anyone's blood on my hands."

"Then why bring Beauty at all?" she asked.

"She won't get herself killed."

Lorelia came to a halt on a ledge that overlooked the valley. "You aren't the only one who cares about her, you know. In the last six months she's been the closest thing I had to a friend in the guild, even though she doesn't know about . . ."

She grimaced and looked away, and Jack didn't break the silence. They had both avoided the topic for days but it had affected every interaction. Every time he looked at her he imagined her scarred and malformed features. He wanted to ask where she'd gotten the scars but thought that would be callous. Instead he cleared his throat and changed the subject.

"Besides, we need to be cautious who we reveal the truth to," he said, reminding her of their conversation in the guildhall. "He may still have loyal followers within the guild."

"You talked about Ursana and Gordon," she said. "Are you certain you trust them?"

He hesitated, and recalled the assignments they had shared prior to defeating the Guildmaster. Even when he'd been imprisoned by the elves and left to be executed, they had risked everything to help him get into the guild, and nearly lost their lives for it.

"I defeated Skorn with their help," he said.

"He wasn't prepared for us then," she said. "This time he is. You need to be cautious."

He smiled at her words. "Is that an order?"

"I *am* the Guildmaster."

"You don't need the title for men to obey you," he said.

Her lips twitched as she stepped over a downed log that blocked the trail. Jack followed, and a moment later the trail turned back on itself to negotiate a steep section of rock. Winding past towering pine trees, the trail forked, with one path heading west and the other curving into a northern valley.

"We should split up," Lorelia said, coming to a halt. "We know very little on the Cult of Skorn and ignorance will cost us."

"And how is splitting up going to give us answers?"

"I'll go back to the guildhall and retrieve the others. You head north and learn what you can from the taverns. Find Beauty and meet me south of Terros. I can take a Gate to Terros and head south to meet you."

He folded his arms at the mention of a Gate. Skorn had brought the four mirrors to the guild shortly after becoming Guildmaster, and installed them in the three guildhalls while keeping one for his private use. They allowed the higher rank thieves to travel to Terros and Woodhaven with ease. They were artifacts left by the ancients and lost to time, but Jack guessed Skorn had known where they had been hidden.

"And why do I get to walk a thousand miles while you portal to the city?" Jack asked.

"Because you have a way of loosening tongues," she said, and a shadow of her former smile crossed her features. "And we don't want to raise suspicions in the guild. If we both return and then leave again, a Skorn spy will know something is amiss."

"I don't care for your logic."

"That's because you know I'm right."

He muttered under his breath. "As you order."

"Travel safe, Jack," she said.

"You as well, beautiful."

He'd called her that before, and the word slipped from his lips before he could stop it. She stared at him, clearly unsure if he was being sarcastic or earnest. Ultimately her expression tightened and she spun away.

"Three weeks," she called over her shoulder. "And don't get lost!"

He wanted to apologize but the words did not come. How did one apologize for calling a woman beautiful? He released an explosive breath and took the right fork. By nightfall the autumn temperatures plummeted and he was cursing her name.

It took four days to reach a settlement, and by the time he arrived he was starving. He even fought a coyote for its kill, and grilled the rabbit over a small fire. When he trudged into the small village he couldn't decide what he wanted more, a bed or a meal. Then he smelled the savory scent coming from the tavern and his stomach made the decision for him.

He ate three bowls of stew, half a loaf of bread, and a wedge of cheese before he wearily ascended to a room and sank into the bed. He slept late, and indulged in another hearty meal while the others in the room ate lunch.

As he stood up from his table a trio of burly men shouldered their way inside. They strode to the counter and drew knives on the owner's wife. In low tones they demanded all her coin. Shaking, she fumbled for the gold.

The door opened and a weary woman stepped inside. Her arrival caused the bandits to spin—and stare in shock at her beauty. She ignored them and sank into a seat near the door. Then she noticed Jack and a smile appeared on her face.

She looked much like she had six months ago. Her black hair was tied down her back, her piercing blue eyes carrying a steel that belied her frame. She'd given up her thief blacks in favor of merchant garb, but her clothes were a hair too rich for her persona, accentuating the curves of her form.

"Beauty," he said.

"Jack," she drawled. "It's been a while."

"Your coin!" one of the bandits shouted, recovering from Beauty's presence enough to brandish a knife. "Or I'll gut you like a fish."

"I was coming to find you," Jack said, ignoring the bandits.

"And I was on my way back to the guild," she said, and her smile widened. "How did you know where I was?"

"*Your coin!*" a second bandit growled, stepping close to Jack.

"I got your note," he said. "I like your brother, by the way."

"Everyone likes him," she replied, her smile turning soft. "If he survives I think he might even unify the clans."

"Do you wish for death?" the bandit said, his voice turning shrill as Jack and Beauty continued to ignore him. "*Give me your coin!*"

"You too," the third bandit said, and stepped toward Beauty with a sleazy smile. "Unless you want to pay by other means—"

Her hand snapped out, striking him in the gut and forcing the air from his lungs. He dropped to his knees, his jaw working in vain. She rose to her feet and casually pushed him aside. The bandits whirled to face her and began to shout, but Jack's voice cut through their fury.

"If you're looking for coin, I've got one for you."

Their eyes wild with panic and confusion, the two men swiveled to face him. The one by Jack jabbed his knife at him. "We'll take it all, fool," he said.

"So greedy," Jack said, and pulled a coin into view.

He flipped it into the air and the bandit's eyes followed the motion—and Jack snatched the knife from his fingers. Then he placed the man's hand on the heavy table and drove the knife through it, burying it into the wood. His shriek was cut off as Jack slapped him, a humiliating blow that did more shock than harm. The man fell to whimpering and struggled to free his hand. Then Jack caught the coin.

"You look good," Jack said, his eyes on Beauty.

"I heard about Terros," she said, and wove her way through the tables toward him. "And Herosian—and Keese." She laughed lightly. "You haven't lost your sense of style."

"*I'll kill you both!*" the last bandit shrieked.

He swung his knife toward one and then the other. The other patrons seemed frozen as they watched the conflict. The woman behind the bar still held a pouch of coins in her hand, her mouth agape.

"I kept busy," Jack said.

"*I swear on Skorn's Blade I'll cut your throats!*"

Jack drew his dagger from the hidden sheath on his spine and slapped him across the face with it. The man crashed into a chair, dazed from the blow. Beauty caught his tunic and tossed him bodily across the room like he weighed no more than a potato. He crashed into the wall and slumped to the floor, where he groaned and did not rise.

"I have news about our former Guildmaster," she said.

He smirked. "I as well. Would you like to ride with me?"

"I thought you'd never ask," she said with a smile.

"We will hunt you down and kill you," the man pinned to the table snarled, his voice twisted with pain.

Jack stepped to him and yanked the knife free. As the man cried out Jack forced him toward the door. Reaching it, he kicked it open and launched the bandit into the street. Unable to stop himself, the bandit tripped on the stairs to crash into the cold ground. A moment later his still-gasping companion landed on top of him. As they fought to rise Jack leaned against the doorframe.

"Stealing is only a profession if you are good at it," Jack said, and held aloft the coin purses he'd taken from them.

Their eyes widened and their hands went to their waists. "You Skorn-blasted thief," one snarled.

Beauty laughed and launched the last man. They cried out as the form crashed into them and they landed in a heap. Catching the pouches from Jack she tossed them to the tavern's counter. "I think its best you pick a different occupation—and not return here."

Her mild tone conveyed a seething threat, causing them to swallow and retreat down the road. When they were gone Jack entered the tavern and strode to the bar amidst hearty cheers from the men.

"Good sir," she said. "Your chivalry is—"

"Not without a price," Jack said.

Her shock lasted for a moment, and then her eyes narrowed. "What do you want?"

"Information," Jack said. "A week east of here lies the ancient fortress of Margauth. What can you tell me about it?"

She shuddered and looked away. "The tales are many, but the truth is uncertain."

He strode to the bar. "I'll take it all."

The tavern owner suddenly barged into the room bearing a woodcutter's axe. His wife slipped to his side and spoke in calming tones. He relaxed at her words, placing the tool on the bar and turning to Jack.

"What do you wish to know of Margauth?" he asked.

"Everything," Jack said.

The couple didn't know much, but what they could say proved very helpful. As they shared details it became clear that most of the time the Cult of Skorn was quiet, with their worshipers meeting in secret and hiding their perverted practices. Occasionally they were known to kidnap men and sacrifice them to Skorn.

Over the last few months, rumors had spread of excitement among the cult members. The furor stemmed from a mysterious visitor that had taken Skorn's unwieldable blade, and it had obeyed him. Shortly after, the cult began to summon their members, gradually drawing them into the fold while not revealing themselves to their respective governments.

Once he had gleaned all he could, Jack paid for a horse and went to the stables with the inn's owner. The man saddled the steed and then handed Jack the reins. As he mounted the man stepped close.

"I would warn you to be careful," he said, his gaze flicking to Beauty mounting her own steed, "but you don't seem like the type to utilize caution."

"I may be a thief, but I'm not stupid."

"These people appear normal," the man said, "yet they hide a sinister worship of a devil. If they have gathered their full might it would take the entire Griffin army to destroy them."

"Or a couple of thieves," Jack said.

The man appeared doubtful but did not disagree. "Perhaps they should be eradicated as the Church of Light preaches."

Jack burst into a scornful laugh. "They are two sides of the same false coin. One side faces the light while the other lies in shadow. It doesn't matter which way you turn it—it's still worthless."

"What do you mean?"

Jack nudged the mount toward the road, forcing the man to hurry to keep up. "Don't worship what you don't know."

The man came to a stop in the center of the road, confusion spreading on his features. "But Ero is a god!" the man called after Jack.

"Gods don't build armies," Jack called over his shoulder. "And neither do devils."

His comment drew a curious look from Beauty, but Jack dug his heels into the steed's flanks and it began to trot down the road. At the bend in the road he glanced back to see the innkeeper still rooted in place. Even at the distance Jack saw the worry on his features.

"So," Beauty said, "What have you learned?"

"It's a long story."

She settled into her saddle with a smug smile. "I like long stories."

He grinned. "After leaving the guild I returned home, and found a memory orb my mother left for me . . ."

Chapter 11: Reunion

Jack and Beauty made their way north but avoided the regular thief haunts. Four days after departing the tavern they came to a small fishing village south of Terros. They made their way to the sole tavern and paid for two rooms and a meal. Then they made their way to field with a vantage point of the road.

"Want to test your skill with a sword?" Beauty asked as the day dragged by.

"I'd rather poke a knife into my eyes."

"You need to practice, Jack. We both know your skills with a blade are lacking."

"I've told you before," he said. "Swordplay is a good way to get cut and bruised."

"Have you forgotten who you face?"

"Of course not," he said. "But it doesn't mean I want to train."

"Spoken like a fool," she said, and then flashed a sly smile. "Or perhaps you require a bribe."

He peaked an eyebrow at that. "What do you have in mind?"

She reached into a pouch and pulled a small red knife into view. "We've been working on this at the guild for a few months now. It's a gorgon key, and it can open any lock."

He grinned and relented with a sigh. "How is it you always know my price?"

"I know you," she said with a smug smile, and tossed him the key.

He slipped the knife into an empty sheath on his chest and joined her in a clearing that overlooked the road. Trained by the barbarians in her youth, her skill rivaled that of a Talinorian weapons master. After several days of training he regretted his choice.

"I should have waited to give you the key," she growled, and twirled her sword in the morning light. "You're less motivated since you already have your prize."

"This is exactly the way I thought it would be," Jack replied, rubbing his latest injury.

"Sarcasm doesn't help."

"Sarcasm *always* helps," he argued.

She glared at him before bursting into laughter. "Stop trying to distract me, Jack, and do the technique again."

Caught, Jack sighed in resignation and spun his dagger before lunging at her. Although he would never admit it, he was grateful for her instruction. She was skilled and patient, and he showed a marked improvement in just a few days. When they stopped for lunch he sank into a seat at her side and gestured to the road.

"They're late."

"They'll be here," Beauty said. "You may not have seen it, but Lorelia has risen to the calling of Guildmaster quite well."

"She changed a great deal after regaining her memories," Jack said.

"We all did," she replied darkly.

"What memory did he take from you?"

She took a pull from her water skin and didn't answer. As the seconds passed Jack wondered if she would share it. Then she sighed and shook her head.

97

"I found out he ordered my sister's death and confronted him, but he said I was too valuable. Then he jammed that blasted memory curse into my skull. I served Erela's killer for months without knowing it."

"We should have followed him into the swamp and killed him ourselves," Jack said.

"I know," she said. "But how many would have survived being hunted by two rayth cats in the Evermist?"

He reclined on the grass and looked at the sky. White cottony clouds floated across the blue expanse, driven by the soft breeze that cooled the sweat on Jack's brow. He smiled and closed his eyes, relishing the sense of freedom.

"How can you be so relaxed when you know what we're up against?"

"Apathy can be quite relaxing," he said without opening his eyes.

Her tone became irritated. "You don't care if he gets the keys?"

"I want to stop him because I think it will be fun," Jack said. "Not because I care if he gets what he wants. In many respects he's just like Lord Horanian in Nightfall Gorge. He has power and coin but is never satisfied."

"That's surprisingly insightful."

"I also enjoy depriving him of what he wants."

She laughed sourly. "I already knew that. I guess I hoped you would want to do this for more than just yourself."

He put his hands behind his head. "Sorry to disappoint you, but I really only want to make him angry."

"What do you intend to do?"

"He helped kill your sister," he said. "Of course we have to kill him. Depriving him of what he wants makes it enjoyable."

She remained silent for several minutes, and then asked, "Why did you leave the guild?"

He opened his eyes and looked up to see her expression somber. "Why did you stay? We both know you don't want to be a thief. You could have come with me."

She looked away, but not before he saw the sudden hurt in her eyes. "I can't return home until I've killed Skorn," she said. "And my father is dead."

He thought of the blistering cold of the barbarian mountains and shuddered. "Why would you want to go back there? I was so cold I thought my skin would shatter."

"It's my home," she said quietly.

He reached out and took her hand in his. "I promised I would help you, and I will."

"Is that why you came back?"

I never wanted to leave you.

He wanted to say it but couldn't seem to voice the words. "I had a promise to keep," he said.

"You really are a—"

"They're here," he said as a distant clop of a horse hoof caused him to sit up. When he heard it again he gestured down the road. "Five horses."

"Don't you want to know what I was going to say?"

"I already know what I am," Jack said, and forced a smile.

He rose and gathered his gear before descending the hill to the road. Beauty was quick to join him, and by the time they stepped onto the gravel path Lorelia appeared astride a horse. She smiled as she caught sight of them and flicked the reins to accelerate her mount. One by one the others appeared behind her.

Gordon and Ursana came next. Although the two had joined the guild on the same day as Jack, they had come from starkly different backgrounds. Upon joining the guild they had forged a bond not unlike a father and daughter, and had worked as partners ever since.

At seventeen Ursana still looked like a tiny girl. A heavy crossbow lay slung across her back, while the rest of her thief's gear was hidden beneath her shaden. A former soldier, Gordon rode behind her. In spite of his training he preferred to sleep more than anyone Jack had met.

Jack grinned and was surprised to realize how much he'd missed them. When he'd joined the guild they had performed a trio of assignments together which culminated in a dangerous theft from a lord in Nightfall Gorge. Several weeks later Gordon and Ursana had come to save him from execution in the elven capitol of Azertorn.

The group rode up to Jack and dismounted, and Ursana darted forward to embrace Jack. Then she stepped back and punched him in the arm.

"You should never have left."

"I'm not a thief," Jack said with a laugh.

"Then why are you so blasted good at it?" Gordon said with a grin.

"Gordon speaks the truth," Thalidon said.

Jack turned to find the dwarf dismounting. Without a beard the dwarf could have passed for a short, stocky human. His clothes were well tailored and threaded with mithral, suggesting they were utilitarian as well as stylish. Jack reached out to clasp his wrist.

"I hope you've brought me new gear," he said.

"Perhaps I have a surprise or two," Thalidon said, his eyes twinkling. Then he gestured to his brother. "This is Roarthin."

The dwarf grunted and did not offer his hand. "Well met," he said. It didn't sound like he meant it.

"Why so dour?" Jack asked. "I thought you wanted to kill Skorn."

"I do," the dwarf said with a scowl. "But I don't care to be saddled with thieves." Thalidon backhanded his shoulder but the dwarf didn't take the warning. He sniffed and looked away. "Your occupation is repulsive."

"*Roarthin*," Thalidon growled, but Jack's laugh stopped the rebuke on his lips.

"At least he's honest," Jack said.

"Let's get moving," Lorelia said. "We're months behind the cultists and we still have to get to the Azure Islands. Did you find us a boat?"

"A ship called the *Erenessa* stops here every three days," Beauty said. "The captain promised to take us to the islands."

Lorelia nodded. "Then let's don our personas and get to the docks. From here on we're working with a pair of dwarves searching for a mine on the islands. Thalidon will be the presumed lead for our party."

While Ursana and Gordon led the horses into the village, the group stepped off the road and prepared their personas. Two hours later they exited dressed as workmen and women, and the dwarves looked like mining prospectors. Then they entered the village and found a place at the inn. Two days later they boarded the *Erenessa* and embarked for the islands of the azure. As the ship pulled onto Blue Lake, Jack carried the last of their gear below decks and paused to wipe the sweat from his brow.

"Going alone makes a persona so much easier."

Beauty grinned at him. "Yet more dangerous."

"I like danger," he said sourly. "It's better than lugging crates about like a mule."

"Do you always complain?" Roarthin said, hefting a bag of mining equipment like it was a pillow.

"Always," Gordon and Ursana said in unison, and grinned together.

"Cut the talk," Lorelia said. "Don't forget we're not the only passengers on the ship, and we cannot afford to be discovered before we even get to the islands." She threw Jack a warning look.

Jack ignored her and sank into a hammock. "At least we've got a week to relax before we get there."

"I can live with that," Gordon said, claiming the hammock beside him. "Wake me when it's time to eat."

"It's three hours until lunch," Roarthin said, his tone laced with disapproval.

"That's not much time," Gordon said.

"But we'll make do," Jack finished.

They grinned in unison and closed their eyes. Someone cursed and another grunted in disgust. Then the group seemed to realize Jack and Gordon were not going to move and Lorelia laughed.

"Leave them to their dreams," she said. "Now that we're loaded there's little else to do anyway."

The sound of boots ascended to the deck, leaving Jack to the creaking of wood and rope. As the ship pulled further out to sea it rocked the hammocks, lulling Jack into slumber. Before it could claim him Gordon spoke.

"Can I still trust you?"

Jack cracked an eye open to find Gordon looking at him. "What do you need?" he asked.

"Whatever happens to me, I need you to swear you will take care of Ursana."

"Nothing is going to happen to you," Jack said with a yawn.

"Still," Gordon said. "Lorelia explained who we face, and I am not certain we will all return from such an assignment."

"Then why did you come?"

"I can't sit idle when one such as him walks free."

"You're a thief," Jack reminded him.

"That doesn't mean I don't have morals," Gordon said. "So promise me you'll make sure my partner is taken care of."

"Didn't you say you already had a daughter?"

"Yes," Gordon said with a faint smile. "And Ursana reminds me of Gwen."

Jack sighed. "I swear it, but don't worry so much. It will disturb your slumber."

Gordon grinned at that. "As you order."

Their conversation lapsed and soon Gordon began to snore. Jack stared at the beams above him. He'd assumed that stealing from Skorn would be easy. After all, the man only had cultists as servants now. But Jack had underestimated him before, and it had nearly cost him his life.

A scowl formed on his face as he thought of Gordon—or any of the others—being killed by Skorn. Then he shrugged and his doubts dissipated. Skorn may have been an ancient, but he certainly wasn't a devil. Jack would get the keys and use them to stop him, and with the fellowship of great thieves at his side he was confident in their fate.

But a sliver of doubt remained.

Chapter 12: The Boneyard

"Land ho!"

After a week of boredom, the words sent a current of excitement through the ship. Jack darted to the prow and peered into the distance. He'd never had reason to visit the Azure Islands, and he was eager to explore them. Then Beauty slid into a place at his side.

"Where'd you get the hat?"

Jack glanced up at the enormous captain's hat that adorned his head. "I spotted it in the captain's quarters and he said I could have it."

"You look ridiculous," she said, but her lips twitched into a smile.

"It kept me from getting burned," he said, and gestured to Ursana, who'd spent so much time on the deck that her skin had been scorched by the blazing sun.

"That's because it's big enough to shade a village," Beauty said.

Jack laughed and shook his head, waggling the hat. "Your jealousy won't make me give it to you."

"You think *I* want it?"

"*Everyone* wants it."

She laughed. "Saying it doesn't make it true."

He grinned and pointed to the approaching island. "We should be there in an hour. Are the others ready?"

"They will be. Thalidon has taken to his role as expedition head quite well."

The dwarf appeared on the deck and snapped orders at Gordon and Lorelia. "Get those crates on deck before we dock. I want to be on the ground in an hour." The thieves glared at him but did as he ordered. Then the dwarf caught sight of Beauty and called out to her using her persona name. "You too Thorna! Stop laying about and get to work!"

"What about—"

"And tell the captain I'd like to speak with him before we land."

"But he's not—"

"*Now!*"

Out of the corner of his eye Jack saw the dwarf's eyes alight with humor, but his gaze did not leave Beauty, indicating he really had mistaken Jack for the captain. She cast a scathing look at Jack and stepped away from the railing.

"I think I hate you a little bit."

"I did say you'd want the hat," he said, and pulled out a spyglass. He winked at her and put it to his eye.

"Where did you get . . . never mind." She attempted to snatch the hat from his head but Jack saw it coming and knocked her hand aside.

"Don't you have work to do?"

She cursed him soundly and strode away. When she was gone he turned his attention to the approaching island and the city that abutted the water. What he saw sent a thread of excitement surging into his veins.

Great towers lined the beach, their mighty structures built from fitted stones and massive logs. The battlements contained several ballistae, the barbed shafts pointing down at the docks. Beyond the sentinel towers the city sprawled up the slope of a hill.

He'd expected a ramshackle village made of logs and thatch. Instead the city was built of stone and finely cut wood. Stained wood formed well-ordered structures, the buildings curving in lazy arcs as the roads ascended to the top of the hill. The shape of the streets suggested they were built for defense, and an invading army would have to fight their way across every inch to reach the fort on the summit.

Dark skinned azure called to each other on the docks, emptying nets of fish into crates to be salted and exported. Renowned for their seafaring skills, the islanders' boats were both artistic and functional. Their sleek prows pierced the water with ease, and one passed the *Erenessa* to slide into an open jetty.

"That's Organith," a voice said, and Jack turned to find the captain at his side. "It's home to the second largest tribe on the islands."

"How are the relations between the tribes?"

"Complicated," he said. "The current peace on the islands is tenuous, and blood feuds date back for thousands of years."

"Is anything neutral?"

"The Boneyard," he said, "our destination. It lies in the heart of the islands and acts as neutral shipping ground for all of the tribes."

"And no one claims the land?"

He grinned and shook his head. "There's no land to claim. But I won't spoil the surprise."

A deckhand called and the captain departed. Curious, Jack remained in place as the ship banked to the side and followed the coastline around a giant island. As it curved inward another island appeared to the north, and another to the west. The captain called out orders as they sailed between them, keeping them clear of the rocks that jutted out from the shores.

As they sailed northwest the islands grew closer together, with some just a stone's throw from each other. Most were small but some of the islands were miles across. Others were just towers of stone piercing the surface like giant teeth.

The captain ordered them to half sail as the waterway narrowed, and eased them through the channels. Jack looked up the cliffs and spotted children running about, laughing and calling out to the sailors.

Huts and homes were in abundance, and dotted the islands in every direction. They sailed around an island that contained a forest of tiny trees, but the further they progressed the trees grew progressively taller. Then they curved around the point of the island and the trees came to an abrupt end. Hundreds of downed trees lay beside a sawmill, and the workers cut into the full-grown trunks, felling one as they sailed by.

"Space is a premium on the islands," Lorelia said, stepping to his side. "And trees are a crop like anything else. Workmen fell trees and plant new ones that will be harvested five decades from now."

"They're more civilized than I thought."

"The storms out here can be brutal," she said, "and they live on the edge of survival. They may live a divided existence but they all recognize the peril of living on the islands."

"You sound like you've been here before."

"Once, as a thief," she replied, "and once as a mage student."

It was the first time she'd ever mentioned her life before the Thieves Guild, causing him to raise an eyebrow at her.

"How old were you?"

"Twentieth year students journey to various lands and study with the magic guilds of other races."

"But the azure don't possess any natural magics."

She smiled, an oddly beatific expression on the human features she was using as her persona. "They have an assortment of magics but no guild, so I used my magic and crafted a persona. I lived among them for six months without anyone discovering my identity. It was the first time in my life I felt free."

"So where are we going?" Jack asked.

"The Boneyard," she said. "And we should almost be there."

The boat banked, splitting a gap between two islands to enter a swath of water. Islands ringed the space but none lay in the middle. Jack sucked in a breath as he saw what lay at the center.

Thousands of boats had been lashed into a gigantic flotilla. Decrepit mammoths, tiny fishing boats, and warships from across Lumineia were bound together by rope and beam. Moss and crusted growths stained the hulls, some layered so deep the ancient wood was no longer visible.

Platforms had been constructed across the decks, connecting the ships into a misshapen island. Homes and shops dotted their surface, and people from various races walked between them. At the heart of the Boneyard a ship dwarfed the others, its masts reaching to the heavens. Its deck had been converted into an enormous arena. The shouts of spectators echoed all the way across the makeshift city.

The city appeared seamless at first, but as they drew close Jack spotted canals weaving their way through the Boneyard. High platforms bridged the gap over channels of water and arced between the masts of neighboring ships. The canals allowed vessels to sail all the way to the massive ship at the center of the Boneyard, and were wide enough even for the *Erenessa*.

"Is the city anchored?" Ursana asked, and Jack turned to find the entire party standing around him.

Lorelia grinned at the shock in their eyes. "Of course, but new ships are added every year. When an older vessel is too damaged to sail, they lash it to the Boneyard."

"How did such a place begin?" Gordon asked, his gaze on a crane unloading barrels of fish.

"No one really knows," Lorelia said. "The azure may be adept at building ships but their written history lacks detail. Most agree it started with the godship." She gestured to the massive vessel at the heart of the Boneyard.

Thalidon grunted in agreement as he joined them. "It is believed the godship belonged to a great chief. The tales say he fought an entire armada to a standstill, so they surrounded him and formed a blockade. The chief's allies slipped a smaller ship through the blockade to supply the chief, but with no way out the supply ship was lashed to the godship. More ships got through, and over time the city was born."

"That sounds unlikely," Roarthin said.

"Most of history sounds unlikely," Jack said with a laugh.

"Where do we dock?" Thalidon asked.

Jack followed his gaze to the edge of the city and found that no wharfs extended into the water. Instead it seemed that ships lashed onto wherever they wanted. He even spotted two men in a heated argument because one had lashed onto the other's ship, mistakenly thinking it was part of the Boneyard.

The captain barked out orders and the *Erenessa* slid next to an aging warship. The sailors were quick to jump over and catch the ropes cast by their companions. With practiced hands they lashed them down and their ship groaned to a halt. Then the captain strode to the thieves.

"There's an inn three ships down that will give you a place to store your gear. From there I'd suggest you try to find Chief Emekalan. If he says you can search for ore on his islands, you'll probably have free reign in the clans. But you'll probably have to buy the rights from the respective chiefs."

"Thank you," Thalidon said. "We appreciate your aid."

The captain nodded and the group disembarked. Grunting in irritation, Jack grasped one of the crates and they strode toward the indicated inn. Entering an alley between two ships, they pulled their thief gear from the crates and dumped the rest into a gap between ships.

"Finally," Jack said, tightening the fastening on his bracers. "I thought we'd never be rid of it."

"You humans are so frail," Roarthin said.

"It was the only way we could smuggle our equipment," Lorelia said.

She swirled her cloak about her shoulders to add emphasis. Then she slid her gauntlets on her arms and tightened them in place. Drawing a breath, her eyes focused and then her features began to change. The human skin darkened to that of an islander, and her hair faded from brown to black. In seconds she'd shifted her persona to one of the azure.

Gordon whistled in appreciation. "I wish my personas were that easy."

Ursana snorted in laughter. "Forlana said a mule will never look like a horse."

Lorelia grinned and gestured to the nearby inn. "Beauty, get us a room. Jack, you're with me. Let's scout around and see if we can spot the cultists."

"It's not like they'll be wearing a sign," Thalidon said. "And why do you think they will be here?"

"Because this is where the tribes keep anything of value. Crimes on the Boneyard are punished by everyone, but land is frequently taken and retaken on the islands."

"And why just the two of you?" Beauty asked with a frown.

"Because I can only keep a convincing illusion on myself and one other," Lorelia said. "And Jack knows the most about our adversary."

She lifted a hand and thread of magic seeped from her finger, leeching into Jack's face. It warmed Jack's flesh as he waited, and a moment later the others began to laugh.

"*Now* you look ridiculous," Beauty said. "An azure sailor would never wear something so gaudy."

Jack sighed as he removed the hat, carefully folding it and sliding it into a pouch at his side. "I'll miss being captain."

"That hat needs to be burned," Gordon said with a smile.

Jack then turned to Lorelia. "Let's go find a group of devil-worshiping fanatics bent on helping their living ancient find keys to a legendary vault."

She grinned. "When you put it that way, what are we waiting for?"

Chapter 13: Competition

Within an hour of exploring the city it became clear that finding the key would be a challenge. The floating city was a random collection of aging ships, a labyrinth of large and small boats cobbled together into an undulating landscape of wood and rope.

The larger tribes had lashed ships together with a purpose, and added them to the Boneyard as a single unit. They represented pinpricks of order in an otherwise disorganized city. The areas the tribes controlled were a world apart from the rest of the Boneyard, and Jack even spotted a shop containing water oars, disks enchanted to propel a ship by water magic. The enchanted items cost a small fortune and were guarded by no less than a score of guards.

Another tribe held cages containing strange water creatures. Shaped like spined snakes, they had clawed hands and feet, which they used to scratch at the glass of the cages. One noticed Jack's examination and spit a stream of blue liquid that caused the water to bubble. The water grend in the cage beside it shaped into a human face and cackled.

"I've never seen a water grend before," Jack said.

The shopkeeper inserted himself into the conversation with a sleazy smile. "They're sentient fragments of water," he said, "and incredibly hard to catch. If they bond to you they will be loyal for life. Six hundred gold for this one, a bargain if I do say so."

"*If* they bond," Lorelia said, "which they rarely do. It's worth half what you are charging."

The shopkeeper sniffed and slipped away in search of less educated buyers. Jack grinned at Lorelia and they stepped out of the shop. Once they were out of the guarded area Jack slipped closer to her.

"You want to go back and steal it, just for fun?"

She grinned. "Perhaps, but we should focus. We have seen no sign of Skorn's followers."

"We need a better vantage point," Jack said, and gestured to the platforms scattered among the masts of the city.

They ascended to an open tavern built between three towering masts. The *Crow's Nest* contained no roof, and the cooks roasted fish over an open bed of coals. Jack and Lorelia took seats that overlooked one of the tribe contingents and ordered spiced lava fish with sea rice. The barmaid's eyes lingered on Jack before she left, causing Lorelia to grunt in irritation.

"I should give you a scar."

"Scars don't always make one ugly," he said pointedly.

She regarded him for several moments before looking away. "Perhaps for you."

He held up the glass and used the reflection to examine his appearance. His features remained the same but his skin appeared as dark as the barmaid's. He ran his fingers through his hair and grunted in approval.

"I look fine."

"That's the problem," Lorelia said. "You're drawing too much attention."

Jack glanced about and saw her words to be accurate. The women stared at Jack in thinly veiled curiosity and desire.

"Or kept me Talinorian," Jack said in an undertone. "It's not like there aren't Griffinborn or Talinorians about." He gestured to the ships below on which a group of Griffin men haggled with a vendor.

113

"True," she said, "but it's possible the cultists have been told about you."

"I'm flattered."

"Don't be," she said. "You nearly killed Skorn, and he won't underestimate you again."

Their meal came, and as they ate Jack looked down at the ships below. Shaped like a giant crescent moon, the section allowed ships a private place to dock. Although the district of the city was clearly made of salvaged ships, the surface resembled a wharf in Griffin, and contained warehouses, taverns, and inns. The entire contingent lay inside a large wall built from special barrier ships, cutting it off from the surrounding area. Noticing his examination, Lorelia gestured to it.

"The larger tribes keep a permanent outpost on the city, and build it offsite before attaching it to the Boneyard."

"I noticed," Jack said. "I suspect that if the key is here, it's in one of them."

Jack kept his gaze on the crowd below, scanning it for any sign of a cult member. Unfortunately, Beauty's doubt proved accurate, and he didn't spot anyone he could consider a worshiper of Skorn. After the meal they moved on to another vantage point near another tribe outpost, and throughout the afternoon they checked each of the others. As night fell they returned to the inn with nothing to show for their efforts.

Over the next three days they went out in groups or alone, searching every corner of the Boneyard for signs of cultists. Their efforts proved in vain, and Jack began to question if the cultists had already found the key and moved on.

Since much of the city was built from derelict ships, searching it was tedious, and at times dangerous. Some boats floated low in the water, their beams soaked through and their hulls listing. Islanders simply avoided them, letting those pieces of city succumb to the depths.

The scent of fish and salt were constants, as was the pungent reek of ship's tar. Larger catches were displayed by hanging them from their tails, and customers haggled while the fish swayed behind them.

Enormous sharks were also hoisted by the tails so their teeth, fins, and jaws could be sold at a premium.

Shortly after their arrival a storm hit the city, causing the Boneyard to undulate. The outsiders huddled in their inns, grasping at anything mounted as the structure tipped and plunged. The islanders seemed not to notice, and walked about in the sheeting rain to conduct their business as normal.

Known for a haughtiness and pride, the islanders carried a disdain for "weak-kneed landers," and frequently called them women, the highest insult among their people. Their clothing was utilitarian and typically woven from wool sheared from the many flocks the tribes maintained. Colors were garish and bright, making it possible for the sailors to be spotted if they fell overboard.

Jewelry and tattoos were used to mark status, wealth, and tribe affiliation. Poorer individuals favored simple gold earrings for both men and women, while the wealthy were veritably festooned with gold rings in ears, nose, and cheek. Rather than dark ink, the tattoos were equally as bright as the clothing, with some even enchanted to move across the flesh.

As the days passed into a week Roarthin and even Thalidon grew irritable. In an effort to avoid the dwarves, Jack slipped out the back of the tavern with Beauty and they strolled about the city.

"What if they already got the key and moved on?" she finally asked.

"Does it matter?"

"How can you ask that?"

"We got the chance to visit the Boneyard," he replied, and swept his hands at the city. "Would we have come here without this assignment?"

"Perhaps you are right," she said. "But I wonder how much longer we can wait."

"We should visit the arena," Jack said.

115

"Thalidon said there's nothing to see but meaningless duels."

"It's the one place I haven't visited yet."

"That's because Lorelia said you should avoid the godship," Beauty said, crinkling her nose. "She doesn't want you betting on the fights—or entering as a contestant."

"I'm not in the guild, remember?" He smiled and turned toward the gigantic vessel situated at the heart of the city. "Besides, we both know you're the better fighter."

"Did you just admit that out loud?"

He released a bark of laughter and crossed a gangplank to the neighboring ship. From there they ascended to an ancient passenger ship to pass over a canal. Climbing to the catwalk above, they crossed to the godship and descended to the deck.

At two hundred feet wide the ship was massive, and its remaining masts seemed to touch the stormy clouds. The forecastle could have housed their entire inn with room to spare, and contained three distinct levels. Instead of crew and captain's quarters, the rooms were reserved for wealthy spectators. Benches had been fastened above it, providing space for hundreds to view the combat taking place on the deck.

Jack and Beauty paid a single copper and entered the ship. From there they made their way to the top of the prow, where the seats allowed them a distant view of the two shirtless contenders battling with their fists.

"What do they fight for?" Jack asked.

"Pride and coin," she replied. "Usually the match goes until one submits, but occasionally a challenge ends in death."

Jack gestured to what was obviously the gameskeeper, and when he approached he handed him a silver coin.

"On the tall one," he said.

Beauty raised a silver piece. "Me as well."

The man sniffed and looked her up and down, the disdain evident on his features. "Women are required to wager the minimum."

"And who sets the minimum?"

The man sneered. "I do. I think two gold is enough—unless that's too rich for your blood."

She pulled two coins from her pouch and passed them over with a sigh.

"Excellent choice," the gameskeeper replied smugly, and noted the wager in a small book. "Name?"

Jack spoke before she could. "Last name Oman, first name Ima."

The man peaked an eyebrow, but Jack merely nodded. He shrugged and added the name next to the bet. Then he strode away and Jack returned his gaze to the match. When the gameskeeper was gone she nudged him.

"What's with the odd persona?"

"Just wait," Jack said.

The two men fought without blade or staff, pummeling each other with fists and knees. The tall one shoved the smaller foe into the thick mast, and then struck him a punishing blow in his gut. His opponent doubled over and went down, and the man picked him up to strike him again. Cheers rang out as the victor dropped the unconscious form to the deck. The gameskeeper began calling out the winning wagers and distributed the winnings. When he called out Beauty's name his accent distorted the words.

"*I'm a woman!*" he shouted. "I'm a woman, get your winnings here . . ."

Howls of laughter erupted around him, and the gameskeeper's face turned red as he realized what he'd said. Then he spotted Jack and shoved his way to him. Slamming the coins on the bench, he growled at Jack.

"I don't appreciate your humor."

"You pronounced her name wrong," Jack said.

The man muttered an epithet and left, and Beauty shook her head. "Why do you have to be so aggravating?"

"Because it's fun."

She stifled a grin and motioned to the two new fighters stepping onto the deck. "Care to wager again?"

"I find I've lost my taste for gambling today."

"For gambling or the gameskeeper?"

He grinned and did not answer. Instead he let his gaze wander across the crowd, absently searching for any sign of a cultist. Like the rest of the city, the spectators came from every corner of Lumineia. Cultists didn't hail from any one race or kingdom, making it nearly impossible to identify them.

Then a face caught his eye.

He almost dismissed him, but something about the youthful features caught Jack's eye. The man was young, barely out of his teens, and the features were distinctly Griffinborn. The man stared at the battling men with dispassionate dismissal, marking him as one familiar with violence. Then the woman at his side spoke in his ear and he twisted to look up, his gaze rising to the forecastle situated behind. When he turned back he bore a familiar sneer of triumph on his face.

"We need to go," Jack said.

"What do you see?"

"Straight across, three rows down, below the forecastle. Use a vision spell."

Her eyes glimmered and she looked to where he'd said. Several seconds passed and then she grunted in irritation. "I don't see . . ." Her breath caught and she leaned in, peering across the distance. Then she cursed and her vision returned to normal. "We need to go."

"I already said that," Jack said.

Jack rose and turned away from the man. Then he slipped through the crowd and departed the godship by one of the bridges that would keep them out of view of the forecastle. Once they were back on the city Beauty stepped to his side but did not speak.

They hurried across the floating city until they reached the inn they were currently staying in. Slipping inside, Jack caught the eyes of the others and strode to the stairs. His expression was sufficient to draw them from their seats and follow. Once they were all inside Jack shut the door.

"We found the cultists, but they are not alone."

"Skorn is here?" Ursana asked.

Beauty shook her head. "He sent another in his place, and it's one we know."

"Who?" Ursana asked.

"Gallow," Jack said, turning to her.

She cursed his name. "The *head* of the assassin's guild?"

Her face grim, Beauty nodded. "It appears Skorn has an ally."

Chapter 14: Stormfall

"Who?" Roarthin asked.

"The youngest member ever to become one of the seven assassins," Beauty said, "and he achieved that by killing assassins to create the opening for himself."

"And they promoted him to lead their guild?" Gordon asked.

"Not by choice," Thalidon said grimly. "He enlisted the aid of a deposed rock troll king and infiltrated the guild. He killed his mentor, Joren, and took his place. In the past, the assassins' work had been subtle and carried out in secret, but under Gallow they have increased their killings tenfold."

"I would think that would draw attention," Roarthin said.

"Any official that has sought to punish them has been killed, and surviving council members have heeded the warning," Beauty said.

"Is it possible he is here on his own assignment?" Gordon asked.

Jack and Beauty exchanged a look and Jack raised an eyebrow. "Did you see his companions?"

"Nine stood with him, although it wasn't apparent at first," she said. "They are obviously not assassins, yet they are obedient to him. There's no telling how long he's been here—or how many more are in the city."

"But he's found the key," Jack said, drawing their gaze to him.

"How can you tell?" Beauty asked.

"One such as him abhors being kept from his goal," he replied. "And his expression was that of a hunter who has spotted his prey."

"He did look pleased," Beauty said. "But if he found it, where is it?"

"Once a cat finds his next meal he stalks its path until the kill," Jack said. "I wager the key is on the godship."

Lorelia's forehead was creased in thought. "There are places far more protected than the godship."

"Exactly," Beauty said, catching on to what Jack was insinuating. "Until now we've been assuming the owner knows its value. If the owner views it as an old trinket . . ."

Lorelia nodded and understanding lit her gaze. "No doubt they've wasted their time searching the city just as we have, and only now have resorted to the godship. It must lie in one of the forecastle viewing rooms that overlook the deck."

"We should go tonight," Jack said, "before they can slaughter their way to it."

"No," Lorelia said. "If we rush into this we might get ourselves killed." She raised a hand to forestall Jack's protest. "We examine the target tonight. Tomorrow we steal it."

Beauty swept a hand to her. "But if we delay—"

"We survive," Lorelia cut her off. "Don your personas and go to the godship. Jack, you're with me in case they spotted you with Beauty. Ursana, you come with us so we look like a family. Thalidon, you and Roarthin examine the ship itself, look for any defenses that we can't see. Gordon, you're a traveler too into his drink to matter. Beauty, you do the same but come from the east side of the ship. Take only weapons that can be easily hidden."

"What if they recognize us?" Ursana asked, reluctantly dropping her heavy crossbow to the floor.

"They won't," Jack said. "Why would he think anyone is going to steal the key? For all he knows Skorn is the only one that knows about it."

"Jack's right," Lorelia said. "But be careful. If the assassin does recognize you, he's as likely to slit your throat as say hello."

They split up, and Jack returned to the godship with Lorelia and Ursana. During their conversation the wind had picked up and the afternoon sky had darkened. The city rippled as the sea rose to embrace the impending storm. Jack and Lorelia exchanged a look and picked up the pace. Dodging ships and makeshift taverns, they reached one of the four bridges that connected to the godship.

They crossed the canal and rejoined the crowd. Jack didn't have to ask to know that Lorelia had already disguised them. The looks he received from the islanders suggested they appeared as azure. A moment later they slipped into a seat that gave them a slight angle on where the assassin had been sitting.

Jack spotted Gallow sitting with his companions, and followed his gaze to the highest room of the forecastle. Comprising the entire fifth level of the massive structure, the space was clearly reserved for the wealthy. A mass of islanders viewed the blade duel taking place on the deck below, their ears filled with gold. One youth stood out and Jack used his chin to point at him.

"Do you recognize him?"

Her eyes flicked to him and nodded. "That's Prince Emeka, son of Emekalan, one of the stronger chiefs. He may be young, but he's already bested many in the contests."

"How can you tell who he is?" Ursana murmured.

"He's wearing the cloak and golden bands of his tribe," she replied. "And if that weren't enough the guards mark him as royalty. He's likely here to scout the latest group of fighters."

"Gallow is moving," Ursana said.

Jack dropped his gaze and watched the assassin slide through the crowd before taking one of the bridges to the western ship. Then he drifted out of the group and came to a halt. Most of his group remained on the ship, but a handful went ahead of the assassin and took seats at a tavern within view.

"A trap," Jack said, recognizing the ploy. "He wants the key to come to him."

"But where is it?" Lorelia asked.

Jack's eyes were drawn to the prince, to the item hanging from his neck. He began to chuckle under his breath as he recognized the shape.

"He's using the key as a pendant," Jack said.

Lorelia released a chagrined laugh. "If he arrived recently, it would mean the cultists didn't find it until now."

"How fortunate for us," Jack said.

Ursana snorted at his tone. "Do you *always* expect life to fall into place for you?"

"Don't you?" Jack asked.

She wrinkled her nose. "No, and normal people don't either."

"Who said I was normal?"

Lorelia stifled a laugh. "You've never spoken truer words." Then she gestured to the lethal trap awaiting the prince. "It's seems Gallow has watched the prince enough to expect him to exit in that direction."

"If only you'd let me come earlier," Jack lamented, "I would have spotted him before he was in place."

Her lips tightened in disapproval. "Regardless, the question is what to do now. If we disrupt the trap he'll know we're here, and we lose our advantage. If we do nothing, he gets the key."

"We could steal the key first," Jack said.

"And how do we do that?" she asked, folding her arms. "The prince has dozens of guards, obviously trained enough that Gallow decided against a straightforward attack."

"We don't need to steal the key," Jack said, an idea forming in his mind, "just the ship."

Lorelia didn't seem to register what he meant. Then her eyes widened. "You want to steal the *godship*?"

He grinned. "Why not?"

"And how do we steal a hundred-year-old ship that in its prime required hundreds to navigate?"

"You say it like it will be hard," Jack said, and began to move through the crowd in the opposite direction of the lurking assassin.

"There are a thousand people on this ship," Ursana hissed. "And the ship hasn't moved in ages."

"It will," Jack said. "Just get a message to the others and let them know to be ready."

"Ready for what?" Lorelia hissed.

"For the storm," he replied, and stabbed a finger toward the darkening sky. "When it hits, we move."

She caught his arm but the motion drew attention from the other spectators. They scowled at her, their eyes conveying disgust for her motion. Reluctantly she came to a halt and Ursana stopped at her side.

He grinned and slipped away. Once he was back in the city he sprinted across the decks. Lightning appeared in the distance and the wall of dark clouds crept toward the Boneyard. The footing of the city became perilous as the turbulent water became increasingly violent.

He leapt to a neighboring ship, skipping the gangplank filled with people. In spite of the islanders' bravado during storms, many had begun to depart the godship, their caution indicating the storm to be a gale. Then Jack reached a walled section he'd visited on his first day.

Leaping to a roof, he sprinted over an inn and dropped into the tribe's makeshift fortress. His appearance startled a group of guards, who rose to their feet and called out to him. Jack darted to the prow of a ship nearby and leapt past them, sprinting for a shop sitting on a curved vessel. The sailors cried out amidst the sound of weapons being drawn. Then the pounding of feet heralded their pursuit.

Jack picked up a coil of rope and hurled it through the glass window. It shattered, sending bits of glass scattering through the empty shop. Leaping through the opening, Jack gathered an armful of small circular discs and stuffed them into a pack. Then he leapt out the window to find the area surrounded by a dozen furious islanders.

"Sorry for the mess," Jack said, "and the cost."

One of the sailors raised a hooked staff weapon and pointed it at him. "We'll gut you and toss you to the sharks, thief—"

Jack crouched and launched himself into a casual back flip that took him to the roof. Astonishment robbed the man of speech but Jack was already gone. Leaping buildings and ships, he raced across the heaving city toward the godship. The sounds of pursuit faded into the distance as he quickly outstripped them.

When the arena came into view he saw that the final fight had come to an end. Spectators and combatants streamed across the rolling bridges as great drops of rain began to fall upon them. A group of Talinorian women scurried away while casting fearful eyes at the black sky. They passed right through Gallow's trap, unaware that a supreme assassin stood within dagger's reach.

With the pathways clogged, Jack accelerated and leapt the thirty-foot gap, drawing a scattering of shouts at the feat. Landing just inside the godship's railing, he sprinted to Lorelia, who stood with a white knuckled hand grasping a rope.

"The prince is about to depart," she said. "Whatever your plan, do it now."

Jack spotted Thalidon and Roarthin drifting toward them. Gesturing them close, he said, "Use your magic to destroy the eastern bridges. Then get everyone else off the ship except the prince."

"How are we going to move the ship . . .?"

But Jack was already gone. Sprinting to the stern of the massive ship, he caught a rope and leapt over the rail. Then he lowered himself

125

down to where the water crashed against the ancient hull. Withdrawing the discs, he slapped them onto the hull one by one, and watched them glow to life. Drenched from the water, he scaled to the deck in time to see men and women cry out as Roarthin launched balls of fire into one bridge. Thalidon attacked a second, sending the lingering spectators sprinting away. The other thieves struck at the supports and ropes holding the remaining two aloft.

The prince appeared in the forecastle doorway, his eyes widening when he spotted the thieves. Then his gaze lit with anticipation and he drew his weapon, charging Roarthin. Abruptly the ship shuddered and groaned, causing everyone still aboard to stagger. All eyes turned to the stern, where a great rush of water could be heard.

And the godship began to move.

Chapter 15: The Godship

Beauty stumbled to a railing and held on, her eyes flying to Jack. "What did you do?"

"Water oars," Jack said. "Lorelia and I saw them in a shop a few days ago. Just one has enough water magic to propel a warship."

Lorelia "How many did you put on?"

Jack grinned. "A dozen."

Wood groaned and ropes stretched, and then the last of the supports holding the godship snapped in two. Weakened by dwarven fire they cracked and twisted before coming apart. Ropes snapped like whips, sending bits of sizzling fire into the crowd. Those lining the neighboring ships stood in shocked silence as the massive ship began to advance.

The prince, his guards, and spectators unfortunate enough to get caught on the ship looked up at the final bridge connected to the city. Unable to withstand the stress of the ship's movement, it crumbled and splashed into the sea below. Then Jack spotted Gallow push his way to the rail of a neighboring ship. He came to a halt as he watched the godship slide past him, his eyes bulging. Jack reached up and offered a mock salute, laughing at the rage on the assassin's features.

"Jack?" Ursana asked in a rising tone. He turned to find thirty islanders standing with a handful of confused Griffin merchants.

"Kill them," the prince said coldly, and strode toward Beauty with a sneer on his face.

Beauty drew her dagger and attacked first. Her motions blurred impossibly fast, her speed charm causing her to overwhelm the prince in seconds. He cried out in dismay as his weapon tumbled from his fingers. Before Beauty could snatch the key from his neck his guards rushed her, and it was all she could do to hold them off.

The thieves leapt into the fray and the scene dissolved into chaos. Jack engaged a burly islander wielding a wooden shield and a spiked staff. Ducking a hasty blow, Jack stepped in and grabbed the man's neck. He yanked him down and brought his knee up, smashing the man's skull on his kneecap. As the man slumped Jack leapt for another but Lorelia got to him first, or at least an image of her did.

The man slashed his weapon through her form, only to stumble as his blade passed through the illusion. Jack laughed and struck him in the throat, dropping him like a stone. Although the islanders had been trained for battle, the thieves fought dirty, turning the tide in spite of their fewer numbers.

As the thieves fought to subdue the prince the ship continued to accelerate, the water oars churning water to propel the ship forward. The bow plunged into a trough and plowed through a crest. It continued to accelerate until the wood of the deck thrummed with power. As the thieves battled on the deck it began to hurtle down the canal at speeds unattainable with conventional sails.

Gordon leapt to the helm and struggled to hold the ship in the center of the canal, but a sudden swell caused them to veer to the side. The massive ship smashed into the city, crumpling another ship like a paper toy.

Everyone on the godship was knocked sprawling, with two of the Griffin merchants being launched overboard. Islanders and thieves slid to the rail as the enormous ship tilted to the side, the wood shrieking as it scraped against the city boats. The mast of the godship crashed into the neighbors' masts, snapping them in half and sending the beams tumbling onto the city.

Islanders screamed and fled from the carnage, barely escaping as whole ships were shattered. Those too slow were knocked into the water and grasped flotsam that littered the godship's wake. Blasting through city boats, the godship continued to accelerate until it barreled down the canal. They reached a walkway that bridged the two sides of the canal and exploded through it, sending a shudder into the godship's deck.

"Beauty!" Jack shouted.

"On it!" she cried, and used a strength spell to ascend the steep deck to reach the wheel. Growling from the effort, she helped Gordon turn the helm, gradually righting them and bringing them back to the center of the canal.

As the ship began to level Jack lunged forward and struck an islander clinging to the rail. He cried out as he plummeted into the sea. Sprinting forward, Jack caught a swing from another and spun, hurling him overboard as well. Maintaining his momentum, he rushed down the leveling rail with the balance of a charging panther, casting the islanders into the frothing sea below. Then abruptly he reached the prince.

"You think to discard me so easily?"

The man wrapped a rope around his free hand and held on, but Jack's vision went beyond him.

"I do," Jack said, and darted to his flank.

Beauty cursed as she realized she'd overcorrected, and the ship crashed brutally into the other side of the canal. Everyone on board was flung across the deck, and Jack's position put him directly behind Prince Emeka. They slid across the deck as the godship shattered smaller boats and barreled through ropes and high bridges. Emeka struck the railing and the impact sent his weapon tumbling into a boat below. Then Jack smashed into his chest, driving the air from his lungs.

"I'll take that," Jack said, and grabbed the spiked dagger from his neck.

"That's mine," the prince snarled, but it came out in a gasp as he fought to breathe.

"Not anymore," Jack said. Then he grabbed Emeka's foot and rolled him over the rail. The man caught the railing, so Jack leaned over and held up his dagger. "Lose a hand or lose your pride. I don't care which."

The man growled and released, and a moment later he splashed into the sea. Just then Beauty managed to right the ship and it careened back to center. Jack rotated to face the remaining islanders and merchants still aboard. They righted themselves and stared about in confusion, swinging their weapons between the thieves.

Seizing the moment, Jack strode to the stairs and ascended several steps. Then he turned and faced the islanders, reaching into his pocket to retrieve his enormous captain's hat. With great care he unfolded it and placed it on his head.

"I proclaim this ship the *Woman's Might*, and name myself captain. You can depart in peace or by force."

His cheerful offer was met by surly growls and the raising of weapons, until Thalidon filled his hands with fire and Lorelia cast an illusion of a dozen swordsmen in their midst. Recognizing that to stay would be foolhardy, they reluctantly moved to the side of the ship and leapt into the canal. Last to go, the two Griffin merchants cast him dirty looks before they too dropped from view.

"Captain Myst?" Beauty shouted, her voice mocking. "You're needed on the bridge."

Jack ascended to her side to find her grimly holding onto the helm of the massive ship. "Report."

She gestured with her chin behind them, where no less than a dozen ships were filling the canal. "Did your plan extend *beyond* this point?"

"Of course," Jack said, mimicking her sarcasm. "We just need the storm to break."

As if hearing his words, the dark clouds cracked open and dumped a veritable ocean of rain. The rain washed across the godship with thundering force, so thick Jack could barely discern the ship's bow. Several of the thieves cried out in dismay but the sound was all but lost in the storm.

"*This* was your plan?" Beauty shouted.

"You don't like it?"

"I love it," she snapped. "Taking a massive, decrepit ship—with just seven people to man it—is exactly how I want to *get killed!*"

They reached the edge of the city and the godship sailed into open water. Without the calming effect of the floating city the water heaved and dropped, and the massive ship went with it. Ancient wood groaned at the titanic forces pressing on its hull. The bow dropped into a trough and then crashed through a wave. Water blasted across the deck, nearly taking them with it.

"STOP LAUGHING!" Beauty roared, but Jack would not be stopped.

With the enraged sea to their front and the enraged islanders at their back, he reached out and helped Beauty and Gordon stabilize the wheel, which shuddered in their grip. He shook his hat, sending water splashing over them.

"Turn us south!" he shouted.

She cast him a scathing glare but did as requested, and the three of them struggled to turn the wheel. It trembled at the strain and Jack wondered if it would break. Gradually the vast ship turned, the enormous masts leaning at an impossible angle.

"This is madness, Jack!" Gordon shouted.

"I know!" he replied, and the glee in his voice caused Beauty to release a string of profanities that ended in his name.

"She's right!" Lorelia shouted, stumbling onto the bridge to join them. The dwarves appeared as well and the thieves gathered about the helm.

"Just hang on!" Jack replied, and shook his hat again to clear the water pouring from the brim.

Beauty snarled as water splashed across her. "If we survive, I swear I'm *burning* that hat while it's still on your head."

"Is everyone ready?" Jack shouted.

"FOR WHAT?" they cried in unison.

Jack spotted a looming cliff of stone in the distance and yanked on the ship's wheel, turning them toward it. Seeing his goal, Lorelia gasped.

"Do you *mean* to crash us?"

Jack laughed as he wrapped a rope around the helm, fastening it in place. Ursana cursed and Gordon growled. Then Jack picked up a coil of rope and sprinted toward the back of the ship. With a wild grin he leapt up and balanced on the heaving rail.

"Stay with the ship or stay with me!" he shouted, and flipped into the sea.

He plummeted toward the white capped water and knifed into the depths. He'd expected it to be warm but the water carried a chill that tightened every muscle in his body. Shivering, he swam upward and breached the surface, drawing a great breath as he looked toward the receding ship. Small figures leapt off the back of the godship, scrambling to escape as it barreled toward a towering island of stone. Jack wiped the water from his face and tensed, waiting for the impact. Then the godship struck the island.

Overpowering the very thunder, the crash roared across the sea. The bow crumpled on itself, the ancient wood snapping like kindling. The six masts folded in half, clattering off the tiny island before collapsing into the water. The sea gushed into the gaping wounds, flooding the interior of the godship. Even as the water oars drove it forward the godship began to sink.

Jack watched with a wide grin on his face. Then he withdrew the last of the water oars from the pouch at his side. Activating it with a touch, he slapped it onto his boots and pointed his body toward the others. Intended to push boats, the magic accelerated him too fast, but he managed to uncoil the rope behind him and tighten it about his waist.

The force of the push made his chest act like the prow of a boat, and he bounced over the water toward them. Beauty spotted him first, and the fury on her face exploded into laughter when she saw Jack speeding toward her, his hat flopping about his head.

"Care for a ride?" he shouted as he turned a wide circle.

The circle allowed her to grab the rope, and once she was on he turned toward the others. Then he pointed his body at the Boneyard. Beauty continued to laugh and it spread to the others. With water splashing over them and islander warships appearing in the gloom, the thieves roared their laughter as they escaped into the sheets of rain and churning sea.

The pursuing ships arrived at the broken godship and sought to salvage it, but their efforts were in vain. They watched in horror as the ship they had worshiped for a century slipped beneath the surface. As the storm turned increasingly harsh, they were forced to return to the Boneyard.

In the subsequent days the city huddled through the storm, but rumors spread like wildfire. Emeka insisted it was a group of thieves attempting to steal a treasured keepsake, but the truth was lost amid claims that a demon had taken the godship. Sailors swore on Ero's staff they had heard his laughter wafting through the storm as the ship sank.

Chapter 16: Cliffwatch

Five days after the godship sank the storm began to fade. Its anger spent, the raging wind quieted and the rain slowed to a drizzle, allowing the captain of the *Deep Blue* to embark toward the dwarven kingdom with a shipment of fish. As he untied from the Boneyard, seven passengers arrived with coin in hand. He counted his good fortune for the extra coin and didn't look past their appearances. A week later he deposited them on the dwarven coastline and sailed away, still wondering who had destroyed the godship.

Jack watched the ship disappear on the horizon and then turned toward the others. "Does *anyone* pay attention to their passengers?"

"Fortunately for us, no," Lorelia said with a grunt of humor. "But I suspect retrieving the next key will not be so easy."

"You think that was easy?" Gordon asked, stabbing a finger toward the receding ship. "Most assignments involve avoiding a few guards, or maybe a curse or two. Every time we go with Jack we end up on rampaging boats or diving off cliffs."

"Don't tell me you didn't enjoy it," Jack said.

"I'm not going to admit that," he replied, and his lips tugged in a smile.

"We should get moving," Beauty said. "Now that Gallow knows we seek the keys he will hasten his steps. We cannot let him reach the dark elves first."

Thalidon grunted. "Then it is well you have us," he used his chin to point at his brother. "The fastest route to Elsurund is through Torridin."

Roarthin grunted in agreement. "The assassin will likely take the longer path through the tunnels in Griffin."

"Lead the way," Lorelia said.

Thalidon shouldered his pack and strode off the beach into the trees. The ribbon of forest grew sparse as they ascended into the towering mountains that abutted Blue Lake. Boulders and broken stones littered the earth around the pine trees, fallen remnants of a shattered mountain. Some of the stones towered over the trees, their surfaces covered with moss and dry leaves.

Thalidon led them up a winding trail that followed a gurgling stream. The air quickly turned frigid the higher they climbed, and the group wrapped their cloaks about them to ward off the chill. Sweeps of snow filled the gulleys and dotted the northern side of the peaks, growing deeper as they approached the summit. Several days after departing the beach they reached a dwarven outpost.

The small fortress clung to the side of a cliff and overlooked the lake in the distance. Its position provided an unbroken view of the crisscrossing paths ascending from the water, and the dwarf that greeted them made it clear they had been spotted hours ago.

"Can you speak for your companions?" the dwarf asked, obviously bored.

"I can," Thalidon said.

The dwarf didn't seem to notice Roarthin's scowl and gestured them inside. "Welcome to Cliffwatch."

Jack advanced through the portcullis and ascended the steps to the outpost. Massive arches jutted out from the cliff to support it, but the entire outpost felt fragile. Barely thirty feet thick, the outpost clung to the cliff thousands of feet off the ground. Situated close to the peak, the structure boasted four levels, while the top of the outpost contained a pile of wood for a signal fire.

The thieves stepped through the oak door and entered a small tavern, the bar of which sat against the cliff. The entire floor carried a distinct tilt, giving the impression the outpost could fall at any moment. Jack instinctively leaned away from it until he realized the angle of the floor was likely a tactical advantage. It implied the dwarves could release the outpost from its moorings in an instant—which they probably could.

Great beams supported the ceiling, the supports mounted to the stone by steel rods. Metal bound the stone and wood in typical dwarven precision. In spite of the precarious position, the crackling fire within the hearth lent a comfortable feel to the outpost.

Unperturbed by the strange floor, Thalidon walked to the lowest point of the slope and looked out through the window. Then he slid into a seat and motioned the others to join him at the table. When they took seats around him he signaled the bartender.

"Wild ale for the table," he said.

The female dwarf stepped to the large barrels mounted against the wall by bands of iron. She deftly filled seven mugs and carried them to the table without spilling a drop of foam. Then she slid them to the group.

"What brings you to Cliffwatch?"

"We're going to—"

"Traveling to Torridin," Roarthin interrupted, casting Jack a warning glance.

"This late in the season it will be rough going," she said. "Snow already falls in the passes."

"And the tunnels?"

She shrugged and pointed north. "A mine lies two days north. If you can reach it, you can travel underground to Torridin." She looked them up and down with an expression that implied disdain. "That is if your companions can handle the deep paths."

Jack grinned but held his tongue while Lorelia assured her they were prepared to journey beneath the mountains. The dwarf shrugged and departed, returning a moment later with grilled meat and stiff bread.

Jack and the dwarves cracked the bread open and dipped it into the ale. Jack chewed the now soft bread, savoring the sweetness. Then he noticed the entire table was staring at him. He dipped the bread again and took a bite, speaking through the mouthful.

"Say what you can about the dwarves, but they know how to eat."

Ursana gingerly dipped her bread into her ale and tasted a morsel. She smiled and plunged it deeper into the mug, eliciting a round of laughter from the group. Following her lead, the rest of the thieves did the same. Jack noticed Roarthin staring at him with a curious expression.

"I lived close to your mountains, dwarf," Jack said, irritated by the attention. "I know your ways."

Roarthin continued to regard him with a spark of interest that had been absent before. Then he shifted to dwarvish.

"You are educated yet you became a thief. Why?"

Jack laughed and replied in the same tongue. "I'm not a thief."

"Then what are you, Jack?"

Jack filled his mouth with a chunk of bread and shrugged. Then he turned away from the dwarf and asked Ursana what she thought of the view. Roarthin did not attempt to reengage him in conversation, but the question lingered in Jack's mind. It was the second time in a month he'd been asked it, and he still didn't have an answer.

He tried to consider what he would do if he wasn't a thief. A merchant's life would be dull beyond compare, while becoming a solider would require him to obey orders. He wrinkled his nose at that and looked at the endless vista stretched out below him.

His thoughts turned to stealing the godship, and the sheer excitement of riding the vessel into an island. But that had not been the only emotion. In the back of his mind he could almost see his mother's look. The striking disappointment in her eyes was the same as when he'd taken the dwarven knife.

You're better than this, Jack, she seemed to say.

Maybe I'm not, Jack answered.

Abruptly Jack rose from his seat and strode away, eliciting curious looks from his companions. Ignoring them, he ascended through the outpost to the signal fire at the roof. The dwarf on watch ignored him as Jack strode to the edge and sat, letting his feet dangle over the endless fall.

Thousands of feet below, the rolling hills descended to the glistening sea. To the north the mountain range went all the way into the water, with one island just off the coast, likely the summit of an underwater mountain. To the south, the trees ended at the Plains of Adbar, and Jack spotted a glimpse of the druid forests beyond it. As the sun set he stared at his distant home.

What would you have me be, mother?

The query went unanswered, and Jack sighed in regret. Perhaps this was the life he was meant to lead, to steal for coin and accept assignments from the Guildmaster, to defy what his mother wanted and forever see her disappointment in his memory.

"Mind if I join you?"

Jack turned to find Beauty standing behind him. "You shouldn't startle someone sitting on a ledge."

She laughed and took a seat next to him. "We both know you would never hit the ground—and you would probably enjoy the fall."

"Probably," Jack admitted with a smile.

For a while they sat in silence, with both lost in thought as the sun set. When the light had been extinguished she sighed.

"Are you going to tell me why you feel guilty?"

His laughter was sharp and mocking. "For stealing the godship? Why would I feel guilty?"

"You tell me," she said. "Guilt is always apparent in the eyes of a sinner."

The words were a direct quote from the book of Ero. "We're all sinners," Jack said with a wry smile. "Isn't that why Roarthin despises us?"

"You don't care what he thinks," she said.

"True."

"Then why do you feel guilt?"

He glanced at her before staring into the darkness. He didn't have anyone he truly trusted, but he shared a kinship with Beauty that went beyond friendship. She too had lost someone to the Thieves Guild, and they had cast Skorn out together. If anyone would understand it would be her.

But he could not voice it.

Deep down it felt childish to say that his mother didn't want him to become a thief, that the moment he'd joined the guild she was likely crying in heaven. She'd wanted him to do more—to *be* more than just a thief. And here he was becoming one.

He told himself it was just to stop Skorn, but he knew that would be a lie. He loved being a thief, and he'd never had so much fun as when he stole the godship. But once Skorn was defeated he would lose his excuse.

"It's not guilt I feel," Jack said, covering the lie with a disarming smile. "It's regret that there was only one godship to steal."

"I overheard you ask the innkeeper on the Boneyard if anyone had been killed," she smiled. "You were worried about the people."

"I was just curious," Jack said.

141

Beauty smiled at his words. "You care more than you admit," she said.

Jack grunted in irritation and turned away. "We should be more careful in the future."

She raised an eyebrow at him. "You? Careful? I never thought I'd hear you talk like that."

He suppressed a smile. "Everyone learns," he said.

Doubt remained in her eyes but after a moment she dipped her head. "One can only hope. Sleep well, Jack."

She squeezed his shoulder and then stood and left, leaving him to his view. With the moon just beginning to rise and a host of stars in the sky, the hills below were indistinct and resembled a lumpy bed.

"You shouldn't lie to the lady," the dwarven sentinel said, speaking for the first time.

"What do you know, dwarf?" Jack growled.

He stood and left, half expecting the dwarf to talk again. Instead he looked upon Jack with a mixture of pity and annoyance. Jack resisted the urge to shout at him and descended to the room they had paid for. Slipping into the sheets he found himself wishing Beauty had not been so easily convinced.

Or that he could convince himself as easily.

Chapter 17: Retribution

Most of the thieves were up at dawn, but they had to wait an hour for Gordon and Ursana to come down for breakfast. Yawning, Gordon descended the steps amidst a round of jeers and laughter. He laughed it off and accepted a bowl of stew and a winter apple. Then he looked about and noticed Ursana was missing.

"Is Ursana still asleep?"

"Your penchant for sleeping late has rubbed off on her," Lorelia said with a laugh.

He grinned. "Perhaps, but I hope that isn't all I've taught her."

"It's your greatest talent," Jack said. "What other skills do you have?"

Gordon shook his head. "Not much. She should have been up by now. I never rise before her."

"Let her sleep," Beauty said. "We've got a hard journey ahead and she could use it."

"If I had known that I would have stayed in bed," Roarthin said.

Thalidon struck him in the arm, eliciting a wince and growl from his brother. "You're a dwarf," Thalidon said. "We don't tire like the humans do."

"Doesn't mean we don't enjoy a good slumber," Roarthin said, his lips twitching beneath his beard.

Gordon rose from the table. "I'll get her. She wouldn't want to make us late."

Jack stuffed a few rolls into his pack and shouldered it. Then he looked at the view out the window one last time. With the sun rising on the lake below, the water reflected a blinding white, causing him to shield his eyes. He smiled at the tranquility of Cliffwatch, and resolved to return when he had time to enjoy the vista.

Gordon's strangled cry shattered the calm. Heads snapped to look at the ceiling, and then chairs clattered to the floor as thieves rushed to his aid. Jack darted to the stairs and sprinted up them, beating Beauty and Lorelia by half a step.

He accelerated and caught a light bracket to launch him up another flight of stairs. Reaching the top, he bolted down the hall and turned to find Gordon standing in the hall, staring into Ursana's room. Jack slid to an abrupt halt beside him.

Ursana lay on the bed while a dozen knives hovered above and around her. They glittered as they turned, some dipping and drawing blood across her flesh. One knife hung so close to her eye that her eyelashes brushed it when she blinked. Another spun lazily above her throat, its tip crimson from where it had grazed her. Ursana did not speak, but her expression was rigid with fear as she looked at the figure standing beside her bed.

"Hello, Jack," Gallow said.

As the others slid to a stop, Jack took a step forward. Gallow's expression became disapproving and he tapped a hand on the air above one of the blades, which sank into Ursana's flesh. She started to cry out but reined it in, the sound drawing the blades closer, like wolves to a wounded deer.

"Learning new tricks from your devil friend?" Jack asked, annoyed that the assassin had infiltrated the outpost without him knowing it.

Gallow's lips curled into a sneer. "He's not a friend, but he has magic I've never seen." He gestured to the hovering knives and they sunk a little deeper, several piercing skin and drawing blood. "My apologies," he said coldly. "I should be more careful."

145

"Let her go," Beauty spit the words at him.

Gallow rolled his eyes. "Do you have any idea how often I hear those words? If I wanted to let someone go, I wouldn't bind them in the first place."

Dwarven soldiers rushed into the hall but Thalidon brought them to a halt, talking quickly to forestall them charging the room. They tried to shove past him but Roarthin stepped in as well, growling at them to hold fast. Then he glanced at Jack, clearly waiting for direction.

"You want the key?" Lorelia asked Gallow.

"Speaking the obvious is beneath you, Guildmaster," Gallow said.

As they spoke Jack evaluated the assassin. Although barely out of his teens he conveyed a darkness that belied his youth. His bright blue eyes resembled chips of ice, sharp and cold. Dressed in green and black, he wore knives and his triangular throwing blade on his back.

"My patience wears thin," Gallow said. "I do have another key to collect, after all, and your friend doesn't have much life."

"What is that weapon anyway?" Jack asked, gesturing at the assassin's back. "I've never seen one like it."

Confused by the sudden query, the assassin said, "An idalia, one of the few surviving weapons from the ancients." He smirked at the reference, implying he knew exactly who Skorn was.

Jack grunted in irritation. "I was really hoping to get one for myself. Do you happen to know of a shop that sells it?"

As he talked, Jack eased his crossbow out of sleeve and into his palm. Gallow's annoyance kept him from noticing. The other thieves looked between them in confusion as the tension mounted.

"You try my patience, Jack," Gallow said. "And it comes with a cost."

A shout echoed from outside Cliffwatch, followed by the sudden clash of blades. The dwarves in the hall bolted down the stairs with axes

146

in hand. Shouts and screams came from outside the outpost, the tone indicating that cultists were falling upon dwarven steel.

The assassin sneered again. "Give me the key, Jack, before—"

"Did you buy it in Griffin?" Jack asked, scrunching his face in confusion. "It doesn't seem like something you'd find in a Talinorian shop. Or perhaps Azertorn?"

"I'm not your wife," Gallow snapped. "Why ask me for shopping advice? We have business to—"

"Where's your professional courtesy?" Jack asked indignantly.

"Do you want me to kill your friend?" Gallow snarled, and raised his hand. "A flick of a finger will end her life. Now give me the key."

"Do as he says," Lorelia said. "We have no choice."

Jack shrugged. "I don't have it."

"How can you not have it?" She swiveled to face him. "You had it when we left the Boneyard."

"You think I was dumb enough to keep it?" He gestured to Gallow. "We have an assassin and a fallen god chasing us. I wasn't about to carry it on my person. At least *I* am a professional." He sniffed, his gaze sliding off Gallow in disgust.

The assassin's eyes narrowed and his features tightened with rage. "You lie when your friend's life hangs in the balance?"

Jack grinned and quoted a thief saying, "I only lie on assignment."

"Do you take me for a fool?" Gallow snarled.

"I don't think you want me to answer that," Jack said, and snapped the crossbow up.

Too late, Gallow realized his mistake and lowered his hand. The floating blades dropped—but Jack's crossbow bolt struck him in the hand, driving him into the wall. Pinned, Gallow could not give the motion that would kill Ursana. He growled in pain and fury and struggled to free his hand, but Thalidon leapt into the room first.

147

The dwarf raised his hands and clenched them tight, freezing the knives in place. He trembled as he used his magic to prevent them from moving, his teeth clenched in the effort.

"Kill him," Thalidon barked.

"With pleasure," Jack said, darting forward.

Beauty beat him to it, and used a speed spell to leap the bed and strike Gallow in the chest. Her fist drove him backward but he recovered quickly, tearing his hand from the wall. With blood dripping from his palm he reached back and drew the idalia. Then he sent it spinning about the room.

Jack swerved but it moved with him, spinning toward his throat. He drew his dagger and deflected it upward but it hurtled toward Lorelia. The speed of the weapon caused her to dive to the side, and it went for Thalidon's back. Roarthin got there first and used a burst of fire to lift it above them. It cut through Thalidon's hair, slicing a deep furrow in his scalp before returning to the assassin.

Gallow ducked a strike from Beauty and then caught her hand, throwing her into a set of shelves. Wood shattered as her body struck them and she collapsed to the floor. In half a second she was on her feet but Jack had taken her place.

In a clash of steel he attacked the assassin, driving him back. Gallow's expression of scorn turned to surprise as Jack defied him. He swung his sword with expert skill, but Jack refused to give ground. Wounded and one handed, Gallow's expression turned to disbelief. As Beauty joined the fight once more he swung his sword out, forcing them back. Then he darted to the window.

"Next time I'll kill one of you first," he snapped. Then he struck a hand down toward Ursana and slipped from view. Instead of the blades descending it was Thalidon that dropped. Knocked to his knees, he struggled to keep the blades from sinking into Ursana.

Realizing the dwarf could not last, Jack darted to Ursana and caught a foot just as Gordon grabbed the other. They yanked her off the bed and crashed in a heap as Thalidon crumpled. The blades plunged into the empty bed, carving deep before finally going still.

"I'm sorry," Ursana said, tears streaming from her eyes. "I tried to call out but they just dug deeper. He just smiled like he wanted to watch me cut apart—I'm sorry I—"

"It's alright now," Gordon said, drawing her to him. "He's gone."

He held her as she cried. Then his eyes flicked to Jack and darkened. "Why do you have to antagonize everyone?" he demanded.

Still sitting beside him, Jack exhaled. "Because it works. Everyone makes mistakes when they're angry."

"You think this is a game?" Gordon growled. "That our lives are pawns for you to toy with?"

Irritated, Jack rose to his feet. "I didn't see you doing anything."

"*I would have given him the key!*" Gordon roared.

"You should have given it to him," Lorelia said coldly, drawing Jack's gaze to her.

"You think that would have saved her life?" Jack asked, heat rising in his words. "Gallow kills for pleasure, and would have cut her down just to watch her bleed." He looked to Beauty and the dwarves for support but their expressions were doubtful.

"Was the key worth her life?" Roarthin asked.

"No," Gordon said, fixing a cold gaze on Jack. "And I think this is where we part ways. Cultists we can handle, but not the head of the assassin's guild. Come, Ursana, we should leave before he returns."

"I'm not going anywhere," Ursana said. She sucked in a breath and turned blazing eyes on Gordon. "And Jack's right."

His eyes widened in surprise. "Ursana—"

Ursana pushed against Gordon and rose to her feet. He was quick to join her but she stood apart, her entire frame rigid. Blood spotted her clothing where the knives had cut her but she clenched her fists and glared at Gordon.

149

"Have you forgotten who he serves?" she asked. "Who Skorn was when he was our Guildmaster? Whatever power he wishes to gain, we cannot allow him to have it."

"But he could have killed you," Gordon plead.

She rounded on him. "Then I would have died for a purpose. Be a man, Gordon. We have an assignment to complete."

She whirled and stomped from the room. Gordon stared after her, his shoulders slumped in defeat. Then he turned to Jack.

"You made a promise."

"I believe I just kept it," Jack said quietly.

Unable to refute the statement, Gordon went after her. Without a word, Roarthin and Thalidon left to care for the wound on Thalidon's head. In their absence Lorelia stepped to Jack, her features tight with suppressed anger.

"I'm still the Guildmaster. Next time I say give someone a key, you do it."

"I'm not in your guild," Jack said, folding his arms. "And like I said, I don't have it."

She snorted in disbelief and shook her head. "Sometimes I hate you, Jack." Then she too left.

Beauty sighed and stepped close. "Do you really not have the key?"

"Do you really want to know?"

She held his gaze and then shook her head. "No. But regardless of where it is, Gallow won't stop coming for it."

"If we can predict him, we can avoid him."

"Now isn't the time to be arrogant."

"Intelligence isn't arrogance."

She sighed. "It is when you think you can beat him. He hunts and kills men, and he's better at it than you are."

She departed, leaving him to stare at the knives where Ursana's body had lain.

Chapter 18: Torridin

Within an hour of Gallow's attack the group of thieves exited the outpost. The dwarves had withstood the cultists without losses, but the same could not be said of Skorn's followers. Eight bodies lay strewn about the threshold. Their bodies twisted and lifeless, their smiles almost gleeful even in death.

The thieves left Cliffwatch behind and took a northern path toward the dwarven mine. Subdued by Gallow's appearance, they walked in silence, and many looks were cast into the shadows. Two days later they reached the mine and noticeably relaxed. Breaching a dwarven outpost was one thing, but the dwarves guarded their underground tunnels with brutal zeal. Thalidon and Roarthin managed to get them in, and they strode past the guards into the mine.

Large glowing runes adorned the walls, providing light and decoration in the tunnel as they descended from the surface. They descended for several minutes before they reached the mine itself, and then came to a halt on the small balcony that overlooked it.

Plunging straight down, the hole bored thousands of feet into the stone. Mine carts corkscrewed their way down descending rails and returned filled with chunks of raw ore. The full carts turned into a side corridor and disappeared from view. Cold air wafted from the dark depths carrying the scent of earth, water, and a touch of smoke.

A dwarven miner leaned out of an office inset in the wall. Dirt covered his clothes and darkened his beard. He stabbed a finger toward the carts.

"If you don't mind the dirt, you can take a cart to the mithral mine twenty miles west of here."

Jack smirked and leapt the balcony to land on the rails below. "Let's go." He caught an open cart moving down the track and climbed in with a huge smile on his face.

"Honestly, he's like a kid," Beauty said in exasperation.

"He's not wrong," Ursana said, smiling for the first time since Gallow's attack. She took the stairs to join him. Gordon sighed and followed, joining them in the cart. He did not meet Jack's gaze.

The other four descended and climbed into carts ambling along behind them. Jack remained on his feet as the tunnel narrowed and the lights dimmed. Barely lit, the tunnel continued to tighten until there was just enough room for two overloaded carts to pass along twin tracks. Roarthin growled from behind them and raised his voice.

"You may want to brace yourselves."

"Why?" Beauty asked.

"The carts are designed for ore," he said.

He took his own advice and sat, grasping the bar attached to the side of the cart. Abruptly the cart began to accelerate as the tunnel dropped, and the others were quick to sit and grab hold.

"Aren't you going to sit?" Ursana asked.

"I'd rather enjoy this," Jack said.

"Arrogant fool," Gordon muttered.

Jack caught the edges of the cart and grinned. "And you used to be fun."

Gordon's features hardened but Ursana laughed. "He's right again."

The cart dipped, speeding up as they passed into the gloom of the cramped tunnel. Jack began to laugh when they accelerated, the cart grinding through a long curve. His hair whipped backward as the air slammed into him.

153

The walls and ceiling had been cut smooth to ensure nothing impacted the cart, and runes appeared at regular intervals. The symbols glowed as they passed, blurring into a staccato burst of light as they reached top speed.

Jack released a cry of exultation, tightening his grip to keep from being knocked from the cart. Standing as he was he could see the upcoming turns, and leaned to the side as the cart banked for the curves. Unprepared for the shift, the others were knocked into the walls of the cart. Gordon growled from a particularly hard impact.

"How can you enjoy this after what happened?"

"How can you not?" Jack had to shout over the wind. "Why sit in fear when you can stand?"

Gordon didn't respond for the rest of the journey, and when the cart finally slowed he rose to join Jack. Together, they rode the last of the turns to the end. With a sigh of regret Jack stepped out of the cart.

The small cavern contained a crossroads of several tracks disappearing into tunnels in several directions. Orange and white light glowed across the runes cast into the walls, illuminating the space enough that Jack had to shield his eyes. When he'd recovered from the glare he spotted a dwarf. The dwarf was busy inspecting a cartload of mithral ore but frowned at their appearance.

"Where ye be off to?"

"Torridin," Roarthin said.

The dwarf used his hammer to point to an empty cart sitting on a track. Then he huffed at the interruption and bent to his work. Jack stepped to the indicated cart before noticing Lorelia's queasy expression. He grinned and sidled up to her.

"Aren't you in the mood for boiled pig's feet and cow liver?"

"Stop," she warned. "Unless you want to see me vomit."

"Be nice," Beauty said, drawing Jack's eyes to her.

"I'm serious," he said. "I can smell the meat cooking now, the distinct scent of pig skin burning against the bone—"

A surge of liquid splashed across his side, soaking him to the skin. Shock and then anger filled his veins and he spun to face Lorelia. Her features were bright with humor as she lowered her water skin.

"Serves you right," she said, eliciting a round of laughter.

"Did you *plan* that?"

"It was Beauty's idea," Thalidon said with a broad grin.

Jack turned and found her smiling smugly. "We can't let you have all the fun."

He laughed in chagrin and then stabbed a finger at her. "Don't start a war you can't win."

"I never do."

Jack laughed again and the lingering tension from Gallow's attack dissipated. Together, they climbed aboard the indicated carts and were off again. This time Jack wasn't the only one to stand. Even Roarthin took a turn at the center, and issued a deep belly laugh as his red hair billowed about his head.

The journey to Torridin took two days, and by the time they arrived they were all weary from the constant jostling within the iron box. In spite of how much he'd enjoyed it, Jack breathed a sigh of relief when they disembarked in the underground city.

Built into a gigantic cavern, the dwarven capital of Torridin lay beneath the fortress that guarded the northern border of their kingdom. Thousand-foot pillars connected the floor to the ceiling of the cavern, their surfaces carved into massive statues of dwarven warriors.

Phoenixes and dragons adorned the walls, their shapes highlighted by real flames, making them lifelike enough to inspire a trickle of fear. Smoke rose from their nostrils and their eyes glowed with sinister intent.

Beneath the titans' gaze lay homes, shops, and roads rolling across underground hills. Blacksmiths and craftsmen were abundant, with every corner containing a forge. Hammers tapped in a constant hum, punctuated by bursts of fire and shouts.

Tracks crisscrossed the city above the roads and buildings, some going multiple layers high. Supported by high arches and sweeping curves of stone, the rails allowed ore to be delivered directly to the smiths.

As they walked through the city Jack spotted a cart rolling to a halt above a shop. A dwarf dumped the contents into a chute. Rocks and stones clattered their way into a pile on the ground floor, and a grey-haired smith collected stones in a reservoir. His face glowed red as he opened the hearth and carefully inserted the melting bowl. He shouted for his assistant, and a young dwarf with a short black beard rushed to do his bidding.

The road had been cut and polished but left rough, allowing traction for the booted dwarves to ascend the frequent slopes. One dwarf hurried up the street and stepped onto a spiral staircase that climbed into a third floor forge. Fire burst from the interior and a dwarven curse followed the explosion.

As the primary exports of the race, weapons and armor were everywhere. Swords of every size and shape hung on the exterior of shops, their blades reflecting the firelight. Men, elves, and azure browsed the wares, gawking at the craftsmanship or haggling over the exorbitant prices.

A man dressed as a soldier from Talinor had brought his family. His young daughter stared at the child-sized knives in wonder. She reached out to touch one and the black-haired dwarf gave it to her.

"You're too little, dear," the man said, gingerly taking the knife and returning it.

The dwarf guffawed at the response. "We give our toddlers knives, and they learn right quick not to stab themselves."

The man shook his head and pointed to a rider's sword and scabbard. "My Lady wishes the gift to reflect her husband's skill on a horse."

The dwarf slid a tiny knife into a sheath and slipped it to the girl. Winking at her, he turned back to her father. The girl caught Jack's eye and grinned before hiding the weapon in a fold of her dress.

"Do you really give your children blades?" Beauty asked.

Roarthin laughed and rolled up his sleeve to reveal a scar just above the elbow. "Thalidon gave me this when I was a babe."

"You deserved it," Thalidon retorted.

Roarthin flashed a rare smile. "I probably did," he said. "And I certainly gave you enough scars."

"How do we get to the dark elves?" Lorelia asked, interrupting them before they could delve deeper into their youth.

"Only a handful of tunnels descend to the Deep from here," Thalidon said. "And all are guarded by Clan Foehammer. We'll speak to their clan prince and meet you at the *Blue Diamond*. It's an inn a mile that way." He stabbed a finger south of their position.

"Feel free to browse about while you wait," Roarthin said. "We'll probably tap a keg."

"We don't have time for that," Lorelia protested. "We need to hurry . . . *are you even listening?*" They were already gone, and she fell to muttering about dwarves.

"I think I'll look for a new dagger," Jack said.

Lorelia took a step toward him but Beauty spoke first. "I could use a new blade as well. We'll meet you at the inn."

"Don't dally," Gordon said. "There's no telling where Gallow is now."

"I doubt he'd risk coming into Torridin," Lorelia said. "Not when we'll be easy prey on our way to the Elsurund."

157

"That's not comforting," Ursana said flatly.

Jack grinned and turned away, gesturing Beauty to join him. As the group talked, they slipped away and turned a corner. Then they slowed their pace. When it was clear they were out of earshot she pulled him into an alley between two forges.

"Have you ever considered if one of our group is a spy?"

He snorted in disagreement. "Why? Because Gallow found us? It would have been easy enough to guess where we had gone."

"Some were a little too eager to give the key to him."

"*You* suggested I give it to him."

She released an annoyed breath. "As did Thalidon, Gordon, and Lorelia."

"Lorelia was the one who suggested we steal the keys in the first place, and Roarthin hates Skorn with more zeal than you do. And you saw Gordon. He's not about to help the assassin."

"Skorn uses manipulation as much as force to attain what he seeks," she said.

"How do I know *you* aren't the spy?" He flashed a sly smile. "Do I have to kiss the truth out of you?"

She folded her arms. "Can you take anything seriously?"

He shrugged. "You know them better than I. Do you think one is serving Skorn?"

She looked away, her expression doubtful. "Perhaps," she said. "Just pay attention, will you?"

He agreed with a nod and she strode away. For the next hour he browsed the thousands of blades on display. To his irritation Beauty's words lingered in his mind, and he found himself wondering if she were right. The more he thought about it, the more he realized they were all suspect.

Roarthin had been imprisoned by Skorn long enough to be turned, while Thalidon had proven he could be manipulated by Skorn. Gordon would do anything for Ursana, but what about her? She'd been the one under Gallow's knives, but was that just a feint? Lorelia had replaced Skorn, but she was more used to wearing a mask than anyone. He briefly considered Beauty but could not imagine she would ever help him after what he'd done to her sister.

He dismissed the doubts with a jerk of his head. He knew his companions, and would even trust Roarthin's hate for Skorn. Returning his attention to the dwarven city, he recalled that many dwarves called it the City of Steel. But who was the best smith in the city? The question drove him to ask the smiths, and it didn't take him long to get a name.

Chapter 19: Urthor's Request

"The steel swords are over there," the smith said. Without looking up from the anvil, he used his hammer to gesture to a line of blades on the wall.

"I'm not looking for steel," Jack said.

The dwarf struck the sword again, sending a shower of sparks on the floor. "My work isn't cheap."

"I'm aware."

The dwarf finally looked up and regarded Jack. Built like a bull, the dwarf wore clothing blackened by soot. Burns and scars marked his legacy of battle with the forge. His pure white hair put his age at six centuries, one of the oldest dwarves Jack had met.

It had taken Jack deep into the evening to find him. In a kingdom renowned for great craftsmen, one name came up more frequently than anyone else, Urthor. The name had been easier to find than the shop, but Jack had found him ensconced in a small tunnel that split off from the main cavern of Torridin.

"What are you looking for?" he asked.

Jack reached to his lower back and tugged his dagger into view. After holding it aloft, he placed it on the table between them. The dwarf hung his hammer on a hook attached to the anvil and set the sword down. Then he strode to the table and picked up the dagger. To Jack's surprise he placed the blade beneath his nose and inhaled.

"Eighty-three percent steel, seventeen percent iron. A decent Talinorian blade." He touched the edge and grunted in approval. "It's been well cared for, but seen its share of combat." He dug a blackened fingernail into one of the notches that marred the edge

"It's kept me alive," Jack said.

"A warrior's truest friend is his weapon. Why replace it?" He twirled the dagger and tested its balance. "It's got decades left on its life."

"Some foes are more dangerous, and require a different weapon to defeat."

Urthor tugged on his snow white beard, his grey eyes alight with curiosity. "What exactly do you expect to battle, my good thief?"

Jack's eyebrow lifted. "You know my occupation?"

"Every blade tells a tale," he said. "A dagger is chosen by one who prefers subterfuge, but is unafraid to engage in combat when the circumstances require. Your weapon carries the damage of soldier's swords as well as smaller weapons, indicating you have fought guards, thieves, and bandits."

Jack grinned at the accurate assumption. "Then how did you know I was a good thief?"

"You came by the door," the dwarf said, his lips twitching. "I suspect you have the talent to bypass even my curses, and could have entered seeking to take as you will. Yet you chose to enter as an honest man would."

"I only steal on assignment," Jack said, pleased with the dwarf's intelligence. "But I admit I was tempted. Your craftsmanship carries a reputation of respect among your people."

Urthor snorted in disgust. "My people gossip more than Griffin wives."

"Are the rumors false?"

"No," Urthor said without arrogance. "But you haven't told me what foe you intend to face."

"A living ancient who led the Thieves Guild until I defeated him."

Whatever the dwarf had expected, Jack's answer was not it. A frown appeared on his features and deepened until he grunted.

"You are thief and a stranger, yet I am inclined to believe you."

"Do you have a weapon I can use?"

"This way," Urthor said, and strode toward a strongdoor set at the back of the room. Swinging it open, he waved a hand to activate the light charms and stepped aside to allow Jack to enter. The light continued to brighten, revealing thousands of blades resting on racks mounted to the walls.

"I think you've earned retirement, my friend."

The dwarf laughed. "Work is the only reason I'm still alive."

Jack strode past row upon row of glittering weaponry. Swords of every type hung together, including many intended for humans and elves. The collection paled in comparison to the axes, which boasted double blades, single blades, and quad-blades, all made from a variety of metals. Some of the weapons were utilitarian, the metal sharp and lethal. Others were more artistic, with spikes and notches like dragon's claws. A massive curving sword hung next to one bearing a hilt that resembled a snarling lion.

They passed on to larger weapons, and Jack's eyes widened as he examined huge swords and spears designed for giant men. One in particular drew his gaze, and he stepped closer to examine the straight-spined greatsword.

"Is that a rock troll blade?"

"Aye," Urthor said, glancing back.

"I thought they forged their own soulblades."

162

"Their warriors do," the dwarf said. "But their mages are not trained to the forge and do not usually craft a soulblade. One of them was exiled and asked me to make her a blade. She broke the first so I crafted a second."

"She *broke* one of your blades?"

He grinned. "Do what she did and any blade will break."

"She doesn't sound like a normal rock troll."

"Sirani is an exception on many counts," Urthor said, and then grinned. "But at times it's difficult to tell if she has lost her wits to age."

"I wonder if she would say the same about you."

Urthor released a bellowing laugh. "Perhaps. Ah, here we are."

He came to a stop before a collection of daggers and knives. Like the swords, the daggers varied significantly, with some bearing intricate designs while others appeared more functional. Jack spotted several that looked promising, but the dwarf reached for a dagger with a dark-tinged blade. Although it was evidently of much higher craftsmanship, it bore a striking resemblance to Jack's own weapon.

"This may serve your purpose."

Jack grasped the hilt and spun it in his fingers, pleased by the exceptional balance. It was lighter than its predecessor yet felt stronger. Also dark, the hilt contained inlaid silver and a swirl of sapphires on the pommel.

"Ninety-two percent mithral core with a steel exterior, fire tempered and reinforced."

"Is that why it's dark?"

"When steel is coated onto tempered mithral it tends to darken, which is why most smiths blend the metals to keep the lighter tint." He gestured to the dagger. "This is actually stronger, but it doesn't *look* as expensive."

Jack smirked at the reference to the legendary dwarven greed, and recalled how many shiny blades had hung in the shops and smiths in the city. Although the dwarves would never stoop to selling shoddy work, they would sell their work for more than it was worth.

"Your people spoke the truth," he said, admiring the dagger.

"Perhaps," the dwarf said with a smile.

Urthor retrieved the scabbard for the blade and they exited the storeroom. Taking Jack's old sheath to a workbench, he added lodestones to the new dagger's sheath so it could hang inverted on Jack's back. When it was finished he handed the weapon to him.

"Your craftsmanship is without peer, dwarf," Jack said.

Jack removed his cloak and shirt and detached the strap beneath. Removing his old sheath, he placed the new one on his bare back. Then he adjusted the weapon until it rested along his spine and put his shirt back on. The hilt protruded at the low part of his back, hidden yet accessible behind a thick patch of leather that kept him from accidently slicing his flesh. He drew the new dagger in a fluid motion and admired it before replacing it in the sheath.

"It will do."

The dwarf snorted. "Talk like that and I'll increase the price."

Jack's turned to face him. "How much is it?"

"More than you can afford."

Irritated, Jack drew the blade and held it up. "Then why show it to me?"

"Instead of coin I require a different payment."

Jack frowned. "I don't understand."

"I will not charge you if you accept another blade."

Jack raised an eyebrow, his curiosity piqued. "You won't charge me for one, but you'll *give* me two?"

164

In answer the dwarf strode to a small chest set against the back wall. Opening it with a key, he reached inside and withdrew a knife. It too was dark, the blade wide at the base and tapered slightly toward the end. Jack accepted the offered weapon and examined it.

"Eighty-seven percent mithral core with a steel exterior, forged on low heat and tempered in elven water."

"What's the charm?" Jack asked as he felt the faint shiver in his skin.

"It takes a keen sense to detect enchantments," the dwarf said, inclining his head in respect. "Many of my weapons carry at least one enhancement, but this one is unusual, for it carries a high level implosion hex."

"Am I supposed to know what that is?"

"Magic that few dwarves are willing to cast," he said. "And for good reason. Once activated it will crush anything in the area to dust. The hex cannot be stopped, nor activated from a distance."

"It's a suicide knife."

"If that is what you want to call it," the dwarf said.

"I was looking for a weapon that would kill *him*, not me."

The dwarf held the knife aloft. "Eighteen years ago a man came to request this weapon be made. It sounded odd so I refused. Then he took my granddaughter and sent me a lock of her hair. If I refused again he would send me her hand. Without any other choice, I agreed."

"Do you often have clients force you into service?"

"Never," he said flatly. "But this man conveyed a disturbing quality that I could not deny. Upon my agreement he returned my granddaughter. He didn't need to say it, but I knew if I failed he would take her again—and I wouldn't get a warning. Reluctantly I set to work."

"Did he say why he came to you?"

"Same reason you did," he said wryly.

"There is always a price for those at the top of their craft," Jack said, and recalled how Skorn had manipulated him.

"As you say," the dwarf agreed. "I reluctantly began to forge the blade, but over the next year I heard whispers of his work. The tales were few yet spread quickly among our people. I began to realize that to give him the knife would be a mistake."

"How did you know who he was?"

Urthor grinned and gestured to Jack's old dagger still resting on the table. "He showed me his sword when he first appeared, and I marked him as I did you. I may not have known his name, but I recognized his occupation."

A trickle of foreboding trickled down Jack's spine. "What did you hear of him?"

"The tales spoke of brutality and cruelty, and I became reluctant to give the dagger to such a person. I claimed I was not yet finished, and as time passed he grew impatient. When I realized he would not be dissuaded I crafted a duplicate knife that would mimic the implosion hex, but lack any power."

"How clever of you," Jack said. "But you didn't say who he was."

The dwarf's eyes bored into him. "You described your foe as a living ancient—one who served as your Guildmaster. The man who wanted that knife . . . was the Guildmaster for your guild."

Jack began to chuckle. "You want me to fight him with the very knife he forced you to create?"

"It's only fitting," Urthor replied, his grey eyes twinkling in a way that made him look a century younger. "Will you deliver it for me?"

Jack accepted the knife from him and slid it into the small sheath. "I'll give him your regards."

"Excellent," the dwarf said, his eyes sparkling.

166

"Does this mean I get discounts on future weapons?"

Urthor's smile evaporated and he folded his arms. "I may be old, but I'm not a fool."

Jack laughed and strode for the door. "You have my gratitude, good dwarf."

The dwarf's expression had turned as hard as the steel he forged. "Just make certain you kill him."

Jack paused on the threshold. "I intend to." Then he slipped out the door.

Chapter 20: Descent to the Deep

They departed Torridin the following morning amidst the loud complaints of Thalidon and Roarthin, who had partaken liberally of ale the previous night. As they threaded their way through the city the two dwarves shielded their eyes from the glare of the fire dragons and phoenixes.

"Do they have to be bright so early?" Roarthin growled.

"It's late," Lorelia retorted. "And it took three of us to wake you."

"Stop shouting," Thalidon groaned.

"Be a dwarf," Ursana snapped, shocking them all. "And stop complaining like human children."

As the dwarves rumbled into silence Jack exchanged a look with Beauty. After Gallow's attack on her, Ursana had matured in remarkable order. The spark of innocence was gone from her eyes and had replaced with a sharpened focus.

The group reached the southern side of the city and came to an unassuming portcullis ensconced in the cavern wall. In spite of its innocuous appearance, no less than a full company of dwarves stood guard around squat battlements in front of the portal.

Apparently prepared for them, the captain signaled a soldier. The dwarf stepped to a great wheel and spun it, causing the portcullis to grind its way off the floor. Machinery clanked and groaned as it lifted the thick barrier. When it was high enough for them to pass under, Thalidon stepped forward.

"I hope you survive, Thalidon," the captain said.

The dwarf turned. "A keg says I return within a fortnight."

"If you don't return by then, I get a keg of your family's private stock—and you have to re-grow your beard!"

Thalidon laughed. "You have yourself a wager."

"If you perish, how do I collect my winnings?"

"You don't!"

The captain grinned and stabbed a finger toward the gaping tunnel. "The road is clearly lit all the way to Elsurund. I wouldn't deviate from the path or you will never see daylight again."

"Are they allies?" Beauty asked.

"Presently," the captain said. "But that can change in an instant."

"I expect that keg to be here when I return," Thalidon said with a grin.

The captain laughed and the group of thieves entered the tunnel, the portcullis shutting behind them. As it struck the floor the impact echoed like a death knell, causing Lorelia to shiver.

"I hate being underground," she muttered.

Roarthin laughed at her discomfort and set off. "We should hurry if we want to reach Elsurund before the assassin."

Casting a final look back, Jack fell into step beside Lorelia and they descended the curving tunnel. Much like the mines, the corridor contained an assortment of runes in the walls and ceiling, providing enough illumination to make it feel larger than it was.

Jack had never journeyed to the dark elf city and he was not alone. Of the group, only Thalidon and Lorelia had been to Elsurund. At Ursana's request, Lorelia launched into a description of the history

169

behind the dark elf city. Jack listened with one ear, curious and bored at the same time.

"Are the dark elves evil, as the tales say?" Ursana asked.

"Hardly," Thalidon said with a derisive snort. "Their environment is harsher than ours, and many dangers lurk in the depths of Lumineia."

"What sort of dangers?" she asked.

"For one thing, all four types of reavers stalk the Deep," Lorelia said. "And trust me when I say that you never want to encounter a mind reaver. They latch onto your mind and will hunt you forever."

"They're not as bad as black reavers," Roarthin said with a grunt. "If those devils get a taste of your blood, they temporarily gain every power you possess—magical or physical."

"There are many tales of dark elves pillaging the surface," Gordon said.

"True," Thalidon said, "but most of the rumors are unfounded. Like any other race they occasionally ascend to trade. Mankind's irrational fear of them has sparked far more conflicts than their natures."

"Then why guard the entrance to their tunnel?" Jack asked, gesturing to where a hundred dwarves watched the portal.

"Because mankind is not the only race that fears them," Lorelia said with a smile.

The tunnel dipped and curved, taking the portcullis out of sight. The road became steeper before entering a large cavern. Stalactites and stalagmites grew from ceiling and floor, merging into scattered pillars. The minerals within glowed purple and green, bathing the chamber in light.

Water gurgled in the distance, the sound fading and amplifying as they passed through a series of similar caverns. Shortly after, an underground river appeared and wound beside them before disappearing from view.

As the dwarf captain had said the road was clearly marked, with dwarf and dark elf symbols placed next to each other at periodic intervals. Dwarven cut, the road itself was smooth, with frequent patches of cleared stone for camps. They paused in one for a noonday meal and filled their water skins from a spring at the side of the camp.

Shortly after, the road left the caverns and entered a fissure. Narrow and curving, it was barely a hundred feet across. Every sound echoed into the darkened abyss. They followed the road as it clung to the side of the fissure, winding deep into the earth. Hours later they reached a bridge that crossed into a tunnel on the opposite side.

That night they camped on a wide plateau overlooking an underground lake. Disturbed by their fire, deep hawks dropped from their perches and flapped about, their chattering echoing off the walls. Jack sat on the edge with his legs dangling over the long drop, watching them.

"There is nothing like them on the surface," Lorelia said, sinking into a seat beside him.

With four wings and long, hooked beaks, the birds resembled hawks, but their eyes were large and luminescent green. They dropped into the water, taking advantage of the additional light to gorge themselves on the multitude of fish in the lake.

"Care for a swim?"

"I wouldn't," she said wryly. "The hawks are not the only predators here."

"What do you—"

The water exploded and a beast surged into view, its great jaws opening over a trio of birds. The hawks shrieked and sought to escape but the teeth snapped shut. Releasing a haunting growl of triumph, the beast dropped from view. As the splash faded into ripples Jack laughed.

"This place is incredible."

She grinned. "The dark elves hunt the gorthon for its teeth, skin, and meat, but the beasts are known to hunt them in turn."

171

"Just how many dangers exist down here?"

"Life is tenuous in the Deep." She gestured to the path behind them. "The elves and dwarves have both placed protective wards on the well-traveled paths, ensuring that trade caravans can pass in peace."

"Do the elves interact with them?"

"On occasion," Lorelia said. "But our cousins do not seem to be inclined to interact with us. We lack the skills of the dwarves to build underground roads, so we depend on the dark elves to maintain the connection."

"You said you had been to Elsurund before?"

"Once," she replied. "Part of our training as mages was to travel to their guild and study with them." Her eyes flicked to him as if expecting him to comment on her secret. When he didn't, she continued. "They actually taught me how to maintain an illusion without exhausting myself."

"What about your family? I can't recall you ever talking about them."

It was the first time he'd directly asked her about her past, and he half expected her not to respond. The seconds slipped by and he stole a glance in her direction. The conflict she felt was written on her features, but then she sighed.

"My father died when I was young, but my mother was a professor at the guild. She was beloved by many, but all she felt for me was shame. My older sister felt the same and was quite vocal on the topic. The guise charm was the first spell they taught me, and they were insistent I used it at all times."

"The appearance of perfection is a dangerous pursuit," Jack said.

She laughed sourly. "My mother would have argued that it's the only pursuit that matters."

"Sounds like she was twisting the book of Ero."

"She was a devout follower," she replied.

"Of who?" Ursana said, sitting beside Lorelia. She picked up a stone and tossed it into the water, smiling when it splashed.

Caught, Lorelia said, "Like many of my people, my mother worshiped at the Church of Light."

"Mine as well," Ursana said. "Right up until they convinced my father to sign our family farm over to them as a donation. He became convinced it would ensure peace in the afterlife."

"Your father really did that?" Lorelia asked.

Ursana dropped another stone into the lake, watching it bounce off the rocks at the bottom and splash into the water. "Within a day the church had sold the farm to a minor lord and pocketed the coin. We were on the street with nothing and the church abandoned us. That's when my father began to punish my mother, blaming her for everything."

Ursana told the story with a dismissive tone, but Jack noticed the tightness to her frame. "What happened to her?"

"She felt betrayed and never recovered. She took ill a year later and died on the streets of Keese. I ended up stealing to survive and wound up with an invitation to join the Thieves Guild. I figured I had nothing to lose so I took the chance."

"Your life has been hard," Lorelia said, her eyes flicking to Jack. "But your tale is not unlike most of those in the guild. We are thieves because Lumineia treated us with cruelty and cast us out, dismissing us for naught."

"You as well?" Ursana asked, turning to look at her. "You are beautiful and strong. How did you end up as a thief?"

Jack hid a smile as Lorelia struggled to answer. "Elves can live for hundreds of years," she said softly, "and I am well into my second century. What you see now was not always so."

"And your mother? How often do you see her?"

Lorelia's expression turned pained. "She took her own life when a secret about our family came to light. I haven't spoken to my sister since."

Jack met her gaze and realized the secret she was referring to was hers. Ursana attempted to consol Lorelia but questions approached the truth. Before Ursana could ask more, Jack took pity on her.

"I didn't know it, but my mother was part of the guild."

Ursana turned to face him, her eyes full of wonder. "So she trained you?"

"No," he said with a sour laugh. "She actually taught me that thieves had no honor, and made me swear I would never become one."

The words slipped out before he could catch them, and Lorelia's expression turned smug at the revelation. Irritated that he'd revealed more than he cared to, Jack grunted and rose to his feet, moving to the fire. Sinking into a seat beside Thalidon, he stared at the dying flames.

Ursana and Lorelia continued to talk, but Gordon rolled out a bedroll and pulled the blanket over his shoulder. Jack followed suit, and the others were quick to do the same. Weary from the journey they were asleep in seconds. Alone on watch, Roarthin grunted in annoyance and muttered curses about thieves.

Without the sun there was no dawn, but the dwarves seemed to have an internal clock that roused them. Jack groaned when they woke him and reluctantly climbed from the comfortable sleep.

They broke camp and gathered their gear before returning to the road where it continued onto a bridge. The span crossed the lake to a tunnel on the opposite side of the cavern. Huge and arching, the bridge appeared dark elf rather than dwarven, its great buttresses reinforced with shimmering purple magic.

When they reached the edge of the bridge Ursana poked Gordon in the side and then skipped away. Laughing at Gordon's protest, she ran ahead, pausing at the center of the bridge to look down into the deceptively quiet waters below. Jack smiled, grateful she had managed to keep a measure of hope in their occupation. He only had to look at Gordon to see why. Ursana shifted to the side, peering over the edge.

A tremor shook the stone. Jack came to an abrupt halt when it seeped through is boots and vibrated his feet. Lorelia and Beauty sensed it as well and exchanged a curious look. Then Ursana's cry shattered the calm, and Jack snapped to look at her.

A crack appeared in the stone, dropping her into the gap. She caught an edge but the whole bridge shuddered, sending cracks all the way to the ends. With a grunt she levered herself up, bringing her terrified expression into view. Jack surged forward with Gordon three steps ahead. Abruptly the bridge shuddered again . . .

And crumbled.

Chapter 21: Gorthon

Ursana screamed as the bridge disintegrated, leaving her to plummet into the lake. Lorelia and Beauty launched their shadowhooks, just managing to catch a protrusion from the ceiling. The dwarves were not as quick, and even as they retreated toward the ledge the bridge collapsed beneath their boots.

Jack aimed his hand toward the ceiling but hesitated, his gaze drawn to his friends falling into the waters below. Growling in irritation, he took two steps and dove over the edge, aiming for a spot close to Gordon and Ursana.

Chunks of the broken bridge rained down with him but he scanned the water, searching for any hint of a gorthon. He glimpsed movement on the far side of the lake an instant before he plunged into the frigid waters. Fighting the chill, he pushed his way to the surface as the remains of the bridge sank around him, the purple magic that had supported the struts flickering in the water before going dark.

"How could this happen?" Gordon growled, his voice distorted from the cold.

"This is Gallow's work," Jack said. "He knew what route we were taking and sought to stop us."

Ursana cursed and spun about, searching the water. "We're too far for a shadowhook."

Jack watched a ripple in the water and squinted into the depths. Disturbed by the bridge's fall, the deep hawks swirled above, shrieking their anger. Jack kept his focus on the water.

"Blasted cold," Roarthin growled, struggling to light a fire in his hand.

"Are you *mad?*" Lorelia shouted, her voice echoing throughout the cavern. "Gorthons follow movement and heat."

Roarthin extinguished the flame and tried to stay afloat without moving, but he continued to mutter under his breath. Across the gap Thalidon exchanged a look with Jack and shook his head, his features tight with worry. Then a rumble echoed throughout the cavern, the sound dark and menacing.

"Roarthin, on your right!" Beauty cried.

Her urgent warning caused the dwarf to turn—and the gorthon exploded from the water. Roarthin cried out and instinctively cast a wall of fire between them. The great creature veered away from the flames and dove again, but not before Jack got a full look at the beast.

It resembled a giant fish but the jaws spanned a third of its body, and extended all the way to the fins. Teeth like giant needles were layered several rows deep. The scales were black and tinged orange, making it resemble smoke rising above embers. Larger than a full wagon, the powerful beast could devour a horse in a single bite.

Ursana cried out at the gorthon's appearance but managed to control her fear. "If we move it comes for us," she hissed, struggling to stay afloat with her gear and clothing.

"Then how do you suppose we escape?" Gordon growled. "We're hundreds of feet from the tunnel." He used his chin to point at the broken bridge extending from the exit corridor.

A current of water shifted and the dorsal fin briefly lifted out of the water. Then Jack spotted a flicker of movement beyond the gorthon, drawing his gaze to a cave at the side of the lake. He peered into the darkened alcove until his eyes adjusted. He sucked in his breath as he

177

realized it was not a cave, but a corridor. And another gorthon was coming from it.

"We need to move," Jack said.

"How?" Gordon hissed, and then followed Jack's gaze to see the second gorthon fin. He cursed under his breath, drawing it out to punctuate every syllable.

The dwarves echoed the sentiment. Then Lorelia began to shout from above. Ripping pieces of rock from the ceiling with their weapons, they sent chunks of stone splashing into the lake. The second gorthon swam to where a rock at fallen, its fin slipping beneath the water. A moment later it appeared, aiming for Gordon. Jack growled and fumbled a hand into one of his pouches, activating his speedstone. The magic flooded his frame and he struck out, swimming for the edge of the lake. The gorthon veered away from Gordon and accelerated toward him.

"What are you doing?" Ursana hissed as he sped past her.

"Becoming bait!" he shouted, drawing the attention of the second beast. "Now *go!*"

Thalidon and Roarthin didn't argue, and began to swim toward the back of the cavern. Ursana hesitated, but Gordon pushed her toward the nearest wall of stone. Then he struck out after her.

"Go!" he shouted.

"What about Jack?" she asked, looking back at him.

"He can take care of himself," Gordon replied. "Now swim!"

As they swam for the edge of the lake Jack led the beasts in the opposite direction. He spotted an island of rock and veered toward it. He heard the rush of water as the lead gorthon surged into his wake.

"You aren't going to make it Jack!" Beauty shouted.

The gorthon lunged for him, coming half out of the water, its jaws reaching for his legs. Jack twisted and dove but the lower jaw scraped across his shoulder, and several of the teeth sliced through his tunic. He bounced along the fish's scales before he managed to come to the surface. Then he saw the second gorthon open its jaws just feet from him.

"*Jack!*"

A crossbow bolt streaked from the ceiling and sank into the gorthon's flank. Another joined the first, disappearing into the beast's scales. The injuries were minor but the fish instinctively dove, creating a wave that sent Jack rolling away. Fluorescent blood stained the water, illuminating the area as the great fish circled for another strike.

Realizing how close he was to the island, Jack aimed his shadowhook and fired it into the stone. It yanked him out of the water, and his body skipped across the surface until he slammed into the stone. Grunting from the impact, he scrambled to right himself and climbed to the top.

As he pulled his feet from the water a gorthon snapped its jaws on his boot. Jack grabbed a crack in the stone but the beast was far stronger, and yanked him back into the water. As Jack dropped into the lake the fish released his boot and came for him. Jack drew his dagger and slashed it across the gorthon's nose. The blade cut deep and the gorthon spun away.

"Fish are meant to be eaten," Jack growled, and climbed out of the water, stumbling to the relative safety of the tiny island.

At a foot above the surface the island afforded little protection against the gorthons, but it got him out of the water. Undeterred by their injuries, the two beasts began to circle, occasionally darting close to test his reaction.

Jack kept one eye on them but looked about. The dwarves had reached the cliff and were halfway up to the ledge they had camped on. Ursana and Gordon had reached the wall of rock that led to the exit corridor and were climbing from the water. Still on the ceiling, Lorelia and Beauty were working their way toward the exit corridor.

"You can't stay there very long!" Lorelia called down to Jack.

Jack grunted in irritation when he realized his position was too far for anyone to assist. At two hundred feet away the nearest wall was far beyond the reach of his shadowhook, and the ceiling was even higher.

"I'll have to make my own exit," Jack called up to her. "Get to the tunnel."

"We're not leaving you behind," Beauty called.

"You're not," he said, irritated by their stubbornness. "At the tunnel you can use your crossbows to keep them off me."

She scowled at him but used her shadowhook to swing to another section of the ceiling. Snagging another grip, she hung five hundred feet above the lake and then cast it again. Lorelia followed her example, and together they made their way across the cavern ceiling. Deep hawks scattered at their approach, shrieking their indignation at being disturbed. Some aimed at them, scratching them with their claws.

"Blasted birds," Lorelia said, killing one with a shot from her hand crossbow.

Jack returned his attention on the water but the fins were gone. He tensed, swiveling in an attempt to search the area around him. Then a gorthon burst into view on his right. It launched itself out of the water and twisted, its jaws seeking to bite his body from his legs. On instinct Jack dropped to the stone, the beast's scales sliding across his chest before it plunged into the lake.

Jack rose to his feet and drew his dagger. It was woefully inadequate against such a creature, but he imagined the giant fish roasting on a bonfire. He smiled savagely and twirled the dagger in his hand.

"I like my fish salted with a touch of lemon," he growled.

In the corridor above, Ursana knelt and yanked the chord back on her crossbow. Evidently overhearing Jack's comment, she laughed as she put a bolt into the mechanism.

"You want to *eat* it?"

"I promise I'll share!"

180

Gordon laughed and aimed his hand crossbow down at Jack. A swirl of motion was Jack's only warning and he rolled off the rock. The second gorthon snapped its jaws and squirmed its way over the island, missing Jack by inches. Its chosen path slowed its momentum, and Ursana sent a bolt into its skull.

It flailed, nearly knocking Jack off as it tumbled into the water. Fluorescent blood spattered across Jack as the creature dived deep before floating to the surface on its side. The other gorthon appeared in front of Jack and charged him. His reflexes saved his life, and he leapt up and back. The beast smashed into the stone hard enough to dislodge teeth, and gave Jack the chance to swipe his dagger across its skull. This time the blow went deep enough to kill it, and the great fish went limp.

"*Jack!*"

The warning in Beauty's voice caused him to turn—and see more fins knifing through the water toward him, drawn by the scent of blood. Instinctively Jack realized there were too many to kill, so he sheathed his dagger and aimed his shadowhook.

"What are you doing?" Thalidon growled.

"Catching a ride," Jack said.

He aimed for the lead fish and waited for it to jump from the water. When it leapt Jack dodged and fired his shadowhook through the creature's mouth. He then leapt to the creature's back and caught the shadowhook thread on the opposite side. He wrapped it around his arm as the beast plunged into the lake.

It dove and twisted, bucking to dislodge the makeshift bit. Shockingly fast, the fish swerved and banked upward, exploding into view and soaring a dozen feet off the lake's surface. Riding the great beast like a horse, Jack's booming laugh echoed off the walls of the cavern.

He sucked in his breath as they dove again, and the water blasted into his form. His smile never left his face as the gorthon heaved and jumped, fighting to dislodge its prey from its back. Then it jumped too close to the cavern wall. Seeing his opportunity, Jack extinguished the shadowhook and his makeshift reins evaporated. Then he rolled off the gorthon's back and cast his shadowhook at the wall, lifting himself to safety.

He climbed to the exit corridor, reaching it at the same time the dwarves did. They climbed off the stone ledge they'd used to get there and stepped onto the end of the broken bridge. Roarthin came to Jack's side.

"What kind of madman *rides* a gorthon?"

Jack grinned at the grudging awe in his voice. "One who likes the fish to know their place."

The ensuing laughter was cut short when a dark elf stepped from the tunnel. "I couldn't agree more," he said to the stunned thieves.

Chapter 22: Riskellion

The dark elf was tall, lean, and muscular. Like the rest of his race his skin was grey, his hair the color of wet ash. His eyes glittered like orbs of obsidian. His features were sharp and angular, and attractive enough that Ursana turned pink when his gaze slid across her. He ran a hand through his shoulder length hair and smiled at Lorelia.

"What brings you to the Deep, good maidens?"

"And who are you?" Lorelia asked.

"Captain Riskellion," he said with a smirk.

He made a motion and a trio of dark elves appeared. The elves stepped to the edge and aimed odd shields down at the frenzied gorthon, placing arrows into the holes at the center. Threads of light reached out to catch the arrows, glowing to life and brightening with power. They took aim and began to fire, sinking arrows deep into the giant fish.

"You have my gratitude for bringing a pack together," Riskellion said.

"You're hunters," Ursana said.

The dark elf turned to her. "Gorthon meat is a delicacy, and this lake is one of the best places to find them. Unfortunately, they're notorious for slipping out the side tunnels into reservoirs we cannot reach." His gaze moved past her and he smiled. "The queen is going to make you pay for the bridge."

"*We* didn't destroy it," Beauty said, and folded her arms. "It crumbled beneath us."

One of the other dark elves sniffed. "Perhaps your dwarven companions eat too much."

Thalidon and Roarthin growled in unison, and Roarthin stabbed a finger at the dark elves. "At least *we* could build a proper bridge."

"Enough," Lorelia said. "Someone damaged the supports so it would fall the next time someone crossed."

"Then we are fortunate it was you rather than us," Riskellion said, and then grinned. "Or perhaps it was *meant* for you."

"Why would you say that?" Gordon asked.

The dark elf stepped past him and examined the broken edge of the bridge. "Because this span was built less than a decade ago, yet it disintegrated like mallorian cheese."

"We're just simple travelers seeking to visit Elsurund," Jack said smoothly.

Riskellion laughed. "Travelers you may be, but simple you are not." He raised a hand to forestall Lorelia's protest. "But I care little for your purpose in visiting our realm. Join us on the return journey and you can enjoy fresh gorthon for dinner."

"We'll take it," Beauty said with a smile that was just a hair too warm for Jack's liking.

"We got four before they scattered," another dark elf said. "And it appears they killed two."

Riskellion's smile widened and his eyes sparkled. "How very *simple* of them. Load them into the carts and thank Ero that this time you didn't have to be the bait."

"What do you mean?" Gordon asked.

"The gorthon are devious," one of the hunters said. "And they won't surface except to hunt. To gather a pack one of us jumps in and splashes about."

"A dangerous occupation," Thalidon said with a grunt.

"Yet oh so profitable," Riskellion said with a smile. "This way. You can dry off and change at our camp."

The other hunters cast shimmering nets and began to hoist their giant catch from the lake, and Riskellion led the group of thieves down the tunnel. From there they followed the road until they reached another open cavern containing a gurgling brook.

A fire burned in a natural bowl, the enchanted flames casting shifting patterns of light upon the cave wall. Beyond the fire a cart sat on the underground road. A large lizard lay in front of it, a yoke holding it in place like an ox.

"Watch out for the jelraw," Riskellion said. "They may be fast but they tend to bite."

The giant lizard swiveled its head to look at them, its tongue flicking out to taste the air. Riskellion patted it on the flank and then stepped to the cart, pulling a hooked spear into view. Then he tossed it to one of the hunters attempting to drag a gorthon toward the cart. Even with the enchanted nets the hunters struggled to load the fish. Riskellion stepped to it and with deft motions removed a large strip of flesh.

"Some like it raw," he said, "but I prefer it seared over an open flame."

He retrieved a large pan from the cart and laid it above the fire. Then he poured a vial of oil into it. When it began to bubble he dropped the fish into it. The fluorescent flesh turned the color of gold as the heat seared it, wafting a delicious scent of spice into the air.

Riskellion reclined against a rock and placed his hands behind his head. "So," he drawled. "What's your purpose in Elsurund?"

"Purchasing," Lorelia said. "We represent a handful of wealthy benefactors with empty walls, and they want exotic items to fill them."

A ghost of a smile crossed his features, making it clear he didn't believe her. "It is uncommon for a group of such diversity—and beauty—to travel to our lands."

Beauty flushed and gestured to the group. "Friendship is not bound by race. You should know that better than most."

Jack glanced at her, his jaw tightening. Then he noticed Lorelia and Ursana had similar responses. Ursana seemed to have suddenly lost her ability to speak, while Lorelia kept glancing at the dark elf, her eyes bright. Evidently aware of the effect he had on the women, Riskellion's eyes sparkled with humor.

"There are many sights in the city I can show you, if you would care to join me."

Jack grunted in annoyance. "I don't think—"

"Don't be rude," Lorelia said, and smiled at the hunter. "That would be wonderful."

The hunter smiled and used the pan's handle to flip the fish. Roarthin muttered disparaging comments at the dark elf's expense and Jack exchanged a look with him.

"In our society, females always eat first," Riskellion said.

Lorelia withdrew her plate from her pack and handed it to him with a smile. The dark elf drew a dagger and sliced a piece for her. As he served Ursana and Beauty, Jack noticed the humor on Thalidon's expression.

"Something amusing?" he murmured.

"I've never seen women choose another over you." The dwarf stifled a laugh.

Jack bit back the acid response as the dark elf stepped in front of him. Although he would have liked to take the fish and throw it into the dirt, he forced a smile and held up his plate. Then he stabbed his fork into the steaming meat and took a bite.

187

To his dismay it was delicious, with an undercurrent of spice that caused his tongue to tingle. As the others praised the food he finished the meal and scraped the plate clean. Then he leaned back and tried to ignore the banter between Beauty, Lorelia, and Riskellion. Fortunately, the other hunters had loaded the cart with the other gorthon by the time everyone had eaten, allowing the group to depart.

Jack slipped to the rear as the group wound their way through giant caverns and plunging underground canyons. Shortly after, Lorelia dropped back to walk beside him. Jack slowed, putting enough distance between them and the group that the keen eared elves would not be able to overhear.

"There's no need for you to sulk," she said.

Jack scowled at the rebuke. "I'm not sulking," he said, but his voice betrayed him, causing her to grin.

"He knows he's attractive and we're using it against him," she said.

Jack stared at her, and then issued a chagrined laugh. "Your persona is flawless, as always."

"You use anger to cause your foe to make mistakes," she said. "We use beauty. There's nothing that causes men to forget like a pretty woman paying attention to them. By the time we arrive in Elsurund he won't care why we're here."

"He's smarter than a bored guard in a tavern," he warned.

"*You* didn't see through it."

He sniffed and looked away. "Of course I did."

She gave a smug laugh, and after a moment he joined in. Then they accelerated to catch up to the group. Now that Jack knew their purpose, he caught the flicker of falseness in Beauty's fawning looks, and the trace of forced humor in her laughter. No trace of such deception was visible in Ursana, who continued to laugh a little too shrilly when Riskellion spoke.

The dark elves used frost stones to prevent the gorthon from spoiling, but they hastened their journey anyway. Two days after departing the broken bridge, the road began to widen and other dark elf travelers appeared. They cast the thieves curious glances but otherwise paid them no mind.

The road split into dozens of smaller paths. The main throughway was lit with ambient light from the rocks, but the side paths were as dark as midnight. Undeterred, groups of dark elves geared for mining or hunting slipped out of view. A group with a similar cart passed them by, their expressions turning envious at the large haul that Riskellion had caught. One of Riskellion's hunters smirked and made a rude gesture. Then he spoke in an aside to Jack.

"Normally we bring home one or two. Six is a fortune."

Overhearing the comment, Lorelia turned to Riskellion. "I assume we'll receive a portion of the sale," she said.

He grinned at her bold statement. "I'll give you a third of the two you killed."

"Half," she countered.

"Done," he replied, his smile smug enough to suggest he'd gotten the better end of the deal.

The road curved into a wide courtyard. Dark elves and a smattering of dwarves bustled about, meeting with merchants, hunters, or miners returning or departing. Beyond them a high arch provided a view of the city. Pressing through the crowd, they crossed the threshold into a mammoth cavern. Miles across, the enormous space lacked a floor, leaving a gaping hole of darkness under the hanging city.

Stalactites the size of a Terros district hung from the cavern ceiling. Homes, shops, roads, and courtyards were visible inside them. Underground plants glowed across every surface in green, purple, and blue. The fluorescent growths illuminated the city like a midday sun, lending it elegance and grace.

Arching bridges connected the massive stalactites. Like threads of stone they extended between the stalactites at a variety of heights. Graceful paths curved around the exterior, allowing dark elves to ascend to the higher levels.

Balconies and windows were abundant, and extended from gardens, streets, and shops. Light glowed from the openings, providing a glimpse of the city's denizens within. Streams flowed in and through the stalactites, ultimately joining into endless waterfalls that fell into the massive abyss.

Riskellion smirked at their silent shock. "Welcome to Elsurund."

Chapter 23: Elsurund

They crossed a bridge that led to a massive stalactite. Weaving their way through a crowd of dark elves, they passed under a portcullis to enter a large circular courtyard. Battlements ringed the space with two companies of dark elf soldiers. Although most of the soldiers were male, the majority of officers were female.

"What's that?" Ursana asked.

Jack followed her gaze to a figure of pure, liquid silver. It resembled a female dark elf but moved like water. As Jack watched, its head melted and flowed into a cart ahead of them, obviously searching the interior. The jelraw shifted its feet and its mouth snapped over the liquid hand. Unperturbed, the hand flowed between the teeth and reformed at the same time the head returned. A nearby soldier shouted for them to continue.

"That's one of the Silver Guard," Riskellion said. "Entities of magic that obey the queen and those under her command. To cross one is to invite a swift death."

"And if you surrender?" Beauty asked.

"You get sent to the Pit," Riskellion replied. "It's the prison on the lowest point of the city."

"Have you ever been there?" Ursana asked. She turned pink when he winked down at her.

"Once or twice."

The cart ahead of them pressed on and the Silver Guard glided to them. A longsword flowed from the liquid in its hand and it used the blade to lift one of the fish to look beneath it. It had taken three dark elves with enchanted nets to lift the gorthon corpse but the Silver Guard did so with ease.

Satisfied, the enchanted soldier withdrew and Riskellion barked an order to the jelraw. The lizard scrabbled forward, pulling the cart through another gate and onto a bridge. Jack's eyes were drawn upward to a quartet of Silver Guard standing on the battlements above.

The enchanted defenders stared down at the thieves as they passed below them, their heads turning as if they were alive. Their features were bland and expressionless, but the spears growing from their liquid flesh made them appear sinister. Riskellion noticed Jack's attention and grinned.

"The Silver Guard are as lethal as they are stunning," he said, his eyes on Lorelia.

The possessive glint to his gaze caused Jack to laugh. "Of that I have no doubt."

Mistaking Jack's meaning, he smiled and stepped to Lorelia's side, engaging her in conversation. She took advantage of the opportunity and asked him about the city. Jack settled in behind him and Beauty took a place at his side. With the cart ambling behind them Jack gazed on the wonders of Elsurund.

"The city sections are called spines," Riskellion said, gesturing to the massive stalactite they were approaching. "Each is controlled by a collection of houses that elect a reign at their head."

They passed through another portcullis and entered the hollowed out interior of the spine. Spiral staircases ascended into the ceiling, many supported by underground trees. Instead of leaves, threads of orange hung from the branches like glowing hair. The trees provided both illumination and beauty to the market, and were interspersed with stands of giant mushrooms.

Shops were nestled between trees and mushrooms, half-hidden and mysterious. Lacking walls or ceilings, the shops dotted the slopes of rolling hills. Trails split off from the main road, curving and disappearing into a maze of enticing displays. Weapons and armor glittered beside strange artifacts, each more desirable than the last. Jack's hands twitched and he resisted the urge to swipe a figurine of a cat fashioned from blue diamond and mithral.

"This is the Enzoar Spine," Riskellion said. "As you can see they deal mostly in metalwork."

Vast openings in the exterior of the spine provided a near uninterrupted view of the other city spines, and Jack ascended a trail in order to look outward. Balconies and trickling streams dotted the exterior of huge stalactites. A female dark elf strode onto a balcony, her jewelry sparkling in the light. He smiled, imagining how easy it would be to slip into the homes that filled the upper levels of the city.

He turned his gaze downward but there was little to see. An ocean of darkness filled his view. A merchant from nearby noticed his scrutiny and stepped to his side. She smiled as Jack turned to her.

"First time in Elsurund?"

"It's a city of wonders," he replied, and then gestured at the view. "What lies beneath?"

"The Well of Shadow has no end," she said. "And none have ever returned."

He peaked an eyebrow. "None?"

"No one knows why," she said.

"You chose a dangerous place to build a city," Jack said wryly.

"It is defensible from many of the dangers in the Deep," she said. Then she glided close and traced a line down his chest. "Will you be staying a while?"

He disentangled himself and stepped away. "Perhaps," he said with a smile. "If there are more like you."

Her eager laugh followed him as he rejoined the group. Riskellion then turned up a curving path to reach a higher level before leading them to Lojanis, the spine of merchants. Riskellion brought the cart to a halt behind what was unmistakably a meal hall. Built of massive bones, the structure bore a sign that read *The Dragon's Fate*. Savory smells wafted out the enormous jaws that formed the entrance.

A dark elf exited and greeted Riskellion, and as they set to haggling Jack motioned Lorelia to the side. Noticing the motion, Beauty joined them. Under the guise of examining a shelf of amulets, Jack moved them out of earshot.

"We're in the city," he said. "What now?"

Lorelia picked up an amulet and threw a glance at Riskellion. "His desires for me are not exactly honorable. If I can get him into a private setting, we can use him."

"You think he knows where the key is?" Beauty asked, her tone doubtful.

"It's possible," Lorelia said. "The way he talks I get the feeling hunting gorthon is the least of what he's done. And he may not look it, but he's well into his third century."

"You can tell his age?" Jack asked.

"His earring has a minor illusion charm on it. I can't be certain, but I suspect it smoothes slight imperfections in his skin, making him look younger than he is."

"A man fighting his age," Jack said, smiling as he examined a bracelet with a shimmering charm on it.

Beauty grinned at his smug expression. "He clearly lacks ambition, which means he's been employed in a variety of professions. One such as him is likely to have heard of the key. We should be cautious not to tip our hand."

"We should also seek Val'Trisian," Beauty said.

"Who?" Lorelia asked.

"One of the ruling women of the city," Jack said with a nod of agreement. "We met her almost a year ago when she took Nemeth."

195

Lorelia smiled faintly. "The same Nemeth that was mysteriously taken by the dark elves for stealing the very amulet you were hired to get back to them?"

"You told her?" Jack asked, annoyed that Beauty had revealed the truth.

"I didn't." Beauty said, indignant. "It wasn't my secret to tell."

Lorelia laughed at his dismay. "You didn't think I'd find the truth? How easily you underestimate me. Still haven't figured out why . . ." She let the question hang but Jack didn't respond. Then her lips tightened. "Given what you know about me, I would think you'd be more forthcoming with your secrets."

Beauty glanced between them. "What going on between you two?"

"Not my secret to tell," Jack said evenly.

Lorelia laughed, breaking the tension. "Go find your ally. I'll get what I can from Riskellion before slipping a drug into his drink." Her eyes settled on Jack. "Meet back here when you've learned what you can."

"And us?" Gordon asked, bending down as if to tie his boot. Ursana leaned against the gorthon cart to block the view of their conversation.

Lorelia gestured to the dwarves and they drifted close to listen. "Learn what you can in the taverns," she said, "and meet here at whatever time they call midnight. Wait until after dinner to make your exit or it'll look suspicious."

The thieves nodded their agreement and ambled back to the tavern. Jack stepped in to find the interior as lavish as the exterior. Great dragon bones arched above them, supporting hanging lights that resembled stars. The tables were made from pieces of the backbone, and were carved with intricate designs. Claws and teeth formed curved benches where wealthy dark elves dined on steaming dishes. Ancient red scales on the exterior formed a barrier that granted the patrons a measure of privacy from the rest in the spine.

"Who died to make this place?" Beauty muttered.

196

Jack cast her a look. "Don't tell me you care for dragons, now."

She shook her head. "I saw one, once."

"And survived?" Ursana asked.

"The one I met was young," she said. "Barely had its wings. It wasn't the devourer I'd been told it would be."

"This one would have been ancient," Thalidon said, gesturing to the ceiling. "A behemoth of tremendous power."

Riskellion finished his haggling and joined them. Overhearing the last of their conversation, he grinned. "Sadly it was not slain by mortal hand. It died in the Great Draeken War, killed by a white dragon in the battle of Xshaltheria. An enterprising dark elf found the corpse and brought it here, piece by piece. Her descendents still own it."

"Now your people dine in the belly of the beast," Roarthin said with a snort.

"If you can afford it," Riskellion said with a light laugh. "It's the most prestigious tavern in the city—but worth it." He smiled at the girls in a manner that made Ursana flush and turn away. "I always pay for my companions, and the seats beside me are warm and ready for a nice—"

"Why thank you," Jack said, sliding in front of Lorelia. "I'll take that offer."

Riskellion blinked in surprise. "That wasn't—"

"You offered to pay for your guests," Jack replied, feigning gratitude. "How generous of you."

Beauty's lips twitched but she managed to hold the grin in check. "Thank you, Riskellion. I'm sure that will cost a fortune."

Lorelia slid past the sputtering dark elf and took a seat at a large table nearby. "You are too kind."

His eyes narrowed at her smile. "You are more shrewd than I gave you credit," he said in chagrin.

Jack laughed and took a seat with the others. "Someone of your age should know not to underestimate a surface dweller."

Riskellion's eyes narrowed, but he forced a smile and took a seat beside Lorelia. "Let us eat, shall we? Then you can be on your way, before you encounter the dangerous side of the Deep."

The veiled threat made Jack smirk. "I like the dangerous side," he said.

Ursana snorted into the drink a barmaid had just placed in front of her. "It's true."

"Perhaps you can go find what we came for," Lorelia said.

"Before the meal?" Jack asked, indignant.

Beauty motioned to the dark elf approaching their table. "We'll take our meal with us."

"He has the coin," Jack said, gesturing to Riskellion.

"Apparently I'm more generous than I thought," he said sourly.

"Come now," Lorelia said, drawing his gaze with a dazzling smile. "Is it not worth it?"

"Time will tell," he said, his eyes brightening.

Beauty took the opportunity to pull Jack outside, but Riskellion only had eyes for Lorelia. A moment later a dark elf came out with roasted meat on a shard of bone. He looked Beauty up and down.

"Come back anytime," he said with a lascivious smile.

When he was gone Jack snorted. "Are *all* males attracted to you?"

"Are all *females* attracted to you?"

He laughed at her mimicking his tone. "I have no argument for that."

She grinned. "Let's go see if one in particular remembers you."

198

Chapter 24: Aranis

"This is delicious," Beauty said.

She savored the last bite and then tossed the bone over the edge of the bridge. Jack watched it tumble into the abyss before adding his own to the fall. Smacking his lips, he gestured to the city.

"It appears Elsurund has more to offer than I'd originally thought."

The trees and plant life had dimmed over the last hour, approaching what Jack suspected to be Elsurund's version of twilight. The streets had emptied of shoppers with the crowds moving to the taverns. The stragglers betrayed a sinister intent, and they eyed Jack and Beauty from dark alleys. Beauty's eyes flicked to them.

"I don't recall our meal coming with a helping of being knifed in the back," she said.

"They think we have an abundance of coin," Jack replied.

"We do," she pointed out.

He grinned and gestured toward the spine they were approaching. "The tavern maid said that Val'Trisian is the current reign of Xolenous, the spine of magic. This is the quickest route there."

"I don't think it's the safest," she said.

"Since when do you care about safety?"

She threw him a look. "Just because *you* ignore wisdom doesn't mean everyone else does."

He laughed as they stepped off the bridge and entered the spine furthest from the heart of Elsurund. The plants on the Kordun Spine were dimmer than in the rest of the city, with many flickering or dark. The stone lacked the polished look of the rest of the city, and the lavish trappings of the wealthier spines were noticeably absent. Even the water of the streams was dirtier.

"It looks like the Sticks," Beauty said, referring to the poorest district in Terros.

"Every city has its slums," Jack replied.

"I don't think this is a normal slum," she said.

Jack found he could not disagree. He'd expected the poor and destitute, the desperate, the weak. Instead he spotted brutes, outcasts, the mighty. One dark elf stood almost seven feet tall, his body layered in muscle. Another was a female dressed in clothes of liquid shadow. She spun a ring dagger in her hand, the steel blurring through the material of her glove and sleeve, making it difficult to discern its location. Her charcoal eyes never wavered from Jack.

Beauty glanced behind them, to where a scattering of dark elves flitted in an out of view. "They think we're lost and easy prey," Beauty said, her voice tightening.

They passed into the spine and came to a city square. Lined with poor shops and homes built from the interior of the rock, the buildings showed the scars of conflict and war. The utilitarian nature of the structures made them seem drab compared to the rest of the city. Dark elves appeared in the alleys, drifting closer, closing off the exits. Jack saw the trap and came to a halt.

"Whatever happens," Beauty said, "don't be you."

"What do you mean by that?" Jack asked.

"These aren't the type you incite to anger," she murmured as a dark elf female stepped into their path.

"We took a wrong turn," Beauty said. "But I'm sure—"

"I like lost ones," she interrupted Beauty, her eyes sliding up and down Jack's body.

The seven-foot dark elf appeared at Beauty's side, his appearance so sudden that she flinched.

"You don't get them both," he rumbled. "I get the girl." He smiled in a way that made Jack's skin crawl.

The one in a shadowy cloak appeared at Jack's side and idly spun a curved knife in her hand. "You had the last one," she said to first one.

"Aranis," the elf to first stop them said, retreating a step. "You know you're not supposed to be here. Thock may be in the Pit, but his orders must be obeyed."

Aranis stared at the dark elf as the tension mounted. Her ring dagger continued to twirl, slicing through the shadows of her clothing with rhythmic menace. Thinking she'd triumphed, the first elf stepped forward.

"Go," she said. "Before—"

A second ring dagger sank into her heart, appearing so suddenly that Jack never saw the throw. Gasping for life, she toppled to the ground. Aranis glided forward and slowly withdrew the blade, her eyes never leaving Jack.

"I want him," she said to the corpse.

Jack folded his arms. "Just because you want me, doesn't mean you can handle me."

Aranis continued to stare. Jack still couldn't see much of her form beneath the cloak, but the other dark elves seemed to distance themselves from her. The shadows shifted and curled about her as if sentient, occasionally revealing a flash of skin.

Aranis stared at Jack without blinking, twirling the bloody ring dagger in her hand. "I always get what I want."

"Do I get the girl?" the giant asked.

"I don't care, Jorlin," Aranis said.

Other dark elves hovered in the background. Some looked nearly as powerful as Aranis and Jorlin, but they seemed reluctant to issue a challenge. Aranis ignored them and drifted toward Jack.

"Wait," Jack said, and flashed a brilliant smile. "Will you grant me a final request?"

Aranis came to a stop, and then acquiesced with a tiny nod. Taking the lead, Jack turned to Beauty and wrapped his arms around her waist. Startled, she released her grip on her knife and caught his arms.

"What are you doing?"

"Before we die you must know how I feel," he proclaimed, his tone grand.

Shock flitted across her features, but before she could respond Jack leaned in and kissed her. Jack had intended on using the distraction to create an exit, but was unprepared for the wave of emotion that flooded him.

She tensed, clearly focused on the myriad of dangers, but then her hands wrapped tighter, pulling him to her. He responded in kind, the force of the kiss drawing gasps and a murmur of laughter from the dark elves.

Then Aranis coughed.

Jack reluctantly withdrew, and smirked at the expression on Beauty's face. "Ready?" he whispered.

She grinned. "Of course."

Aranis continued to spin her dagger, but the tempo had increased as if with excitement. "Kiss me like that and I'll let you live longer," she said.

Jack inclined his head and stepped to her, briefly obscuring Beauty from view. The next instant an object tinkled as it struck the ground—

and a blast of sunlight exploded throughout the square. The dark elves cried out and shielded their eyes, while Aranis raised the shadows of her cloak into a shield.

Jack bolted through a gap with Beauty at his side. Racing toward the nearest alley, they rushed down the street, leaving chaos in their wake. The magic faded in seconds and dark elves flooded after them.

Jack turned a corner and came to a dead end, so he leapt to a window of a building and dove inside. Beauty cast a strength spell and leapt after him, rolling on the floor to stand beside him. They jumped out the opposite window and sprinted down another street. Pandemonium echoed off the walls, with dark elves eager to reach them before Jorlin or Aranis caught them. Abruptly one leapt out of an alley and hurtled a glowing net.

"I enjoyed the kiss," Jack said, leaping over the web. He struck the elf on the face as he soared by.

"You want to talk about it *now?*" Beauty demanded.

"We never talk about it," Jack said.

Another dark elf dropped from above them. Brandishing a sword, he landed in their path and charged. Beauty twisted past him and bashed her elbow into the wielder. "When Skorn is dead, we'll talk."

"Is that a promise?"

She threw him a faint smile. "You have my word. Now can we get out of here?"

Jorlin burst from an alley and grabbed Beauty's throat, slamming her into a wall. "Nice try little mouse," he said, "but no one escapes me."

Jack drew his dagger and swung it, but Jorlin caught his wrist and launched him down the street. He tumbled to a stop and slammed into a wall, losing his grip on his dagger. He groaned and forced himself to his feet, stumbling to his weapon. His vision swam into focus as he retrieved it. Then he saw Beauty.

"I'm not a mouse," she snapped.

She grabbed the thumb that wrapped around her throat and yanked, forcing him to release her. She landed in a crouch and grabbed his free hand. With the strength of her magic she pivoted on her foot and hurtled him into the wall. He grunted as he went down but rolled forward.

"That wasn't nice," he growled, and leaned back to punch her.

Beauty punched first.

Their fists collided and bones snapped. Jorlin cried out and crumpled. Before he could recover Beauty stepped forward and reared back to deliver a punishing blow to his jaw. As Jorlin collapsed Beauty turned to the handful of elves that had filled the end of the alley.

"*Who wants me now?*"

Her snarl sent them scurrying away, and Jack stumbled to her side. "I certainly do."

"I don't," Aranis said coldly.

Jack turned and raised his crossbow but she was faster. Threads of magic from her clothing streaked out and formed hands of liquid black. One caught Jack's dagger on the blade and another wrapped around his crossbow, yanking them from his hands. Another shadow hand grasped Beauty's dagger and tossed it away. Jack retreated to Beauty and drew a knife from a sheath on his chest.

"I don't need weapons to fight," Beauty said, balling her hands into fists.

"I don't need them to kill," Aranis said.

Her clothing unraveled further, revealing toned arms and legs. The threads of shadow magic turned into hundreds of hands, each clenching and unclenching. They streaked toward Beauty and lifted her off the ground, wrapping around her throat. Others came for Jack, coiling around his legs and arms, dragging him toward her. She spun her ring daggers faster, her eyes fixed on him. Other threads lifted more spinning daggers, turning into a whirlwind of steel.

"Come, my pet," she said, smiling for the first time as Jack was lifted off the ground by the shadow hands. "It's time to forget about her."

A silver sword exploded into view, severing the shadow threads. Ring daggers clattered to the street and Jack and Beauty fell with them, crashing onto the stone. Jack rolled to his feet and retreated as the Silver Guard glided between them.

Aranis scowled and sent threads to pick up her weapons. "Why are *you* here?" she demanded. "Who commands you?"

"Me," a dark elf said, appearing with a dozen soldiers at her back.

"Reign Trisian," Aranis said, withdrawing into her shadow cloak until only her mouth was visible. "What brings you to Kordun?"

Val'Trisian smiled. "Find a new pet, Aranis. This one already belongs to me."

Aranis scowled and spoke to Jack as she retreated. "I can be patient for this one . . ."

The magic of her cloak wrapped about her and she evaporated from view. The other dark elves of Kordun followed her lead, and in seconds the street had emptied. Jorlin cast a baleful look at Beauty before limping away.

"Jack of Thieves," Val'Trisian said, turning to him. "I never thought I would see you again."

"The pleasure is mine," Jack said, stepping toward her.

One of Val'Trisian's guards raised her sword. "That's far enough human. We know of your exploits."

Jack grinned broadly. "My reputation precedes me. How intriguing."

The guard jabbed her sword toward Jack. "I suggest he be remanded to the Pit for—"

"That will not be necessary," Val'Trisian said, flicking her hand in dismissal.

"But my lady," the guard protested, "you cannot trust them."

Her eyes flicked to the guard. "I suspect they would protect me with the same zeal you would."

The guard scowled but withdrew, and Val'Trisian gestured to Jack. "Come," she said. "We should leave Kordun, quickly."

The guards formed a ring around them as they ascended through the spine and crossed a bridge to Xolenous. Only then did they slow their steps. Val'Trisian dropped back to join Jack and Beauty.

"As much as I'd like to believe your presence is social, I suspect your purpose is more nefarious."

"Yet you dismiss your guards?" Beauty asked.

"Sometimes being a reign is a stifling occupation," she murmured. "And one needs the occasional intrigue."

Jack smirked. "We seek a knife like this," he said, pulling the first Eternal key from a secret pouch at his side.

She accepted the ancient knife and examined it. "The craftsmanship is uncommon," she replied. "It contains an enchantment foreign to me."

"Have you seen its like?"

"I have," she replied, returning the knife to him. "The captain of the Reaver Guard has collected weaponry for centuries, and I believe I've seen a sister blade on his walls."

Jack caught the disgust on her features. "You do not like him?"

"He is a vile and repulsive elf," Val'Trisian said. "And I look forward to embarrassing him."

"For *you* to embarrass him?" Beauty asked.

"I can't let thieves have all the fun." she said, and smiled. "I'm coming with you."

Chapter 25: Sinder's Obsession

Jack and Beauty left the reign and returned to *The Dragon's Fate*. There they found Riskellion passed out on a table and the other thieves conversing around him. Jack found a seat across from the slumbering dark elf.

"What happened to him?"

Lorelia smirked. "He got grabby, so I slipped lightsbane into his mug." She tapped his head. "Unfortunately, he doesn't know anything."

"We didn't learn anything either," Gordon said, and Ursana grunted in irritation.

"Any sign of Gallow?" Beauty asked.

Jack smiled. "We found the key."

They leaned in and he detailed what they knew. The ambient light of the city gradually dimmed, mirroring nightfall. The tavern and houses of entertainment grew raucous as the wealthy wasted their fortunes. Then a dark elf slid into a seat across from them.

"Who are you?" Lorelia asked.

Tall and beautiful, the dark elf wore grey, fitted clothing with silver accents. Her hair hung braided down her back. Armed with a sword and a sheathed crossbow on her chest, she appeared ready for a fight. She grinned at Jack's query.

"I understand this is what you call a persona?"

Jack began to laugh when he realized it was Val'Trisian. "Flawless," he exclaimed.

"Forlana would be hard pressed to do better," Beauty said with an appreciative nod.

The dark elf brushed the silver ring protruding from her ear and her face flickered, briefly showing her real face before returning to the persona.

"Few are capable of casting the guise charm," she said wryly, "but it can be a powerful mask."

Jack met Lorelia's gaze. "As long as the mask doesn't become you."

Mistaking his words, Gordon nodded. "We use personas only on assignment. Only a coward would hide themselves from everyone."

Lorelia's features hardened and she looked away. Jack wanted to kick Gordon under the table but that would lead to questions Jack could not answer. In an effort to shift the conversation he turned to Val'Trisian and motioned to her clothes.

"I must say, I did not expect you to commit so fully."

Even the magic could not hide her flush. Then her expression turned excited. "Let's go steal a knife."

They exited the tavern and Val'Trisian led them into the neighboring spine, which proved to be a labyrinth of smaller streets. Homes lined the ascent, lights glowing beside the doors. Etchings of fogged light graced the ceiling, giving the street a magical feel. The stone underfoot had been carved like cobblestone, suggesting a wealthy neighborhood.

They continued to ascend until they reached a large cavern at the extreme summit of the spine. Three homes graced the terminus of the roadway, and each sought to outshine the others. The two on the sides displayed balconies and turrets, their surfaces dripping with magic, while the one in the center held a real dragon shackled to the front gate. The young black had a chain wrapped around its snout to stifle its acid

209

breath, but its eyes glowed with hatred as it paced. White tattoos of blades adorned its scales.

"Please tell us it's not the one with the dragon," Jack said.

"I can't do that," Val'Trisian replied with a smile. "We must bypass it to enter."

Beauty threw her a look. "If one of your status gets caught, what's the consequence?"

"It depends," Val'Trisian replied. "If my identity is known I will be stripped of my rank. If not, I'll spend a few months in the city's prison, the Pit."

"Are you certain you wish to do this?" Lorelia asked.

Jack answered first. "A life without excitement is no life to live."

Val'Trisian laughed, her tone laced with anticipation. Overhearing the exchange, Roarthin snorted in amusement.

"Stealing with Jack is more excitement than one needs."

"Stop complaining," Thalidon said. "We both know you enjoy it."

The dwarf's lips twitched behind his beard. "I will not admit that."

"Let's get this done," Gordon said. "Before Gallow appears."

"Gallow?" Val'Trisian asked.

Lorelia's gaze flicked to the dark elf. "He's the head of the assassin's guild, who now serves our foe."

"Did they not mention that?" Ursana asked.

Jack made a dismissive motion. "No need to worry about him."

"*I* worry about him," Beauty said.

Val'Trisian's expression was alight with amusement. "I'm beginning to think I chose the wrong occupation," she said.

Jack smirked at her answer. "Thalidon, Roarthin, if it comes to it, distract the dragon. Lorelia and Beauty will handle the guards. Gordon and Ursana, get high and provide cover. If we are discovered, we're going to need it."

"And how exactly do we get in?" Val'Trisian asked.

Jack wrapped his arm around her waist, pulling the beautiful elf close enough to kiss. "You stay with me," he said, and cast his shadowhook toward the ceiling of the cavern.

She gasped as it yanked them into the darkness at the roof of the cavern. They caught the wall and then Jack cast it again, allowing them to swing around the exterior of the cavern. She laughed breathlessly as they flew through the air, causing the dragon to lift its head and glare. Then Jack swung them over the wall to the surface of the home.

They alighted on the topmost balcony of Captain Sinder's home, and Jack darted to the door. Withdrawing a set of picks, he set to work on the lock. Seconds later his lock picks sizzled and melted. He frowned in irritation, and then withdrew the knife Beauty had given him.

He disconnected the blade from the hilt and placed the hilt against the lock, caressing the rune on the pommel. The hilt turned liquid and flowed into the lock, filling every nook and pressing against the tumblers. When it turned solid Jack inserted the blade into the lock and turned.

Sparks came from the hole and then it went silent. Reminding himself to thank Beauty for the gorgon key, Jack eased the door open and withdrew the master key, reshaping it back into the innocuous knife. He slipped inside—and came face to face with a black reaver. He froze, but Val'Trisian chuckled as she strode past him.

"It's not real," she said. "Captain Sinder worships the black reaver he guards."

His eyes adjusted to the darkness and he made out the reaver's bulk. Although the likeness was flawless, it was just a statue. Then he spotted the walls and their decorations. Enchanted etchings prowled the walls, all of black reavers and dragons.

"Obsessed much?" Jack asked.

"There is a reason he has no wife."

He stifled a laugh and moved to the opposite side of the room. Putting his ear to the door, he listened for guards in the halls. Val'Trisian had informed them that Captain Sinder used the bulk of his wealth on his home, reserving enough to hire a score of sentries.

Jack heard the faint footfalls but they were receding. Once they were gone, Jack eased the door open and stepped into the hall. When it proved empty he gestured to her.

"Care to lead the way?"

She grinned and took the lead. "Watch my back."

"I intend to," his said, his eyes on her curvaceous form.

She laughed lightly and darted down the hall. She may have been a noble, but she moved like a wraith, silent and swift. She glided through the corridors of Captain Sinder's home without fear or hesitation. Then they turned a corner and a guard stepped out of a room. Shocked, he yanked his sword free.

Val'Trisian was faster. She drew her own blade and obliterated his defenses. When his sword tumbled to the floor she struck him in the gut with her free hand. He doubled over and she brought her knee into his face, sending him to the floor.

"Do all reigns fight like that?"

She sheathed her sword. "Not many," she admitted with a smile.

They pulled the guard back into the room and left him bound. Then they advanced into the home until they reached the collection. The door was unlocked and Val'Trisian eased it open, shutting it behind them. She touched the rune on the side of the room and the lights brightened.

Weapons filled the room, lining every wall, the ceiling, and the inside of hundreds of displays. The collection could have armed the Talinorian cavalry with weapons to spare. Every type of blade, staff, and instrument of death was visible, many bearing enchantments that depicted dragons and reavers.

"I don't think I care for the captain," Jack said.

"No one does," she said. "But his father had connections and helped him gain the rank and wealth."

Jack felt the urge to destroy it all but turned to her. "Where's the knife?"

She picked her way through the collection to the far wall, where an assortment of knives lay hilt to hilt. He spotted the key to the Eternal vault and checked it for curses. Evidently it wasn't one of Sinder's more valued items as no curses were attached. He picked it up and slid it into an empty sheath on his chest.

"That's it?" Val'Trisian asked, and sighed. "I hoped for more."

Jack spotted an asunder blade, the edge enchanted to sever steel. An idea crossed his mind and he turned to her. "Just how much damage would you like to do?"

She gestured to the horde of weaponry. "As much as I'd like to, we can't possibly destroy it. The more valuable are protected by magic that would stop even a dragon's fire."

Jack reached for the asunder blade and lifted it down from the wall. "What about the acid breath of a black dragon?"

She caught what he was insinuating and her eyes lit with mischief. "You want to use his dragon like a weapon."

"Of course," he said, and handed her the sword. "I'll hold the door for you."

She grinned and they exited the collection—to find a dozen soldiers rushing toward them. Dressed in armor and helm, they were backed by an unarmored dark elf. Shorter than the rest, the dark elf was still in his nightclothes, which bore images of dragons and reavers.

Jack burst into a laugh when he realized it was Captain Sinder. "Do your undergarments also have reavers on them?" he asked.

213

Captain Sinder flushed. "Do not kill them," he barked. "I want time to punish them."

The dark elves charged and Jack pulled his dagger and crossbow, darting down the hall. Val'Trisian took the lead, her blade streaking in a pattern of defense that overwhelmed the lead guards. They cried out in dismay when their blades tumbled from their fingers.

Jack slipped around Val'Trisian and fired his crossbow at their feet, freezing them to the floor with a frost bolt. They cried out and fell awkwardly, unable to move their boots. Jack leapt over them and engaged the next one with his dagger. Working in tandem, Jack and Val'Trisian decimated the guards. Then one guard managed to evade Val'Trisian and came for Jack.

Jack aimed his crossbow but the guard ducked, driving for Jack's chest. Jack just managed to rotate, the sword impaling his shadow. Then he felt a tug on his tunic and looked down to see the guard's free hand grasping the Eternal key.

Jack's eyes widened in surprise but his shock cost him, and the guard grasped his arm, spinning around and placing the key at his throat. Val'Trisian looked back and saw Jack pinned. She parried two thrusts and leapt forward but Jack raised his hand.

"Don't," Jack said. "He's not a guard."

She ignored him and darted in. The guard withdrew a glowing shackle from his belt and clamped it over Jack's hand. It yanked Jack to the floor and sank into the stone, fusing to the floor. Then he pulled off his helmet to reveal his identity.

Gallow.

The assassin smirked at Jack before turning, catching Val'Trisian's blade on his own. He leaned into a kick that sent her tumbling down the corridor. She rose and came again but soldiers filled the gap, charging at her. Her motions became desperate as she gave up ground.

"Jack!" she called.

"Go!" he shouted.

"I'm not leaving you behind!"

Jack pulled against the bindings but they would not budge. Gallow turned away from the dark elves swarming Val'Trisian and strode toward Jack. Through the press of bodies he met Val'Trisian's gaze and knew she would not leave.

"Trust me," he said, his voice somehow piercing the clash of blades. "Go."

Indecision twisted her features and turned into a scowl. Then she leapt over a downed elf and darted down a side corridor. Half the remaining guards raced after her while Sinder pushed his way through to Jack.

"Well done," he said Gallow.

Gallow knelt and pulled the second Eternal key from the sheath on Jack's chest. "I was told not to kill you," he said, his voice dripping with hatred. "But if I leave you here I won't have to. They will kill you for me."

As the other guards swarmed Jack Gallow slipped through the crowd, disappearing with a smug grin on his face. Alone and surrounded by elven guards, Jack was bound and dragged before Sinder. The diminutive elf straightened as if it would make him more impressive and his expression turned haughty.

"A thousand soldiers have been summoned and stand outside my gates. They will find your friends."

"Can I ask you a question?"

He frowned at Jack's tone and gestured for him to speak.

"Did you steal a child's nightclothes?"

Shock rippled through the guards and several smothered laughter. Then Sinder recovered and his face turned red. Without a word he stepped in and struck Jack. In spite of his size the punch knocked Jack to the ground. He laughed anyway, and Sinder struck him again. Then everything went dark.

Chapter 26: The Pit

The guards pushed Jack into a cell and slammed the bars shut before departing. He rose to his feet and looked around, surprised by the lighting. He'd expected a cell covered in dirt and infested with rats. Instead the room was clean and well lit, containing a bed and even a privy adjacent to the cell.

Nary a crack marred the ceiling, walls, or floor. He was quick to test the bars and walls but found no hint of egress. Then he came to a rune on the back wall. Curious, he reached out and touched it—and a door swung open.

"This is new," he said, poking his head out the back of the cell.

He stepped into a hallway and looked both ways. In either direction were matching doors leading to other cells. The hall was empty, so he followed the curving corridor until he reached a spiral staircase. The stairs extended from the ceiling of a large common area, and a giant platform came into view.

Hanging beneath the spine, the circular platform was hundreds of feet across. Dozens of staircases dotted the platform, providing a route for prisoners to move between the common area and their cells.

Criminals lounged about, with most playing cards, dice, or bones. He spotted a pair staring at a board game, and nearby a group trained for combat. Although dark elves dominated the populace, a smattering of surface races were also present, including a trio of surly elves talking in low tones.

The platform lacked walls or railing, so the edge of the platform dropped straight into the Well of Shadow. A fifty-foot illusion shimmered faintly, indicating that the prison was not visible from the outside. The shield likely ensured that the citizens of Elsurund did not have to see the prisoners at the base of the city.

Jack descended to the surface of the platform and strode to the edge, peering into the depths of the Well. The proximity to the illusion wall allowed him to feel a spark of power, and realized it prevented criminals from attempting to climb out. Then he heard a pair of footsteps approaching and whirled, causing a dark elf to jump in surprise.

"I was going to warn you about standing at the edge," she said. "Criminals have been known to fall."

"Or be pushed."

She grinned at that. "The durans occasionally throw someone off to maintain fear."

"Durans?"

"They are the ones sentenced for life."

She jerked a thumb at a group of dark elves gathered in the center of the platform. Burly and covered in white tattoos, the group formed an invisible epicenter among the criminals. Jack noticed the further one sat from the durans, the more solitary and furtive the prisoners appeared.

"The guards let you murder each other?"

She looked up at the ceiling. Jack followed her gaze to see a trio of guardhouses hanging from the ceiling high above. Silver Guard and dark elves looked down from within the bowl-shaped rooms. Large crossbows were mounted on the sides with the weapons pointing at prisoners.

"If they see a crime they will kill the offender, but the durans are subtle enough not to get caught."

"Who are you?"

"Amala."

"Jack. What crime did you commit?"

She smirked and gestured to the fortress. "I tried to steal from a warden."

"A fellow thief?" Jack grinned. "How intriguing."

"Are you from the surface guild?" she asked.

"Only thing I'm guilty of," he said. "After you get out you should visit the Thieves Guild on the surface."

"I may take you up on that," she said. "And if I'd known there were men as attractive as you, I'd have visited decades ago."

He laughed lightly, drawing the attention of the nearby surface elves. "Have you ever met a member of the surface guild?" he asked Amala.

She pointed to the pair of humans playing the board game. "Actually we have one of your guild here."

Jack peered into the distance until he spotted him, and his eyes narrowed. As if sensing the weight of his gaze the man looked up. Anger flared across his features and he rose to his feet. Then he strode across the platform to Jack.

"*You*," he growled.

"Nemeth," Jack said coolly. "I'm sorry to say it, but you look well."

Tall and strong, the man looked very little like the thief Jack had betrayed a year ago. Gone were his limp and gut, and in its place were layers of muscle. With a shaved head and a skull tattoo on the bald surface, he looked more like a brute than the devious former thief.

"It appears you know each other," Amala said, retreating from the budding tension.

"He killed my mother," Jack said.

"And *he* sent me here to rot," Nemeth said with a sneer.

218

"You deserved it."

Nemeth stepped closer but Jack twisted to the side so the edge of the platform was no longer at his back. Nemeth rotated with him and stabbed a finger into Jack's chest.

"I've spent a year preparing to face the Allegian Trial—all so I can come back and kill you."

"You should leave revenge to me." Jack sniffed in disdain. "I'm better at it."

"You were always so arrogant," Nemeth sneered.

"And you were always so stupid," Jack said. "You had no idea who you were serving. All you cared about was the coin."

Nemeth's features tightened at the mention of Skorn. "I knew to fear him, which is more than you can say."

Jack laughed, the sound low and mocking. "Do you even know when you lost your spine? Or did you ever have one in the first place?"

Nemeth regarded him with rage simmering across his features, but he held it in check. "I should thank you," Nemeth said. "I'd grown soft in my retirement from the guild. Down here the elves healed my limp, and because of you I had the motivation to survive. I've regained my courage to kill."

"Thief or killer, you'll always be a pawn."

"You won't last a week, Jack. I swear it on my mother's grave."

"Don't swear on a woman who's disappointed in you."

Nemeth's eyes widened in fury and he reared back to strike, but a column of silver flowed between them. It dropped to the ground and shaped into the figure of a man facing both directions. The two faces stared at Jack and Nemeth as two hands raised liquid swords to each of them.

Nemeth scowled and leaned to see past the Silver Guard. "I have no need to complete the trial, now. Enjoy your final hours, Jack."

219

He turned and strode away, and a moment later the silver figure turned into a thread of liquid and flowed back to its perch. Amala took its place and sighed.

"You're lucky it didn't kill you both."

"Luck has always been a friend of mine."

She smirked at that. "If that were true you wouldn't be in the Pit."

"Even friends betray us sometimes."

She grunted in agreement. "Lucky or not, I'd suggest you find yourself a weapon. Nemeth is as dangerous as the durans. He'll make good on his threat."

"Not if I get out first."

"You can't," she said. "Not from here."

"What about the Allegian Trial he mentioned?"

Her gaze remained on Nemeth's back. "It's a test to prove your integrity."

"That doesn't sound difficult."

She smirked and faced him. "You go into an arena and face a black reaver. If you survive, your loyalty to the dark elves is proven, and you walk free."

"How many have survived?"

"One, and he was a prince."

The flat answer caused Jack to raise an eyebrow. "Black reavers aren't invincible."

"They are when they get a taste of your blood," she replied. "And they give your blood to the beast *before* the conflict."

"So it's a death sentence," Jack said.

"Of course it is. Yet every six months a handful of criminals make the attempt. For durans it's the only way out of the prison, and the potential prestige of being the first criminal to triumph outweighs the risk."

"When is the trial?"

"Four days," she said, and then her expression turned incredulous. "You're not thinking of entering, are you?"

"Perhaps," he replied. "I like a challenge."

"It would be a pity to lose that face of yours," she said. "But it's your life to lose."

"And you?" Jack asked with a smile. "Ever thought of attempting the trial?"

She laughed lightly and flipped her hair over her shoulder. "I actually like breathing. Besides, I only have another few months left on my sentence."

Jack smirked. "Has anyone escaped the prison?"

"A handful," she replied, "but more often than not the effort costs them their lives. Either they fall into the Well of Shadow or they're killed by the Silver Guard. The few to accomplish it do so with help— but I doubt you have time to develop a plan."

"What makes you say that?"

Her eyes flicked to the side, and Jack spotted Nemeth talking with the durans. He stared at Jack with abject hatred, as did the muscled dark elf at his side. There was no mistaking the look of murder in their eyes.

"Looks like he wants to kill me before the trial," Jack said.

There was no response, and when he looked Amala was gone. He spotted her slipping into a group of prisoners a short distance away. She flashed him an apologetic look and then turned away, making it clear they were not friends.

He grunted in irritation. Having an ally would have been invaluable within the prison, but Amala obviously had no desire to go up against the durans. Those close enough to overhear the conversation also drifted away, leaving him alone.

But could his friends reach him before Nemeth did? And even with them, would an attempt get them caught? Or killed? He'd been in numerous prisons before but never one watched by Silver Guard, or placed above an endless pit.

Normally he would dismiss Nemeth as an empty threat, but the hatred in his eyes was sufficient to instill caution. Jack was in a foreign prison without tools, allies, or a means of escape. He'd be a fool to disregard the danger he was in.

A glimmer of light drew his attention, and he turned to find a spider of blue light climbing over the edge. On impulse he strode to it. He stooped and peered into the Well of Shadow, using the motion to hide picking up the spider.

The spider stopped moving the moment he picked it up, and Jack hid it in his hand as he strode toward the staircase that would take him to his cell. When he reached it Nemeth called out to him.

"Only a coward hides like a cur."

"At least I don't smell like one," Jack called back, eliciting muffled laughter. Nemeth scowled at the retort.

Jack ascended and returned to his cell. Only when the door was shut did he open his hand and place the spider on the floor. It brightened and crawled to a wall. With astonishing speed it began to spin a web, the strands forming words. A smile crossed his face as he read the message from Lorelia.

Jack, we managed to escape but Gallow did as well. We believe he departed the city for Margauth to deliver the keys. Six days after the Allegian Trial you are to appear before a tribunal for sentencing. We'll make our attempt then. Do us a favor and don't get killed before we can help you escape.

The words shimmered for several seconds before they and the spider disintegrated. Jack's smile faded with them, his thoughts turning to Nemeth. With four days until the trial and six after, Jack would have to stay alive for ten. But in his gut he knew the truth.

He didn't have ten days.

Chapter 27: The Allegian Trial

The next day Nemeth made his first attempt. Gathering a group of durans, he approached Jack when he was on the common platform. Prepared for the straightforward approach, Jack used a sling he'd made from threads of clothing to launch a pebble into the guardhouse above. It didn't do any harm, but it succeeded in drawing a Silver Guard down to take the weapon while a guard shouted at him.

Jack hid a smile as Nemeth scowled and retreated from the spectacle. Jack watched them plot over the next few days but they seemed content to bide their time until after the trial. Jack resisted the urge to taunt him.

The impending Allegian Trial had set the prison into a state of tension, and a pair of Silver Guard began patrolling the common platform to prevent any unrest. The prisoners ignored them while they placed wagers on who would enter.

A trio of durans seemed the most likely to enter the trial, although a handful of others were part of the speculation. Not wanting to miss out on the coin, Jack placed his own bet with Amala, who was one of those taking wagers. She peaked an eyebrow at his choice.

"Are you certain?"

"Always."

"And how do I collect my winnings when you lose?"

"Contact Arcus," Jack said. "He's a moneychanger in Terros that holds some of my funds. When I win you can deliver my winnings to him."

She grunted in doubt but activated the small light charm. She was a light mage, but her skill was woefully inferior to Lorelia's. A list appeared on her arm and she used her finger to add Jack's wager. Then the light faded from her skin and she looked up at him.

"I'd wish you luck," she said, "but you said you already have it."

He grinned and strode away, making room for another to place their wager. Then he chose a seat near the staircase to his cell. Nemeth smirked at his choice of position, making it clear he thought Jack was afraid. In reality, it was the only place to sit on the platform.

As the hours ticked by the apprehension among the prisoners increased, heightening the tension to the breaking point. Two of the durans most likely to enter began to argue about their success, and the conflict escalated until one struck the other and threw him over the edge into the Well. It happened so quickly that not even the guards could react, and by the time they descended the duran leader bore a smile on his face.

"Your execution has been ordered, Thock," the guard said.

"I'll take my chances in the trial."

The guard laughed and retreated with the Silver Guard. "Your fate will be the same."

"I'll see you in the streets after I gain my freedom," he called after the guard, but the elf merely laughed again.

Across the platform Thock's eyes met Jack's. At nearly seven feet tall the elf towered over the others of his kind, and Jack wondered if he was Jorlan's brother. Thock had spent his time in the prison with a singular purpose, and his muscled body demonstrated his brutal training. Jack had heard whispers that he'd been a high ranked officer in the dark elf army until his family had reported his brutality. The queen had sent him to the prison for life as a consequence, but the elf had vowed to return and punish his wife for what she'd done to him.

225

Shortly after the duran's murder, the prisoners gathered on the side of the platform, all craning to look at the spines of the city. Jack moved to join them and watched a circle of stone descending from the cavern roof of Elsurund. Its placement suggested it could be viewed from nearly everywhere in the city, and its appearance renewed the betting.

"It won't be long now," Amala said from next to Jack.

"About time," he replied. "I hate waiting."

"You should not be so eager."

Jack didn't respond, and watched as it descended just below where they were situated. For the first time he gained a view of the arena used for the Allegian Trial. Several murmured in dismay, but Jack found a smile spreading on his face. Then a shout drew his attention to the guardhouse.

A trio of Silver Guard descended, carrying Captain Sinder to the center of the platform. Dressed in black and green, the captain bore an insignia on his shoulder for the Reaver Guard. He was shorter than the other dark elves, but his demeanor was a shade darker.

"Captain Sinder," Thock said, and his smile turned mocking. "Do our people still mistake you for a child?" His question elicited a scattering of laughter.

The diminutive elf flushed. "Tell me," he said, "how many scars do I have to give you before you learn to hold your tongue?" He smiled, but it only darkened his demeanor. "Or perhaps I'm not cutting where it hurts. Your son is of age now, isn't he? It wouldn't take much to get him sent here . . ."

Thock stepped forward, his features blackening. A Silver Guard raised a sword to his throat and he came to a halt. The chords on his neck stood out as he spoke.

"When I defeat the black reaver, it's not my wife I want to torture," he said. "It's you."

Captain Sinder stepped close and looked up at the massive dark elf. "My reaver will cut you to pieces and discard you like trash. And after you are dead I will still torture your son until he joins you with Skorn."

Amala sidled up to Jack as Thock shouted a retort. "He uses his position to hurt those he thinks are inferior—and we are all inferior."

"Is he the warden?"

"One rank higher," Amala said. "He controls the entire prison, and worships the reaver he guards. But he's more vile than any of us."

"We've met," Jack said, and smiled when Sinder's eyes drifted to him. Raising his voice, Jack called out to the captain. "Did you sleep in your reaver bedclothes last night?"

Laughter engulfed the prisoners and Sinder's features blackened with hatred. "I will see you executed, human," he said coldly.

"My death won't end your embarrassment," Jack said, and began to describe the man's bedclothes in great detail. Only when a Silver Guard stepped in did he fall silent, but his smile remained.

"Does he really have reaver clothing?" Amala asked as Sinder turned away.

"I was caught stealing from him," Jack said. "I saw them with my own eyes."

"Too bad you didn't succeed," she said, smiling faintly. "His pride could have used the blow."

He winked at her. "Don't worry," he said. "I suspect he won't survive the day."

She raised an eyebrow at his tone but he merely smiled and turned back to the Captain's speech.

"The Allegian Trial will begin shortly," Captain Sinder called, turning away from the subdued Thock. "Whosoever wishes to prove their loyalty to the people, step forward now."

Thock snarled his willingness, and a second duran joined him. After a moment's pause another elf stepped forward as well. Marking the three names, the attendant gestured to the group with a knowing smile on his face.

"Is there anyone else?"

"Me," Jack said, stepping through the crowd to join the circle.

Nemeth's eyes bulged at his appearance, causing Jack to smirk and wink at him. "Jack Myst," he identified himself. "And it's a name you'll want to remember."

Smirking, Captain Sinder grunted and noted the name. Then he gestured to the Silver Guard and one of them flowed around his waist, carrying him into the guard station. The others did the same with the three entries for the trial. As Jack ascended Nemeth stepped into the gap.

"At least I get to watch you die!"

"Enjoy the show!" Jack shouted to him.

"*Your arrogance will get you killed, Jack!*"

"Not today!"

They reached the guardhouse and the Silver Guard pulled them into a small cell attached to the side. Then the enchanted soldiers turned back into men and took their places, watching through the bars. Jack took the time to appraise his companions.

The unknown of the entries was skinny and betrayed his nervousness with every twitch. He wore the tattoo of murderer on his neck, marking him as a duran. The second resembled Thock and appeared eager for the impending fight. Jack vaguely recalled his name was Corl. The dark elf paced along the bars without taking his eyes off the Silver Guard.

An hour passed, and then two, and finally a soldier appeared and unlocked the door. The Silver Guard ushered them out as Jack followed the soldier up into the spine. A moment later they were led onto a balcony overlooking the trial arena.

Sprawling and uneven, the arena appeared tiny between the gigantic stalactites. Held aloft by shimmering chains, the platform hung near the center of Elsurund. The arena contained buildings, hills, and shallow canyons, becoming a labyrinth of overlooks, twisting pathways, and alcoves. A handful of trees, giant mushrooms and other vegetation were scattered about, as were ponds and other sources of magic.

Swords, axes, and spiked mauls hung throughout the arena. At first Jack assumed they were for the combatants, but many were large enough to suggest they were for the reaver. Then a dark elf stepped onto a balcony on Primok, the spine of the queen. His appearance hushed the crowd.

"Today we have four challengers for the Allegian Trial!"

The voice boomed throughout the city, filling Elsurund and eliciting a surge of noise. Jack stepped to the edge to look up, and found that ledges, balconies, windows, and bridges were lined with spectators. Jack spotted Aranis on a balcony of Kordun, her features twisted in regret. Jack inclined his head to her and smiled, but she looked away. As his crimes were listed to the crowd, a dark elf soldier stepped behind Jack, drawing his attention.

"Your belongings," he said, handing each of them a parcel.

Jack whistled in appreciation as he recognized his tools, equipment, and weapons within the pouch, and he quickly donned them all. A smile crossed his face as he slid the gauntlet containing his shadowhook onto his wrist. As he tightened the last strap, a dark elf entered.

Dressed in a ceremonial robe of crimson, she unsheathed an odd sword with a channel down the center. She took a step forward and raised it to Thock.

"Step forward."

He did as requested and stepped within reach of the blade, whereupon she placed the tip against the inside of his elbow. He didn't flinch as it pierced his flesh.

"The blood of the pledge, willingly given," she intoned.

Thock's blood leaked onto the tip of the sword, darkening the weapon.

"The energy of the soul, freely offered."

When she had sufficient blood she withdrew, touching his elbow to heal the incision.

"The demon within stands to be slain."

She handed the sword to a Reaver Guard and drew a second blade, repeating the ceremony with each of them. Jack didn't resist as the blade pierced his arm. Once she had collected the blood of all of them, she departed with the blades that contained the criminals' blood. Captain Sinder took their place.

"As you know, you must survive until the corin drops or—"

"What's a corin?" Jack asked.

Sinder frowned in irritation. "You will have about twenty minutes to defend yourself against the reaver. If you survive, your innocence is assured. If you die, your guilt is proven. Any attempt to leave the arena will result in execution by the guards."

His smile turned smug. "Many choose a merciful death from the Silver Guard over the reaver."

"Cowards," Thock said, and spit on the ground.

Captain Sinder turned to Jack, a sneer on his face. "You're just a cheap thief, so I've wagered that you choose death by arrow instead of the reaver. You are going to earn me a significant sum today."

"I appreciate that," Jack said.

The captain frowned in confusion. "Why would you appreciate my wager?"

"Because it means you need me to enter the arena."

"So?"

"So I can do this."

Jack's punch sent him reeling, blood cascading from his nose. A Silver Guard was by Jack in an instant, his blade at Jack's heart. Jack paid it no mind and stabbed a finger at the dark elf growling on the floor.

"I don't care to be called cheap," Jack said indignantly.

Captain Sinder trembled in pain and rage. "At least I get to watch you die today." Another guard helped him to his feet and he retreated, still cradling his broken nose.

Thock turned to Jack, his expression mildly impressed. "I've wanted to do that for ages."

"What's the consequence for striking a guard?"

"Ten years," Thock said, and a faint smile crossed his face. "Per blow."

"I should have hit him again."

Corl released a rumble of laughter, and looked toward the captain. "Perhaps that's why he now stands out of reach."

Across the arena the queen's attendant finished his speech. Then he gestured across to where Jack stood. The ledge they were on began to push out from the wall, making the fourth criminal squeak in surprise and nearly tumble over the edge. Jack raised an eyebrow at him, wondering what had driven him to enter in the first place. Then a second ledge began to extend towards the arena thirty feet to their left. Jack turned to watch the black reaver pace into view.

With a mane of steel, it resembled an armored lion. Spikes of metal grew across its back, each the length of Jack's arm. They clanked into the chains that bound it. The bonds were the color of midnight, indicating they had been forged with anti-magic enchantments.

A guard approached the creature's flank, extending a sword to it. The reaver crashed against the chains, nearly impaling the guard on one of its spikes. As the guard flinched the reaver bit the sword, snapping it in two. It licked the blood from the pieces before casting them aside. They clattered off the stone and fell into the Well of Shadow. It snarled and the spikes brightened.

"Corl," Sinder snapped, and the dark elf turned. "You're first."

A lightbridge appeared and the tall duran dropped into the arena. Alighting on the top of a squat building, he dropped down the steps.

231

Then all eyes turned to the reaver and the chains clacking open. Its snarl of anticipation echoed and re-echoed throughout Elsurund as it leapt into the arena. The queen's attendant lifted her hand and dropped a small, fluttering object.

"The Allegian Trial has begun!"

Chapter 28: A Thief's Trial

Corl drew his sword and caught up a crossbow hanging on a wall before disappearing into the labyrinth. The black reaver surged through the corridors and leapt onto the roof, charging across the gaps. The dark elf kept to the exterior and sought to evade it, but the reaver seemed to anticipate the tactic. Exploding through a wall, the beast smashed into the criminal.

The elf screamed and swung his sword, but the weapon bounced off the metal spikes. The reaver ignored the attack and wrapped a massive clawed hand around the elf. Lifting him to his mouth, he tore him in half and tossed the pieces over the edge of the platform, sending him tumbling into the Well of Shadow. Then it rose on its hind legs and turned to the crowd, releasing a roar that shook loose stones from the city's spines.

The challenge faded into a deafening silence, and then the crowd roared its approval. Baring its metal teeth, the creature leapt back to its pedestal and paced, waiting for the next victim. Awed by the display, Jack turned to make a comment to the next elf attempting the arena. Instead he spotted the skinny elf sprinting back toward the prison, screaming to be put back into his cell.

"There's always one," the guard said with a laugh.

Thock grunted in disgust. "Coward."

"Can you blame him?" Jack asked.

"He's witnessed the Trial before," Thock said. "He knew what he'd agreed to."

"Witnessing a death and facing your own are quite different."

Thock cast him an appraising look. "He's still a coward."

Jack grinned. "Or perhaps he's smart, and we're the cowards."

Thock drew his weapon and stepped to him. "*I'm not afraid of the reaver.*"

"You're afraid to admit your fear," Jack replied, unperturbed by the blade at his gut. "And that makes you a coward."

"And you *aren't* afraid?"

Jack smirked. "The soldier does not fear a battle he's sure he can win."

"Then by all means, go first," Thock said with a sneer. "Show how a *human* can overcome a challenge that has defied our people for thousands of years."

"I'll expect your thanks afterword."

"Why would I thank you?" he growled.

The lightbridge appeared and Jack started down it. "Because I'm about to save your life," he called over his shoulder.

"Your arrogance will get you killed, thief!"

Jack grinned but didn't turn. "So I've been told."

One of the guards grunted in disbelief. "Who *is* that?"

"A fool," Thock said.

Jack grinned and continued his advance down the lightbridge. He wondered what past elves had thought as they took the long walk. Had any stepped off and chosen the Well over facing the reaver? Without rail or barrier, the narrow bridge would have allowed a terrified prisoner to simply disappear into the fathomless depths below. Apparently he was not the first to think it, as one of the spectators above shouted down to him.

"I've got ten silver that you jump!"

"Then you're a fool!" Jack shouted back, eliciting a round of laughter from the other spectators.

He reached the labyrinth and came to a halt, his gaze drawn to the queen's attendant standing on the balcony above. Out of the corner of his eye he spotted the reaver being fed his blood. Then the queen's attendant raised a small yellow object and held it high, allowing the tension to build across the spectators. A flurry of last minute wagers were placed, and Jack saw new elves lining the balconies above.

A flicker of light drew his eye and he turned to see Lorelia standing beside Beauty and the others. The confusion, fear, and anger on their faces were almost comical. They had evidently never considered he would take the trial. The touch of betrayal on Beauty's face caused him to raise his fingers to his lips and blow her a kiss.

Beauty snorted and shook her head, while Lorelia threw up her hands in disgust. Amusement flitted across the features of the others, while Ursana subtly tapped her crossbow. Jack recognized the offer but shook his head. Then the queen's attendant released the corin, and the black reaver's snarl forced him to focus.

Unlike his predecessor he didn't run, and casually strode toward the reaver. On his way he picked up a shield while drawing the dagger from his back. In the distance he could hear the reaver's claws scraping the stone as it charged for him, and a wall of stone shattered as it plowed through it. He watched the plume of dust and debris and shifted direction.

His unhurried advance drew a murmur from the spectators, and he spared a look to find that the crowd had grown since his appearance, with more shoving for a view on the balconies. He smirked, realizing that he'd sparked curiosity among the dark elves.

The reaver slowed as it drew close and set to hunting him, its snarl reverberating down the corridors of the labyrinth. He shifted direction again, angling to get behind where it had appeared. As if sensing his desires, the reaver turned, the spikes of its back scraping the stone walls.

Jack's corridor opened into a small courtyard next to a short castle-like structure. As he entered the courtyard the reaver appeared across from him. It growled and caught a sword embedded in the stone. Rising up, it hurled the blade at Jack.

Jack sidestepped and the blade crashed into the wall behind him, sinking all the way to the hilt and cracking the stone. Then Jack reached the reaver and raised his shield, catching the reaver's claws as they attempted to rake across his flesh.

He spun and twisted, deflecting the massive strength of the beast and striking back with his dagger. The creature leapt over him and came down at his back, and Jack whirled to strike across its face.

The reaver lowered its head and the weapon clanged off the steel spikes. It growled and surged forward. Jack stepped aside and leapt, twisting over its shoulder and landing closer to a building.

The beast reached to its back and snapped a spike free from its own flesh. It hurled the spike at Jack, nearly taking his head from his shoulders. The metal shard grazed his skin across his cheek, leaving a furrow of blood to drip down his jaw.

Jack winced and threw the beast an irritated look. "I hope that doesn't scar."

It snorted and came at him again, and for several seconds it sought to land a blow on Jack. The reaver's sheer strength and speed made it impossible for Jack to strike back, but their matching agility made it difficult for the reaver to land a blow. Then it reared onto its hind legs and charged like a hulking, spiked barbarian.

Jack scrambled backward and raised his bent shield. The claws dug furrows in the steel barrier and sent him skidding toward the building. He struck back, swinging his dagger at the beast's shoulder and finding a gap in the armor, cutting a thin line across the flesh.

The reaver paused and its great head looked down at the miniscule wound. It seemed amused, and then its lips curled in anger. Jack leapt to the side as it lunged, barely escaping the spikes as it flew past him and crashed into the building wall. Trapped, Jack raced up the steps and sought for an escape.

He reached the first level and leapt into a room. The reaver skidded into the opening, demolishing the roof's supports and forced its way inside. Jack sprinted across the room and reached the stairs on the opposite end of the structure. Then he hurled himself up to the highest point on the structure, using it to leap to a neighboring building.

The reaver landed behind him but Jack kept going, sprinting across the tops of the buildings until he reached the highest point, a hill that overlooked the entire arena. Situated close to where the reaver had entered, it had rarely been touched by past conflicts. Spotting a balcony jutting out from a hill, he darted to the edge and turned to face the beast.

The reaver bypassed the steps entirely and leapt into a high flip onto the balcony. In spite of the circumstances Jack grinned at the display of agility, recognizing it as coming from his own blood. He retreated to the edge and looked down, and found himself staring into the Well of Shadow.

With his back to the Well he raised his shield and prepared himself to fight. He'd planned carefully but a current of apprehension tightened his jaw. Fleetingly he wondered if he would fail, but the thought left his mind as soon as it appeared.

"I can see why they never defeat you," Jack said.

The reaver came to halt, its body low to the ground as it prepared to pounce. For the first time it spoke. *How can you have such certainty in the face of death?*

The voice was female rather than male, and carried enough curiosity to cause Jack to smile. "I trust what I know," Jack said.

Your arrogance is going to get you killed, thief.

Annoyance caused Jack to frown. "Why does everyone keep saying that?"

Perhaps you should listen.

He grinned and darted to the side, seeking to bypass the reaver and return to the tenuous safety of the arena. The reaver intercepted him and reached out to clasp the shield. Its claws wrapped around the edge of the barrier, reaching all the way to his arm. Jack yanked his arm out as the reaver ripped the shield free. It sent the shield spinning into the Well of Shadow with a flick of its claw.

Jack pointed the dagger toward the reaver as a hum of expectation filled the spectators. A glance revealed his friends trying to get closer but he knew they were too late to reach him. As the reaver stalked forward he knew he was out of time. Then a smiled played across his features.

And he sheathed his dagger.

The motion drew a shocked silence from the spectators but the reaver didn't pause. Its great hand reached out and wrapped around his waist, digging into his flesh. Then the beast reared up on its hind legs and released a bellowing roar of triumph.

Jack's vision filled with the reaver's teeth and he knew it would be futile to attempt to escape. He was so close he could feel its breath on his face, and see the grey tongue coiling in its mouth. He clenched for what he knew was coming . . . and the reaver hurled him over the edge of the arena.

The force of the throw sent him soaring upward, all the way to the ledge the reaver had come from. He rolled to absorb the impact and rose to stand beside the rune that activated the lightbridge. He slammed his hand onto it and the lightbridge glowed to life, allowing the reaver to charge up to him. Reaching Jack, the beast passed him by and lunged for the guards just exiting the tunnel.

They shrieked as they perished, and their bodies were tossed over the edge. Then Jack opened the gate that allowed them into the tunnel beyond. Without hesitation the reaver surged through and began to slaughter the guards that had chained it.

Jack turned to the tumultuous response from the spectators and raised a hand to them. "You have my gratitude for a fine Trial!" he shouted. "A pity I cannot stay to finish it!"

He offered a mock salute to the queen, and his smile could not be constrained. Amidst cheers from the crowd and shouts from the guards, he turned and streaked after the rampaging beast. Arrows clattered in his wake but his laughter lingered to echo throughout the city.

Chapter 29: Unlikely Allies

The black reaver plowed through the Reaver Guard in the tunnel, sending their bodies crashing into the wall. Blood from the impact touched the reaver's tongue, and the spikes on its back began to glow with power. A pair of Silver Guard appeared but the reaver slammed into them before they could form weapons. Silver splashed on the tunnel and struggled to coagulate.

Corridors and doors blurred past them as they sprinted through the upper levels of the prison. Shouts and orders echoed around them and guards appeared on all sides. One raised a crossbow and aimed at Jack but he activated his hand crossbow and fired first, sending a bolt into the dark elf's knee. He cried out and collapsed, his bolt going wide.

Soldiers appeared ahead but the reaver did not slow. They scattered like pebbles before a tumbling boulder, with weapons, helms, and shields clattering off the walls. Jack leapt their groaning forms without pause.

They reached a set of wide stairs and sprinted up them. A quartet of Reaver Guards appeared at the end of the corridor and skidded to a halt. They formed a rank and a burst of brown light cascaded from their forms, striking the reaver. It slowed, whining as the animal magic sought to subdue it.

Jack slipped past the reaver and raised his crossbow, firing a bolt into their midst. It exploded on the wall, knocking them sprawling in a cloud of dust and bits of stone. The reaver's claws dug into the floor as it accelerated once more. They leapt the downed soldiers and ascended upward.

"If I were ever to have a partner," Jack said with a laugh, "it would be you."

The reaver released a rumbling snarl that carried a tinge of humor. *If there were ever a human I would not kill, it would be you.*

They reached another set of stairs and charged up them into a broad courtyard. Battlements ringed the space with barracks beneath them. The ceiling contained runes and glyphs that illuminated the chaos.

A portcullis was halfway shut and guards massed on the battlements above it, aiming crossbows and gathering magic. The reaver charged the gate and slammed into it, releasing a *clang* so loud that everyone in the vicinity winced. But the gate held and continued to lower.

"Watch my back!" Jack shouted.

He dived under the portcullis and stood in the midst of the guards. They turned on him in astonishment, but he was too fast. He caught one man by his armor and knocked him into another, kicking his legs so they both went down.

An elf lunged for him but Jack slipped to the side, catching his wrist and yanking him from his feet. Jack took advantage of the space to raise his crossbow and fire ice bolts into the remaining soldiers. Frost exploded around them, freezing them together in a comical pose.

Growling and straining to free themselves, the soldiers tipped to the side and slid down the wall, putting one soldier's face on the ground. Jack heard his muffled curses and laughed as he jumped over him to the guardhouse door.

The reaver released the portcullis and turned around, its bone-chilling snarls forcing the soldiers to gather into a single unit. Jack kicked the locked door from its hinges and leapt inside. Three guards rose to face him but he slipped past their swords and yanked the lever that raised the portcullis. Then he sidestepped a sword thrust and yanked the weapon free, jamming it into the workings. Dodging their furious attempts to stop him, he leapt out the window and rolled to his feet.

And found a Silver Guard gliding toward him.

"You can't stop it!" A guard snarled, and Jack looked down at the frozen soldier.

"I don't intend to," Jack said, and thumbed the rune for exploding bolts. As quick as he could pull the trigger he sent four into the Silver Guard. He ducked behind the pile of frozen soldiers as the bolts detonated, sending sizzling silver into the wall.

He patted the soldier on the head and leapt to the opening portcullis. There he found Captain Sinder stepping in front of the black reaver. He screamed at the beast and uncoiled a whip of pure light.

"You are mine, beast!"

He whipped her across the face, drawing blood. Then he reared back to strike again—but the reaver caught the whip and pulled it close, dragging the screaming captain with it.

I WAS NEVER YOURS!

The mental roar thundered in the minds of everyone present. The dark elves clasped their heads and fell to their knees, while Jack instinctively shut out the sound. Then the reaver grasped the dark elf and raked its claws across him, launching the corpse into the wall. Its primal roar boomed across the courtyard, causing even the Silver Guard to hesitate.

"Done?" Jack asked, striding to the reaver's side.

The reaver snorted and surged past him, its spikes scrapping against the portcullis. Jack followed and together they burst onto a city street filled with dark elves. Jack grinned as they scattered, then glanced at the reaver.

"Don't forget our deal."

The reaver snorted and tossed its head. Then it surged into a sprint across a bridge to a neighboring spine. The soldiers and Silver Guard hurled their weapons, and Jack ducked behind the reaver as arrows and spears clattered off the creature's armor. Enraged and empowered, the reaver could not be stopped, and it plowed through their ranks.

Dark elves and liquid silver were tossed aside but the beast did not go for the kill. Instead it accelerated toward a bridge that would take them to Enzoar, the spine closest to an exit. Jack followed the reaver as it continued its unchecked rampage. Dark elves crowded balconies and higher buildings, shouting and screaming as the pair raced by, but few braved the streets. Those that did were knots of soldiers intent on stopping their escape.

A group of mages stepped in front and cast a shield charm. Jack recognized the shimmering barrier as crafted from animal magic and realized it would sap the reaver's energy. Since the light was dim he cast his shadowhook, catching the face of the dark elf in the center. He came to a halt and yanked, pulling him from the line and disrupting the spell.

The black reaver shattered what remained of the shield and blasted through them, charging across another bridge. It reached a shimmering golden portcullis just as it lowered. The impact echoed across the underground city, and the metal bent inward. The enchantment flickered and weakened, allowing Jack to slip through the gap.

"One moment," he called to the reaver.

Hundreds of guards were in the courtyard and they started at his sudden appearance. Knowing he had only seconds before they would swarm him, he leapt to the guardhouse and grabbed the uniform of a dark elf at the winch controls. The elf sought to draw a blade but Jack heaved him out the door and yanked the lever that would raise the portcullis.

Shouts of dismay erupted in the courtyard and the soldiers rushed to the portcullis on the opposite side of the spine. A Silver Guard appeared in the guardhouse doorway with sword in hand, so Jack drew his dagger and deflected the strike. The Silver Guard struck from all sides, its blade turning into two, and then a spear.

Jack dodged and leapt, twisting to avoid a sudden javelin. Then he leapt to the ropes and kicked off the wall, twirling into a flip that carried him over the Silver Guard to the door. The Silver Guard's sword cleaved the door in two but Jack rolled and streaked away.

He sprinted across the courtyard as the reaver burst from beneath the portcullis. By sheer momentum the reaver scattered the hasty attempts to stop it. Together, they crossed the spine and reached the final gate when it was several feet off the ground. Bellowing in defiance, the reaver lowered its head and charged under it.

The gate groaned and rent as the reaver's spikes crashed through it, jamming it into the wall. Leaving the mangled portcullis behind, they raced across the bridge and through the archway that led to the wilds. The guards made a token attempt to stop them, but Jack spotted the fear on their faces.

The sounds of pursuit faded quickly as they left Elsurund behind. Shortly after, they came to a halt in a cavern shaped like a crescent moon. Illuminated by the glowing purple and green stones common in the Deep, the space branched into numerous side paths and corridors.

Abruptly the power of blood faded and the reaver slowed. It came to a halt and seemed to wilt. Jack's chest heaved from the flight and he began to laugh. Loud and laced with delight, the sound echoed off the stone walls and came back distorted.

Our escape amuses you?

Jack could hear the fatigue in the reaver's mental voice, but it also sounded like it was smiling. Abruptly he decided it was no beast, and deserved to be spoken to as a woman. He grinned when her great head turned to face him.

"How could it not?" he asked. "Did you see the shock on their faces?"

I've performed for their pleasure enough, she replied, her tone darkening.

"They were cheering *for* our escape," Jack said.

The reaver settled onto her haunches and regarded him with curiosity in her green eyes. The motion made her look like a dog—a

246

huge dog with metal spikes and jaws like a lion. He grinned at the mental image.

I cannot forgive them.

"Your tormentors have received their recompense," Jack said. "They tortured you and paid with their lives. I doubt the rest of the dark elves knew the truth."

They will continue to hunt my kind for the Trial, she said with a snarl.

"Perhaps," Jack said, "but they regard you as a dangerous beast. It will take time to capture another."

The reaver's laugh echoed in his head. *I* am *a dangerous beast.*

"No," Jack said. "You are an *intelligent* beast, and someday they will learn that."

The reaver stared at him for some time. *I thought you a criminal, a thief deserving of death, yet you speak with wisdom.*

"Don't tell my friends that," he said with a laugh. "I have a reputation to protect."

She chuckled again. *I smell your friends' presence, and there are dark elves with them. I wish to be gone before they appear or I may break my oath. Be well, Jack the thief. Do not be as trusting with others of my kind. They are unlikely to spare your life.*

"Farewell, Triskella," he said. "Say hello to your children for me."

The reaver rose to her feet and plodded toward a side tunnel. She paused on the threshold and swung her head back to Jack.

When all around me saw me as a tool of destruction, you did not. You have my gratitude . . . and my allegiance. If you ever have need of me, I make my home next to Diamond Falls, twelve days east of here.

"I assure you, the pleasure was mine," Jack said.

She rumbled a laugh and then departed. Evidently waiting for the reaver to leave, his friends stepped into view. The other thieves

247

cautiously approached with Val'Trisian and a contingent of dark elves. Jack turned to them with a smile on his face.

"Ready to depart? We have an assassin to find."

They stared at him with looks ranging from incredulous to furious. Then Lorelia released an explosive breath and stabbed a finger toward the tunnel where the reaver had left.

"You couldn't wait until we got you out?"

"Nemeth was in the Pit."

She blinked in surprise at the name, and Val'Trisian nodded. "Instead of an execution the queen decided to leave him in prison until his death. Frankly I thought he would perish within a month."

"Nemeth was always devious," Lorelia said. "I suspect he managed to ingratiate himself with those in power."

"He had," Jack said, recalling how he spoke with the durans. "And apparently he'd spent the last year preparing for the Trial so he could come after me and exact his revenge."

"And you expected him to survive the trial?" Thalidon asked, raising an eyebrow.

Jack snorted scornfully. "Of course not. But once I was in the prison he didn't have to."

"He would have killed you there," Ursana said, her eyes lighting with understanding.

"He tried," Jack said. "And I couldn't wait."

"So you decided to attempt a Trial that had never been won?" Roarthin asked, and folded his arms.

"You make it sound like it was hard."

Gordon laughed. "Then what *happened*?"

"I too would like to know," Val'Trisian said. "How did you tame the untamable beast?"

248

Jack pointed to the ceiling. "Guide us to Griffin and I'll tell you on the way."

Val'Trisian glanced at the soldiers behind her and then back to him. "You have yourself a deal." Then she turned down a different corridor from the one the reaver had taken. "Speak," she commanded. "How did you ally with the black reaver during the Trial?"

"I didn't do it *during* the trial," Jack said, and a sly grin spread on his features. "I did it the night before . . ."

Chapter 30: Reaver

The Night Before the Trial

Lights darkened on the common platform, signaling an hour before they had to return to their cells. Many of the prisoners ambled their way to the spiral staircases. Jack fell into step behind those in his block but slowed his pace, allowing the distance to grow between them.

Ascending at the back of the line of criminals, he came to the point where the spiral staircase ascended into the ceiling. Instead of continuing to the private cells, he reached for a crack in the roof. With great care he slipped off the staircase and hung from the dark surface of the prison ceiling.

Deep in shadow he was nearly invisible to the prisoners fifty feet below him, and he took his time crossing the uneven surface. His fingers strained to hold his body weight as he crept toward the guard stations. Then he reached the lip and paused.

A bowl had been hollowed out of the ceiling. Like three bubbles, the guard houses were grouped near the center. Silver Guard and soldiers stood within, scanning the prisoners below. When they looked away Jack scaled over the lip and climbed to the recessed ceiling.

Slowing his pace, he eased himself up the curve until he came to the side of the guardhouse. Then he spun his body and put a foot on a knob protruding from the wall above the guards. He righted himself and took a moment to rest his burning arms, taking advantage of the time to examine the guardhouses up close.

Each hung from the ceiling and contained two soldiers and two Silver Guard. Walkways extended between the guardhouses to a circular hub at the center, where a spiral staircase ascended into the rock above.

Making his way towards it, he descended to a window and peaked inside. A sudden shout from within sent his heart hammering in his chest. He looked down to find two durans arguing, and a Silver Guard flowed out of a guardhouse. As it intervened Jack levered himself through the window, using the distraction to reach the staircase and ascend.

He reached the level above and found himself in a circular chamber with eight corridors stretching away from him. A pair of guards appeared in one, so he chose another. Advancing on cautious steps he checked each door he passed.

Spotting a door without a lock, he eased it open and slipped inside. Instead of a room, he found himself in a short hallway with several more doors. He checked each and found stores of food, bedding, and clothing. He snagged a handful of dried fruit and moved on. At the last room he found several crates holding guard uniforms, and wasted no time in changing into one. He doubted it would hold up to close scrutiny, but in the dim lighting it would buy him precious seconds.

He exited the storage room and entered an empty corridor. When a patrolling guard appeared at the end he veered into a side hallway to avoid him. After the dark elf passed Jack continued his search for an exit.

Over the next few minutes he mapped out the roughly circular level, but to his dismay the four stairs ascending upward were all protected by Silver Guard, and the few windows contained curses he could not bypass without his tools. The only anomaly was a section of the floor that was guarded by a different contingent of guards.

Dressed in grey and black armor and bearing the insignia of a steel spike, the Reaver Guard patrolled a section of the prison distinct from the rest. Curious, Jack managed to slip through their patrols and wound his way to a small enclosure set at the exterior of the spine. He turned the corner and came to a halt when he found the cage.

And the black reaver.

At fourteen feet long the beast was larger than a tigron, its body muscled and layered in metal spikes growing from its back and flanks. A metal ball sat in one corner of the cell but the teeth marks made it clear it used it to chew, not for play. Then he recalled that the minerals and iron that black reavers consumed coated bones, teeth, and eventually grew spikes on their back. It regarded him with an intelligent, curious gaze.

You're not one of the Reaver Guard.

The words came to Jack's mind just like his panther's had, and the voice was distinctly female. He flinched from the mental contact, unprepared for the link. The last time he'd felt it had been as Shadero died, giving his life so Jack could survive.

"I'm a thief," Jack said.

The reaver snorted and looked away. *That explains the reek.*

"I've only been here four days," Jack said, indignant. "And I don't plan on staying long."

They all think that, before they die in the Trial.

"And how many pay you a visit?"

She turned back to him and her lips parted to reveal her teeth. *None,* she admitted, and it sounded like she was smiling. *Did you wish to see the harbinger of your death before it kills you?*

Jack laughed lightly. "I don't intend to offend you, but I have no intention of participating in the Trial. I sought to escape, but that proved impossible. Then I found you."

Her mental laugh lacked humor. *You are smarter than you appear, human. Who are you?*

"Jack Myst," he replied, bowing to the reaver. "And you?"

Triskella, she replied, her humor returning. *I do believe you are the first to ask.*

"How long have you been here?"

Nine years, she replied. *Ever since they took me from my young.*

"You're a mother?"

Your surprise is offensive, she said, and a low rumble escaped her throat. *Are we not capable of bearing children?*

"You just seemed younger than that."

Her laugh rustled the spikes on her back, scraping metal on metal. *You think me vain enough to be consoled by that?*

"Of course I do," Jack said, and he gestured wide. "Females of every race like to feel attractive—and young. I assumed it no different for you.'

A growl escaped her throat as she laughed again, but before she could respond a group of footfalls echoed around the corner. On instinct Jack leapt for the bars and scaled to the ceiling, shifting into a darkened corner. His passage took him close enough for the reaver to shred his limbs, but her attention was on a turn in the hallway, where four members of the Reaver Guard appeared.

The elf in the lead, a shorter than average member of his race, came to a halt just outside the reaver's reach. He smirked, his features lit by a possessive light. Then he turned, providing Jack a glimpse of his features.

Captain Sinder stood below him.

"Are you ready for the Trial, beast?"

She ignored him, causing rage to flit across his features. He reached to his side and withdrew a rod of yellow light. A flick caused it to extend into a whip of light. Then he reared back and snapped it at the black reaver. The magic passed through the bars like they didn't exist and struck her exposed forearm.

The flesh split and she snarled, rising up onto he paws. Gone was the intelligent creature that Jack had spoken to, and a supreme predator had taken its place. Blood trickled to the stone at her feet. As she moved Jack noticed the scars lining her powerful forearms, the marks matching that of the new wound.

A smile appeared on the captain and his companions. He flicked the whip again and struck at her, drawing blood across her limbs until she charged the bars, slamming against them in a frenzy. The entire chamber shook from the impact, nearly dislodging Jack from his perch. He tightened his grip but did not take his eyes off the reaver. Her display of power may have been caged, but it was terrifying and shocking. Instinctively Jack searched for exits, wanting to be gone in case she broke free and set to slaughter.

"Are you hungry yet?" the captain asked, heedless of the roaring creature driving for his throat. "It's been four days since you've eaten, but I'm sure you'll feed well tomorrow. I know you don't care for prisoner flesh, but perhaps when you are hungry enough, you will."

His companions laughed but he continued to watch the rampaging beast with a lidded gaze. Then abruptly the reaver regained control and withdrew with a parting snarl. She stood on her hind legs and grasped the bars, attempting to drive them apart. The captain sighed and whipped her again until she relented and dropped to the stone.

"Will you not speak to me today?" the captain asked. "Do I not deserve to hear your voice?"

The reaver reached to her flank and snapped a spike from her flesh. Then she hurled it through the bars. The captain dived to the side but the spike plunged into the arm of the laughing elf behind him. He shrieked in agony and the captain signaled the others to take him out.

"Well done, beast," he said, his voice triumphant. "Now I can petition the queen for more restrictions to be placed upon you. I hope you enjoy the chains."

His mocking laugh followed him from the room, and when it faded Jack descended to face her once more. She did not meet his gaze, but instead stared out the tiny window at the lights of the city.

"I'm sorry."

I DON'T NEED YOUR PITY, HUMAN!

Her mental roar accompanied her strike at the bars again. The rage and hatred in her voice were tinged with shame, causing Jack to reach down and pick up the spike from where it lay. Raising it to his hand, he sliced his palm and allowed his blood to coat the spike. Then he offered it through the bars.

"I'm told you gain the abilities of the blood you take," he said. "I heal quickly."

The seconds passed and he expected her to refuse. The reaver finally turned to face him and then approached. Biting the spike from his hand, she licked it clean and tossed it away. She shook herself and some of the tension melted away. Between his blood and her innate capacity to absorb energy, her wounds began to knit. Then she leveled her gaze upon him.

You are a strange man, Jack of thieves.

"I don't care for cruelty," he said, his tone turning dark as he looked to where the captain had left.

One day I will kill him.

Brutal and laced with hate, the words left no doubt in his mind that she would find a way to do it. He wanted to help but his predicament was no less dire. Then a thought crossed his mind and he smiled slyly.

"What if your day was tomorrow?"

Her lion-like head swiveled to him. *How can that be?*

Heedless of the danger he stepped close to the bars. "I think it's about time the Trial had a victor, don't you?"

Her head was at his level, and they were so close she could have reached through the bars and ripped him apart. Instead she cocked her head to the side and bared her teeth. The anticipation in her eyes was unmistakable.

Tell me your plan, thief.

Chapter 31: Doubts

Lorelia shook her head in admiration. "You *stole* the Allegian Trial?"

"If I hadn't seen it, I wouldn't believe it," Gordon said.

Ursana snorted in disbelief and didn't look up from her work on her crossbow. "You've worked with Jack enough. I'd think you would know him by now."

Thalidon grunted in amusement. "The girl's words have merit."

Beauty laughed lightly and her eyes connected with Jack's. "When will I learn not to doubt your talents?"

Jack snorted. "I'll try to be a patient instructor."

Jack leaned back against the rock, his smile fading as they discussed what he'd done. As much fun as it had been to escape Elsurund he could not shake the thought that Gallow had a six-day lead on them. Even with Val'Trisian's help he doubted they could reach Margauth before the assassin.

At the same time an elusive irritation tugged at his mind. After a moment's thought he realized it was directed at himself. He'd failed to get the key, and what's worse, Gallow had retrieved them both.

Fatigue finally drove them to their bedrolls but Jack continued to stare into the flames. They were using the dead stalks of large mushrooms for cooking. The strange fuel cast a greenish tint to the fire that was beautiful and mesmerizing. He glanced at his slumbering companions scattered around the fire, but his irritation mounted. It had been a long time since he'd failed.

The next morning Jack rose to find the levity of the previous night had been extinguished. The thieves still laughed and spoke of Elsurund, but there was a tightness about their features that implied a sense of urgency. Jack knew what they were concerned about, and by unspoken accord the group quickened their pace back to the surface.

The eastern roadway that ascended from the Deep lacked the refinement of the dwarven-built road, and on several occasions they passed the remains of travelers. Evidently ambushed and killed by the denizens of the Deep, their bones lay about the ashes of fires, their packs picked clean by other travelers.

After another ten days, the rock turned to soil, and several hours later they passed into the open. Jack breathed a sigh of relief as he looked up at the endless sky. A smile spread on his features as he sucked in the scent of cedar.

The last vestiges of sunset lingered on the horizon, lighting the edge of heaven in purple and pink. Stars dotted the rest of the sky, growing brighter by the second as if eager to greet the night. Cedar trees obscured the region around the cave and climbed onto the surrounding hills. Val'Trisian bid them farewell, departing with a kiss on Jack's check.

"Come back anytime, Jack of thieves," she said with a warm smile. Then she was gone.

Jack sighed in regret. "I like the Deep."

"You would," Ursana said with a sour laugh. "But I think I'm done with dark elf assignments."

"You and me both," Gordon said with a relieved smile.

"They have their own guild," Beauty said. "And I got the impression they didn't think much of us."

"That was before Jack used the Trial to escape," Lorelia remarked.

Jack grinned and then shivered as a gust of icy wind carved into his flesh. Cursing the cold, he reached into his pack and withdrew his shaden cloak. The others followed suit, and by the time they were wrapped in warmth the sun had set, plunging them into darkness.

"We should hasten," Beauty said. "We have no way of knowing what Skorn intends."

"Skorn has the keys by now," Roarthin said. "He's probably already on his way to the Vault of the Eternals."

"Perhaps not," Jack mused. "He's worked very hard to keep himself out of sight. Do you really expect him to risk all that?" He shook his head. "He'll use a pawn, just like he always has."

Beauty was nodding. "He calculates and manipulates, but never rushes."

"Excellent," Jack said. "Then we find an inn and stay for the night."

"I think we're north of Crossroads," Gordon said, and motioned to the cedar trees. "If we make our way there we can find rooms. In the morning we can seek mounts before pressing on."

"You really think he'll wait?" Thalidon asked as they set off down a trail.

Roarthin grunted sourly. "He kept me in a cell for twenty years while he waited for a thief capable of stealing the ancient map. Time is meaningless to him."

"We can craft a plan on the way," Lorelia said. "If we are close to Crossroads, we're a fortnight from the citadel. We'll have plenty of time to consider our options."

Jack buried his concerns beneath a smile and agreed. "The last bed I slept in was inside a dark elf prison."

"You know you enjoyed every minute," Ursana said with a grin.

He set off into the trees. "Guilty as charged," he said. The others laughed.

260

For the next few hours they worked their way through the darkened forest. Several times someone made a disparaging remark about Gordon's sense of direction, but as the hour neared midnight they reached the edge of a large settlement.

Built around a strategic intersection, Crossroads had grown from a collection of inns and taverns into a sprawling and disorganized city. Its position a few miles east of Terros made its population largely transient, with travelers and merchants headed to the middle cities, soldiers marching to the northern forts, or workers going to the mines in the south of Griffin. With winter fast approaching, the settlement was packed with individuals seeking to complete their business before snow blanketed the roads.

The better inns were already full, forcing them to choose a seedy location at the edge of town. Jack nearly suggested they sleep on the ground but a gust of wind drove him into the leaning structure.

The food was as bad as he'd expected, but at least the linens on the bed was clean. He slept well, and for the first time in months rose before dawn. Plodding downstairs, he was not surprised to find the others already eating. Even Gordon sat at a table drinking his morning cha and yawning. Jack slid into a seat beside him and took a roll from his plate.

"Has anyone else grown tired of chasing these blasted keys?" he asked, his mouth muffled by the food.

"We can't just let him have them," Lorelia protested.

"We have to find them," Beauty said, her jaw set in a firm line. "We must destroy them before Skorn gets whatever he's after."

"You assume they *can* be destroyed," Roarthin said with a grunt.

"Everything can be destroyed," Ursana said.

The dwarf cast her an appraising look. "True," he relented, "but objects of ancient make have defied time and effort to break them."

"I destroyed the map," Jack said, and briefly shared the tale of the map Skorn had sought, including when he had tossed it to the vintor. "I watched it snap into sparks and bits of nothing," he finished. "I'm

261

certain the keys could be destroyed—unless you are saying we've found something even a dwarf cannot break."

Thalidon smirked at the challenge. "Your map aside, most relics that remain from the Dawn of Magic do so because they were *made* to endure. I suspect the keys are such artifacts."

"You shouldn't have kept it on you," Beauty said.

Jack laughed and signaled the barmaid for a meal. "That's what I said. A smart thief stashes the assignment if he thinks he'll be caught."

"You *never* think you'll be caught," Beauty said shrewdly.

"Did you have it on you in Cliffwatch?" Gordon asked, causing the table to go quiet.

Jack's eyes flicked to a tiny scar on Ursana's neck, a legacy of Gallow's attempt to kill her. "I almost threw it into the sea, but couldn't bring myself to do it."

"You should have," Ursana muttered. "Let him go swimming for it."

Her comment eased the sudden tension. Lorelia's brow furrowed in thought, and then she shook her head. "To do so would have been terribly shortsighted."

"How is throwing Skorn's desire into the ocean shortsighted?" Beauty countered.

"Because everything that is hidden eventually comes to light," she replied. "It may not be in the next few years—or even in our lifetimes— but Skorn would find it. Do not forget he has lived for over *forty thousand years*. What's a few decades to someone like him?"

Jack grunted in exasperation. "Then what do we do once we get the keys?"

"We find a place even he cannot go," Lorelia said, a smile playing across her features.

"But the only place he cannot go is . . ." Jack's eyes widened. ". . . the vault."

"What do you mean?" Beauty asked.

"We get the keys and open the vault," Jack said. "Then we toss the keys in and let it shut."

His smile widened as he imagined leaving the keys in the one place Skorn could not get to. The man would be trapped outside the vault for eons, knowing that what he sought lay just beyond the door.

"I think you just want to steal from the Vault of the Eternals," Roarthin said, skewering him with a look.

"There would be no harm in taking a peak," Jack said with a smile. "Then I drop the keys and walk out."

"I don't think that's wise," Beauty said. "What if you end up stealing the very thing he wants?"

Ursana laughed. "Why does Jack get to enter the vault and not me?" Her eyes twinkled with amusement.

"Because it was my idea," Jack reasoned.

A chorus of protests erupted, drawing irritated looks from the other patrons. Lorelia was quick to quiet them before they drew too much attention, and then leaned in. A smile crossed her flawless features and her eyes flicked to Jack.

"We get the keys," she said. "And then we find out exactly what lies within this vault, together."

Roarthin shocked his brother by slamming a fist onto the table. "You're fools."

Thalidon glared at him. "Why say that?"

"Because seated at this table are the best of thieves in Lumineia," he said. "And he will want to use *one of you* to get into the vault. You're playing into his hands."

"Only if we get caught," Jack said.

263

Roarthin turned on him with a vengeance. "This is the time for caution."

"I know," Jack interrupted with an annoyed sigh. "I'm not a fool."

Roarthin was on his feet. "Luck has kept us alive for now, but luck never holds. Even for you, Jack." He turned and stomped away.

When he was gone Beauty nodded. "He's right. We can't expect to walk into Margauth and steal what he's been seeking for ages."

"Why not?" Jack asked. "We're thieves, after all, and as Roarthin said, some of the best."

"Your arrogance knows no bounds," Beauty said to Jack, her tone biting enough that the humor faded from the table.

Stung, Jack folded his arms. "We can't very well leave him with the keys. Lorelia's right, he won't stop until he gets what he wants."

"Don't pretend you care about the world."

A thief has no honor.

Jack's mother's words came back in force but Jack shoved them away. "Perhaps I do," he said.

She glared at him before rising to her feet. "It may be a game to you, but our lives hang in the balance."

Jack made to argue but she stalked to the door and left. His anger rising, Jack followed her into the street and caught up to her. When he grabbed her arm she yanked it free and spun to face him.

"You risk your life like it does not matter," she growled. "But even you cannot think you can survive forever."

"You don't have to come," he replied heatedly. "We don't need you."

"I'm not going to abandon you," she said. "Unlike you, I actually care about my friends and—for reasons I cannot fathom—you."

She turned on her heel and strode away, leaving Jack standing in the empty street. He watched her retreating form, angry and confused. Then Beauty turned a corner and Jack lost sight of her. He released an explosive breath and trudged back to the inn, but her words would not be dismissed. As they embarked on their journey he began to wonder if she was right.

And if he was leading his friends into an ambush.

Chapter 32: Hilltop

They worked their way south and then east to reach the southern tip of Griffin. As they neared the border Jack began to notice an increase in travelers on the road. The change was almost imperceptible, but the occasional merchant or traveler became groups of two or three. Few were dressed as workmen returning from a season in the mines. They tried to hide it, but their expressions were excited for no apparent reason.

He noticed a woman riding behind them. Her gaze passed over him, dismissing him as if he didn't matter. He realized the woman knew he wasn't a member of the cult, but could not hazard a guess as to how. Smiling blandly at them, Lorelia passed them and took the first turn in view of the cultists. Once they had passed on, Lorelia shook her head.

"We are known by too many," she said. "We should split up and enter Hilltop under guise."

She pointed to the sign at the crossroads, *Hilltop 6 miles*. A second sign sat below it, the wood rotted and the lettering barely discernible. Jack squinted and managed to make out, *Margauth 18 miles*.

Jack pulled the reins toward the forest. "Watch out for Gallow."

Lorelia grunted in agreement and led her horse in another direction. The thieves slipped into the forest and Jack made his way alone. He found a trail and followed it toward the village, arriving shortly before nightfall.

Jack spotted a hut outside the village and took a set of woodsman's clothing. Slipping into the persona of a woodsman, he wiped grease from the hut's equipment and darkened his features. Then he added a scar on his cheek. Leaving the horse at the hut, he strode into the village and made his way to the sole tavern.

He doubted he would find a room but strode inside anyway. After some sharp elbowing he managed to find a small corner table. Feigning weariness, he listened to the talk wafting across the establishment. Beauty he spotted first, although she was far less attractive. She sat at the bar dressed in drab clothing, her hair soiled and her cheeks stained. Several wrinkled their nose as they came close to her, indicating she'd used smell to add to her persona.

He spotted Thalidon and Roarthin when they entered dressed as miners. They took a seat across the tavern. Jack withdrew a piece of parchment and scribbled indecipherable notes on it but he needn't have bothered. The villagers assumed he was part of the sudden influx of travelers, while the cult members assumed he was a villager.

He learned a great deal just by listening. The village veritably bustled with cult members journeying to Margauth. The confused village members struggled to cater to their demands, and many of the poorer families rented out their own beds, opting to sleep in the barn in order to make extra coin. Hilltop sat on the road to the southern mines, but it was also the last stop on the road to Margauth.

A few hours later Lorelia walked into the tavern with two companions. In the depths of a human merchant's guise he almost didn't recognize her, but there was no mistaking Gordon. The man lacked any talent for subterfuge, and hardly looked different from earlier in the day.

Ursana had donned the persona of their daughter. She was seventeen but her persona made her look younger. Her gaze slid over Jack twice before she recognized him, and a slight smile crossed her features. She nudged Lorelia and the trio made their way to his table.

"With this crowd we'll have to conduct our business outside," Jack said loudly.

Lorelia cursed the crowd and stabbed a finger toward the door. "After you."

Jack led them out of the tavern and into the forest. A short distance away they came to an abandoned shed. Slipping inside, Jack drew a candle from his pack and then shut the door, plunging them into darkness. With his sparklight he lit the candle. The illumination revealed a squat hut that smelled faintly of mold. A makeshift cot sat on one side, while rusted farm equipment hung on the wall.

Jack relaxed against the wall. "As you can see, cult members are flocking to Margauth. Apparently Skorn has made an impression."

"He's gathering his forces," Lorelia said. "I've spotted a fair number of soldiers and weapons trainers heading up the pass."

Gordon slipped onto the cot. "It's been a hard road. Any chance we can sleep before we start all this?"

"Perhaps," Jack said, "but this is no normal assignment, and we need to stay sharp."

"Is that a trace of caution I hear?" Lorelia asked.

Reluctant to admit his concerns, Jack forced a smile. "I relish a challenge—and stealing from a devil worshiping cult qualifies as one."

"We're ready for Skorn," Ursana said, her face set.

She flicked a bulge in her pack. Her crossbow emitted a dull whine in response, as if it too was eager for the fight. Jack peaked an eyebrow at her but her smile widened.

"I had a mage add a charm while we passed through Torridin. I haven't had the chance to use it yet."

"How much did that cost you?" Lorelia asked.

"Too much," Gordon said.

"It was worth it," she said defensively. "Looks like we're facing a thousand cultists."

Gordon gave a sour laugh. "He took on the persona of a fallen god—which he actually is. Evil or not, the man has style."

"Regardless," Jack said, "it will be nigh impossible to get in."

Lorelia's eyes glowed in the firelight. "You have a plan."

"Of course," Jack said, and a sly grin spread on his features. "But I don't think Gordon will like it."

The man frowned. "Is this going to get me killed?"

"Only if you don't run fast enough," Jack said, and laid out his plan.

Gordon's expression darkened. "I don't—"

"I like it," Lorelia said. "If we depart in the morning, we should reach Margauth at nightfall. I'll let the others know the plan." She put her hands together and fashioned three spiders. They glowed to life and dropped to the floor, skittering under the door and into the night.

"But—"

"Relax," Ursana said. "I'm sure you'll outrun them."

"Easy for you to say," Gordon grumbled.

"Rest while you can," Jack said. "We'll head up the canyon at nightfall."

In spite of his words Gordon was asleep in seconds. Lorelia remained awake for some time, her expression reflecting an internal conflict. Jack met her eyes but she looked away, her features tightening with sudden regret. Jack wanted to ask what troubled her, but since Ursana was still awake he chose to respect her silence. Shortly after, fatigue got the best of her, and she fell asleep reclining in the chair. When it became clear that Ursana would not rest, Jack pointed to Gordon.

"He really cares about you," he said quietly.

"You shouldn't have left."

Surprised by the harsh statement, he shrugged. "I needed answers—answers that wouldn't be found in the Thieves Guild."

"Did you ever want to be a thief?"

"No," Jack replied.

"You can't deny what you are, Jack."

Jack was on his feet. "Why do you care?"

"Because the guild is a family," Ursana said. "And you are part of it. You may not want the guild, but it needs you."

The force behind her words bound his tongue, and caused Lorelia to grunt in irritation. "If you're going to argue, go outside," she said.

"I'll take watch," Jack said, and escaped outside before Ursana could object. Once in the trees he climbed to a vantage point. From there he watched the gloomy forest and struggled to contain his anger. He half expected her to follow him but the door did not open. Too keyed up to sleep, Jack remained in the tree until midnight. Then he woke Gordon to take his place.

At dawn they gathered their things and slipped into the trees. Jack guided them past the thick trunks until he reached the road. Foregoing the open ground, they advanced parallel to it until the trees came to an end. Then they used the shadows to hide. An hour later the dwarves appeared and Jack stepped from the trees. Turning up the canyon, he hiked up the gravel road. Thalidon and Roarthin kept their distance, suggesting they were two parties rather than one. He caught glimpses of Beauty on the mountain above.

The wind whistled about them, haunting and sinister as if warning them of their path. Jack shivered within his shaden, irritated that he could not shake his worry. Several times they encountered cultists, but they were quick to dodge behind the many boulders strewn about the pass.

They hiked throughout the day and still the canyon continued. Grey stone rose on either side, climbing to the heavens. Patches of snow were visible on the peaks above, and icicles dotted the stone where the snow had melted.

The sun sunk toward the horizon at their back, falling behind a mountain and robbing the pass of warmth. Nightfall came quickly, leaving them hiking beneath the starry sky. Shortly after sunset they reached the fortress.

The road curved and Margauth came into view. Situated in the cleft between two peaks, the fortress looked down upon the road's terminus. A great wall spanned the canyon, separating the road from the sprawling courtyard.

Jack's gaze was drawn to the features of the citadel. The massive jaws and teeth made the mountain look like it caged a beast within the stone. The enormous eyes were tilted in fury, glowing with light from the interior. Although Jack heard the clank of armor and the whisper of voices, the fortress lay disturbingly quiet.

Instead of elven light orbs, the exterior wall was lit with green torches, the flames as tall as a man. They crackled and sparked, the fires shifting between various scenes of Skorn's life. They also illuminated the road below, preventing anyone from approaching without being seen.

The firelight reflected off the gaping jaws of the citadel, simmering in the eyes and making the beast appear more visceral. Bathed in green light, the cliffs surrounding the fortress seemed to shift and move, their contours conforming with the shadows.

Green-cloaked figures patrolled the battlements of the courtyard wall, their numbers suggesting they were expecting a conflict. The glint of steel was visible, revealing the many weapons in easy reach. Eschewing the pool of light, the thieves slipped behind a cracked boulder to examine their target. A moment later Beauty dropped down to join them.

"Look," she whispered, and gestured to the cliffs surrounding the castle.

Jack peered at them and spotted a small orb bracketed into the stone. Another lay nearby, and another. Then Jack saw the pattern and it was easy to spot the others. Layered and placed across the whole of the stone, the orbs would bathe the cliffs in light if activated. The protection was costly and unnecessary—unless one knew that thieves favored shadowhooks.

"He's ready for us," Jack said. "Gordon, you know what to do."

"I still don't like it," he said acidly. "And I don't see why *I* have to do it."

"Relax," Jack said. "If he catches you, he won't kill you until he has answers."

Gordon released a low growl and then removed his cloak. "If they kill me, don't let them have my body."

"Stop complaining," Ursana hissed at him. "This won't work if they think you're terrified."

"I *am* terrified."

Jack grinned as Gordon stepped into the open and strode toward the gates. The light revealed his white robes, marking him as a priest of the Church of Light. Striding across the cold stone, he came to a halt outside of crossbow range.

"Cult of Skorn!" he shouted. "We have long known of your blasphemies, and I call on you to hear my words!"

Laughter scattered across the battlements, and someone shouted a reply. "Go home, priest. We do not serve your false god!"

"False god?" Gordon roared. "You dare to call Ero, Herald of Light, Dawn of Magic, *a false god*?"

"You come to our door and spout your twisted doctrine?" a woman shouted, anger in her voice. "Your bravery will get your killed. I warn you again, depart in peace while you yet have your legs."

"Skorn is the devil, cast out by Ero for attempting to destroy Lumineia. Yet you worship him? What sort of person believes such filth?"

"Filth?" came the sputtered reply, and a ripple of anger filled the battlements. "You have twisted a religion for the purpose of gold, and you call us filth? Your entire faith is a sham."

"Your deity is dead!" Gordon shouted. "Killed by Ero in their final battle. And we are better now that such waste has been executed."

"Your ignorance is astounding, priest," the woman shrieked. "For Skorn walks with us this very day, and soon your entire church will be destroyed."

"You dare to threaten a servant of the Light?" Gordon shouted. "We should call on Ero to strike you down."

"You have no power here!" the woman screamed. "Nor anywhere in Lumineia. We serve Skorn here."

"I know," Gordon called, and his voice dripped with pity. "But you can always repent."

The woman screamed at him, but the words were no longer intelligible. Jack sensed the current of rage stretching to the breaking point and smiled, mentally praising Gordon for his persona. Then Gordon raised his hand a final time and issued a thundering roar.

"Skorn is *nothing but a slain devil*!"

Abruptly the door cracked open and cultists burst into view. Gordon turned and fled. Sprinting into the darkness, he raced down the road with hundreds of enraged worshipers shrieking at him. Jack stifled a laugh as he watched them flood past their hiding spot. Then he turned to the others.

"They left the door open for us," he said, and smirked. "How can we turn down such an invitation?"

Chapter 33: Skorn

From deep in the shadows Jack watched the cultists stream by. He grinned to the dwarves, who nodded and slipped away with Beauty. Then Jack led Lorelia and Ursana from their hide. Gliding through the shadows, they darted to the open doors and slipped inside. As Jack had guessed, most of the cult members had left their posts to punish Gordon. Their numbers were intimidating, but they lacked the discipline of a true army. Under Lorelia's light bending charm the thieves slipped through the remaining guards.

"How did you know so many would follow Gordon?" Lorelia whispered once they were inside the fortress.

"They're cultists," Jack said. "How trained could they be?"

"What if Gordon can't outrun them?" Ursana whispered.

"He has a speedstone," Jack said. "So unless they have magic he should have no trouble reaching Hilltop."

They crept through the shadows that surrounded the courtyard. Then they slipped into an armory and made their way to the opposite door. Easing it open, they glided into the keep that abutted the mountain. Lorelia paused to snag a trio of green cloaks and tossed two to Jack and Ursana.

"Might as well blend in."

Jack donned his and then strode down the side hall, searching for a way upward. Mentally he counted the seconds and then they found the stairs. Then the sounds of returning cultists echoed from the exterior.

"Split up. Meet back in the courtyard in ten minutes—whether you have the keys or not."

They nodded and slipped away, and Jack took the largest corridor into the mountain. Finding a set of stairs, he ascended to the second level. Several times he passed a cult member but they did not bother him inside his cloak, and a moment later he reached the great hall.

He slipped into the shadows cast by a statue and scanned the area, searching for hint of a strongroom. A handful of green cloaked figures moved about, with several exiting or entering the large double doors leading higher into the keep. Jack pictured what he'd seen of the keep and frowned.

The interior of the citadel had been carved from caves within the cliff, and apparently divided into three levels. The lowest contained training rooms, armories, barracks, and storage rooms. A single set of doors allowed entry into the fortress's mouth on the second level. Jack guessed from the layout that the area behind the eyes on the top of the fortress would also be isolated.

Feigning nonchalance, Jack ascended to second level. A cult member swung it open just as he reached it, and he smoothly stepped into the opening with a nod of gratitude. Then he entered the amphitheatre.

The stonework of the benches was old but well maintained, and faced the stage that abutted the teeth. The amphitheatre faced the jaws of the fortress, making it feel as if Jack stood within the mouth of the mountain.

The roof of the cavern remained unchanged from the original cave, while the floor had been cut into benches that descended to a raised stage. Packed with cultists, the amphitheatre was disturbingly silent.

Jack slipped into an empty seat in the back row. His irritation mounted as the seconds ticked by but no one appeared, and no one moved. Then the arched opening that sat against the platform shimmered and the stone parted like a veil, allowing Skorn to enter. By unspoken accord the audience stood, causing Skorn to smile at them.

It had been several months since Jack had seen Skorn, but the man had not changed. Tall and lean, he exuded a menace that went beyond his dark eyes. His features were stark and angular, and would have been considered handsome without the scars. A quartet of white lines twisted his face, the mark of a great cat swiping at his skull. Ugly and wide, the scars seeped with menace.

"You have worshiped me for forty thousand years," Skorn said, "and the time has come for the kingdoms of Lumineia to witness my might."

Whispers swept across the cultists and they murmured avowals of worship. Skorn strode across the stage, his boots clipping against the stone, hard and menacing. His gaze swept across the crowd, lit by triumph.

"But on this day some have come with the purpose of harming me."

The whispers gained an angry tint. Skorn smiled but the expression merely bent the scars, making it cruel rather than kind.

"You have nothing to fear," he said. "For they cannot harm me."

He gestured to the arch and Ursana was pulled into view and shoved to the floor. She blinked in the glare of the light orbs and forced herself to her feet. She flinched as the cultists began to shout for her death. Then two more were shoved through the opening. Gordon and Lorelia stumbled to Ursana's side and stood with her, forming a protective circle. Their hands in shackles and their faces bruised, they faced the crowd with defiance on their features.

Skorn raised his chin and the crowd went eerily silent. "Jack Myst . . . welcome to my home. Would you care to join me?"

Before Jack could move the cult member in front of him turned to face him, and those beside him followed suit. Then the entire crowd turned to stare at him, their expressions rigid with simmering rage. The one at Jack's side turned as well and Jack's eyes widened in recognition.

276

"Gallow," Jack said, and sniffed in disgust. "When did you even become his pet?"

Gallow sneered at his words, a touch of red climbing into his skin. "I obey him because I know what he is." Disdain and fear rippled his features, making it evident that Gallow did not serve Skorn by choice.

Gallow shoved him toward the aisle, but he slipped out of Gallow's hold and descended the steps. The seething rage from both sides seemed to strike at him, and several spit on his cloak. He blew out his breath in disgust.

"You should keep your dogs on a leash," he said.

Someone reached for him but Skorn barked an order and they withdrew. "Must you enrage everyone you meet?" he said with a sigh.

Jack grinned as he stepped onto the platform. "Must every fool offend so easily?"

"You are the fool," Skorn said, "for thinking you could enter my halls unnoticed. Have you already forgotten what I am capable of?"

"Of course not," Jack said with a snort. "Which is why I didn't come alone."

Skorn gestured to the three shackled thieves. "Your arrogance will be your end, Jack."

Jack grinned. "Couldn't have said it better myself."

Skorn's eyes narrowed and flicked to the others. His calculating look only served to heighten Jack's amusement. Then Skorn snapped to look at him—and the lights winked out. Extinguished with a shocking suddenness, it stunned everyone in the room. Then Skorn's bellow rent the darkness.

"There are others! Find them!"

Men and women scrambled about, and the sounds of their billowing cloaks filled the chamber. Shouts rang out as someone tripped, smashing a knee into a stone bench. Another cursed, accidently using

Skorn's name in vain. Then the spell came to an end and the lights blazed to life.

Jack and the others were gone.

The empty stage drew a collective gasp, and Skorn's roar galvanized them to action. "FIND THEM!"

As the cultists scrambled to obey Skorn's orders, Jack slipped out a side door and raced down the corridor leading deep into the mountain. Thalidon joined him, and a moment later Roarthin appeared.

"Took you long enough to get in," Lorelia said.

Thalidon tapped the wall with his fist. "It's granite and marble. We were lucky to get through at all."

"At least we have our exit," Gordon said. "I'd rather not be left at the mercy of these people." He gestured to the unconscious cultists scattered across the floor of the tunnel.

The tunnel forked ahead, and as they reached it Beauty appeared. Across the way Jack met her eyes, and grinned. She'd been on the front row of the amphitheatre when Jack had taken the stage, and dropped the lights with a darkstone.

"Did you find the keys?"

She smirked and twirled them in the air. "I took them off Skorn when the lights went out."

Jack laughed and accelerated to catch up to her. "Then let's go."

"Are you enjoying this?" Roarthin asked with a scowl.

"You aren't?" Jack and Ursana said at the same time, and laughed in unison.

"They're gaining on us," Lorelia said, her voice rigid. "Ursana?"

"On it."

The girl pulled her crossbow into view and spun. Then she fired three bolts in quick succession. Gusts of wind burst from the weapon, guiding the bolts down the corridor and around the bend. Jack heard the impact and recognized the sound of bolts exploding ice, filling the corridor with a frozen wall. Muffled cries of dismay confirmed it.

"Wind magic?" Jack asked, peaking an eyebrow. "Is that what you had added in Torridin?"

Thalidon grunted in surprise. "Dwarves don't possess wind magic. Where did you get it?"

"A rock troll," Ursana said with a sly smile.

They reached the end of the corridor and Roarthin ushered them into a storage room. The moment the door slid shut, an explosion sounded in the distance, and hundreds of feet flooded into the tunnel.

"We don't have much time," Thalidon said. "I'll seal the door. The rest of you with Roarthin." He turned to the door and fire seeped from his fingers, turning the handle red.

As the metal fused to the frame Jack turned to Roarthin. "I hope you have an exit for us."

"Same way we came in," the dwarf said. "You're fortunate you have me. Thalidon was never good with stone magic."

Thalidon grunted. "You really want to compare talents now?"

Roarthin grinned and shoved a barrel out of the way to reveal a gaping hole in the back wall. The stone was rough and appeared half melted, as if fire had drilled into it.

"It connects to a ventilation shaft further up. Follow it to the surface and then descend to the road."

Beauty took the lead, her jaw set in a firm line. "Don't get lazy. We won't be safe until we've put Margauth at our backs."

She took a step toward the exit—and collapsed, crying out in pain. Jack leapt to her side but could do nothing as Beauty screamed. The others gathered about, craning to see.

"What happened?" Jack demanded.

Gasping in pain, she lifted the sleeve of her tunic to reveal a tiny cut along her shoulder. The blood was minimal, but it had a tinge of green to it that suggested poison. She ground her teeth together.

"It's stronger than my magic," she hissed.

Jack shook his head. "When did it happen?"

Her features twisted in agony and she arched her back. "In the hallway I felt a sting," she hissed. "When I looked no one was there."

Jack shook head. "That was after we stole the key . . ."

And it was just us.

He swiveled to face the thieves gathered around Beauty. Ursana and Gordon were closest, with Ursana holding Beauty's hand. Thalidon and Roarthin stood behind them, the fear on their faces making clear it wasn't them.

Lorelia was gone.

Then he spotted her by the door, using her magic on the handle. Jack lurched to his feet and shoved his way through but it was too late. Lorelia yanked the door open, revealing Skorn and Gallow framed in the opening.

Chapter 34: Betrayed

Jack stared at Lorelia, anger and shock dumping into his veins. "Why?" He spit the word at her.

Lorelia didn't meet Jack's gaze as she stepped to the side. "I have no choice."

"How could you do this to us?" Ursana said. "You hate him as much as we do."

"He has a way with manipulation," Lorelia said. She looked away, her expression pained.

"Traitor," Beauty said through clenched teeth, causing Lorelia's expression to tighten.

"You don't know anything about me," she snapped.

"You should not squabble," Skorn said, his smile turning smug as he stepped into the room. "I own you all, now."

"You don't own me," Thalidon barked.

The dwarf pulled an axe from his back and lunged for Skorn, but Gallow darted in and deflected the blow. He spun and kicked the dwarf in the temple, driving him to the floor. By then the rest of the group leapt into the fray.

Gallow deflected Roarthin's axe and launched his idalia spinning around them. In the confined space of the room they struggled to evade it, and Gallow slipped between them, striking on all sides.

Jack leapt over him and landed by Skorn but he shifted away. Jack's blade glanced off his forearm with clink of metal, revealing the steel-wrapped gauntlets beneath his robe. Jack stepped to the side, barely avoiding having his throat cut by the assassin's spinning blade. The motion allowed him to catch a glimpse of the room. With half the thieves groaning on the floor, the other half fought with ferocious valor, but Gallow was simply too fast. He slipped among them and knocked their blades aside, evading with the agility of a trained swordsman.

Skorn used Jack's distraction to strike his gut, driving the air from his lungs. Then he caught his tunic and threw him across the room. Jack crashed into the wall upside down, grunting from the impact before sliding to the floor. He just managed to get his hands down to prevent his skull from fracturing and rolled to his feet.

"Stop," Jack hissed. "Before they start killing."

"Wise words," Skorn said. "Gallow, leave them be."

Gallow looked up at him. He had a knee on Gordon's back and was about to strike at Ursana. He scowled at the order, but he caught the spinning blade and withdrew to Skorn's side. Groaning, the thieves pulled themselves to their feet.

"Why spare our lives?" Gordon asked, clenching the bloody furrow in his arm.

"A tool need not be destroyed until it is no longer useful," Skorn said. "But make no mistake, if you continue to defy me your lives have no purpose."

Beauty hissed in pain, drawing all eyes to her. "What sort of poison is this?" she asked.

Skorn withdrew a small vial from a pouch and tossed it to Jack, who caught it deftly. "Give it to her and see for yourself."

Jack exchanged a look with Beauty, but she shook her head. "It can't do anything worse than what's happening now."

He growled under his breath and stooped at Beauty's side. Her face was drawn and a sheen of sweat reflected off her skin. She clenched her side like it would alleviate the wracking pain. Then she arched her back, every muscle in her body contracting simultaneously and contorting her arms.

"Do it," she whispered. "He could have killed me already if he wanted to."

Jack hesitated, and then reluctantly tipped the liquid into her mouth. She gasped as it went down her throat, and then her body relaxed. She sighed in relief and weakly got to her feet. Then her eyes fell upon Skorn.

"Why heal me?" she asked.

"Because of him," Skorn said, stabbing at finger at Jack. "I need him, and this is the only way I can ensure obedience."

"You assume I care about her life," Jack said, and folded his arms.

"*Jack*," Beauty said, her voice wounded.

Skorn released a mocking laugh. "You can lie to me, but you can't lie to yourself. Two doses will cure the poison, and the first dose is temporary. If she fails to get the second, she will suffer an agonizing death." He reached into his pocket and withdrew another vial, holding it aloft so everyone could see it.

"What do you want?" Jack asked.

Skorn's eyes glittered in triumph. "As I'm sure you know, the Vault of the Eternals requires two keys to enter. Unfortunately, mine were taken and destroyed by my brother, necessitating a replacement." He pointed to the keys in Beauty's hand.

"Who are the Eternals?" Beauty asked.

Skorn laughed. "Answering that would be like explaining the stars to a dog."

"If yours were destroyed," Thalidon said, "why not re-forge them?"

"A thousand dwarves could not remake such keys in ten lifetimes," Skorn said. "And they are given only to Eternals. Only one saw the light and stood against the Eternals, and you know him as Lord Draeken."

Jack's eyes flicked to Lorelia at the mention of Draeken. She too had known the keys came from him, but where had she gotten her information?

"What do you want from the vault?" Jack asked.

Skorn gestured to Lorelia. "I'll allow your friend to explain it to you on the way."

"You expect me to trust her?" Jack asked, stabbing a finger at her.

Lorelia reached out to him. "Jack, I—"

"Don't," Jack said, his voice so cold she flinched and withdrew her hand.

Skorn made an irritated sound. "You'll have plenty of time to consider her actions on the road. Don't forget the clock is ticking." He held the vial aloft again.

Jack tensed, readying himself for the leap to take it. As if reading his thoughts, Skorn smiled.

"Attack me and the vial could break," he said. "Are you willing to risk it?"

Jack stared at it, but managed to control the temptation. "One assignment," he said. "For Beauty."

Skorn advanced until Jack could see every flaw in his scarred flesh. "Do you not understand? I *own* you—and your talent. Only when you have retrieved what I need will I allow Gallow to kill you."

Jack laughed. "And you call me arrogant? Are all ancients like you?"

Skorn gave an appreciative chuckle. "I have underestimated you, Jack. You *do* know who I am."

"How do you know I won't sneak in and take the vial?" Jack asked.

Ursana suddenly cried out and grabbed her elbow. Then Gordon went down, followed by the dwarves. Each showed the same symptoms as Beauty. Jack realized Lorelia had poisoned them all and his eyes flicked to her. She flinched at his unspoken anger.

"I had no choice," she repeated.

Skorn laughed. "You will do as I say because you will not let your friends die." He swept a hand at the room. "You have six weeks and a long journey. You should hasten."

Ultimately, Jack realized he had no choice. Releasing a growl, he said, "As you order."

Skorn smiled in triumph, twisting the scars on his face. Then he withdrew four more vials and handed them to Gallow to distribute.

"You and Lorelia will go to the vault's entrance," he said. "There you will use the keys to access the vault. Resist the urge to marvel at the Eternal's refuge and find the strongroom. Then it will be up to you to steal this." He held up a drawing depicting a small black pyramid. "Retrieve it and return. Then I will heal your friends."

"How do I know you will fulfill your oath?"

"You don't," he said. "But you have no other choice."

Conscious of his groaning friends, Jack realized he could not disagree—for now. If he feigned consent the opportunity to defy Skorn would come. Scowling, he swept a hand outward.

"So where is the vault?"

"In another realm," Skorn replied.

"Then how do we get there?" Jack demanded.

Skorn's smile widened. "The same way you travel to any realm. A Gate."

Chapter 35: The Eternal Gate

Jack and Lorelia exited Margauth and followed the canyon to Hilltop, but their journey north was a silent one. Several times Lorelia attempted to start a conversation but Jack did not respond. The hours stretched into days but Jack held his tongue, and eventually she accepted his rebuke and stopped trying.

They rode their mounts across the breadth of Griffin and passed through one of the northern forts into unclaimed lands. Great footprints of giants and tigrons marked the earth, as did the tracks of wandering goblin tribes. In spite of the evidence they saw no one, and shortly after passed onto the Fractured Plains. An hour later they reached the pit.

At a mile across and several miles in length, the pit disappeared into darkness below. Wind howled into and out of the giant chasm, haunting and shrill. They stood and gazed down upon the depths for several minutes until Jack spotted a flicker of movement across the gap.

"We need to move," Jack said.

"You're speaking to me now?"

"No," Jack said. "But this is rock troll land, and they call themselves the flesh of war for a reason. I may be angry, but I'm not a fool."

"The rock trolls are not what they once were," she said, turning away from the pit and leading him into a shallow ravine. She spoke in a rush, as if eager for the conversation. "King Tryton brought them to

288

peace, and as you know, even contracted his people as guards for royalty, master craftsmen, and mages."

He smiled as he recalled facing them in Griffin. Then his levity faded and his voice hardened. "When did you know you would betray us?"

She released a pained sigh. "Six weeks before you returned, Skorn sent me a message—"

"And you answered it?"

"I did," she said. "But I didn't know it was him. The message came from an acquaintance from my time in the mage guild. She said she knew my secret and had found a way to heal me. I couldn't resist, and when I showed up I found Skorn waiting for me."

"He tricked you," he said. "It's what he does."

"No," she said. "He did something to my face, and I watched my flesh turn whole for the first time in my life. There was no illusion. My scars were gone, and even the marks of my birth mended before my eyes." Her voice filled with yearning when she described what Skorn had done. Then it turned bitter. "Then he took it away."

"He promised he could make it permanent," Jack guessed.

"I could not refuse," she said quietly.

"You could have," he said. "You don't need him—"

She spun to face him, her beautiful face tightening with sudden rage. "Were you going to help me? Not likely. And where was everybody else? No one ever looked past my pretty face. No one *cared* to. Gordon even called me a coward."

"Can you fault us?" Jack demanded. "You hide yourself and blame us for not accepting you. If you had shown us who you were, we would have helped."

Her illusion evaporated and her deformed features returned. She stabbed a finger at the scars covering half of her face.

"This is what happened the last time I showed myself."

"It's who you are," Jack said. "Accept it."

She stepped close to him and jammed a finger into his chest. "Like you accepting that you're a thief?"

"I'm not."

"It's who you are," she said, mimicking his condescending voice perfectly. "Accept it."

He growled and strode away. For several miles they seethed in silence. The expanse of stone contained thousands of plunging ravines, canyons, and pillars of windswept stone. Vegetation was sparse on the surface, but Jack caught glimpses of dying brush in the base of the ravines. The spring runoff had long since dried up, but the hardy plants had dug their roots deep and were prepared to weather the winter before snowmelt flooded the region.

The broken expanse made navigating it difficult, and several times they were forced to backtrack in order to find a place narrow enough for them to leap the gaps. By nightfall they camped in a shallow crevasse but forewent a fire. As the stone cooled under Jack's back he stared at the sky.

"He was your breakthrough," Jack said, recalling how she'd spoken of a breakthrough when researching Skorn. "How much did he tell you?"

She didn't answer for several minutes. "He said he was the last ancient on Lumineia, but there were others in another realm. All he wants is to return home."

Jack snorted in disbelief. "He's not a family man."

"I didn't believe him either," she said, "at first. But after he showed me what ancient magic could do I could not refute his statement. The magic is . . . strange, and in some ways does not appear to be magic at all."

Jack thought of the map, of how light had flowed from it to display the world. "What I've seen looks like dwarven engineering," he said.

"I thought the same thing," she said, and offered a smile.

He didn't return it.

"What about this vault?" Jack asked. "Why does he want this relic?"

"It's a beacon that will alert his people to his presence," she replied. "Once they know he's here, they will come."

"You think more ancients on Lumineia are a good thing?"

"He just wants to go home," she said.

"Why is there doubt in your voice?"

She didn't answer, and Jack didn't press the issue. The next morning they rose and advanced north across the perimeter of the Fractured Plains. At the northern end of the stone they climbed into the far northern foothills. The towering mountains in the east were already covered in snow, while the west led to an endless expanse of sand dunes.

"Fill your skin," she advised, and stepped to a trickling stream. "We'll be in the sands for some time and water will be scarce."

Jack followed her lead but crinkled his nose. "I hate sand in my boots."

"Then you will hate the next few days," she said. "Windstorms are common here, and sand will find a way into everything you wear."

"You don't make it sound appealing."

She laughed and rose to her feet. "Let's get moving."

"What's in the sands?"

"The Irilian Shield," she said. "It's home to the largest tribe of sand trolls but they merely use it as a barrier against storms. It's one of the last remaining structures built by the ancients."

They set off into the shifting sands, and in minutes Jack was drenched in sweat. Bound on three sides by mountains, the sands received little rainfall. Even this late in the season the air and ground were hot, burning through Jack's boots. The toll of hiking endless dunes caused Lorelia to extinguish her spell of beauty. At first she threw him apprehensive looks but he made no comment on her distorted features.

The night descended quickly and brought a welcome relief from the searing sunlight. They camped in the sand, and Jack fell asleep listening to the wind scrape across his body. Rising with the dawn, they set out again. They stumbled on an oasis shortly after noon, and gratefully filled their water skins before pressing on.

The blistering sun beat down on them as they fought their way north. They took to resting during the day and walking at night, but that left them shivering when the temperatures plummeted upon nightfall. A week after entering the sands Jack wanted to turn back and murder Skorn in his bed.

Shortly after sunset they spotted a pair of sand trolls hiking nearby. At seven feet tall the hulking trolls were shorter than their rock troll cousins. They wore animal skins for protection from the elements and strode across the sands like it was a street in Griffin.

Jack and Lorelia exchanged a look, and then began to follow the pair's footprints. Evidently unconcerned by pursuit, the two sand trolls led them northwest as stars appeared in the sky. Just as the last of the light slipped away they crested a dune and the Irilian Shield came into view.

Five massive towers of white twined together like twisting vines, supporting a massive umbrella above the entire village. Curved and graceful, the barrier exuded power. The sand trolls had taken up refuge beneath the shield and built homes, shops, and even troughs to water their gardens. A small ancient structure sat beneath the shield at the center. Water bubbled up from the roof, indicating it had been placed over a spring and brought the life-giving liquid to the surface.

Although night had fallen, the streets were spotted with torchlight. Male and female trolls toiled together, curing meat, tending the gardens, or transporting water in earthen pots. Light glowed from within the brick homes, as did the soft echo of laughter.

Jack glanced at Lorelia when he heard it. "They are not like the rock trolls?"

"They train to fight," she replied, "but no more than the other races. They are nomadic and peaceful most of the time. They may lack the warlike nature of their cousins, but they are still more powerful than us."

"Did the ancients *ever* do anything small?" Jack asked, gesturing to the shield.

She grinned at his tone. "The Gate lies on the summit."

Curious despite the circumstances, Jack stepped off the dune and advanced toward the village. With nightfall upon them they had no trouble approaching the village, but as they neared Jack made out the sentries—some of which were rock trolls. Lorelia cursed under her breath and shifted deeper into the darkness.

"What are they doing here?" Jack hissed.

"Outcasts," Lorelia murmured. "I heard some still lived with the tribe."

Jack gauged the distance to the edge of the dome, but it was well out of range for a shadowhook. Then he thought of an idea and smirked.

"Remember the spider you sent me as a message?"

She met his gaze, a smile crossing her scarred face. "You think it would work?"

"Everyone is afraid of spiders," Jack said, "especially if they are giant and glowing."

Her grin widened and light began to gather about her form. Drawn from the moonlight, it warped across her hands and flowed into a tiny creature at her feet. It glowed on the sand and skittered about as if eager for battle, and a moment later another joined the first, and then another. Soon there were dozens of spiders crawling over their boots.

Then Lorelia's eyes brightened and she poured her magic into them, causing them to swell in size. Even though Jack knew they were harmless, he shuddered when a giant spider crawled up his arm.

"Get ready to run, Jack"

Chapter 36: Broken

The trolls noticed the glow and drew their weapons. They called a challenge but no one answered. Then a horde of giant spiders burst into view. Skittering across the sand, the glowing creatures charged the trolls.

Cries of alarm turned to confusion when the lead spider jumped to one of the sand trolls and ascended to his face. Although it did no harm, the mere sight of a giant spider biting at his face was sufficient to cause him to shriek in fear. A rock troll caught a second and dispassionately buried his huge sword into the light, ripping through the magic. As the magic disintegrated he shouted that they were merely illusions, but his voice was lost in the din.

As trolls converged on the spiders, Jack and Lorelia bolted from cover and threaded their way into the village. Then they made their way to one of the pillars that ascended two hundred feet to the shield. By shadowhook and hand they climbed, slipping into ceiling shadows as the spider army disintegrated. Clinging to the side of the pillar, Jack and Lorelia grinned at each other.

"Your smile makes you pretty," Jack said. "You don't need the mask."

She flushed and her flawless face reappeared. Without a word she ascended to the top of the pillar where it fused into the shield. Jack joined her and together they launched their shadowhooks. Twin threads of ink exploded from their gauntlets and streaked away to catch the lip of the shield. Then they released and swung over the milling crowd below.

Like two passing shadows they soared down and up, and Jack thumbed the rune that drew him in. As the arc tightened he accelerated. He tightened his grip as his swing sharpened, lifting him over the lip and onto the shield. He extinguished the magic and alighted, and Lorelia landed at his side.

Smooth and rising in a giant arc, the Irilian Shield rose to a gentle mound. Dust and sand covered the whitish material, making it dingy and aged. It also made it slick, and both of them slipped several times. By the time they reached the top, it became clear that no one had set foot on the shield in ages.

The summit of the ancient structure was nothing more than a smooth curve, with no adornments or decorations to mark its purpose. Underwhelmed, Jack looked at the giant mound sloping away from them.

"Is this it?"

She nodded and bent to examine the surface of the shield. "Skorn said there are several entrances to the vault throughout Lumineia, but this one is rarely used since the trolls took up residence. Do you have the keys?"

"I don't have them."

She snapped a look up at him. "I'm in no mood for games, Jack. Do not forget that our friends' lives hang in the balance."

"*My* friends," Jack said. "If they were your friends you wouldn't have handed them over to Skorn."

Anger flashed across her face but she reined it in. "Are you going to open the vault or not?"

Jack reluctantly reached into a hidden pouch and withdrew the keys. To his surprise they were glowing. He raised them to his eyes and watched the orange glow fade. Curious, he lowered them again and they brightened.

"The keys find the lock," he said, and tossed one to her.

Turning away, he searched the summit of the shield while watching the knife. Following the brightening glow, he wound his way until he spotted a flicker of light beneath the dust. Kneeling beside it, he brushed the sand aside to find a crack in the material.

The gap glowed brighter as Jack brought the knife closer, and he called Lorelia. As she knelt at his side he put the knife into place and slid it home. The light flared to blinding and turned red.

"Let's find the other lock," he said.

"Is that eagerness I hear?"

"We're about to unlock a vault that has endured for eons," Jack said. "How could I not be eager?"

"Spoken like a thief."

She laughed lightly and returned to where she'd been searching. He followed her, and a moment later spotted a glowing crack directly across from the embedded dagger. Kneeling beside it, Lorelia sank the second key into the lock and it too glowed red.

They retreated as the light streaked away from the blades, arcing together until it formed a glowing ring. Then another ring appeared inside the first, and another. The concentric circles continued to appear, shimmering into view before dimming. Each came with a blast of energy, increasing in power until Jack and Lorelia were forced to retreat. It reached the center and a geyser of red exploded upward before fading and turning silver. Like a rock had been thrown into a pond the silver light rippled, fusing the rings into a single mirror-like surface that reflected the stars.

Jack released his held breath as he examined the circular Gate. "Where does it go?"

She snorted in irritation. "He said I was not capable of understanding."

Jack stepped to the edge of the Gate and stooped to touch it. Just as the other Gates he'd used, this one allowed his hand to pass through as

298

if it were liquid, and returned to its shape when he withdrew. He rose to his feet and turned to her.

"Ready?"

"I'll be here when you come back," she said, and envy flashed across her face.

"You're not coming?"

She shook her head. "Skorn made it clear the keys only allow one to pass."

"Lucky me," Jack said wryly.

"You were always lucky," she said.

He frowned. "I don't care to go in blind."

"You have no choice," she said. "Just as I don't."

"You had a choice," he said. "And you chose to follow him."

"How could one like you understand what it's like to be ugly?"

"One's beauty does not mean that much," Jack said.

She stared at him, her expression heavy with sadness. "You think me shallow." She said it without rancor.

"You betrayed us to be beautiful," Jack said.

She shook her head, her eyes lifting to his. "I do not desire beauty but an identity, one I only gain when I don this mask. My entire life I've been broken, and all I desire is to be whole."

"How can healing your face change that much for you?"

"You cannot understand," she said, looking away.

He reached out and caught her chin, forcing her to look at him. "I would have, if you'd showed me earlier."

She stared at him for a long time. "I will show you what happened the last time I shared my secret."

299

She opened her palms, sending light curving about them. The Irilian Shield and night sky faded, shimmering to pure white before darkening to a hallway in what was clearly a mage guild. Young elves rushed between lessons, flowing through Jack and Lorelia as if they weren't there.

Jack spotted a young Lorelia walking with a group of girls and a boy. There was no sound to the memory, but Jack read the malice in the girls faces as they whispered at her back. They walked into an empty classroom and someone closed the door.

"They told me the professor had called an extra lesson," Lorelia said, "and I believed them."

The girls were quick to surround Lorelia, poking at her and laughing. At first she shook her head, denying what was being said. The fear on her face was palpable.

"I trusted Felan," Lorelia said, motioning to the boy hovering in the back of the group. "He said he loved me and I told him my secret. He told the others."

"What are they saying?" Jack asked as the girls shoved the young Lorelia down and pinned her to the floor.

"That an ugly mutt does not deserve love."

Jack flinched and glanced at Lorelia. She stood rigid as she watched her memory unfold, her features haunted. She did not look away as the leader of the girls pulled a knife into view.

"She said it wasn't right that one side of my face was pretty," Lorelia whispered. "It was only fitting that both sides matched."

The girls ripped the amulet from the young Lorelia's neck and she panicked. She fought with magic and fist but there were too many. They held her pinned as her real features appeared, laughing at the disfigurement. Then the leader leaned down, digging the knife into Lorelia's face. Lorelia squirmed and fought, her mouth open in a silent scream. Blood spilled to the floor, mingling with her tears.

Jack clenched his hands into fists. "It is forbidden for elves to spill the blood of another elf."

300

"They said I wasn't a member of the fair race," Lorelia replied. "They said I might find love among the pigs . . . now that I looked like one."

The girls finally released her and retreated, leaving a bloody and sobbing Lorelia on the floor. Laughing and casting insults, they swept from the room. The young Lorelia scooted to the wall and huddled against the stone, cradling her injured face as she sobbed.

"The elves are known for their beauty," Lorelia said, her gaze on her broken younger self. "Yet they are vain and petty, especially in youth. Image matters more than skill, knowledge, or talent. My mother swore me to secrecy, but I shared the truth with one I loved—and he betrayed me. After that everyone knew."

The view changed, and in its place Jack saw Lorelia walking through a sea of revulsion inscribed on young faces. Elf maidens chattered from the classrooms, pointing and laughing. The more sinister passed her in the halls, pushing her down, taking her things.

"I told you my mother took her own life," Lorelia said. "But she did it because she was ashamed of me, because her friends blamed her for my appearance. After that I changed my face entirely and returned to school as a different student. The same students that had hurt me now respected me, and laughed as they told the tale of my scarring. I didn't realize then, but it was my first persona."

Jack looked away, unable to endure any more. "Why show me all this?" he asked, sweeping his hand at the images.

She stepped to him, drawing close and wrapping her arms around his neck. "Because I love you, Jack."

She leaned up and kissed him, drawing him into a crushing embrace. Unprepared for the contact he froze, his mind spinning in circles. He kissed her but not with the same force, and sensing his reserve, she withdrew.

He opened his eyes to find himself back on the Irilian Shield. Lorelia stared at him, her features hardening. The weariness about her frame implied an enormous amount of magic had been required to provide the glimpse into her soul.

301

"I don't feel that way toward you," Jack finally said.

"You acted that way before you knew the truth," she said. "You kissed me."

"I shouldn't have," Jack said. He shifted his feet but it didn't alleviate his discomfort. "I never felt for you the way I feel for . . ."

He didn't say it, but he didn't need to.

Her features turned bitter. "Perhaps you would have if I didn't look like this." She pointed to her face. Then she whirled and strode away. "I think I'll make the return journey alone," she cast over her shoulder.

Jack raised a hand to her. "Lorelia—"

"Don't," she said, whirling to face him. "I know how you feel about Thera—and as you said—they call her Beauty for a reason."

"You don't understand," he said. "You're my friend."

Anger flitted across her features and then turned cold. "They all said that."

She turned and strode away, but Jack made a final attempt. "What if I don't come out?"

"Then I'll count myself lucky."

He stared after her until she'd disappeared in the gloom. When he realized she would not return he grunted, his confusion turning to irritation. He regretted kissing her, and wished there was a way he could explain? If anything, he valued her *more* since learning the truth.

He scowled and faced the shimmering mirror at his feet. Where he was about to go he could not afford to be distracted, and he cast Lorelia from his mind. Then he stepped forward and dropped into the Gate.

Chapter 37: Refuge of the Eternals

Jack exited the Gate and promptly landed on his back. Grunting from the impact, he rose to find the Gate now vertical, as was the tunnel he now stood in. His irritation at the awkward exit evaporated as he took in his surroundings.

The tunnel was circular with a flat floor. Blue accents graced the polished white walls. Windows lined one side, but the view beyond was of darkness and stars. Drawn to the window, he stepped to it and saw a massive peak rising nearby. He started to turn away until he realized it wasn't a peak.

And it was moving.

The stone gradually rotated to the side, spinning and sliding away to reveal it wasn't a mountain at all, but a single massive stone floating through the night. Held fast by the display, Jack was unprepared for the sight when it shifted out of view—allowing sunlight to fall upon him.

An endless expanse of night sky stretched away from him, with the sun glowing in the distance. Nausea assailed him and he pushed his nose against the window in the hopes of seeing the ground, but the curve of the glass prevented him from seeing beyond a few feet. Although he tried to convince himself it wasn't possible, he could have sworn the mountain he stood on was moving as well.

He forced himself to turn away and focus on his task. Then he advanced toward the end of the tunnel, pausing on the threshold of a massive chamber. Spherical and miles in diameter, the space contained forests, lakes, and streams across the interior—extending up the walls to flow across the ceiling as well. An orb of light pulsed in the heart of the chamber like a tiny sun, its magic dimmed as if it were twilight or early morning.

Large corridors extended from the sphere at odd angles. Strange equipment dotted the sphere's landscape, curving onto the walls and ceiling. Gardens dominated much of the area, with fruit trees and grass pointing to the miniature sun. Streams trickled among the trees, gurgling across the ceiling and down one side to a lake.

There was no balcony outside the tunnel, and the sides sloped outward like a funnel. The strange exit flowed into a grove of sweet smelling fruit. Tentatively Jack advanced on the slope but it was no different than descending a shallow hill. By the time he reached the trees the miniature sun was up and the ground at his feet was down.

Clouds floated on the other side of the sun, their cottony surface bent as they followed the curve of the sphere. A light rain fell, drizzling on the multitude of plants with the soft patter of a spring storm. From his vantage point the rain fell upward, drenching the trees on the upper curve of the sphere.

As disconcerting as the sphere was, it caused Jack to smile. Whatever magic the ancients had possessed, it was powerful enough to defy every sense of known logic, meaning their relics were likely just as powerful.

And valuable.

As he advanced through the fruit trees he spotted strange animals in the field. They looked at his appearance but did not seem afraid. Jack strode within touching distance of a deer but it merely regarded him with passive curiosity.

Although he didn't see anyone else, he made his way to one of the tunnels that extended out from the sphere. When he reached it he looked back to the one he'd entered from, but the tunnel was now up the curve of the sphere.

He turned down the tunnel and found that the transition to walking on the floor of the new corridor was as seamless as the last. Again, it brought a smile to his lips as he pondered how the ancients had accomplished such a feat.

The corridor matched the first, and also culminated in a Gate. This one lay inert, the markings on the wall suggesting it did not lead to the same place. Although he was tempted to test it, he retreated to the central sphere and moved on.

The next two tunnels ended at Gates as well. Jack strode into the fourth tunnel expecting the same but came to a halt. Instead of a single corridor this one branched into a series of rooms and smaller halls. All of the doors were closed, and Jack realized it was likely the sleeping quarters for the fortress.

Returning to the central sphere he continued his search. Some of the tunnels went to Gates, while others went to chambers of strange machinery. The more he searched the more confused he became.

Then he found the vault.

Although much of the citadel's construction appeared strange and foreign, the vault was unmistakable. The hall came to an end at a circular door. Set into the wall, the metal glowed with a luminescent green. A single hole marked the surface, a lock for a key.

He bent to examine it, unsurprised to find its craftsmanship unique. The lock resembled the knives he'd used to enter the ancient fortress but showed a more tapered bore. He knew at a glance he could not pick it, but its construction was clearly mechanical.

"Let's see how you like a gorgon key," he murmured, and withdrew knife from its sheath.

He detached the blade and placed the hilt up to the hole. Then he caressed the rune on the pommel. The hilt turned liquid and began to flow into the lock, filling every nook and crevice. Sparks came from hole before the hilt turned solid and Jack inserted the blade into it. With great care he began to turn the lock. A grin crossed his face as the entire door rotated with it, turning as easily as a wheel of cheese at the end of a dagger.

"I expected more," Jack said to the lock, his voice one of pity.

The door abruptly turned transparent and faded, leaving the knife in his hand. He smirked and returned it to its sheath.

He stepped through the door and it closed behind him, leaving him inside another spherical chamber. At just a hundred feet across it was much smaller than the main chamber, but far more intricate—and it was occupied.

Instead of a miniature sun, a woman hovered at the center of the space. Crafted of pure light, she gazed on the glowing ball in her hands. Jack remained rooted in place until he was certain he had not disturbed the sentinel. Then he scanned the chamber.

Several recessed alcoves were scattered about the room, each holding a single item. He spotted pyramids, a staff, and what looked like a pocket mirror. Three resembled hourglasses but instead of sand they held silver liquid. The artifacts were foreign to him but two stood out. Situated across from him and partway on the ceiling, the first black pyramid was the size of his hand. It hovered in its slot, spinning casually so the light reflected off its surface. Halfway up the curve sat a second.

With great care Jack stepped out of the alcove and onto the interior of the sphere—and the entire chamber shifted. The openings slid to the side and rotated to face sheer rock. Curious, Jack took another step, and this time noticed the woman at the center rotated the ball in her hands, and the room spun to match.

A chagrined smile crossed his face as he realized the truth. The vault held two spheres, one outer, one inner. The outer sphere contained the artifacts, while the inner had windows leading to the alcoves. Every time the inner sphere moved the windows shifted, blocking access to the vault's treasures.

The door was merely a formality, while the chamber was the true lock. Each item likely had a single path to reach it, a combination where the person could walk the secret pattern to reach the item they wanted. With the size of the chamber Jack estimated there would be an infinite number of combinations to reach a single relic. To steal them all would be impossible.

He took another step to gauge the chamber's movement but it did not match his own, and turned in a new direction, rotating until he stood on the relative ceiling. The only thing that did not move was the woman, and from his vantage point she stood upside down, her unseeing eyes studying the ball in her hands.

He looked back and scowled. The opening that led to the door had shifted as well, leaving the sphere's wall obscuring the door. The chamber wasn't just a lock to guard against thieves, it was a trap. If he went the wrong way the door might never reappear, leaving him caged in the vault until death or discovery.

He cautiously retreated the way he'd come, and to his relief the chamber reoriented in the reverse order. The large opening slid back into its place and the entrance came into view. He stepped to it and turned back to the chamber, examining it once again.

The minutes passed in silence but he did not move. The vault he faced was designed to be uncrackable, a killer of thieves. The thickness to the rotating sphere was excessive, and he doubted even a score of rock trolls could break through. He frowned, guessing the makers of the vault had likely prepared for such an attempt. Additional traps might also be hidden out of view.

He scowled as another thought crossed his mind. The vault sat inside a fortress nearly impossible to enter, yet it contained barriers unmatched by any among the five kingdoms. The relics were secured by layer upon layer of protection, each stronger than the last. With such measures to stop a thief, they wouldn't let the artifacts be taken.

They would destroy them.

He scanned the chamber again but his attention was drawn to the woman of blue light hovering at the center. She was the source of the power for the room, or at least the conduit. But how would she react if something went amiss?

He activated his crossbow and aimed at one of the other relics, sending an explosive bolt into the alcove. The woman at the center was faster, and sent a burst of energy to shield it. The fire appeared tiny in the vault and was extinguished by the woman's power. Then her features changed.

Her countenance darkened with frightening suddenness, the blue light sharpening with fury. Power rippled across her body like lightning, coursing up her torso and into her hands. Then it came to a stop, the power sparking on her fingertips. She spoke for the first time.

"One mistake is permitted. A second will be punished."

Jack shivered at the voice and the warning. The woman returned to her posture as if she were holding an invisible ball, but the lightning continued to arc up her arms, and her features remained dark.

"What are you?" Jack abruptly asked.

"Identity request confirmed," she said. "I am a guardian construct."

He was tempted to ask more but decided against it. He'd pressed his luck enough already, and had no desire to be burnt to ash by the vengeful sentinel. With an effort he turned away from the hovering woman and examined the vault with a critical eye.

Feeling the press of time, he focused on what he knew about the vault. As he pieced together what he could be certain of, an idea formed in his mind. He mulled it over as a smile crossed his face, testing it for flaws. Again and again he rehearsed his intentions, mentally moving his body through every motion until he was ready. His heart thudded in anticipation and a smile spread on his features. Then he sucked in his breath.

And leapt into the vault . . .

Chapter 38: Vault of the Eternals

Jack soared through the air and activated his shadowhook. The black thread streaked into one of the alcoves containing a relic but attached to the side, away from the item. Jack swung himself forward and then extinguished the magic before touching the inner sphere. Sailing through the air he twisted his body into a flip and pointed his feet into another alcove.

He bent his knees to cushion the blow but it was too much and he wobbled, nearly touching the sphere before righting himself. Then he looked to the sentinel, half expecting it to turn and strike him down. He now stood on a curve of the ceiling with an angled view of her features, but she did not move.

He smirked and resisted the urge to taunt her. He'd guessed the truth, that the only safe places to step were the alcoves, where a visitor would need to enter in order to retrieve a relic. The architects of the vault had anticipated every attempt to steal from the chamber.

Except if no one touched it.

He stepped on what was likely a priceless artifact and used it to leap into the air, activating his shadowhook at the apex. He yanked himself into a flip and released the hook, aiming for another alcove. He sent his shadowhook streaking away, connecting for the briefest of moments before sending it into the next hole. When necessary he alighted in an alcove to regain his bearings, and then leapt into the air once more.

He leapt from floor to ceiling and back again, using the alcoves like anchors to hold himself aloft. The edge of the sphere came within inches of his feet before he brought himself back to the center of the room, passing so close he could see his reflection on the sentinel's frozen features. The proximity to her power raised the hair on his arms.

"Sorry, beautiful," he said.

She didn't respond as Jack soared over her head. He sent his shadowhook into the alcove that contained an artifact. The thread of ink yanked him across the space. He twisted in the air and alighted inside the alcove, gliding into the space like a sword into a sheath.

He grinned at the triumph and looked up at the sentinel's back. She still faced the door with power arcing across her arms. Several times he'd expected her to strike him down but she'd stayed her hand, evidently not enchanted to stop someone using the air in the room to get past her.

"Don't feel bad," Jack said. "You're not the first strongroom I've breached."

She did not turn or answer, and he wondered if she had even heard him. Then he noticed a tightening about her frame that implied tension. On her profile he spotted a touch of wrath distorting her features. Then he realized the truth and his smile widened.

"You *can* hear me," he said, "but you can't retaliate unless someone activates you."

A rumble escaped the sentinel, confirming Jack's suspicions. "You know what I'm here to do," he said, "but you cannot stop it unless I make a mistake. Has it ever happened to you before? Or am I the first to best your defenses?"

Another rumble escaped the sentinel, louder than the first. The lightning on her arms intensified but she still did not turn. Jack laughed and turned away from her.

"Do not worry," he called out. "I'll be gone in a moment."

He slipped into a crouch before the black pyramid, gauging its weight and balance. Although he saw no hint of an enchanted trap, it undoubtedly had some kind of tether. He pulled a knife from his thigh and ran the tiny black blade over the pyramid, searching for curses. It

311

wavered twice but not enough for him to identify the curses around it. Something guarded it but he could not identify what.

For a long moment he stared at the pyramid, considering his options. He'd already activated the sentinel once, and doing so again would attract attention. He mentally listed and dismissed all the curses or hexes possible. The lethal ones would have been affected by the anti-magic knife, leaving only debilitating or alerting type magic. He looked up at the sentinel's back and grinned.

"Why protect it when it has you," he said.

Readying himself for the impending flight, he gathered his strength and checked his gear. Then he reached up and sent his shadowhook streaking away. The instant it caught he reached down and scooped up the pyramid.

The sentinel whirled to face him, her features turning indigo blue. "Your retribution has been ordered, thief."

"Come and get me," Jack replied.

His shadowhook yanked him out of the way as the sentinel unleashed a blast of lightning. Rock exploded as the lightning ripped a gash in the interior of the sphere, but Jack was already landing on the ceiling.

"You missed."

Fury rippled across her features and she dived for him, twisting to land on her feet. The moment she touched she rose to face him and rotated her hand. Jack stumbled as the sphere rotated, reacting to her touch.

"No one escapes a construct," she said, and sent another arc of lightning at him.

He dodged to the side but the current of power lifted the hair on his neck and sent tingles through his limbs. He rolled on the surface of the sphere and leapt to his feet, his speedstone in his palm. Activating it at a touch, a surge of magic enhanced his body and he charged up the slope of the curve.

Lightning bombarded the sphere around him, seeking his heart as he dodged and weaved. Stone shattered and exploded, pummeling him with shards. The sphere spun under his feet, but with the speedstone's magic his reflexes were heightened even further. He sensed the shifts and moved with them, using the spinning walls and ceiling to his advantage.

She leapt over his head, coming down in front of him, cracking the stone from the impact. She gathered her strength and sent a ball of power at his heart. He dropped to the ground and rolled beneath it, coming up as it detonated behind him. Another arc of lightning exploded to him. He used his momentum and slid into an alcove. The bolt streaked over him, so close that it locked his jaw.

He pushed through the pain and leapt out of the alcove as the sphere spun again, nearly being crushed as the sphere closed the gap. He sprinted away but the surface of the sphere was no longer smooth. Great rents littered the sphere, gouged by tremendous blasts of power. Holes that had led to alcoves were visible under piles of rubble sliding around the surface of the rotating curve.

Jack heard her coming and threw himself upward, evading another arc of power by inches. With the speedstone active, the force of his leap carried him to the center of the space. He spun in a casual flip as the pull shifted and yanked him onto the ceiling. Now across the sphere from her, he looked up and grinned.

"You're a great dancer," he said.

She snarled and unleashed a current of power. He darted away but it followed in his wake, carving a line across the sphere like a pen on parchment. The relentless blast filled the air with dust and chunks of stone.

Jack dodged falling and sliding rubble, staying ahead of the lightning lance by sheer speed. She kept up the assault, coming closer by the second. Heat singed his cloak and he glanced back to see a line of fire burning in the broken sphere. With all the damage it no longer turned smoothly, and every rotation ground against the rubble that had fallen into the alcove openings.

The grinding slowed the vault and Jack turned toward the entrance door. An alcove opening was rotated toward it, giving Jack the chance he'd been waiting for. He leapt into the air and cast his shadowhook, throwing himself across the sphere. A current of power severed the thread of magic but it was too late, and Jack streaked toward the window.

He flipped again and straightened his body, reaching the hole in the inner sphere just as it passed in front of the entrance door. Like a thread through a needle he passed through the opening and crashed into the door, tumbling to the floor.

A shriek echoed from inside the sphere and the construct spun the strongroom, turning it to bring the larger opening in line. Jack rolled to his feet and darted to the door, swinging it open just as the sentinel appeared in view.

"Better luck next time," he said.

She unleashed her whole power at him but he swung the vault door shut, allowing it to take the brunt of the attack. The door held, but from the other side he could hear thunder and detonating stone. He expected her to stop but her fury would not abate, and she continued to pummel the thick door.

The speedstone magic faded and Jack leaned against the wall, his chest heaving. He slid to the ground with a smile on his face. Even with her power, he doubted she could break through, not quickly anyway. Temporarily safe, Jack retrieved the pyramid from his side and held it aloft.

"So this is what he wants," he mused. "But are you really a beacon?"

"It is," a voice replied. "And it doesn't belong to you."

Jack was on his feet in an instant, his dagger in hand. He found himself facing an old man with stark white hair. Although his physical body appeared frail there was a power about his features that could not be ignored.

314

"I just need to borrow it," Jack said, shifting his feet in order to bolt past him. If he could make it back to the Gate . . .

The man's eyes flicked over his shoulder to where the vault door continued to shudder. "That's enough, Myria," he said, and the sentinel went silent. "No one has ever bested her before—and almost unscathed, I might add."

Jack glanced down to see his clothing in tatters. Burns and cuts littered his body from where the lightning had cut into his flesh. He sucked in his breath at the sting and turned his attention back to the man.

"An untested vault always has a weakness," Jack said, deciding honesty would buy him the most time. The man knew what he'd done. Feigning ignorance would serve no purpose.

"Who *are* you?" the man asked.

"You first," Jack replied, shifting his weight once again.

His efforts came to abrupt halt when the man replied.

"My name is Ero."

Chapter 39: Brother

Jack stared at him shock. Skorn looked like any man, albeit a dark, menacing, cruel one. Ero *looked* like a god. His features were weathered but flawless, his hair the color of snow. The eyes were bluer than the construct's lightning, piercing him as if the man could see into Jack's soul. Still . . .

"Prove it," Jack said.

The man cocked his head to the side. "You're not an Eternal and you're not from . . ." His eyes widened. "You're from Lumineia."

"Where else would I be from?"

Ero shook his head. "That's not possible. How did you even get here?"

"Draeken's keys," Jack said. "You really shouldn't have let him keep them."

"You can't be here," Ero said. "You are not permitted to see the others. Not yet."

"Just how many ancients are there?" Jack asked, rubbing his forehead.

Ero peaked an eyebrow. "I'm not the first you've met?" Then his smile evaporated and his expression hardened. "*Skorn.*" He said the name like it was a curse.

"You thought he was dead," Jack realized.

Ero seemed to be lost in memory. "He tried to escape several times. On the last attempt I thought he'd perished."

"You never suspected the truth?"

"I should have," Ero said, his lips tightening. "He's always had a way with survival."

"I've noticed," Jack said wryly.

Ero's attention focused on him, a measure of wariness touching his eyes. "You know what he is. Are you his ally?"

"Hardly," Jack said with a snort. "But I know his identity."

Ero regarded him for several moments. Then he turned and strode away. "Come. There are things you should know before you return to your home."

Jack hesitated, and he considered sprinting past him for the Gate that would take him home. But his curiosity drove him to catch up. Stepping to Ero's side, he followed him to the main sphere.

"How much of the ballad is true?" Jack asked.

Ero threw him an amused look. "Most of it, actually. When we fought I proved victorious, but I lacked the courage to end his life. Instead I imprisoned him."

"And let him escape."

Ero's jaw tightened. "You don't understand him."

"He also has a way with manipulation," Jack said.

Ero released a dry laugh. "I was mistaken. You really do know him." Then he sighed. "He was not always as he is now."

The ancient exited the main sphere and turned down a corridor Jack had not visited. The tunnel opened onto a door that resembled the vault. He strode to it and produced a key.

"I do wonder how you managed to bypass the door," he asked. "And Myria."

317

"Magic always triumphs."

Ero laughed and turned to face him. "You have no idea how true that statement is."

He caught the door and swung it open. Jack half expected the man to shove him inside and shut it, but instead he entered first, gesturing Jack to follow. Jack stepped in to find himself in a small home. Glass walls revealed a quartet of rooms including a bookless library and a dining hall. Then Jack noticed the text written on the glass and recognized the handwriting.

"This was his prison," Jack said.

"I kept him here for forty thousand years," Ero replied, his gaze on the dining area.

"And I thought ten years was a long sentence."

Ero continued as if he had not heard. "I thought he died in his attempt to escape. Now it appears he has been plotting his revenge."

"Can you blame him?" Jack asked. "You kept him caged like an animal for eons."

"Are you concerned for him?"

"Don't be absurd," Jack said with a laugh. "But you might as well have fused his blood with a desire for revenge."

Ero turned to face him. "Our kind does not track time the way yours does, and a thousand years means little to us."

"How many Eternals are there?"

Ero cast him a strange look. "The Eternals are few in number, but the ancients number more than you can comprehend."

"Are you this honest with all of your intruders?" Jack asked.

Ero began to laugh. "You are the first to gain entry to our home uninvited, let alone the vault, making you the first intruder I've ever encountered."

"Then why show me all of this?" he asked, sweeping a hand at Skorn's prison. "Why tell me so much about you?"

"Because only truth will keep you silent."

He turned away from the prison and led him back to the main sphere. Once they stepped into the open Ero turned in the direction of the Lumineia Gate. As they followed the path of crushed green stones, Jack shook his head.

"You expect me to return from here and not say a word about it?"

"You must," he replied. "For to speak of this place will invite others to search for it. Only the Eternals know of its existence, and it must remain that way."

Jack caught his arm and attempted to force him to turn, but the strength of the old man belied his frail form. Nevertheless, Ero rotated to face him.

"Why not just kill me?" Jack asked bluntly. "It's the only way to ensure my silence."

"The Eternals guard Lumineia, not kill those who live upon it. Even dispatching a thief would break our oath."

"How fortunate for me," Jack said wryly. If Ero wanted to kill him, Jack knew there was nothing he could do to stop it.

"Can I trust you will hold your tongue?"

Jack regarded him for several moments and then shrugged. "As you order."

"You have my gratitude," Ero said. "Now if you will return what you have taken, you may be on your way."

"What makes you think I took something?" Ero folded his arms and frowned, causing Jack to grin. "What if I refuse?"

"Then you will see my brother's prison again—from the inside."

Jack heard a crunch behind him and turned to find Myria. Her hair was in disarray and her features tight with fury. Jack grinned at her expression.

"Hello, beautiful."

"I request permission to kill him," she growled, her voice distorted with emotion.

"That will not be necessary," Ero said, and his expression turned amused. "Unbonded constructs are perfect for defense and always obedient, but they can be unstable."

"And the bonded ones?" Jack asked.

"They are enhanced by the one that bonded with them, so each is unique."

"What sort of magic are they?" he asked.

Ero chuckled at the question. "They can be created from a variety of energies, but it is not magic."

Jack raised an eyebrow at that. "How can she not be made of magic?"

Ero's smile widened. "Because, my dear thief, ancients cannot wield magic."

Jack had not expected that, and mulled the idea over in his mind. Could he use that to defeat Skorn?

"I take it you will be dealing with your brother now?"

"On the contrary," Ero said. "Without the beacon he is helpless. It is not serious enough for us to intervene."

"You're leaving me to clean up your mess?" Jack folded his arms. "I expected better from you."

Anger washed across Ero's features. "We deal with problems you cannot imagine, and are preparing for a war you lack the capacity to understand. As much as I would like to resolve every dispute on Lumineia, there are other realms with far more pressing threats."

"What about Draeken?" Jack asked.

Ero's eyes narrowed. "A mistake, I grant you. We chose poorly in inviting him to join our ranks. Fortunately, he is imprisoned and cannot harm you."

"Like Skorn was imprisoned?"

Rage rippled across his features. "Give me the beacon and return to your realm. There's nothing for you here."

Jack stared at him but saw no hint of compromise. He sighed and reached to the pouch on his side. Then he withdrew the black pyramid he'd taken from vault and handed it to the ancient. Ero smiled at the gesture.

"Trust me," he said. "You don't want my brother to get this. Summoning the rest of my people would be devastating to yours."

Jack sniffed. "For a god you aren't very nice—or smart."

Myria glided toward him, but Ero shook his head. "I never said I was a god, Jack. That's a title your ancestors gave me because they did not understand."

"Then enlighten me," Jack replied, and gestured to the great sphere they stood in. "What sort of race builds a place like this—without magic—yet manages to kill themselves in the Dawn of Magic."

Ero regarded him for several moments until he sighed in regret. "We have our merits," he replied, "but our failings are the same as yours."

"So that's why you won't step in," Jack said with a scowl. "You lack the courage to kill your brother so you hope I will do it for you."

Ero didn't blink. "Have a good life, Jack."

Jack made his way to the corridor that led to the Gate and paused to look back. The miniature sun had begun to brighten like dawn, and the storm on the other side abated, leaving trees and paths blanketed in drops of glistening water.

321

Ero and Myria followed him but kept their distance. Their expressions made it clear they doubted he would depart without assistance. Jack frowned in irritation and turned on his heel, leaving without another look.

He reached the Gate and stepped through, climbing back onto the Irilian Shield. Then he stooped and yanked one of the daggers from its slot. The Gate began to close, shrinking upon itself as it faded. Jack retrieved the other key and held them over the above the shrinking portal, but hesitated. On impulse he pocketed them and then settled in to wait. Minutes stretched into hours, but the Gate did not reopen. When he was certain he was not being followed he reached into a pouch at his side and withdrew a black pyramid—the second item he'd taken from the vault.

"How long will it take Ero to realize I stole more than a beacon?" The pyramid did not answer, but Jack nodded as if it did. "I agree. Long enough for us to return to Margauth and deal with Skorn."

A smile spreading on his face, he turned and left.

Chapter 40: Astaroth

He expected to find Lorelia waiting, but she was absent. He descended from the Irilian Shield and entered the shifting sands expecting to find her at the base. By the time he reached the first oasis he knew she was gone. At first his irritation mounted, but as the days dragged by he realized her absence gave him time to consider his options.

Ero's words regarding the beacon inspired a sense of caution that he could not shake. If he returned without the beacon, Skorn would kill his friends. But if Skorn obtained the beacon, Jack would be the reason the ancients returned.

He wrinkled his nose in annoyance. He'd defeated Skorn before with allies, but his attempt to infiltrate Margauth had been disastrous. This time he would be entering Margauth alone and facing an enemy that knew exactly what Jack was capable of.

After four days he entered the Fractured Plains and made camp in a small gully sheltered by a tower of stone. Foregoing a fire, he wrapped himself in a blanket and stared at the starry sky, gnawing on a strip of dried meat.

The answer seemed easy. He needed allies. But as easy as the answer was, Jack could think of no one he trusted. The few thieves he did trust were already in Margauth, and he'd alienated nearly everyone else.

"Perhaps it's time I meet some new friends," he said.

You have to be nice to make friends.

His lips twisted into a smile as he imagined Beauty's words, and realized she was right. But if did not have friends, perhaps he could buy allies. Although there was any number of mercenary guilds he could employ, he might as well hire the best . . .

Rock trolls.

He grinned, considering the risk in attempting to subvert the rock trolls. Tryton would never permit his people to serve a thief, regardless of the foe. It would be far safer to hire Talinorian Mercenaries, or cheaper to get ones from Griffin. Still, he found the prospect of stealing a contract to be appealing *because* of its danger. And Skorn would not be prepared for such a powerful foe. Unable the shake the thought, he rose and gathered his things. He shifted direction and turned west, heading deeper into the Fractured Plains.

Fatigue drove him to sleep around dawn, but after a few hours he rose again and pressed on. As he hiked he considered how his plan could fail, but each time he came up confident, and his smile widened.

His path took him toward the heart of the Fractured Plains, and it didn't take the rock trolls long to find him. He heard them coming and came to a halt, turning in their direction. The patrol of six rock trolls rose from a depression in the earth and approached.

Like all of their kind, the trolls stood over eight feet in height. Four were female while two were male. Each bore unique soulblades they crafted as part of their training, with the leader bearing a spiked warhammer.

He was smaller than the others, the number of kills marked across his chest, right arm, and face were fewer than those of his companions. In spite of his stature Jack got the sense he would grow to surpass the others.

"What is your purpose in our lands?" the youth spoke first, marking himself as the captain.

"I have engaged a contract with High Captain Arana," Jack said with a short bow. "I came to collect a patrol of your people."

"And you trust us?" a second troll asked, a smile on his face. "Not too long ago our people were the flesh of war, and slaughtered anyone that entered our lands."

"That was before Tryton became your king," Jack said.

"You know of our king?" the captain asked.

"We've never met, but I've had the pleasure of engaging some of your people in the past." Jack suppressed a smile as he thought of his infiltration of the Terros castle.

"I'm Thorvaldur, seventh Felshard under Captain Moritha."

"Alic Thorn," Jack replied.

"Come," he said. "We can speak of your contract in Astaroth."

The trolls shifted around him, making clear it was a command, not a request. Jack looked up at the female troll and her litany of tattoos, marking every kill and feat. A smile crossed his face.

"Aren't you a charmer."

"How did you know?" she asked, a hint of a smile on her features.

"Are you going to fall for a human, Korna?" one of the trolls asked.

She laughed. "Of course not. But he is handsome."

Thorvaldur laughed and ordered them to their ranks. Then the trolls led him across the expanse of a broken rock. Once they were on the move Thorvaldur dropped back to walk beside him.

"Where are you from, human?"

Jack heard more in the troll's voice than curiosity. The rock trolls were adept at combat in every form, and were as intelligent as any race. If Jack revealed too much, they were just as likely to imprison him and turn him over to any of the kingdoms that wanted him. Besides, stealing a rock troll's loyalty was dangerous enough.

"My contract has a time element," he said. "Would it be possible to hasten our journey?"

326

"As you will," he said. "Can you keep up with us?"

Jack grinned. "Can you keep up with me?"

The trolls laughed and began to run. Jack accelerated with them, grinning at the blistering pace. He thought of his panther companion and recalled racing through the trees for hours, relishing the rush of wind on his face. It had been too long since he'd simply run.

Thorvaldur looked at him several times as if expecting him to quit, but when Jack kept pace his smile widened. Then they reached a twenty-foot ravine and the trolls slowed. Jack slipped between them and reached the edge, leaping effortlessly over the gap.

"You're falling behind!" he cast over his shoulder, eliciting a bark of laughter.

The trolls caught up and Thorvaldur gestured to him. "What sort of magic drives you, human? You do not appear as a barbarian."

"I'll leave that for you to figure out," Jack said.

"You're a curious man," Korna said with chuckle.

Jack grinned, and then they reached another shallow canyon and the terrain prevented further conversation. For the rest of the day they rushed across the plateau. In spite of his stamina Jack began to struggle. Unwilling to admit it, he pushed his body to the limit. Then they topped a rise and Astaroth came into view. His chest heaving, Jack slowed with the others, grateful the trolls had not met him further from the citadel.

"Have you tired yet?" the female asked.

"Of course not," he said, forcing a laugh while digging the heel of his palm into his side. "You?"

"Never," she replied.

She was breathing hard, but no more than if she'd just jogged across a courtyard. The others were the same, and Jack found himself wondering how such a race trained.

"This way," Thorvaldur said. "King Tryton and his Warshards are currently in the dwarven kingdom, so you will be meeting with Drenuh, high cleric of our clan."

Realizing he needed to stall, Jack allowed more of his weariness to show. Wiping the sweat from his brow, he winced and caught his side.

"Perhaps in the morning?" he asked. "I admit I may have pushed too hard."

Thorvaldur smiled and agreed. "As you will," he said. "Korna, find him quarters and inform Drenuh of his arrival."

"As you will," the female said, and gestured Jack to follow her.

Jack bid them farewell and followed her down the slope to the courtyard that abutted the fortress. As they approached, Jack's eyes lifted to the citadel. Built within a tower of stone, the fortress boasted high balconies and natural battlements. From the shape of the openings Jack guessed that caves had once lined the interior, and the rock trolls had expanded them for their use.

A series of huge boulders had been rolled into a wall, forming a courtyard that stretched to the west, but Korna led him through a smaller side entrance. They passed hulking rock trolls standing as sentinels and entered a corridor that sloped upward.

Huge shields and weapons adorned the walls, and were interspersed with banners of fallen armies. Rock trolls strode about on their respective errands, their heavy footfalls echoing off the hard walls. A handful of other races appeared dressed in servant's garb.

"If you would care for a meal," she said. "I can take you to the meal hall."

"I have my own food," he said gesturing to his pack. "And it's been a tiring day. Right now I'd rather sleep."

"As you will," she said. She turned down a smaller side corridor and came to a stop beside a large door. "These will be your quarters for the night. I wouldn't suggest wandering about. King Tryton may have changed our laws, but we still treat intruders with lethal force."

"Thanks for the warning," he said, and yawned to reinforce the façade of fatigue. Then he slipped inside and she shut the door. Her shadow remained in the hall, and he guessed she would stay there throughout the night.

He turned to find the room more spacious than he'd expected, but containing little more than a bed and a small balcony. Elven light orbs were bracketed on the walls, illuminating the space in soft light.

Removing his pack, he went through the motions of getting ready to sleep and extinguished the lights. Then he waited until he was certain they would not check on him. He considered it unlikely, but there was always the chance they would discover his identity during the night.

He could have sought to initiate a new contract but that would have led to too many questions. Stealing another would be much easier—if he could find one. He shifted to the balcony and stepped outside.

The balcony faced north and was located near the base of the citadel. The expanse of the Fractured Plains stretched away from him, barely visible under the darkening sky. Air warmed by the stone wafted across him, curling around the citadel on its way south.

He turned and looked up, scanning the surface of the fortress and its myriad of balconies. Most were easily identifiable as private rooms, likely reserved for higher ranked members of the tribe. Although there was always the chance that such records would be contained deeper in the fortress, he guessed information on contracts was considered less valuable. Anyone could see who the trolls guarded, so hiding it would be unnecessary.

He glanced back at the door and then fired his shadowhook to one of the balconies above. The thread of ink was nearly invisible in the fading light, allowing him to ascend without being seen. He reached a balcony and heard a pair of voices from within. Drifting to the side, he fired again, and scaled his way up the exterior of the fortress.

He reached a large balcony and peeked inside. It connected to a multi-level training room, with hundreds of young rock trolls locked in duels. He pressed on to the next before any noticed him. It was equally disappointing, but the third showed promise.

He eased onto the balcony and crept to the archway leading to the interior. To his surprise he found a series of rooms, all spacious enough to indicate one of exceptionally high rank. A private bathing room, sleeping quarters, and what looked to be an office surrounded a central room.

A soft voice touched his ears and his gaze flicked to the side. Visible through an open doorway, he spotted a female rock troll sitting on the bed of a child. Her soft song echoed back to Jack. He remained in place, listening to the surprisingly gentle tone. Curiosity brought him close until he was able to see the singer.

She was tall and graceful, her skin flawless. The lack of tattoos marked her as a mage, but she was intimidating without them. Her legacy was visible in the litany of scars lining her shoulders, arms, and legs. Then the troll rose to her feet and turned, and Jack realized who she was. She was Kythira, joined to the most powerful rock troll in ages, King Tryton.

And Jack was about to steal from her.

Chapter 41: A Mother's Rage

Jack knew her name from the tales of her husband, and Kythira's legend nearly matched his. She was rumored to be tremendously powerful in both wind and healing magics, and as smart as Tryton. If she discovered him in the chambers of her children it would be like poking a dragon in the eye.

She exited the room and strode toward the balcony, forcing Jack to drop off the side and hang by his shadowhook. Her footfalls approached and came to a halt directly above his head. As she looked over the dark vista he controlled his breathing.

Kythira remained on the balcony for several minutes. Then he spotted a paper bird drop into view and soar away. Evidently enchanted with wind magic, it banked away and flew west. Her message complete, she turned and reentered her quarters.

Jack waited for several minutes before easing himself back onto the balcony. Then he slipped to the side of the opening and peered inside. Instead of moving to the bedchamber, Kythira strode to the office and sat at a massive desk. Under the light of a trio of light orbs, she set to work.

A curse nearly found its way from Jack's lips but he caught it in time. When it became clear that Kythira intended on working into the night, he eased himself around the corner and glided across the darkened training room. Keeping a sharp ear for her movements, he searched the rest of the royal chambers, hoping the records he sought would be contained elsewhere. When the effort proved futile he returned to the training room and hid behind a rack of shields.

The minutes ticked by as Jack considered his options. He could return to his room and attempt to bluff his way into a contract, but didn't care for the odds of that endeavor. Tryton had forged his people into protectors, and personally verified every potential contract—both target and buyer.

Or he could continue with his original plan, and steal an existing contract. He'd never anticipated an adversary as powerful as Kythira. It was still better than returning to Margauth empty handed.

Frowning, he returned to the balcony and activated his crossbow, thumbing the detonation rune. He took aim at one of the unoccupied balconies lower down. He hesitated, questioning the wisdom in inciting the trolls. Then he shrugged and fired.

He darted inside as the explosive bolt detonated, sending a burst of fire into the night and a tremor through the stone. Jack slipped behind a rack of shields before Kythira burst from her office and raced to the balcony. She shouted to someone and then sprinted to the door. The moment she disappeared Jack sprinted to the office.

Built for rock trolls, the desk was huge. The surface was at his throat, and he slid under it to a cabinet on the wall. He yanked the doors open and his gaze fell upon piles of parchment. Most appeared to contain information on kings and nations, their relative strengths and status of treaties. With great care he sifted through them until he found a stack of recent contracts.

He smiled as he saw the names and the information regarding their background. Some contained the names of high ranking craftsmen and nobles in neat, flowing script. He found a bundle of requests that had come from Terros. Each contained High Captain Arana's seal of approval, and a handful had been confirmed by King Tryton. He spotted several that indicated they would be visiting Astaroth, but one name stood out from the others.

Telorias Vanderl, a minor lord from southeastern Terros, had requested a temporary contract to help him rid his region of bandits. Both Arana and Tryton had approved the request, and were expecting a steward to arrive within the next fortnight to lead the trolls to his lord's home.

Jack scanned the record for any other relevant clues, memorizing what he needed before carefully returning the bundle to its location. Just as he placed the rest of the parchment on top he heard the soft rub of a boot on stone. He scowled in irritation and pulled the top sheet from the pile before slipping it into a pouch at his side, keeping his back to her.

"I do not care for thieves in my home."

Kythira's words trembled with rage but Jack did not turn. He deepened his voice and added a rasp to his tone.

"I meant your family no harm," he said.

"Your *presence* is the harm."

She took a step toward him but he pulled his last darkstone from his pocket and flicked it against the wall. It shattered, and every shred of light throughout the king's quarters was drawn into it, plunging the room into darkness.

Jack ducked and spun but she was faster. Even robbed of sight she sent a wave of air into his body, slamming him into the wall. He sucked in his breath as pain lanced through his body. Then he forced himself to his feet and rolled behind the desk. As she charged toward him he cast his shadowhook at the ceiling and wrapped it around the corner of the desk, activating the magic.

The thread of ink went taut, yanking the end of the desk off the floor. It smashed into her and broke apart, stunning her for the precious moment he needed to slip into the training room.

Starlight filtered into the space, giving him just enough light to spot a young rock troll across from him. He raised a sword with a hammer on the end and charged. Jack dived to the floor and rolled, barely avoiding catching the hammerblade in his face. He came to his feet and drew his dagger. Although clearly young, the troll was his size, and fought with a skill that far surpassed his own.

"Andric! Flank him!"

334

After everything he'd been through, the idea of being caught and killed by a rock troll child was so absurd he began to laugh. His amusement drew the anger of the son and the boy grunted in irritation.

"You find your death amusing, thief?"

Jack swerved as another blast of air came at him. "You've trained him well, Kythira. You should be proud."

"*You are not permitted to speak about my child!*"

Although the room was dark the trolls fought as if they could see, and Andric's hammerblade reached for his body. A gust of air came at his back, driving him into the weapon. Jack just managed to get his dagger in the way before it sliced into his heart. Then Kythira struck him with a fist like stone, sending him tumbling toward the balcony. He clutched his side and rose to his feet to find both trolls coming at him, their forms swift and deadly in the darkened room.

"It's been a pleasure," he said in his raspy voice. "But I must be going."

The boy came to a halt and raised his weapon. Just as he charged Jack dropped his lightstone on the ground. It shattered into a blinding light, causing the trolls to shield their eyes. They recovered quickly and darted forward.

But the balcony was empty.

Kythira raced to the balcony and looked down, shouting for aid before whirling and returning inside. Clinging to the underside of the balcony Jack wrapped his shadowhook around his waist and sprinted down the slope. Dodging balconies and pools of light, slowed his fall enough that he didn't slam into the porch of his room. Stumbling from the rough landing, he stripped his outer clothing and dived into the bed.

He wiped the sweat away and controlled his breathing, willing his heart to slow. Within a minute there was a knock at the door. Before he could move it crashed open and Thorvaldur barged in, waving at the lights to brighten. Jack started upright and blinked as if he'd been asleep, his eyes wide with alarm.

"Is something amiss?"

335

Thorvaldur searched the room and then strode to the door. "Just searching for a thief."

"I hope you catch him!" Jack called, a trace of anger in his voice.

"We will," Thorvaldur assured him before exiting.

Korna gave Jack a curt nod before closing the door. Jack extinguished the lights again before allowing a smile to spread on his face. Then he lay down and listened to the sounds of rock trolls searching Astaroth. The smile remained until sleep claimed him.

He half expected to awake to shackles, but the next thing he knew dawn shone into his eyes. He groaned and rolled from the bed, reluctantly dressing for the day. He probed his ribs where Kythira had hit him but it did not appear to be broken. It was already healing quickly, a legacy of his fallen panther.

He realized he'd thought very little of Shadero in the recent months. It made him wonder what his life would have been like if the thieves had never killed his mother, and his panther had never died for him. What would he have become?

He was saved from answering when a tray of food slid beneath the door. Grateful for the distraction, he retrieved it and brought it to the balcony. He relished the food and then gathered his things before knocking on the door. Instead of Korna it was Thorvaldur at the door, and the rock troll gestured for him to follow. As Jack ascended through the citadel with him, Jack looked about in wonder.

"Did you catch your thief?"

"Not yet," Thorvaldur replied, glancing back at Jack. "But we're still not sure why he came. It appears he stole meaningless records of trader purchases."

Privately Jack was glad he'd taken something so mundane. It would keep them confused until after he was gone. A moment later he entered a large office with walls of swirling wind. The female troll behind the desk looked up.

"Thorvaldur said you were Alic, come to collect a contract?"

"That's correct," he said with a disarming smile. "Telorias Vanderl dispatched me as his steward."

She rifled through the documents at her side and then produced one identical to the parchment Jack had seen on the previous night. She read the notes and then her gaze shifted to Thorvaldur.

"A group of bandits needs to be dealt with. Are you certain you wish to go with him after last night?"

Thorvaldur glanced down at him. "There are plenty of trolls hunting the thief. Besides, I'm curious about this human."

Drenuh nodded and shifted to face Jack. "Your contract allows you to take a single patrol of rock trolls, which will be led by Felshard Thorvaldur," she inclined her head to the troll at Jack's side. "He is contracted to you, but his patrol answers to him. They will not willfully cause harm, and if you seek to order them to do so, they will turn on you. Do you accept these conditions?"

"Trust me," Jack said. "The ones I seek deserve their fate."

"Very well," she said, and picked up a pen before dipping it into a bottle of ink. "Where is the destination?"

Jack saw no reason to lie so he spoke the truth. "Margauth."

Drenuh nodded. "Good luck with your bandits. I'm sure Thorvaldur will have no trouble with them."

Jack's grin widened. "Of that, I have no doubt."

Chapter 42: The Thief in the Myst

After leaving Astaroth they journeyed south to Blue Lake. From there they managed to secure an azure ship that would take them to Terros. The sailors seemed wary of the rock trolls but the trolls were well disciplined, and Jack guessed they had strict instructions from their king.

Jack spent most of the time with Thorvaldur, and the troll asked endless questions about the other kingdoms. Jack answered without breaking his persona. As the steward of a minor lord it was plausible that he had journeyed on his master's behalf.

A week after departing the northland they landed in Terros. Jack led the five trolls off the ship and they entered the city. Many of the citizens blanched at the huge trolls, with some outright fleeing at the sight. Jack hid a smile at their fear and wondered how long it would endure since King Tryton had forged a peace with Griffin.

They entered the Gold District and worked their way through the shops. Then Thorvaldur turned north, toward the rock troll outpost. Recalling that the troll outpost was led by High Captain Arana—who Jack had met on his theft from the king—he shifted south.

"If you don't mind," he said. "Time is still a factor. Perhaps we could we hasten our journey?"

It was still afternoon, with plenty of time for them to begin their journey to Margauth. Still, Thorvaldur regarded him with a trace of doubt in his eyes. Then he nodded and gestured the others to follow Jack.

"As you will," he said. "I suggest you get a mount if you wish to keep up. Running with us for a single afternoon is one thing. Staying with us for several days is another."

His eyes flicked to Korna. "Get a horse for him and replenish our supplies. We'll meet you at the east gate."

"I can get a horse myself," Jack said.

"Nonsense," Thorvaldur said. "You have a contract, and we fulfill it."

The smile on his face did not reach his eyes, and Jack recognized he had no choice. He smiled in turn and rotated away—but noticed a flicker of motion in the corner of his eye. Thorvaldur made a series of hand signals to Korna. Although Jack did not know the meaning, he could guess the intent.

He considered slipping away, but the trace of curiosity in Thorvaldur's expression caused him to remain. If there was a chance the trolls would uphold the contract he was inclined to stay. Besides, he liked them, and enjoyed talking to Thorvaldur. Either way, staying with them would be exciting.

If they didn't kill him.

Korna strode away and disappeared into the streets of Terros. Jack and the others headed for the eastern gate. The trolls had been open and talkative on the ship, but now they demonstrated a marked reservation. Out of the corner of his eye Jack noticed a flurry of hand signals between them. Shortly after reaching the gate Korna appeared holding the reins of a horse and carrying a large pack slung across her shoulders.

Jack tensed, readying himself to bolt as Korna conversed silently with Thorvaldur. Jack stepped to the horse and mounted, praising Korna on her choice even as he surreptitiously watched them. Then Thorvaldur seemed to come to a conclusion and smiled, gesturing to the gate.

"Lead the way, steward."

Jack sensed a reserve in the troll that had been absent before, but it seemed clear he wasn't going to act on his suspicions, for now. Jack managed to restrain his smile and did as requested. Together they joined the crowd streaming from the city. Like sheep before a wolf they parted, giving the trolls a wide berth.

"Do you always have such an impact on humans?" Jack asked.

One of the other trolls released an amused grunt. "Not just humans."

Thorvaldur looked down at him. "Troll or man, we all sense the presence of a predator."

Jack grinned at the knowing look in the troll's eyes. He doubted the troll knew he was a thief, but he clearly knew he wasn't a lord's steward. For whatever reason he had decided to go with Jack anyway, perhaps to discover his true motivations.

"Predators are so much more interesting," Jack said. "Wouldn't you agree?"

Korna grinned, the expression twisting the tattoos on her face. "Especially when you know what they hunt."

Jack smirked as Thorvaldur frowned and made a motion to her. She fell silent, speaking volumes to what they had revealed. Apparently the trolls were curious enough that they had decided to join him.

"Tell us about Margauth," Thorvaldur said.

"What do you wish to know?"

"Everything," he replied. "For us, victory is decided before blades are drawn and blood spilt."

"And we like to know what *bandits* we will be killing," Korna said.

Thorvaldur cast her another warning look but Jack laughed. "These bandits are actually cult members that worship a man named Skorn."

"Like the devil from the ballad?"

"He has taken on the identity of the devil," Jack said, deciding it best not to say that it was true. "And has now taken the cult as his own."

"Tell me about their refuge," Thorvaldur said.

340

Jack settled into his saddle and began to describe the fortress of Margauth. As the days passed the trolls were relentless in their attempts to understand Skorn's strength. By the time they crossed the southern border of Griffin, Jack understood that it wasn't just the trolls' stature that made them powerful, it was their intelligence.

They camped in the forest several miles from Hilltop and Jack laid out his plan. At first the trolls disliked his suggestion, but by the time he was finished Thorvaldur bore a smile on his face. He leaned back and folded his arms.

"It is not a tactic we would choose on our own, but there is an elegance to it that I find appealing."

"Are you certain?" Korna asked.

"I am," Thorvaldur replied, and turned to Jack. "I assure you, we'll be ready."

"A smart man never doubts a troll."

His comment elicited a round of laughter from the others and then Jack rose to his feet. Gathering his gear, he nodded to them and slipped into the trees. For the next hour he worked his way through the forest until he reached the road that ascended into the mountain pass.

Winter had arrived since he and Lorelia had departed for the Vault of the Eternals, and much of the ground lay covered in snow. The depths of the season had yet to arrive but the frigid air pierced his clothing. Stars twinkled between dark clouds. A few snowflakes fell, drifting in lazy patterns before joining the drifts on the ground. It muffled the sound of his footfalls.

He found the cold and silence refreshing after months of conflict. In spite of what waited for him, a sense of peace permeated the canyon. He had not felt such a calm since before his mother had died, and he relished it, breathing deep of the crisp night air.

As the minutes passed his smile faded. Instead of comforting, the stillness left him unsettled. His irritation mounted as he trudged through the snow, and he wondered how such a setting could inspire his reaction.

He climbed higher in the mountains but his agitation did not abate. As he ascended, the storm thickened, blotting out the stars and driving snow into him. His smile returned as the blizzard struck him and he turned to face heaven's fury. Then he realized his unease had evaporated, and been replaced with a sense of belonging. In the depths of the storm he began to laugh, and finally saw the truth.

The stillness had been a welcome reprieve but it was not for him. The heat of the conflict is what he craved, the tension when creeping into a strongroom and stealing from those who had little thought for what they possessed.

He liked the stars.

But he lived for the storm.

His smile returned, spreading across his features until it seemed to defy the bitter wind. He closed his eyes, relishing the blasting snow across his face. His mother had not wanted it for him, but he could not deny what he was.

"I'm sorry," he called to the heavens. "But I am a thief. By birth or choice, it's what I am."

The storm howled as if in response of his avowal, and Jack grinned. He'd expected to feel guilt, but instead came a sudden sense of freedom, and in that instant he made a choice. He may be a thief, but perhaps he could live with the honor his mother had taught. He closed his eyes and for an eternal moment relished the storm lashing his form. Then he resumed his pace with renewed purpose.

The storm billowed through the pass and he fought against it, pushing his way through the snow until Margauth came into view. Blanketed in snow the great fortress seemed to roar into the storm's fury. Pinpricks of fire dotted the battlements, the flickering light struggling in the wind.

The gates groaned as they opened for him, pushing the snow into a drift to allow him passage. A pair of cultists greeted him, their expressions bright with excitement. Skorn stood behind them. Hundreds of cultists rushed into place, thickening their ranks as they craned for a better view.

Gallow appeared and strode to Skorn's side. His features twisted with hatred when he met Jack's gaze, and his lips curled into a sneer. The blackness to his eyes matched the darkness of the storm above.

"You surprise me, Jack," Skorn said. "I expected another attempt to defy me."

Jack strode through the gates and the cultists parted for him. "I don't care to be predictable. It takes the pleasure out of the game." He met the gaze of a woman cultist and winked, eliciting a blush and then a scowl.

"Did you retrieve it?" Skorn asked, licking his lips in anticipation.

Jack reached into his pouch and lifted the back pyramid into view. "I always complete my assignments."

Gallow's expression tightened and he looked about as if expecting an ambush. "I don't trust him."

"Neither do I," Skorn said, his eyes never leaving the beacon. "Search the pass and cliffs above. Cover every inch."

"There's no need for that," Jack said, a smile spreading on his face. "My allies are right behind me."

"You don't have any allies," Gallow said.

"True," Jack admitted, "but I'm not the only one that wants to defeat your master."

Skorn's eyes widened and for the first time a trace of fear tightened his features. Then it turned to disbelief. "My brother would not follow you."

Jack let the implication hang, enjoying the fear in Skorn's eyes. "He did not need to," Jack finally said. "He just needed to send his own servants."

Something behind Jack caused the cultists to stir, fear causing them to stumble back. From the billowing snow a massive figure appeared. Cloaked in white and bearing a huge spiked warhammer, Thorvaldur advanced as if the storm did not touch him. Then another troll appeared,

343

and another. As each resolved into clarity the cultists began to shout, screaming to shut the gates.

Skorn's eyes widened with shock at the appearance of the trolls, and then his expression turned scornful. He'd evidently expected Eternals or perhaps his brother, but the mortal trolls did not frighten him. He began to call for order but a booming voice drowned out his words.

"Your master is not a god!" Thorvaldur roared. "And we, the servants of Ero, have come to destroy him for his impudence! Lay down your weapons or suffer the wrath of a just god!"

Shouts and screams erupted from the people and cult members bolted to the gates. Jack drifted to the side as if to leave space for them—and plunged a knife through the edge of the door, sinking the blade into the wooden beam beyond. The cultists caught the door and pulled but the knife would not be dislodged. Unable to close the gates, they began to panic.

"They're just trolls!" Skorn shouted, but his voice was lost in the din.

Gallow drew his dagger and idalia. "Hold the line!" he shouted. As they gathered around him Skorn yanked his sword from its scabbard and threw it forward, where it took up position in the open gate. Then he turned to Jack, but his fury died on his lips.

Jack was gone.

Chapter 43: Friend

"JAAAACK!"

Skorn's roar echoed throughout the fortress, bringing a smile to Jack's lips as he sprinted through the citadel. The moment Skorn's and Gallow's attention had been on the trolls he'd pocketed the beacon. Then he'd removed his cloak to reveal the green cloak he'd "liberated" from a cult member that had been drunk in Hilltop. He'd blended into the fleeing cult members and slipped into Margauth.

The clash of arms reverberated throughout the fortress as he ascended the steps. Despite his urgency he paused at a window overlooking the courtyard. Led by Korna, the trolls charged through the door and slammed into the hastily organized line of cultists. Weapons clashed, sending blood into the snow at their feet.

For a few seconds Skorn's cultists stood their ground. Then they began to flee, bleeding away from the troll's might. Those most faithful remained, screaming and throwing themselves at the trolls. Unperturbed by the odds, the trolls advanced like farmers at the harvest, and left stalks of fallen grain in their wake. Korna peeled off from the group and engaged Gallow, matching him blow for blow.

Outside the gates, Thorvaldur was in the fight of his life against Skorn's blade. The weapon struck and twisted, carving a line into his flesh before being deflected. Thorvaldur's eyes did not waver from the floating sword. Then the blade wove past his defenses and came down upon him.

The rock troll reached up and *caught* the blade with his bare hand. At first Jack thought he'd made a mistake, but then he realized the troll had allowed the opening in order to draw the weapon close. Flames burst up the sword, burning the rock troll's flesh. He scowled but did not release it.

The great troll advanced to the doors of the fortress and plunged the struggling weapon into the wood. It trembled, shaking as it fought to withdraw. Thorvaldur spun a full circle, accelerating his weapon into a blur of steel, aiming for the stuck sword.

The hammer at the end of Thorvaldur's weapon smashed into Skorn's blade. With a deafening *crack* Skorn's blade snapped in half. The crash of metal reverberated throughout the fortress, sending a hush through the cultists as the hilt of the broken blade bounced into the courtyard. It clattered across the courtyard stones and lay still.

Thorvaldur's roar of triumph raised the hair on Jack's neck, and brought another smile to his lips. "How can you not love rock trolls?" he said aloud.

The snap of the blade had broken the cultist's spirit. They began to flee before the trolls and Thorvaldur's arrival turned it into a rout. As cultists scattered below, Jack spotted Gallow attempting to rally their forces, but saw no sign of Skorn. Realizing he'd wasted enough time, Jack turned upward and ascended into Margauth.

The sounds of battle faded as Jack rushed through empty corridors, searching for his friends. He reached the amphitheatre in the mouth of the fortress and passed it by. Ascending higher in the citadel, he reached the rooms behind Margauth's eyes.

The chamber behind the citadel's left eye had been built to accommodate a commanding officer. Large stone tables stood about the room, their surfaces shaped with magic to represent maps of the surrounding region. Jack spotted several inaccuracies and realized it had not been changed since the castle's construction.

Ancient weapons adorned the walls, their blades cankered with rust. Some had been removed to allow room for parchment and sketches, the details of which reminded Jack of Skorn's work before he'd left the Thieves Guild.

347

Jack wove his way through the chamber to the enormous window. Shaped like a giant eye, the window looked down on the courtyard far below. Most of it was obscured by the billowing snow, and he squinted to see the raging battle. Through the storm Jack could see that Gallow had managed to rally the cultists and the battle had intensified.

"I hoped you would not come."

Jack whirled to find Lorelia standing in a doorway at the side of the chamber. Beyond her he caught a glimpse of Margauth's other eye and a matching chamber. The glint of cages was just visible around the corner.

"Beauty?" he called.

Chains clanked and her face appeared between the bars. "We're all here!"

Lorelia's features clouded with anger and she started forward, her magic gathering in her hand. "I hate you, Jack."

"No," Jack said. "You don't."

Light exploded from her hands, charring a jagged line in the wall as Jack slipped to the side. He pulled a throwing knife and sent it spinning toward her but she glided to the side and darted forward.

Magic erupted from her fingers, filling the room with images of her, all bombarding him with light. Jack dived under one of the tables, but caught the edge before appearing on the opposite side. A current of light shattered the rock where he would have appeared and he tracked its source. Pulling himself back the way he came, he leapt to the top of another table and threw another knife.

The blade spun to one of the Lorelias and sliced across her arm. She cried out as it cut her skin and the other images flickered. Then she turned her pain into rage, unleashing an unrelenting torrent of power at him.

Jack leapt from table to table, rebounding throughout the room as the tables shattered. The light in the room dimmed as Lorelia drew on it, allowing Jack to launch his shadowhook into the ceiling. He used it to swing to the side of the room and kick off, coming down close to Lorelia.

"I'm going to kill you, Jack!" she cried, and cast a blade of solid light from her magic. Then she advanced upon him.

Jack slipped his dagger from his back and struck back. The weapons clashed amidst a shower of sparks but she drove into him with surprising strength. Distantly he was aware of his friends shouting in the background, but it took his whole focus to keep from being impaled by Lorelia's searing blade.

His shoulders bounced against the wall and he slid to the side. The lightblade plunged into the stone, sinking into it as if it were made of cheese. Before she could withdraw the weapon, Jack caught her wrist and bent it to the side, forcing her to release the blade. Then he flipped his dagger along his forearm and struck the hilt across her skull, sending her to the floor. He grabbed a length of curtain hanging from the window and tied her wrists she was stunned.

"I'm sorry," he said quietly. "I can't give you what you want, but you'll always be my friend."

He reached up and caught the hilt of the searing blade. Before it could dissipate he leapt into the neighboring room and sliced across the bars. A second strike near the bottom and the bars tumbled to the floor.

"Your freedom has been granted," he said.

Relief and amusement flashed across their faces but Beauty's smile held his gaze. "It's about time," she said.

Her hand lingered on his as she stepped out of the cage, her posture leaning closer than was necessary. Jack saw the yearning in her eyes and inclined his head to let her know he felt the same. Then Roarthin coughed.

"We're out of the cage, but not free."

Jack turned to him. "Are you always this impatient?"

"Only when the devil is here," Thalidon said, stepping out of the cell. "But what about the cure to the poison?"

"You mean these?" Jack withdrew the vials he'd pickpocketed from Skorn while he was focused on the trolls. He smirked and handed them out. "For a thief guildmaster I expected better of him."

They wasted no time in drinking the vials. Then Thalidon grinned. "I don't suppose you have a plan to get us out?"

"Have I not proven myself yet?" Jack asked, indignant.

He reached to a hidden pouch at his back and pulled a small pocket mirror into view. Smirking, he pointed it at the wall. Then he thumbed the rune on the back, causing the glass to turn liquid and flow to the floor. Like a stream it trickled to the wall and climbed upward, turning into a mirror against the stone.

"Is that a Gate?" Beauty asked.

"A beacon wasn't the only thing I took from the Vault of the Eternals," Jack said. "This will take you to the guildhall in the Evermist."

"I could kiss you," Ursana said and without hesitation dived through the Gate.

Gordon slapped Jack on the shoulder and strode after her, a wide grin on his features. "I always thought your arrogance would get you killed. Who knew it would be the thing that saved us?"

"An honorable thief," Roarthin said, following Gordon. "I didn't think they existed." He paused on the threshold and looked back, nodding in gratitude. Then he disappeared from view.

Thalidon followed his brother but Jack called out to him. "I expect something special for this," he said to the dwarven smith.

"I'll consider it," he said with a booming laugh, and then slipped through the Gate.

Beauty turned to him. "You really are amazing, you know that?"

"I do."

She laughed lightly and stepped to the Gate. Then her eyes flicked over Jack's shoulder and her features turned to shock. Recognizing the warning, Jack pushed her through the portal just as a throwing knife struck the mirror, shattering the magic. He whirled to find Lorelia and Skorn standing in the doorway.

Black rage rippled across Skorn's blood spattered features. "I'll have your head mounted on my wall before this is over."

"Then you could see my smile every day."

"You arrogant fool," he snarled. "I almost want you to live so you can witness the arrival of my people."

Jack pocketed the small mirror. Even if it worked he did not have time to activate it without letting Skorn follow him. Then he casually drew his dagger and activated his crossbow with a flick of his wrist.

"Tell me," he said. "Did you enjoy your prison? I understand time is different for you, but a forty-thousand-year sentence . . ." He whistled.

Skorn pulled his old sword from his back and started forward. "I'll take the beacon from your corpse."

Jack laughed. "It appears your vaunted sword was no match for a rock troll."

Skorn didn't respond and continued to advance upon Jack. Seeing the murder in his eyes, Jack raised his crossbow and fired, but Skorn jerked to the side and the bolt missed. Then he darted forward and swung his sword at Jack.

Jack parried but the next blow came just as fast. He'd hoped that anger would drive the man to error but Skorn kept up a relentless assault, punishing Jack for the smallest mistake. Demonstrating the same inhuman speed he had at their first duel, Skorn obliterated Jack's defenses and sent his dagger spinning away. Then he caught his throat and lifted him off the floor. With a savage throw he sent Jack hurtling across the room.

Jack slammed into the wall and crumpled to the floor. The sounds of Skorn's approaching steps echoed in his ears as he struggled to his knees. Spotting the dagger nearby, he reached for it and stood. Halfway across the room Skorn reared back and launched his sword at Jack.

"Goodbye, Jack."

Jack struggled to move but his body did not respond in time. He growled as the blade left Skorn's fingers and flew toward him. The steel glittered in the light as it soared to his heart—but Lorelia stepped into it, the blade plunging into her chest.

She crashed into him and they both went down. He struggled to his knees and saw at a glance that nothing could be done. Anger rippled across his frame as he saw the damage. He reached out and hand her hand.

"Why would you save my life?"

"I'm sorry, Jack," she said, her voice fading. "I thought you could love me if I wasn't damaged."

"You were my friend," Jack growled. "I don't care what you look like."

"Then forgive me," she whispered. "And remember me as a friend."

Her magic faded, revealing her scarred and broken features. Anger, sadness, and regret rippled through Jack as he met her gaze. Then he leaned down and murmured to her.

"Your courage made you attractive," he said. "And you've never been more beautiful."

She smiled at him, and it was an expression unrestrained by fear or doubt. She reached up and fumbled with the amulet at her throat. Pulling it from her neck, she slipped it into his hands with trembling fingers.

"Goodbye, my friend . . ."

The light dimmed from her eyes and her body sighed in death. He stared at her, the rage building within him. Then he gently placed her on the floor and rose to face Skorn. He stood where he'd thrown the blade, an expression of pleasure on his face.

"How many will die before you give me what I seek?"

"You want this?" Jack held the beacon aloft, and his voice rippled with fury. "You will never get it."

"*Give me the beacon, Jack!*"

"Come and get it," Jack snarled. Clutching the beacon in his arm, he whirled to the window. Before Skorn could react Jack dove into the blizzard and fell from view.

Chapter 44: Defeated

Jack plummeted down the icy face of Margauth. He sent his shadowhook into the wall but even with the storm it was too light outside. The shadowhook barely held, slowing his passage but not halting it. It did allow him to put his feet on the wall.

He twisted his body and sprinted down the slope, leaping imperfections like they were stones on the ground. Seconds later he reached the mouth of Margauth and jumped. He caught a glimpse of the amphitheatre as he streaked past. Still sliding across on the cliff face, the shadowhook caught near one of the opening's teeth, slowing him down and sending him bouncing off the cliff below Margauth's jaw.

He cast his shadowhook again, sending the ribbon of ink onto the cliff above. Sliding and scraping down the cliff he turned his attention on how to land without shattering every bone in his body. Spotting a snowdrift in the courtyard, he used the shadowhook to angle his path toward it. Then he gritted his teeth and braced for the impact.

His body hit the snow and sank into it, sending a plume of white billowing into the sky. He sank all the way to the ground and struck the rock but the drift had sapped his momentum. He winced at the blow and then struggled to free himself from the drift. Then a large hand caught his cloak and lifted him free.

He wiped snow from his face to see Thorvaldur's features swim into focus. Blood marred his body from a dozen wounds, and the tattoos that marked his kills were mostly covered by it. In spite of the damage the rock troll bore a smile on his features.

"The battle is over."

Thorvaldur deposited Jack on a ground littered with dead cultists. Every troll had suffered injuries but none were fatal. They picked their way through the dead to join Thorvaldur.

"And the assassin?" Jack asked.

Korna grunted in amusement and wiped the blood from her cheek with the back of her hand. "Fled with the others. I do not think he enjoyed a true adversary."

"Then it's time to depart," Jack said.

Jack strode toward the gates and the trolls fell into step behind him. As he passed through the doors of Margauth he dropped the beacon in the snow by the door. When he was a good distance from the fortress he turned back to it and waited.

"What are you waiting for?" Thorvaldur asked.

"It's not over," Jack replied.

Then Skorn appeared in the gates and strode toward Jack. The rage on his features did not diminish at the sight of the trolls, even when they drew their weapons.

"I will hunt you to every corner of Lumineia," Skorn snarled. "I will not rest until those you value lie dead and the beacon is in my grasp. What you call a *god* could not stop me. No petty thief will do what Ero could not."

"I already did," Jack said coldly. "But you were so focused on me you missed it."

He raised his crossbow and took careful aim. Skorn dodged out of the way but Jack did not follow his movements. Instead he aimed for the gates of Margauth, to the knife he'd plunged into the door at the start of the battle.

Skorn whirled and spotted the beacon half buried in the snow. He leapt to it but Jack fired first. The bolt sped over Skorn shoulder and struck the hilt of the dagger—right on the trigger for the implosion hex.

The implosion swallowed the beacon and ripped the wall apart, the ball of light expanding into the fortress. Skorn's scream was lost in the deafening roar as the hex carved into stone, wood, rock, and corpse. It swelled into a sphere that engulfed Skorn. Then abruptly it came to a halt and began to retract, drawing everything it had touched inward.

Skorn twisted and plunged his sword into the ground. The magic pulled on his body, lifting him into the air as it attempted to pull him in. He roared in helpless fury as it passed over him, and dropped onto the ground swept free of snow. As the ground beneath him cracked and tumbled into the ball of fire, he fought to put distance from the knife.

Wind howled as it was sucked inside the vortex. The battlements cracked and shattered, battering into the bodies of dead cultists as its pieces flew inside the tightening sphere. Great wooden beams that had stood for ages snapped like sticks and crumbled, groaning as they compressed inward.

Metal shrieked as if in pain, rending in half and folding inward, unable to withstand the titanic pressure. The lower jaw of the fortress cracked off and collapsed, falling into the churning sphere, shredding into bits of unrecognizable stone.

The epicenter began to harden, drawing all the broken elements into a lump. The sphere of light continued to contract, shrieking as it compressed the ball tighter and tighter. The light gathered the last of the material and then touched the ball—and detonated into oblivion.

Jack shielded his eyes from the searing light. When it faded he lowered his arm and gazed upon the devastated fortress. The eyes and upper teeth remained but everything below it was gone. The cliff had cracked across it, making it resemble a broken skull.

A perfect sphere had been cut into the earth and cliff, and snow was quick to fall onto the steaming rock. As silence fell upon the canyon Skorn stared at the gaping hole beneath the remains of the citadel.

He was on his knees at the edge of the crater, his skin and clothing burned and smoking. Burns spotted his face as he stumbled to his feet and rotated to face Jack. The shock on his features caused Jack to smile grimly.

"Urthor sends his regards."

Black rage twisted Skorn's features and distorted his voice as he spoke. "You and your smug smile," he said. "You think this means you are triumphant? I have outlived *millions* of your kind, and you are nothing but an insect to me."

"Even insects can kill," Jack said.

Skorn straightened and stabbed a finger at him. "Within a week you will have a bounty on your head so great that every assassin and thug in Lumineia will come for you. I will not need to kill you. Your own kind will hunt you down and *cut you to pieces!*"

He surged into a sprint, causing Jack to draw his dagger. Instead Skorn darted around him and sprinted down the canyon. Thorvaldur swung his warhammer but Skorn slid beneath, twisting and ducking beneath the other troll's weapons. Korna came close enough to rip his cloak free but Skorn did not slow. Weaving his way through the trolls he burst into the open and raced down the canyon. His roar echoed back to them.

"You'll be dead in a month, Jack!"

Thorvaldur called out to the other trolls and they came to a halt, giving up the attempt to catch him. Then he turned to Jack. As he casually wiped the blood from his face a faint smile spread on his features.

"I admit I was uncertain what you intended for us. If your foes did not merit death, we planned on killing you."

"You assume you could."

The trolls laughed, and Korna said, "Spoken like a troll."

"We are not foes this day," Thorvaldur said when his humor subsided. "But that does not make us allies. We are not in the practice of contracting with thieves."

Jack arced an eyebrow, realizing for the first time that the trolls knew exactly who he was. "Why did you come?"

357

"Margauth," Korna said. "When I spoke to High Captain Arana I learned of Skorn's citadel, and the rumors regarding his return. I also learned of a certain nemesis named Jack Myst."

"I decided this cult deserved a visit," Thorvaldur said, and a faint smile appeared on his face. "We didn't come for you."

"Nevertheless," Jack said. "I proclaim your contract complete."

Thorvaldur grinned. "It was *you* that stole the information from my Tryton's office."

"Would you kill me if I admit it?" Jack asked, his lips twitching.

"You do not have to," Thorvaldur said. "But I suspect there is a steward somewhere that is very confused, and I'm certain Tryton and Kythira will not be pleased when they learn what you have done. I would suggest you steer clear of our lands for the next decade . . . or two."

Jack sheathed his dagger and inclined his head. "Have a safe journey, my friends."

Korna laughed at his choice of words and gestured to where Skorn had fled. "I've seen many an enemy, and I can guess what it will take to stop him. Are you certain you can handle it alone?"

Jack thought of his friends. "I have my own allies," he said. "And I will make certain Skorn does not succeed."

"Farewell, thief," Thorvaldur said. "I can honestly say it has been a pleasure."

"I can say the same," Jack said, and inclined his head.

He raised his hand in farewell but remained in place as the trolls turned and departed. Feigning a desire to linger, he turned to the ruined fortress and waited until the trolls were gone. Then he withdrew the tiny mirror from his side and activated the Gate. The silver liquid flowed into place and shimmered.

Jack took one step toward it but hesitated. A sly smile crossed his face when he thought of how useful such a tool would be—if no one

358

knew he had it. The Gate would only connect to the thief guildhalls, but it could prove an invaluable secret. He looked at the icy road winding through the falling snow and groaned at the prospect of the freezing journey back. Reluctantly he extinguished the mirror's magic and pocketed it. Then he turned and hurried to catch up to the trolls. He had a long journey to reach the Evermist.

Chapter 45: Guildmaster

Jack trudged out of the canyon and into a deserted Hilltop. The cultists had abandoned the region, leaving the villagers to weather the storm alone. They seemed more than content and Jack noticed many dressed in expensive furs.

Cursing the absence of a rentable steed, Jack pressed on through the muddy road. For a week he hiked through the early snows across forest and hill until he passed into Talinor. He stopped in Wedge, indulging for two days to warm his bones. Located in the southeastern tip of Talinor, the city straddled the border.

Once he was refreshed he exited the Talinorian section of the city and passed through the gate into the Evermist. The guards stared at him in astonishment as he casually strode into the mist. Although the city was cold and dusted in snow, the swamp retained much of its warmth, and Jack relished the heat as he made his way to the Thieves Guildhall in the depths of the Evermist.

Many times Jack considered using the Gate, but each time managed to resist the impulse. With a sigh of relief, he raised the bridge and strode across it. Before he'd made it halfway Beauty appeared and sprinted to him.

"We thought you were dead!" she cried, wrapping her arms about his neck.

He grunted in chagrin, realizing for the first time that his friends would have expected him to come through the Gate a fortnight ago. When he did not appear they would have thought the worst.

"The Gate was destroyed when I fought Skorn," Jack said smoothly. "And I had no other way of reaching you."

She led him back into the Thieves Guild but barely made it a dozen steps before a crowd of thieves surrounded him. Shouting and laughing, they clamored for answers, which Jack provided. Starting with when he'd pushed Beauty through the Gate, he finished the tale of his victory over Skorn.

His description of the trolls fighting on his behalf drew a round of guffaws and more laughter. When he finished, Beauty shouted for order and promised them a retelling later in the day. Then she pulled him through the crowd and led him to the guildmaster's office. Jack stepped in to find Thalidon talking to his brother, but his eyes swept the office that had formerly been Lorelia's.

His gaze settled on the desk and sadness tightened his chest. In spite of her faults, Lorelia had been an excellent guildmaster, yet none had known the truth about her. The papers were stacked neatly, with some still awaiting a signature that would never come.

Jack thought of Skorn and his jaw clenched. Before he may have fought Skorn to spite him, but now the ancient had made it personal. He'd manipulated Jack's friends and killed Lorelia. He needed to be punished, and Jack wanted to be the one to serve it. Then the dwarves noticed Jack and approached, so Jack forced a smile.

Beauty caught the guard at the door. "Summon Gordon, Ursana, Forlana, and since Kuraltus is in Woodhaven, Slyver."

"As you order," the guard said, and slipped away.

Jack heard their exchange from the depths of a crushing embrace from Thalidon. When Jack finally managed to extricate himself from the dwarf's embrace Roarthin caught him and did the same. Surprised by the emotion from the taciturn dwarf, he struggled to free himself.

"You should have done this to Skorn," Jack said, his voice strained. "He couldn't have done much with a crushed spine."

Roarthin released him with a hearty laugh and slapped him on the shoulder, nearly knocking him from his feet.

"How did you escape his clutches again?" he boomed.

Jack opened his mouth to respond but Beauty cut him off. "Not yet. When the others get here you can tell your tale again—and then you can include what you omitted."

Thalidon groaned at that. "A dead friend walks through the door and you make us *wait?*"

Beauty grinned at his dismay. "Be patient, dwarf. You aren't the only one that thought him dead."

"Does no one have faith in me?" Jack asked, folding his arms.

Ursana appeared in the doorway with a smile on her lips. "*I* insisted you were alive. They did not believe me."

"How could we?" Gordon asked, and strode forward to clasp Jack's hand. "Last we saw, you faced an ancient and our traitor guildmaster."

Slyver and Forlana appeared behind them. Slyver grunted at Jack's appearance and leaned against the wall.

"So Jack Myst survives again," he said sourly.

Jack laughed at his tone. "You're just jealous we didn't invite you."

Slyver glared at him and then released an explosive breath. "Perhaps your words have more truth than I care to admit."

"You served him for years," Beauty said. "You can understand why we thought you might follow him."

"Yet you trusted Lorelia," he said acidly. "And she betrayed you all."

At the mention of their guildmaster, Forlana turned to Jack. "Did she survive?"

Jack's smile faded and he shook his head. In the ensuing silence he told the tale of Lorelia's final act to save his life, and of his escape from Margauth. He finished by detailing the devastation from Urthor's cursed knife.

"An implosion hex?" Thalidon asked, his bushy eyebrows climbing on his forehead.

Roarthin grunted in appreciation. "Such a curse is beyond us, and few of our race possess the ability to cast it."

Beauty shook her head. "I still do not understand why Lorelia betrayed us. Of anyone in the guild, I thought we could trust her."

"Skorn promised her what she desired most," Jack said quietly. "And she believed him."

"What did she desire?" Beauty asked.

Jack hesitated, reluctant to reveal Lorelia's secret. "What none of us could give her," Jack said, deciding it best for them to remember her as the strong, beautiful elf she had been.

When it became clear he would say no more, Gordon gestured to him. "That still doesn't explain why he went through all this trouble in the first place. What did you get from the Eternals?"

He laughed as he realized that none of them knew about the Vault of the Eternals. Deciding it didn't matter now, he started with his ascent to the Irilian Shield and told of his entrance and escape from the vault.

"You met *Ero*?" Slyver asked. "The same god who gave magic to the races in the Dawn of Magic?"

"He's not a god," Jack replied. "But he is one of the ancient race."

"The ancients?" Forlana asked. "What do they have to do with this?"

"Skorn is one as well," Beauty said.

Disbelief washed over Forlana and Slyver, and Slyver jerked his head. "It's just a name. The ancients perished in their civil war during the Dawn of Magic."

"I wish that were true," Gordon said, his tone turning dark. "But it isn't. Anyone who has witnessed how that man fights knows he is anything but human."

363

Slyver opened his mouth to protest but no words came out. Jack saw the doubt on his face, and recalled that the skilled swordsman had dueled Skorn several times when the ancient had been their guildmaster. Each time he had obliterated Slyver with inhuman skill.

"It cannot be," he said, but his voice betrayed him and he issued a growl.

"If what you say is true," Forlana said. "Then why did he want the beacon?"

"To contact the rest of his people," Jack said. "Or at least that's what he claimed."

"There are more of them?" Slyver asked. "Where? If there was an army of ancients running around, surely someone would have seen it."

"We're assuming there even is one," Ursana said. "It's possible that they are simply deluded brothers that think their people still exist. Did you see any others in the vault?"

Jack shook his head. "It's possible," he said, recalling the clarity in Ero's eyes. "But I do not think so."

"So you believe in a fallen god?" Slyver asked with a sneer.

"I trust my instincts," Jack said, a trace of irritation in his voice.

"Then what do we do now?" Ursana asked. "Does he still pose a threat to the guild without the beacon?"

"We've considered him dead before," Thalidon said, "and he manipulated our guildmaster into betraying our guild. Thinking he is gone is a dangerous assumption."

"He's right," Beauty said.

"I thought you said you weren't a thief," Forlana said, fighting a smile.

"I'm not," Beauty said. "But I want to see this through. By now you all know he killed my sister."

364

"I'm glad to see you're staying," Thalidon said. "But you aren't the only one that said you weren't a thief." He shifted to face Jack, as did the rest of them.

Feeling the weight of their curiosity, Jack flashed a wry smile. "Over the last few months I've come to realize just how much I enjoy this occupation. I think I'll keep it."

Ursana's smile was matched by nearly everyone in the room. "You're staying?"

"For now," Jack said.

Beauty and Thalidon exchanged a look, and Thalidon nodded. Then Beauty said, "We did not know Lorelia was dead, but we knew she had betrayed us. Shortly after our return we decided who would replace her. Although several names were suggested, one in particular stood out."

Unable to contain her excitement, Ursana began to laugh. "They picked you—if you survived." She stabbed a finger at the guildmaster's desk. "It's yours now."

He peaked an eyebrow. "You want *me* to be responsible for the guild? I'm not exactly the responsible type."

"Perhaps," Beauty said with smile. "But you've also proven capable of leadership. And right now, we need someone capable of defeating Skorn."

Jack released an irritated sigh but could not refute the logic behind it. The Thieves Guild needed a leader to go against Skorn, and Jack had proven twice that he could do it. But could he do it a third time? Lorelia came to mind, and his doubt hardened into resolve.

He recalled how it had felt to have the assistance of the rock trolls. Having allies had made the difference between victory and defeat. As much as he was reluctant to take on the responsibility of leading the guild, he recognized the merit to the idea.

"Two conditions," he finally said.

"What's that?" Slyver asked, folding his arms.

"No paperwork," he said, his lips curling in disgust.

"I'll handle it," Forlana said with a smile. "I did enough under Guildmaster Lorelia that I know how it works."

"And the second condition?" Beauty asked.

"Roarthin and Thalidon stay until Skorn is dealt with."

Roarthin issued a grunt of surprise. "You want us to stay? Why?"

"Because I need your magic for what I am planning," Jack said.

The dwarves exchanged a look, and then Thalidon shrugged. "It's your choice."

Roarthin grinned and swept his hands wide. "It appears we get to be thieves for a little while longer."

"So you're agreed?" Ursana asked.

Jack relented with a sigh. "For now."

Ursana laughed and everyone but Slyver smiled. The smug tilt to Beauty's expression caused his eyes to narrow.

"Is that why you invited them?" Jack asked, gesturing to Slyver and Forlana. "So you would have a majority of higher ranked thieves to support me?"

"Perhaps," she said, causing a round of laughter from the others.

"Then my first act as guildmaster is to ban all intrigue from the thieves."

"We're thieves," Slyver said with a snort of laughter. "You might as well order them to donate to the Church of Light . . . *guildmaster*." His comment drew more laughter, and Jack joined in.

"Wait," Thalidon said when it subsided. "You said you need us for your plan. Just how do you intend on defeating a fallen god?"

A smirk spread on Jack's face. "We've been fighting him alone. Perhaps it's time we have an ally, one who's already defeated him."

"Who do you suggest?" Beauty asked.

"The only way to defeat a god . . . is with a god."

"You cannot mean . . ."

"Ero," Jack said, his grin widening. "I say we steal a god."

Epilogue: Burned

As night fell on Margauth the storm came to an end. Flurries of white continued to drift into the canyon but the wind's fury began to abate. Steeped in darkness and muffled by the drifts of snow, the approach of two men went unheard.

Skorn and Gallow trudged through the piles of frozen white until they reached the crater where Margauth had once stood. Above, the eye slits for the fortress were just visible in the gloom. With darkness augmenting their size, the remaining teeth of the mouth appeared gigantic.

Gallow's face was sore from his wounds. The woman who had bandaged them had been unskilled, and he could feel the edges of the cuts every time he blinked. The scars would be ugly—but would not compare to Skorn's.

Gallow cast him a surreptitious look. The explosion had burned the flesh of his face and arms. Although the same healer had attempted to repair the damage, the burns remained, adding to the scars that had already lined his face. Skorn had faced Jack Myst twice, and each time added to his scars. Gallow scowled and looked away, mentally cursing the thief.

"Why are we here?" Gallow asked.

Skorn did not answer his question. Instead he reached into his cloak and withdrew a vial of purple liquid. Then he poured it into the snow at his feet and stepped back. When the snow began to melt and burst into steam Gallow retreated as well. From a short distance away he watched the liquid burn bright, searing a line in the snow.

It did not flow downhill, but moved like a snake slithering through the grass. The snow melted at its passage, leaving a meandering line. The stone glowed underneath, marking the liquid's path.

"What is—"

"Quiet," Skorn snapped, and Gallow reluctantly fell silent.

The current of purple liquid carved its way into the crater and then back out, glowing dim and then brightening. Several times it left pools of shimmering liquid behind. Then it found something and came to a halt, the remaining liquid glowing bright enough to cast the crater in purple.

"Retrieve the pieces," Skorn said.

"Of what?" Gallow asked, jutting his chin out.

Skorn cast him a look that sent him scurrying into the snow. Cursing Skorn under his breath, Gallow pushed his way through the snow until he reached one of the spots of light. There he found a tiny piece of twisted black metal in a puddle of purple liquid. Gingerly he reached into it and picked it up. When the shard passed from the liquid it went dark.

Gallow moved to the next, gathering each of the pieces until he came to the last. To his surprise he found the remains of a broken black pyramid, the edges bent and torn apart. Collecting it, he blinked in the sudden darkness and trudged back to Skorn's side.

Skorn took the largest piece and examined it, his dark eyes glittering with excitement. The minutes passed and still he rotated the destroyed beacon in his hands. Gallow began to stomp his feet and shiver, the cold piercing even his enchanted cloak. Just as Gallow was about to snap, Skorn reached inside and touched the interior of the beacon. A flicker of light came from within, illuminating Skorn's triumphant features.

"Will it work?" Gallow asked.

Skorn's eyes flicked to him as if just realizing he was present. "Of course not, but it's enough that I can rebuild one."

"Then why did we have to wait until night to return?" Gallow asked, rubbing his frozen fingers together.

"The thieves believe it was destroyed," Skorn said. "So they will not be prepared for what I intend."

"You're afraid of him," Gallow accused.

Skorn turned to him, his scarred expression so furious that Gallow retreated a step. "Jack is nothing to me," Skorn growled.

In spite of his declaration, Gallow noticed a trace of doubt in Skorn's eyes, confirming the truth. Gallow looked away before his smile could be spotted. It quickly turned into a scowl. How could such an arrogant thief be so vexing? His skill in combat did not even compare to Gallow's—or any of the assassins—yet he continued to defeat Skorn. Even now Gallow could recall Jack's mocking laugh, and could not stop himself from glancing about to see if he were present.

"Gather the survivors," Skorn said, his attention back on the beacon. "And tell them to recruit others."

"What is your plan?"

"We build a beacon."

"Then what?" Gallow asked. "What happens after you contact your people?"

Skorn's smile sent a chill into Gallow's bones that had nothing to do with the winter. "Then I finally get to watch this cursed world burn."

Gallow imagined drawing his blade and killing Skorn, but his courage failed him. He lowered his head and followed Skorn back down the snow-filled canyon. He paused at the corner and looked back at the ruined citadel. Scowling, he turned and left. He did not notice the cloaked woman at the top of the cliff.

From the summit above she stirred. Rising to her feet, the observer touched her ring. Orange light flickered in the gem and Gallow's conversation with Skorn repeated. She listened intently before extinguishing the charm. From beneath her cowl a smile appeared.

"Perfect," she said, and slipped into the night.

The Chronicles of Lumineia

By Ben Hale

—The Master Thief—

Jack of Thieves

Thief in the Myst

The God Thief

—The Second Draeken War—

Elseerian

The Gathering

Seven Days

The List Unseen

—The Warsworn—

The Flesh of War

The Age of War

The Heart of War

—The White Mage Saga—

Assassin's Blade (Short story prequel)

The Last Oracle

The Sword of Elseerian

Descent Unto Dark

Impact of the Fallen

The Forge of Light

Author Bio

Originally from Utah, Ben has grown up with a passion for learning almost everything. Driven particularly to reading caused him to be caught reading by flashlight under the covers at an early age. While still young, he practiced various sports, became an Eagle Scout, and taught himself to play the piano. This thirst for knowledge gained him excellent grades and helped him graduate college with honors, as well as become fluent in three languages after doing volunteer work in Brazil. After school, he started and ran several successful businesses that gave him time to work on his numerous writing projects. His greatest support and inspiration comes from his wonderful wife and five beautiful children. Currently he resides in Missouri while working on his Masters in Professional Writing.

To contact the author, discover more about Lumineia, or find out about the upcoming sequels, check out his website at Lumineia.com. You can also follow the author on twitter @ BenHale8 or Facebook.

Printed in Great Britain
by Amazon